# *The*
# EDUCATION
# *of* DELHOMME

# The
# EDUCATION
# *of* DELHOMME

CHOPIN, SAND, & LA FRANCE

A NOVEL BY

# NANCY
# BURKHALTER

ISBNs: 978-1-7329508-3-2 (pb); 978-1-7329508-5-6 (hc); 978-1-7329508-4-9 (eBook)

Front cover illustration "Watercolor landscape of the castle Conciergerie and the river Seine in Paris" courtesy of Sibirtseva Marina/Shutterstock
Cover and book design by Mayfly Design

Library of Congress Control Number: 2020937696
First Printing: 2020
Printed in the United States of America

Publisher's Cataloging-In-Publication Data
(Prepared by The Donohue Group, Inc.)
Names: Burkhalter, Nancy, author.
Title: The education of Delhomme : Chopin, Sand & La France : a novel / by Nancy Burkhalter.
Description: [Roseville, Minnesota] : History Through Fiction, [2020] | Includes bibliographical references.
Identifiers: ISBN 9781732950832 (pb) | ISBN 9781732950856 (hc) | ISBN 9781732950849 (eBook)
Subjects: LCSH: Piano technicians—France—19th century—Fiction. | Spies—France—19th century—Fiction. | France—History—Second Republic, 1848-1852—Fiction. | Chopin, Frédéric, 1810-1849—Fiction. | Sand, George, 1804-1876—Fiction.
Classification: LCC PS3602.U75587 E38 2020 (print) | LCC PS3602.U75587 (ebook) | DDC 813/.6--dc23

*To Tuners Everywhere*

# PIERŚCIEŃ by Stefan Witwicki (1801-1847)

Language: Polish

---

Smutno niańki ci śpiewały,
A ja już kochałem,
A na lewy palecmały
Srebrny pierścień dałem.

Pobrali dziewczęta drudzy,
Ja wiernie kochałem,
Przyszedł młody chłopiec cudzy,
Choć ja pierścień dałem.

Muzykantów zaproszono,
Na godach śpiewałem!
Innego zostałaś żoną,
Ja zawsze kochałem.

Dziś dziewczęta mnie wyśmiały,
Gorzko zapłakałem:
Próżnom wierny był i stały,
Próżno pierścień dałem.

# THE RING

Language: English

Again you stand before me
Clothed in childlike pride, my love,
As when in boyhood
I asked you to be my bride,

Then I, your youthful lover,
Gave you a tiny ring.
And you promised me
To wear it until death.

But now I am far away,
Wishing I was near you.
And now you have married another man,
Forgetting me and my ring.

But you will never be
Separated from my love.
You, and that dear ring,
Will be cherished in my thoughts forever.

# DESCRIPTION by Robert Cummings*

Even those with a casual interest in classical music are aware that Chopin is almost exclusively known for his piano compositions. His 19 songs, however, are all worthwhile compositions and all quite short affairs, able to be accommodated on a single CD with room for fillers. This song, *The Ring*, at a minute-and-a-half, is rather typical of the composer's terse manner in the vocal realm, but its quality is fairly high. It should be noted that although *The Ring* is counted as No. 14 in his output, it was chronologically his 12th song. Its text is derived from a poem by Stefan Witwicki (1802-1847) and deals with man's rejection by his lover and his lamenting over the rebuff. The ring in the title pertains to the ring he gave to his betrothed in his youth, a ring he cannot forget. The song, while not chipper or joyous in mood, surprisingly does not come across as melancholy or sad, either. The piano begins with a rather sunny, energetic introduction, presenting music seemingly at odds with the text. The vocal line, however, exudes regret and anguish, even expresses moments of anger. Chopin feels the heartrending emotions here, but also exhibits a measure of scorn for the young woman. Still, the brighter music from the introduction makes two more appearances in the song. This is an attractive though probably minor masterwork.

* https://www.allmusic.com/composition/pierscien-the-ring-song-for-voice-piano-op-74-14-ct-142-mc0002664958

# AUTHOR'S NOTE

*P*eople are always surprised to hear that I've written a book about Frédéric Chopin's piano tuner. "How did you come up with *that* idea?" they ask. It's a good question and one I can't readily answer because all my inspirations come from a place with no address, no accountability, and no way to access it on demand.

But that idea would never have surfaced without becoming a piano tuner myself. As a newly graduated linguistics and foreign language teaching major from Northwestern University, I spoke four languages and expected the world to fall over itself to hire me. It did not. I was bored and frustrated. Seeing my malaise, my friend, apropos of nothing, said, "Why don't you become a piano tuner?"

Why not, indeed! I finally convinced Don Wilson, a tuner and rebuilder in Chicago, to take me on as his apprentice. A year later, I hung out my shingle and the rest is—yes, I'm going to say it—history.

During that year of working in the damp, cobwebby basement of Don's shop, I was surrounded by piano actions, books, parts, tools, and a radio. I listened all day to classical music and fell in love with Chopin. Sometimes, I even wept. I decided Chopin must have had a tuner since that skill takes a long time to learn and requires stamina, something the tubercular Chopin lacked.

During my doctoral work in linguistics, I learned how to find even the most obscure book or article. That research expertise was applied to the max for this book. I leapfrogged from one source to another about France, Poland, and Russia; music; tuning; Chopin; Sand; Vidocq; Berlioz; trains; clothing; and on and on. Since pulling on one thread of history tugs on several others, the hard part was knowing when to stop reading. I also traveled to Warsaw, Paris, and Nohant to see things for myself, including Chopin's grave. In Warsaw's Fryderyk Chopin Museum, I saw the *pièce de résistance*—a piano he'd played on. This is the stuff that feeds a historical novelist's soul.

Taking liberties with facts is a big no-no in recounting history. But for historical novelists, the rules are more elastic. I labored to plot all events, fictional or not, on their true timeline. One problem cropped up, though, with Hector Berlioz, who graduated medical school in 1824, twelve years before my fictional tuner did, yet I made them classmates. I also fashioned diary entries by George Sand. No such texts exist, but they are true to her autobiography and others' accounts. I created them because I wanted her to have her own say since all else is told from Delhomme's point of view. I hope the reader will forgive these liberties in the service of story.

To write is to learn. Now I understand much better the long and violent roots of the workers' struggle for better pay and working conditions. I appreciate even more now that the world has forever been ravenous for good music, even if it means devouring the very musician who creates it. Finally, it seems that the social hierarchy favoring men over women, rich over poor, and educated over unschooled has shown great staying power. *Plus ça change . . .*

Here are answers to questions my tuning customers always ask: Yes, I play the piano, but tuners don't need to, although it is pleasing to check the tuning from a musical standpoint. Next, we don't adjust a string until it "sounds good." We count beats, the pulse created when two sounds of different frequencies cross. Each interval on the piano has a specified number of beats. Learning to count them is but one of the challenges. Last, perfect (aka absolute) pitch is useless to a tuner. The A below Middle C must be set to *exactly* 440 cycles per second. Someone with perfect pitch may *perceive* a sound as an A even if it vibrates anywhere from 435 to 445 cps. For tuners, that measurement is too imprecise. Have tuning fork—will travel.

Sadly, I no longer tune. I miss it and all the wonderful people who trained me and were unstinting with their knowledge and support. Now, I only write about tuners and their antics. Oh, did I just say antics? I meant actions.

# Fate – Bells

## Fate

S py. What a stupid, lethal choice. Now I sit shivering on the mud floor of a crowded cell with four walls and a black door. Five other men stare blankly into space. A sixth sticks his hands out the window and cries for food from passersby—anything to stop the hunger—coffee grounds, vegetable peelings, shriveled berries, cheese rinds.

The noxious stench from their unwashed bodies and buckets of excrement numbs the nostrils. The Seine threatens to overflow from snow and rain. But what does it all matter? I am days, likely hours, away from the guillotine. "I am innocent!" I say to the others. But no one listens. No one cares. There are only the sounds of chin-wagging shoppers and clicking horseshoes. The sparse straw is a paltry shield against the cold earth. I stretch the thin blanket from the jailer over my head and face and sit in a corner farthest from the window. Chill winds blow. There will be no January sun today.

Spying was supposed to be a brief stint, something to earn money so I could marry Lili. That delusion has cost me dearly. I want to atone for that. But not with death!

My trial is nigh. I will stand proudly in court, pound my fist, and declare that Vidocq tricked me into joining his detective agency. All to help

King Louis Philippe control the masses. I will ask the judge, 'What truck would I, a lowly piano tuner, have with radicals wanting to kill the king? I care about wood and wire and wonderful music. How does this mean I betrayed the monarchy? Let those who killed innocent people with their muskets and knives go to their death!' That is what I will say.

Who will come to my defense? Frédéric Chopin would have, but he died three months ago. George Sand is volatile and untrustworthy; I hope she can muster fairness. Even so, I doubt her testimony can undo Vidocq's devilish words. He will swear I sided with resisters, hobnobbed with radicals, and became a counterspy. Never mind that he lured me with easy money. He is the ruler's vaunted, powerful toady. Loyalty trumps scruples in this man's government.

I did everything Vidocq asked of me—reluctantly, I am proud to say now. Then one day, I fed him wrong information on purpose. It was my attempt to fight the domination of those who ignored the suffering of others. Then, Vidocq's wrath came crashing down. Now here I sit. Accused of treason. Jailed. Condemned.

## Bells

We are housed in the Conciergerie. This prison has evoked fear since the Reign of Terror over fifty years ago. Some forty thousand people died in that one short year after being paraded around the Place de la Concorde like animals going to slaughter. The ominous Bonbec Tower still holds the threat of water torture, dismemberment, decapitation, drawing and quartering. Some undergo the boot torture where legs are squeezed by a wooden instrument. That tower exhorts all citizens to behave.

Guards check on us hourly. Escape is impossible from the exercise area surrounded by unscalable walls. The famed Marie-Antoinette tried once but was caught and moved farther away from the entrance. A trial remains my lone hope. For justice. For freedom.

I seesaw between terror and resignation. But then, it is my fault. I could have become a doctor like my father, or a musician like Chopin. And I certainly could have refused Vidocq's filthy money.

Bells from Notre Dame toll midnight. I cover my ears and hope sleep will come soon.

# Medical School
# – Shame – Death

## Medical School

M y twentieth birthday found me penniless and restless. Still living at my parents' house in Marainville-sur-Madon, I clerked in Petrichor, the local seed store. My day was spent filing papers, stamping receipts, dealing with customers. "How many sacks of wheat seed do you need this year, Monsieur Flambé? Oh, you say you are rotating in barley this year? Wonderful idea. Will you need delivery?" Day after day, tedium was paired with penury, with no escape.

I wanted to play the piano, accompany singers, perform with an orchestra that would play mighty symphonies. Each night I fell asleep to imaginary applause after my brilliant rendition of a tempestuous fugue by Bach or Beethoven's moody Sonata Pathétique. For an encore I would dazzle listeners with a saucy piece by Mozart, or when I felt bold, an étude by Chopin that would stun the audience. People would marvel at my virtuosity, then stand and clap and shout "Bravo! Bravo!"

Dawn brought reality. I left my bed, dressed, ate breakfast, and steeled myself for another day just like yesterday: stamping and collating, adding and subtracting, tallying and filing. Occasionally, I entered local piano competitions. I won first place several times. On weekends, Father Bernard counted on me to play the organ for church services, weddings, and funerals. He saw my fire and thought I should attend music school.

But Papa scoffed at this plan. He said I would attend his same medical school in Paris. End of discussion. "Become a doctor! Study anatomy! Dissect!" he said with his booming voice. "I will pay your way."

Paris! How I dreamed of living there but could have never afforded it.

"You can return to Marainville after you graduate," he said. "This is a wonderful place to settle."

Marainville-sur-Madon in the Lorraine region had been home to several centuries of Delhommes. A small, agricultural village with fertile soil, thanks to the Madon river, which snaked north from the Vosges mountains and emptied into the Moselle. It was a daylong coach ride from Paris, just far enough to keep unsavory city dwellers away. Papa liked treating the farmers who plowed the land and maids who minded the children of wealthy landowners. With his wiry red hair, straight back, thick shoulders, and hands strong enough to bale hay and milk cows, he looked more like a peasant than a doctor. Those laborers and domestics saw him as one of their own. He wanted to live out his days in this small town doing the magic of healing. He wanted—expected—me to join him.

I wanted no such life. But my father's wishes ruled. So, after celebrating my twenty-first birthday, I packed my bags and left for Paris to enter la Faculté de Médicine, his alma mater. I listened to lectures about humors and Hippocrates, bloodletting and bile. But each class soured my stomach more than the previous. If just the theory about wound care nauseated me, the thought of debriding purulent lesions and attaching slimy leeches to someone's body made me gag. And the horror of touching a cadaver!

The day finally came to face that fear. After several months of lectures, our first gross anatomy class met in a specially designed area on the first floor of the medical school building. Tall, wide windows allowed plenty of light. An aisle divided ten tables equally and led to a fireplace that lent a modicum of comfort in the winter months. But heat was used sparingly to keep the room cool enough to preserve the bodies. The stone floor was strewn with sawdust to soak up fluids. Despite that precaution, we walked in a cesspool of blood, sheets of peeled-off skin, a discarded heart, and a glob of fat excised from the omentum of an obese man who had suffered cardiac arrest. The sawdust muffled the talk and noise of instruments, creating an eerie atmosphere. We had been advised to inhale camphor to disguise the odor, but the putrid smell prevailed.

On each side of the room lay revolting-looking corpses with shriveled skin and cracked skulls. Sawed-off limbs were placed beside the torso. Each group purchased its own cadaver, when one became available, which was not often, and would set about working on it with some haste due to decomposition. Maggots wriggling in the cavities added to my revulsion.

On the first day in the dissection room, one of my tablemates removed the sheet from our corpse. We had been told nothing about the person, including the cause of death. The woman's gray hair and missing teeth led us to guess her age at sixty. Sagging skin could have been due to illness. Muscular legs and strong shoulders suggested a life of hard labor.

"Shall we pray before beginning?" I said to the group. I thought it the least we could do before ravaging this woman's body in the name of science. I had barely bowed my head when one zealous student grabbed a scalpel, plunged it just below her rib cage, and dragged it down to her pubic bone. The others laid claim to organs as if on a treasure hunt. "I get the heart!" said one. "I want the spleen!" shouted another.

I turned away only to see rats in the corner gnawing on a vertebra. A flock of sparrows had swooped down and were squabbling over a pair of lungs. I felt sick and headed for the door but vomited on a skull before getting out. The miasma of flesh and fluids lingered in my nose for years.

## Shame

I wrote to my mother:

> *Why would Papa want me to forsake the sublime art of music in exchange for enduring their shrieks of pain or gloomy death rattles. I fear he will be the last doctor in this family. Please, Maman, burn this letter. I fear Papa will discover it.*

She wrote back:

*I am sure you will adjust. Try again, ChouChou* (her powerful term of endearment). *You can do this. I have faith in you. We will be so proud of you.*

She mentioned at the end of her letter that she had been feeling tired lately and planned to ask Papa for some advice, something she rarely did. "He has enough sickness around him," she would say but found it comforting to have a doctor in the house. Bolstered by her confidence in me, I hurried off to class to avoid truancy.

The fear of facing my father's rage if I failed should have been an incentive to curb my physical responses. But one's nervous system is not under conscious control. The instructors stressed clinical detachment. "Cadavers," the professor explained, looking directly at me, "feel no pain. You need to suppress your own physical and emotional reaction to the willful mutilation of another human being."

The following week, our class filed out of the auditorium to the cadaver room after another lecture on dissection techniques. I was contemplating emptying my stomach beforehand when I caught the eye of a tablemate who also lagged. We nodded to one another. He introduced himself as Hector. He had red hair like mine, but his was a flaming, bushy mane that swung independent of his face. He had a sharp beak of a nose and thin, pinched lips.

"Looking forward to putting those new techniques into practice, are we?" he asked.

I looked askance. Was he making fun of me?

He put his hand on my shoulder, and said in a low voice, "Please keep this secret, but I was violently ill yesterday, too."

"But you came back."

"*Bien sûr,*" he said. "My father threatened to disown me if I did not become a doctor like him."

His story was twin to my own!

Hector and I dallied outside the cadaver room. But the gimlet-eyed lecturer burst through the doors and shooed us inside, mumbling something about having to attend to errant children.

This scene proved even more revolting. Rotting flesh stung my nostrils anew, body parts littered the ground, and rodents dragged hunks of flesh out the windows to their nests.

This carnage brought back the memory of my father caring for people injured in an accident when I was eight years old. It was a July afternoon. A torrential rain had come through town that morning. I was reading on the porch, enjoying the cooler weather when a neighbor ran up.

"We need Dr. Delhomme. Quickly!" he said, panting. He explained that a mudslide had swept a wagon, a horse, and three people into a ravine. I shouted for Papa, but he was already on his way downstairs. He grabbed his medical bag that he kept by the door.

"May I come, Papa?" He hesitated but thought better of leaving me alone in the house. "Yes, but you must behave." I helped hitch up the horse, jumped into the wagon, and out of the barn we shot. I was so proud of Papa that he could save lives.

We arrived to find several anxious onlookers peering into the ravine that had been worn by the Madon river. The narrow road on the outskirts of town had been carved out of the hill.

Papa pulled up on the reins. "Can I get a few volunteers?" he said to the crowd. Several men stepped up. Gripping his medical bag with one hand, he held out his other to me. "Make way," he shouted. "Make way for the doctor." He guided me carefully down the hill to treat the hapless family. We neared the overturned wagon. The thick mud sucked at my shoes as I scrambled to keep up. I watched the men right the wagon. Miraculously, the horse had survived without a scratch. But the man's lacerated legs and woman's gashed neck made my head spin. I wretched.

Papa turned to me. "Go back to the wagon," he said unsympathetically. "I have no time for a weak little boy."

I trudged up the hill, head low from shame at my uncontrollable response. It felt like hours before my father returned. Close behind him were townspeople helping the injured parents into our wagon. One placed the dead boy beside them. I sat up front with my mud-splattered father. He grabbed the reins without comment and shouted "Hyah," to the horse.

I had such conflicting emotions about my father. I was so proud of him yet hated his cruel words. I only wanted to learn. Why did he shame me so?

In the dissection room, Hector and I sidled up to the table. An eager student had already removed the sheet. My tablemates lowered their heads to look at the corpse. Mine was bowed to entreat God to calm my stomach.

"Delhomme," the professor said, walking by our table. "Dissect the hands. They contain less blood. Oh," he added, "the mortician forgot to remove her wedding ring. Maybe you can do that for the family."

I appreciated his concern about both me and the woman's family. I set about the task. Her fingers were so flexible I could move them easily, as if she were alive. The silver wedding band, though, held fast below an arthritic knuckle. Thin and scuffed, it spoke to a life of commitment and loyalty—cooking, cooling a fevered brow, and spooning pabulum into a baby's mouth. Maybe this old woman had even played the piano. My scalpel remained immobile.

Meanwhile, the students continued rummaging in her torso for new prizes to examine. One of them whooped as he pulled out entrails covered in pus. "I think I found the cause of death!" he said with delight. This was the final straw for both of us. Hector grunted, yanked off his robe, and leapt out the open window. I followed suit, as if Death and all its hideous crew were at our heels.

The following day, the director asked me to leave the school. I was not surprised. No recourse remained but to face Papa. Certain he would reject any explanation, I sent a letter to Maman in advance of my return, so she could soften the blow. That weekend, I hired a cabriolet to take me to Marainville, a ten-hour journey if we traveled quickly. We stopped at several relays for fresh horses and small meals, although I had left my appetite in Paris. I could not imagine ever eating again. Each mile heightened my dread. I rehearsed my excuses, but they all fell flat.

The coach pulled up to my parents' house at dinnertime. The driver unloaded my suitcase and set it beside me. I opened the door. Maman did not dare look at me. She was busy putting stewed chicken, fresh peas, and a tomato salad with chèvre on the table. The wine stood uncorked.

Dinner would have to wait.

"Beaulieu!" Papa bellowed from his study. "*Viens ici, maintenant!*"

I slowly opened the door. There sat father on *Le Grand Trône Blanc de Jugement,* with its massive oak frame and cushions upholstered with a needlepoint pattern reminiscent of a Gobelin tapestry. My sister and I, if we had committed any infraction against my father's code, were ordered to sit across from his desk in an uncomfortable chair made of wooden slats. My chair used to be too tall and wide for my young frame back then. Now, my feet reached the ground and elbows rested easily on the wooden arms stained with perspiration. This time, as surely as night followed day, I knew I would be cast into that same lake of fire as the Christian nonbelievers for what I had done.

I entered and sat stiffly. Father stood behind his desk leaning on his fists. Slowly, he walked behind my chair. He put his face close to my ear. His voice was lowered, tight. "You are nothing but a sniveling, spoiled brat," he said in a controlled tone. I felt his hot breath. "Are you too stupid to continue studying medicine? Or just too lazy?"

I looked at the ground.

He came around front to look at me with his piercing gaze. He said, "What will you do with your life now? You have wasted this opportunity. The professors are laughing at your mewling and puking like a baby. Jumping out a window, indeed!" He wagged his finger at me: "I hope you have a good, strong spine. You will need it to help the peasants scythe the wheat at harvesttime."

Excuses were *non grata.*

"Get out of my sight," he said, returning to his chair. "You are no son of mine."

I went to my room. Maman, sympathetic with my problem, brought a plate of food. I thanked her but left the meal untouched.

## Death

I left for Paris before dawn (I could not bear seeing my father after that debacle in his office) to collect my belongings from the school. I wanted to say goodbye to my friends and begin looking for work.

The coach lumbered along the familiar route, stopping at the same places to change horses and allow riders to purchase a meal. I never spoke with the other three—a mother traveling with her well-behaved small boy and a man in his mid-seventies whose forlorn expression reflected my mood. The mother played games with her son and recounted a few La Fontaine fables she knew by heart. She delivered the tales in a pleasant, sing-song voice. She made sure the boy understood the lessons behind each one. But one spoke to me in a special way. La Fontaine called it *The Wagoner Mired*. A peasant's cart was mired in mud. The man called on a powerful god to help. The god said, "Stop whining! Put your shoulder to the wheel and urge on your horses." Soon, he freed his wagon, proud he had solved the problem himself.

"Do you know what that fable means?" asked the mother.

"That the peasant should be more careful?" said the boy.

The mother smiled. "Yes," she said. "It also means that you should rely on yourself first to solve a problem before calling on the gods."

He seemed to understand her explanation, but then asked, "How do I call on a god, Maman?"

It was late afternoon when we arrived in Paris. I trudged up the five flights to my attic apartment, gripping my suitcase laden with sorrow and worry. Exhausted, I fell into bed without unpacking.

Within days of my return, I lay in bed pondering how I, like la Fontaine's peasant, could help myself when I heard quick footsteps up to my apartment and someone shouting "Monsieur Delhomme! Monsieur Delhomme!" I opened the door to a breathless messenger. "Monsieur, I was told to deliver this right away."

The letter announced more bad news: My father had died. Lucky to have reached fifty years old, he had not been ill and never complained. Maman told me as he lay in bed, he cried out and fell onto the floor clutching his chest. Traditionally, the eldest son had the duty of closing the deceased's eyes, but I was not able to return in time to perform the ritual.

The funeral was scheduled that weekend, so I had the luxury of delaying that pain by a few days.

When I returned, Maman was dabbing her swollen eyes.

"*ChouChou!*" she said as she ran into my arms. What would become of her? I thought. Would she be able to live in this big house by herself? Should she move to Paris where I could keep watch on her? Neither solution seemed ideal. Surely, she would miss the rolling hills of Marainville, the chirping birds, and tulips blanketing the meadows in the spring. My parents had lived in this home for almost thirty years. Their son and daughter had played in the trees and swum in the river on hot summer days. Paris' filth and crime would shock her system, to be sure. I wanted to help her stay in her house.

I spoke about the situation with my sister, Marie, a dressmaker. She and her husband, a railroad worker, had moved from France to find employment in jobs-rich industrial England years ago. I used to play tag with their son, Marc. I would hide in the most unlikely places. But he always found me. I missed his laughter and bright eyes.

In those traumatic first days after my father's passing, Marie attended to our overwrought mother with tea and kind words. Meanwhile, before I helped tidy the house, I slowly opened the door to their bedroom. Would I feel Papa's ghost? Would it fly at me and scold me for disappointing him? I crossed the threshold. The bedroom looked the same—the simple maple bed he had made with my mother's red and white quilt lying across the foot of it. I walked over to his bureau. His gold fob watch and loose change lay on the lace runner. Time and money—both useless to him now. Amid the coins was a well-worn medal of Saint Raphael the Archangel, patron saint of healing. It was small, cold. A remembrance of his dedication to healing, I slipped it into my pocket along with the watch.

The funeral was held the next day. Hundreds of mourners crowded around his coffin to pay their respects, most of them probably his patients at one time. I felt numb as I looked at him lying with his hands placed just so across his chest holding a rosary. Many others cried at the loss to their community. Scenes flashed in my mind about his cruel words and punishments for defying his strict rules. Yet, I felt immense pride in his humanitarian practices. "Help the poor," he would say. "Make a better place for those around you." But I never understood why he would bestow patience and empathy onto complete strangers while I, his only son, felt the sting of his paddle and words. Those opposing emotions sat uneasily in my mind.

We pallbearers placed his casket in a special wagon and set out for the cemetery located on a high hill overlooking the river. The graveside service was mercifully short.

After the burial, our family took a coach home. Friends gathered in the living room drinking tea and consuming sweets the neighbors had so thoughtfully brought.

Afterwards, Maman and I sat in the kitchen. She looked more ill than grief stricken but not too sick to deliver one more bitter blow. "Your father just wanted you to continue his legacy." She said that without rancor or bitterness, but I heard blame for his death tucked inside her comment.

Marie and I helped Maman impose order on her life. We pulled his books from the shelves and stacked them in wooden boxes. We cleaned out his closet and drawers and donated the goods to charity. She warned us against looking at the financial records. "They are private," she said.

Two weeks passed. My sister and her family returned to London. I expected to leave by the end of the week.

Guilt weighed on my chest like an anvil for having let down my father. But it was assuaged after I sneaked a forbidden look at the bank account information. It told me I would not have been able to continue medical school, even if I had controlled my gastric responses. Ministering to the poor had not been very lucrative. Perhaps he died from his own shame of not being able to keep his promise to support me. But then it occurred to me that there would be no money to inherit. Therefore, Maman's care fell entirely on my shoulders. I felt light-headed at the thought. Where would I get the money for that? Would I have to move back here and take care of her myself? Was I to become a farmer to earn money after all?

As if hearing my thoughts, Maman asked when I would move back to Marainville. She repeated her complaint about not feeling well and said she could not cook or clean very much.

I looked at her. "I thought Lili was helping with that."

Lili Millefeuille was a young neighborhood girl who came once a week to do light chores. Petite, blond, with greenish-gray eyes. *Pretty*, I thought when I first saw her. She was learning how to use medicinal herbs from her mother. The medical community, including Papa, disparaged such practices. "What about dosing?" he would say as he stomped around the house, fulminating against such imprecise measures. "Do you mean to tell me that someone can yank a fistful of weeds from the ground, make a tincture, spoon it down someone's gullet, and think *that* would cure someone of anything?" His diatribe was always the same about herbal remedies, so I knew what was coming next. "Medicine is best left to men who know about the scientific method," he railed, throwing his hands in the air. "Quackery!"

"Lili is quitting. Getting married." She paused, then said, brightening, "I know. What about clerking for Monsieur Argent in the seed store again? He still asks about you."

Inside I groaned. "Maman, there is no work here." I patted her hand and noticed her own silver wedding band that someone would remove one day when she died.

It crushed my spirit just to think of returning to that cramped office with that repetitious stamping and mindless recordkeeping of who bought how much of which seed, day after dull day. "Let me talk to Lili," I said. "Perhaps she has a friend."

"Please, *ChouChou*." She wiped tears from her cheeks. "Stay."

My parents had been married thirty-one years. I could only imagine her loneliness as a widow. I comforted her with a promise. "I will send money each month for the new helper." A bold offer indeed: I had no profession, no training, no prospects.

Lili arrived mid-morning dressed in a yellow frock and crisp white apron to start her chores. I introduced myself.

"Please have a seat," I said, pointing to the living room. She sat on the edge of the maroon sofa, hands folded, feet together, looking as if I would bite her.

"Thank you for singing at my father's service," I began. "What a lovely voice you have."

She blushed.

"I understand you are getting married," I said, returning to the matter at hand. "When is the happy day?"

"Alexandre serves in the Foreign Legion," she said proudly. "He wants to stay in until he is thirty. Then he said we can settle down."

I judged her to be in her mid-teens, a ripe age to be married.

"How long is that?" I asked.

"Another year. I will be sixteen then."

I envied him such a loyal, patient girl.

So, at least Lili's departure was not imminent, but I had to make other plans for Maman's care when she did marry, all of which involved money.

I had no choice but to sell my father's books and medical equipment to the hospital. Of all the items, my mother begged me to leave behind his medical bag. It was a black, roomy, tooled-leather satchel made of elephant hide lined with red leather and fastened with a metal jaw hinge. There was a medallion on the flap inscribed with his initials. Over thirty years of opening and closing that bag had left few scratches, so careful was he with in his possessions. I explained to Maman that having it would not ensure any clearer memories of her husband. She still protested and barred the door to prevent my leaving. I had no other option, I said. Reluctantly, she went back to the kitchen table and sank into her chair, sobbing. The sale netted enough money to support me several more months in Paris and to hire Lili two days a week. After that, only the Fates knew my destiny.

# Dr. Dittmar

## Dr. Dittmar

*O*nce I returned to Paris after the funeral, red-haired Hector and I agreed to meet with Dr. Dittmar, head of the medical school, at ten o'clock the next day. It was a requirement of anyone dropping out. I arrived early, but the doctor graciously invited me in. He was an imposing, tall man with zealously combed white hair and matching moustache that hid his rumored harelip. He wore a handsome brown suit with an ascot and high collared shirt. "And Hector?" he said. I indicated my ignorance of his whereabouts. He bade me sit as he closed my file.

Glass cabinets lined the walls with tomes on human anatomy, modern surgical techniques, and his specialty, coronary medicine. I had attended some of his lectures that were full of information only a man who had held a beating heart in his hands could know.

He sat behind a large oak desk strewn with papers and books.

"I knew your father quite well," he began. "Exceptional healer, that man. If we had difficulty diagnosing someone, we brought in Gérard." He stopped long enough to pack and light his Meerschaum pipe adorned with a naked woman carved out of ivory stretched across the bowl. He puffed a bit on it.

"I watched him once with one patient, a woman sick for months. No one had an inkling what was wrong. Some sort of stomach ailment. You know how many things cause stomach problems?" It was a rhetorical question. "So, we called in your father. What a bedside manner. He held her hand and looked into her eyes. And do you know that he asked nothing about her symptoms—*nothing*—only about her diet over the past weeks!" He put down his pipe and looked right at me. "Who cares about what one eats? Why, I almost burst out laughing, I tell you. Then he comes into my office and sits right where you are sitting and says without any expression on his face, 'Cow's milk.' I had no idea if that was the cause or the cure. I held my laughter while he explained that people often have difficulty digesting it. This woman, he contended, was unusual because her disturbance was only in spring and summer—when the herd ate clover!" He lifted both arms to indicate his disbelief at such a peculiar diagnosis. "But then he said cryptically, 'Winter silage, no problem.' I stopped laughing then. Who ever thought to consider anybody's diet until your father came along? Changed everything we do now." He paused to take a few more puffs as he turned to take a book off his shelf. He handed it to me. "We still use his book, *The Art of Diagnosis*."

Of course, I had seen that book. Father had spent many an evening writing it—evenings I would have preferred he spend with me. Any other time, I would have been pleased to hear of my father's accomplishments. But today I heard a disparaging comparison between him and me.

"Heart attack, right?"

Yes, I said.

"Autopsy?"

Just the thought of strangers excising my *own* father's heart with all the zeal of a butcher carving a side of beef flooded my senses. He must have seen my eyelids flutter and changed the subject.

The director tapped out the spent tobacco and repacked it. He clenched his teeth on the stem with a clicking sound. He checked his watch. "Berlioz?"

"*Je ne sais rien sur Berlioz, comme toujours.*"

He changed the subject. "You have probably heard the story about your father risking his life to help a friend in Warsaw."

I had not.

He looked surprised. "Yes, his friend, Nicolas, a childhood friend from your village, I was told."

He lit the pipe as he recounted that Nicolas had been the protégé of a Polish businessman, who taught him the language and offered to take him to Warsaw so the sixteen-year-old could continue his education and tutor the man's children. After some years in Poland, Dr. Dittmar continued, Nicolas wanted to return to France because there was talk of a third partitioning of Poland, and he feared danger was afoot. Two previous divisions had outraged Poles, who felt helpless against the combined might of Austria, Prussia, and Russia. The political situation had become unstable, and his fears about the peril came true: Many futile uprisings ensued.

He repacked his pipe and lit a lucifer. I watched the phosphorous burn orange and yellow. "Your father was in Paris then. Just finished medical school. Nicolas wrote him from Warsaw. Said his leg had caught a bullet in the Kościuszko uprising and was infected." Dr. Dittmar turned his chair to stare out the window, as if the rest of the story lay on the lawn. "Your father left for Poland the next day. He knew an untreated shrapnel wound would kill him."

I interrupted. "What about local doctors?"

He shook his head. "Hospitals were full. Besides, Nicolas was an insurgent *and* a foreigner. No doctor wanted to chance helping him." He held the pipe near his mouth teasing his lips as he spoke. "Your father debrided the wound daily, and Nicolas started perking up. Then, one day your father left before curfew for more supplies in town. Never came back."

I leaned in. "What happened?"

"The tsar's men captured him. Violated curfew, they said."

"But you said he left *before* curfew."

"Rules were what they said they were," he said, striking another lucifer on his shoe.

He continued: "Your father sat there and told grisly details about being tortured by his captors . . . tying him upside down, caning the soles of his feet. Kept him awake for several days, he said, and trussed his arms so tight behind him that he lost all sensation."

My father did favor his arms when doing heavy labor. He winced when he lifted anything over his head. Old age, I thought, maybe arthritis. I never thought to ask.

The doctor went on: "He pleaded with them, 'I am a doctor!' he said. 'I need my arms for work.' Why was he in Warsaw, the soldiers demanded, and why was he helping someone resisting the tsar? Listen to this: They thought your father was a *spy!*" He laughed and hit his thigh at such an absurd idea.

My eyes widened at the incredible idea. "Was he?"

The director put his pipe down and opened the window to fan out the smoke. "Never asked. People do stranger things than spy in wartime. His pleas for leniency must have worked. He came by to see me when he returned. I begged him to teach medicine here. No, he said. He was resolute about returning to the countryside to help the workers there."

I was captivated by the story. "Where is Nicolas now?" I asked.

"Died."

"Because of his wound?" I asked, with some apprehension.

"*Mais non*. Three years ago, in some place called Żelazowa Wola outside of Warsaw. Tuberculosis. Never did make it back to France."

I now saw my father in a different light. He had risked his life to save a friend and yet had said nothing.

"Well, young man," he said, putting the pipe down and crossing arms, "what do you intend to do now?"

I wished he had not asked me that, for I had no idea. *No* idea. I felt lost.

"By the way, your father said he communicated sometimes with Nicholas. You might want to talk to his son. He lives here in Paris. Quite famous."

"Oh? Who is that?"

A knock interrupted him.

"*Entrez-vous*," said the director.

Hector stood in the doorway. "Excuse my tardiness, Doctor Dittmar."

"Monsieur Berlioz, come in."

Hector looked at me as if to apologize for leaving me in the lion's den alone.

I arose. "Thank you for that story, Doctor." I reached for the door handle, then turned back, "You never told me Nicolas' last name."

"Chopin. Nicolas Chopin."

Berlioz perked up. *"Je connais très bien Frédéric Chopin.* Would you like me to introduce you?"

## CHAPTER 4

# George Sand's Diary – Chopin, Finally!

Dear Diary:

At long last I have met Chopin. He has been on my mind for many months. I finessed an invitation to his apartment for a musicale with some of Paris' artistic elite last night. How is it that we have such talent in our city now? Liszt, Hiller, Meyerbeer, Kalkbrenner. And those are just the musicians. Liszt was incomparable. Such a showman. But Chopin cast a spell on everyone, including me, when he improvised on some themes.

The setting was magical. Candlelight pooled around the piano. I sat in the shadows in a white chair that turned orange from the flames in the hearth. I cannot imagine a séance looking any different that night. The whole evening transcended earthly bounds. The night concluded after the Chopin and Liszt played a sonata for four hands. My only regret was that more people did not hear this display of brilliance, worthy of the ears of the King of France, that is, *if* I liked the king, which I do not!

I wish it had been a séance. I would have conjured up my grandmother to scold her for being so mean to me. And Mother too. They tossed me behind the cloister grill in that convent as if I were a sack of potatoes, and for two years! The walls of the classroom were covered with a vile yellow paper the color of egg yolks; the ceiling was dirty and peeling; and the stink of henhouse commixed with the smell of coal from the stove.

We got up at six and, in winter, had to crack the ice in the water basin to wash. Our swollen feet would bleed in our too narrow shoes. We went to mass by candlelight before breakfast and either shivered on the bench or fell asleep on our knees in a posture of meditation. Dark rooms, relentless praying, the expectation of perfect behavior. I do not believe Mother knew what else to do with me. I suffered the first few months, but the joke was on them because I came to love the convent and all the freedom it gave me to think and read as I pleased.

I must admit that I feel quite motherly towards Chopin. He is so delicate and sickly with his constant cough. I need to suffer for someone. I need to use up the excess energy inside me. I need to nourish and look after a tired and ailing being. I am thirty-two years old now and long to fill that void in my life. But all thoughts of his infirmity left me when he played. This man beckoned the spirits out of the piano that wrapped around us listeners, invisibly, silently. I was unmoored from reality. No one else has captured my soul with music as Chopin did last night.

I am not sure what impression I left on him, or anyone else for that matter. I could barely move I was so entranced. Chopin is difficult to read. I wanted to pay tribute to him by wearing red and white—the colors of Poland—so he could see my solidarity with his homeland. But he hardly looked at me the entire night. I will persist. I feel this longing to be next to him, to see what sort of person creates this music.

I will tantalize him with an invitation to dine at Nohant next spring. No one can resist me! Parisian weather is inhospitably cold now. I will be lucky to withstand the freezing temperatures and blowing snow. The Champs-Élysées is empty. Too slippery. I dream of walking through the flowering trees and arbors of the Tuileries among the pale green willows and birches in the spring. For now, I will busy myself with writing until dawn, as always, and taking care of Solange and Maurice during the day.

Meanwhile, Mallefille is becoming possessive. I am pleased that my children are flourishing under his tutelage, but I do not consider that a successful pathway to my heart, regardless of whether we sleep together.

He continues to assume I am for the taking. How like a man. We do have intense talks about literature, but I do not share a soul with him. Just his bed. How will I ever juggle two lovers? I do relish the challenge, though.

## CHAPTER 5

# Cash – Conservatoire – Failure Again

## Cash

*I* awoke every day in Paris with unemployment biting at my heels. I considered selling the home in Marainville but decided against it for now. It would hardly work for Maman to live with me in my cubbyhole apartment or even manage the five flights.

Sadly, job prospects were slim in Paris: a waiter in a restaurant or shelving books in the library. No training needed, the ads said. I might as well have returned to dole out seeds at Petrichor if I had wanted to die of tedium.

Hector provided the ideal distraction to my travails by inviting me to a matinée recital at Notre Dame. The organist played an all-Baroque program: Buxtehude, Händel, and several Bach pieces. Low, growling bass notes thundered in my chest as sun streamed through stained-glass windows, drenching listeners in crimson and lapis. My spirits soared through the rafters and mingled with the clouds.

Strolling home that May afternoon, we lingered under greening maples and buckeyes to discuss the concert. I happened to mention my uncertain future and precarious finances.

Hector kicked a stone off the path as he thought. He looked up with wide eyes. "I have an idea," he said. "I was accepted at the Conservatoire for this fall. With my recommendation, they will most certainly accept you."

"But your father wants you to be a doctor," I said.

"Dr. Dittmar put an end to that. I only did it to please my father. I had been secretly composing for many years. I simply cannot live without music," he said. "Then I had my debut."

"What debut?" I asked.

He recounted how his *Symphonie Fantastique* in the Conservatoire's concert hall, no less. Most musicians could ill afford to rent such a regal hall and had to perform in cramped theaters or raucous circus arenas. Its horseshoe shape provided superior acoustics. Moreover, it accommodated only a thousand people. *Très intime.*

"They never knew about it," he said. "They live in the mountains near Grenoble, for God's sake. It takes five days by public stagecoach to get here." We turned onto my street. "They found out from a friend."

"What was your punishment?" I waited to see if he had been chastised as I had.

"Of course, my father was angry, and my mother said any musician was automatically on the road to Hell!" He laughed in a crazy, disarming way by throwing back his head and shaking his curls. Berlioz seemed disconnected from life, as if he were floating above it, eschewing the same rules we mortals followed. "And now that I have been 'excused' from medical school, they have finally relented." Hector ran his fingers through his hair and rolled his eyes. "Oh, the struggles I had with composing it. For some time, I had that symphony in my brain. I wanted to stagger the musical world!"

He described the brutal reviews he received from critics carping about how his symphony was overly orchestrated. He mocked their scorn: "'Why do you have two harps?' 'Why the chimes?' 'Berlioz always has to go to excess.' And on and on." He downplayed their complaints, then added with contempt, "You know what they hated the most? The wood side of the violin bows tapping against the instrument. I thought it was a clever way to signify bones rattling!'" He sighed. "I am just ahead of my time." He paused. "Critics," he said through his teeth, "I spit on them all."

I mulled over his offer about the Conservatoire. How plausible was a career in music? True, I had won several competitions in Marainville and had tutored students. I loved music. But this was Paris. Acceptance to the Conservatoire was one thing. But competing with the many talented musicians afterwards was quite another.

We reached my apartment after half an hour. Late afternoon traffic had picked up on the main thoroughfare. People hurried to dine with friends or attend a play. As with many buildings in Paris, the most expensive rez-de-chausée and mezzanine spaces were occupied by shops and businesses. Those cost about fifteen hundred francs a month. But prices declined as flights increased. My fifth-floor, tumbledown, attic lodging cost me twenty-five francs a month.

I was eager to hear about Berlioz's musical past and invited him for tea.

"I have work to do," he said and yet lingered, leaning against the doorway arch. "I tried playing the flute and clarinet, and my father gave me a flageolet as a child. But I was too busy composing. Even as a child, I had notebooks full of compositions."

He wore the confidence of a man who had already tasted success. I asked him why he was bothering with more musical training.

"I have a respectable ear for some original tone combinations," said Hector, without modesty. "But teachers have told me to learn more about my craft, so the Conservatoire it is . . . for now."

He straightened and put his hands on my shoulders. "Let me introduce you to the director," he said. "What can it hurt?"

We settled on three o'clock the following Wednesday. In the ensuing days, I thought of little but the challenges I would face. What if my technique proved lacking? What if I failed? My father's voice roared in my head, dripping with derision.

## Conservatoire

The music school was in the nineteenth arrondissement on rue Jean Jaurès between the Canal de l'Ourcq and the stunning, steep cliffs of Buttes-Chaumont overlooking the north of Paris. The music school's grand double cathedral doors and floor-to-ceiling second-story windows evoked the grandeur of a palace. Was I worthy of passing over its threshold? The likes of composer Luigi Cherubini and violinist Rodolphe Kreutzer graced the faculty. Frédéric Chopin had performed in its Salle des Concerts several times.

When I arrived that blustery afternoon, my father's gold timepiece showed exactly three o'clock. Berlioz had yet to arrive. I paced. My mouth was dry. Sweat bled through my shirt. I could leave. I turned to retrace my steps, but as I looked up the street, I saw only my pointless life staring back. So, I stayed.

By three-twenty, Hector ran up, breathless. "My work . . ." We entered the school. He started toward the director's office, but I paused in the cool, white marble entryway to take in the screech of violins, the bang of bombastic pianos, the flatulence of a blatting trumpet. The sounds were not what I had imagined from supposed vaunted music students. I caught up to Hector just as he rapped on the director's door.

Hector introduced me.

"*Eh bien*, Monsieur Delhomme," said the director coming from around the desk, holding out his hand. "Monsieur Berlioz tells me you are a burgeoning genius on the piano."

"I try, sir." I could have demurred, and in retrospect, should have.

"Which composers do you have the greatest affinity for?"

I reeled off Bach, of course, and Mozart and Handel.

"Anyone contemporary?"

"Chopin, *naturellement*. I have attempted some of his scherzi. But I am most partial to his Ballade in G minor." Then I shook my head. "But is it really Chopin if he himself does not play it?" I looked at both for confirmation.

The director smiled. "You are not the first to say that."

I liked this man. He was direct, friendly, accepting. He was my height with a thinning head of light brown hair and ready smile.

"Where have you performed?" he asked.

I reeled off my competitions, recitals, and church work.

"And composing? Did you bring any compositions?"

I deflected his question. "Sir, I am standing next to Hector Berlioz. What could I compose that would measure up to his wonderful feats?" I tried to make a good case for appreciating music and a great desire to learn. Yes, I would apply myself to the fullest.

"Apply yourself—to accomplish what, exactly?" he asked.

"Why, piano technique, of course . . . and the organ," I said, bolstering my case for being schooled in both instruments.

On the strength of Hector's recommendation, I was granted matriculation along with a stipend in exchange for office help. But it was miserly pay, barely enough to sustain me, and only if I ate one meal a day.

To make matters worse, the political situation in France was bad. Workers were publicly grousing about low wages, high taxes, and poor working conditions. These were not new complaints, but this time it seemed more urgent since King Louis Philippe had sent down but measly concessions. In the end, the laborers had but one recourse: to demonstrate. It was dangerous, given the king's well-armed forces. My father would have supported the workers, perhaps even marched himself.

I held out hope Hector would introduce me to his friend and fellow composer Frédéric Chopin. We could talk about music and piano technique and performing and, of course, share stories about our fathers, especially the one I had just heard from Dr. Dittmar about Nicolas Chopin's time in Poland.

I wrote Maman that I would be attending the Conservatoire. She replied with cool enthusiasm but admitted she was happy I had a direction now. She added a curt note about Lili, saying she had been arriving later and later each day with puffy, sad eyes. My own life, heaped as it was with challenges, had no room to deal with the melancholia of an employee, and I could do nothing at this distance in any case. I kept thinking about Lili— her vulnerability, her loyalty to a man she rarely saw, her unerring belief he meant what he said about marrying her. I knew men. Clearly, he did that to keep her all to himself. Meanwhile, he was living the daring, dangerous, wanton life of a soldier overseas. I felt sorry for her. She was a virginal maiden, and he, a bawdy brawler who I imagined spat on the ground and reeked of whiskey and tobacco. But I kept telling myself that he was her problem. *Stay out of it!*

A terse letter from Maman came soon thereafter. "Lili has quit," she said. No reason given. Naturally, she was beside herself and pleaded for me to come home. The classes at the Conservatoire did not begin for another few months. I had no recourse but to ask Berlioz for a small loan so I could take a cab back to Marainville that weekend with the aim of finding more reliable help. I promised to repay it incrementally as soon as I began receiving my stipend at the Conservatoire.

The coach rumbled past luscious forests and through villages with small produce stands piled high with dark morels, emerald green lettuce, ruby-red strawberries, and jars of clover honeycomb. Near Marainville, lemony-yellow sunflowers and lush vineyards growing on the foothills of the Vosges mountains contrasted with the rich brown fields. The government had promised to build a train line to the region, but so far it was only talk. I arrived around nine o'clock. Maman had already gone to bed. I followed suit.

The next morning, I went downstairs to make coffee. The same lace curtains from my childhood drooped by the open window over the sink. This kitchen was much larger than mine in Paris, bigger than my whole apartment. A long, pine farm table stood in the middle of the gray slate floor. Maman was an immaculate housekeeper, but lately, without Lili's help, soiled dishtowels were strewn in the corner, the floor had not been swept in days, dishes lay piled in the sink.

The morning light did no favors for Maman's demeanor or coloring. It had been only three months since Papa died. She seemed disoriented. Her skin was drawn and sallow. New lines had formed around her eyes. Her mouth was frozen in a frown. She took tiny steps and spoke in clipped sentences. Lili had not been here for two weeks.

I hardly knew where to begin. Should I address her sullenness and undernourishment, or broach the topic of what to do about Lili? Either one would invite argument. She sat straight but motionless, hands in her lap, eyes empty.

I walked to start the coffee. She sat to the right of Papa's captain's chair. No one had sat in it since he died. I chattered on about the Conservatoire and Berlioz and his *Symphonie* while putting on the kettle and setting the table. The breadbox was empty, and one lonely egg occupied the wire basket. Only God knew how old it was. I made a mental note to go marketing that afternoon.

My chair had a woven-rush seat and a wooden back with bluebells painted amid a garland of green ivy. It wobbled a bit more than I remembered. I took her hand. "You never said why Lili quit. Is she getting married?"

Maman started to answer, but her head turned toward a knock at the door. "Are you expecting someone?" I asked. No reply.

"Good morning, Lili," I said brightly when I opened the door. She wore a white sun dress with a pink sash and carried a small basket covered with a cloth. Her blond hair was pulled back. She registered surprise at finding me home. "I have something for your mother," she said.

"Please." I beckoned her in.

Maman looked away when she entered.

I offered her coffee.

"*Merci*, Monsieur Delhomme." She came into the kitchen and greeted Maman. "*J'ai un cadeau pour vous, Madame.*" She turned back a corner of the blue napkin to reveal warm croissants.

"They smell delicious!" I said as I placed one on a dish for Maman.

"I wanted to say goodbye," Lili said to her.

Maman held her head in an upturned palm and picked at the pastry's buttery flakes.

"Shall I let you two talk privately?" I asked, as I headed toward the coffee.

Lili indicated she wanted me to stay.

I returned to my seat. "Maman said you quit," I said.

"Yes. But it is not that simple. "

"Did you say something that upset her?"

"I . . . I . . . she said she could not pay for my services any longer."

Maman had misled me. Perhaps she was trying to preserve her dignity after exhausting her funds. I reached into my pocket for my loaned money and peeled off enough francs to pay for two more months. I held back enough for my return trip and next month's rent. Both mother and guest seemed relieved.

"I miss taking my potion," Maman said. "Will you bring some the next time? It makes me feel better."

"What potion?" I looked at Lili but Maman answered.

"Lili makes me this special tea that she says thickens my blood."

I touched Lili on the shoulder. "Thickens her blood?" How did a maid of fifteen know how to diagnose anyone, let alone treat such a condition?

Lili looked at me with a calm but resolute gaze. "I was worried about your mother. She complains often of being tired and dizzy. Sometimes she is confused about what day it is. And she looks so pale. My mother is quite familiar in herbal medicine. She suggested I make her this special tea."

"Made from what?" I asked, irritated her mother had diagnosed Maman without ever seeing her. It seemed imprudent.

"Dandelion and burdock root," she said.

"Beaulieu," said Maman, "the tea did make me feel better."

I understood my father's misgivings about herbal medicine being too imprecise. But at least Lili cared enough to help. Maybe I was angry at myself for not taking her seriously or helping her more. I decided to ignore it.

I walked Lili to the door and thanked her for the croissants, and yes, the herbal tea.

"She keeps so little food in the house," she said in a low voice. "Sometimes I have to beg her to eat." She paused.

How charming Lili was with her perfect teeth and blushing cheeks. Her supple waist was slender and shapely. If only I could touch her to see if she was real. She reminded me of the china doll by my mother's bedside. The bisque head had painted eyelashes and blue eyes the color of a summer sky. "Never touch her," Maman warned about the fragile doll. I wondered if Lili would break, too.

"How is your fiancé?" I said.

She turned to leave. I did not pry for details. She hurriedly thanked me again for the wages and left without explanation.

I spent the rest of the day marketing. I bought two aubergines, four tomatoes, and several zucchini, and fresh bread. Some endive and pears would make a delicious salad. Maman and I chatted about this and that while I peeled the vegetables. The ratatouille lacked her extra touch, but she ate every bite.

## Failure Again

With Maman's situation stabilized, I returned to Paris. Hector, a true friend, offered to pay for concerts and recitals. I learned he was not afraid to express his opinion one night when a group of us went to the Opéra to hear Carl Maria von Weber's *Der Freischütz*. It was thoroughly enjoyable. But without warning, Berlioz stood up and shouted to the orchestra, "You do not want two flutes there, you brutes! You want two piccolos! Two piccolos, do you hear?" Then he sat down, crossed his arms, and studied his shoes for the remainder of the concert.

I hardly knew what to make of this outburst and in such a public place. Some fellow composers thought Berlioz's behavior was affected; others found him interesting and liked his fervor. Even his appearance drew looks of awe, with his high forehead, curving hawk nose and unruly mop. He said appearances did not concern him. He was singularly devoted to composing.

Unfortunately, even the cachet of Berlioz's imprimatur did not save me from my fate at the Conservatoire. Every day for two months, my musical regimen comprised fingering exercises, études, scales. Over and over, day after day I practiced until exhaustion set in.

M. Proulx, my piano teacher, was an excellent musician and instructor with much patience. We met in one of the many closet-sized, thick-walled practice rooms. M. Proulx had assigned a Scarlatti sonata to sharpen my timing and accent. As I sat at the small piano and began to play, he stood waving an imaginary baton to keep beat, and murmured "bum bum bum" to give auditory feedback. He stopped me several times, sat, and demonstrated on the keyboard how to correct my performance. But I could hear no difference. Discouraged, I did the unforgivable—playing wrong notes. He hid his mounting frustration, but I could feel it.

After my lesson that day, M. Proulx put his hand on my shoulder and said kindly, "God does not mete out talent equally." I was being dismissed.

I begged the director to keep me on in the office, but there were many other students with exceptional talent who also needed a salary. I left his office swallowing tears.

On the way home, I picked up some pebbles and lobbed them at cooing pigeons roosting on a bench. They flew off with a loud clapping of wings. I cursed an old beggar with bare feet, holding out his hand. I snapped, "I have no money either!" and walked away. True, I did not have much, but I did have shoes. I returned to drop some coins into his palm and wish him good luck.

## CHAPTER 6

# Tuning – Loan

## Tuning

*L*eaving the Conservatoire that afternoon feeling dazed and disoriented, I could not bear going home to a dark, empty apartment, so I headed northeast on rue Jean Jaurès to visit Giles Truel's piano shop. Rain drizzled. The thick mist made streetlamps irrelevant, each with an eerie yellow nimbus. The veil of mist soon became droplets, then strings, then heavy rain. Pools collected on the path. The gloom felt like a soothing coat around my drooped shoulders. I met a line of children leaving school for the day. Their shouts of joy pinged against my sadness. My shoes were soaked by the time I arrived at the shop.

Giles had tuned and repaired the Conservatoire's pianos and harpsichords for decades. I first met him when one note on my practice piano developed a distracting flutter. I heard him hard at work in the neighboring room. So, I knocked and asked if he could please check my instrument at his convenience. He followed me in and listened to the offending note.

"Hard to play anything when Middle C is unhappy," he said. He opened the lid, removed the front panel, and fine-tuned the bothersome string. The procedure took no more than five minutes.

"What was wrong with it?" I asked.

"One of the strings in the trichord fell flat. It happens, what with the pounding you students give it day and night."

We talked about my challenges at the school.

"Too much competition?" he said as he replaced the panel and closed the lid.

I forced a smile.

"I know that look," he said. "I see it every time someone tries to hide panic and inferiority." He looked over his glasses at me in a fatherly way. "Did you think you were the only one who felt that way?"

Giles seemed dedicated to a job that few would appreciate. No one ever listened to a piano and said, "My goodness, what a wonderful tuning!" It was the absence of excellence that one noticed, as when a note went sour.

I asked, naively, "How do you know when a piano is in tune?"

From his chuckle, I realized the whole of his knowledge about tuning had been telescoped into that one question. He picked up his tuning case. "Come to my shop someday. I will show you."

Without any signs and in the dense fog, I recognized his shop that rainy afternoon from an odd mixture of piano parts cluttering the bay window: an upright action, a black grand piano lid, and matching music desk. I walked in.

I could barely squeeze by the grand piano case taking up the lion's share of the floor. Against the wall stood two uprights stripped of everything but their strings. The smell of freshly sawn wood and hot hide glue hinted at new repairs. Some needle-nosed pliers, a flathead screwdriver, and equipment for drilling and sanding hung on the wall. The silver-haired tuner stood at his workbench. "*Oui?*" he said, looking in my direction. He did not recognize me at that distance in the gloom of day. "*Qui est là?*"

"*C'est moi*, Beaulieu Delhomme, from the Conservatoire."

"*Oui, oui, oui, oui, oui,*" he said, recognizing my voice. "Please come in," he said warmly. "I was about to leave, but perhaps I should wait until the rain stops." By now the downpour roared as it pelted the footpath.

I put my coat by the wood stove and rubbed my cold hands together in its warmth. He invited me over to see his restringing job. He had removed the original rusted strings and was measuring their gauge to ensure he replaced each one with the proper size. It all had to do with the physics of the instrument, he explained.

He asked how things were going with my education. Still smarting from my release, I said quickly that I had quit. He sympathized. "Pay it no mind," he said. "The Conservatoire is not the whole world of music."

"What are you working on over here?" I asked, looking at his workbench.

"New set of hammers." He walked over and picked up his rasp to demonstrate: "I take a new hammer," he picked up a hammer head, "and try to fit a wooden shank into the wooden hammer butt." He worked it a bit. "Hmmm, too tight." He sanded the shank just enough so it fit snugly. "Take care not to sand it too much," he cautioned, "or you must rely on the glue to hold it, and it will come loose after a time." He then smeared some hide glue on the end, fit the shank again into the hammer butt, screwed the assembly onto the keybed, and aligned it with its neighbor before the glue hardened. He took off his soiled blue apron and gave it to me. "Go on. Try it," he said.

I was overly cautious, and it took a while, but, boasting aside, I performed the task with alacrity. It brought back good memories of making wooden Christmas toys with my father for sick children.

"Ever think about learning the trade, Monsieur Delhomme?"

I had not. What kind of life would that be, tinkering with dusty piano parts and torturing my ears with out-of-tune strings all day? More importantly, what woman would want to marry a common laborer?

"The sooner you learn, the sooner you can become part of the elite group of tuners in Paris. Good ones are in high demand, my friend. Pay is pretty good too."

"How long does it take to learn?" I asked, then added, "I play the piano, so that should help."

"Sorry, but tuning has nothing to do with music."

How could that be?

Tuners listened to beats, he said, never the musicality. Beats were the pulses created by two strings vibrating at different frequencies. Tuners learned how to count them and adjust various intervals according to a pattern.

And how long would it take?

He spoke as he fitted and glued hammers in the treble section. "Maybe a year," he said, putting down his tools. His eyes met mine. "You must work hard, and I mean *really* hard."

I mentioned that I needed money right away.

"What if I pay you to help in the shop?"

"You mean, be your apprentice?" I pondered the offer. The salary, far from a king's ransom, would supplement the waning savings from the sale of my father's instruments and help me repay the loan from Berlioz. "And you teach me how to tune?" I asked.

"I can deduct the fee for weekly tuning lessons from your shop pay."

So, even less money. Was there any alternative? Oh, yes, the seed store in Marainville. I accepted his offer and even mustered some enthusiasm. I told myself I was building my future.

From the first day in his shop, I loved the precision and detail. Every evening, I left content that I had restored—may I say healed?—an instrument so it could sing as its creators had intended. At least there was no blood to contend with.

Tuning, though, presented an unexpected challenge. It took some doing to learn how to count the beats. Arduous, demanding work. But the greatest trial came from learning to move the tuning pins driven into a wooden pin block of wood so the strings would stay put. Without proper technique, pins would return to their original place, and the tuning would be doomed. Over and over I battled with those pesky pins. And over and over, the results were disastrous. I felt defeated.

At my weekly lesson, a full two months after starting, Giles commiserated with my struggles in his homespun manner, with a voice loaded with wisdom and patience reminiscent of my grandfather—one where the speaker knows the path that lies before the listener yet wisely allows self-discovery. He assured me that progress on all fronts would be slow. Great leaps on some days, falling back the next. That was natural. "A good tuner—an excellent tuner—is the lifeblood of a pianist," he said. "But it takes time."

A laudable goal, but was his comment supposed to encourage or warn me?

As time passed, I noticed that Giles was squinting more as he worked. He bumped into large objects that he should have seen. He fumbled with small parts and asked me to read the wire gauge for restringing.

One day, I came into the shop and found him weeping.

"Can I help, Giles?"

"I am going blind," he said. "Cataracts. Both eyes."

"What about glasses?"

He shook his head. "Spectacles are not the solution."

"But you can see now," I said. "Perhaps the doctor misdiagnosed you." My father said misdiagnoses happen all the time.

"I can hardly read."

A month later, he said he could see only shadows and bright light. I had to take over more responsibilities. But no word was said about increasing my salary. Of course, Giles had taught me a lot, but I needed more money. Pity did not quell the bellowing of an angry landlord or repair the soles of my well-worn shoes. *Tomorrow. I will tell him I quit unless he increases my pay.*

## Loan

The mid-July Parisian weather offered little respite from a two-week spike in temperatures. I started out early for the shop to avoid the heat. The long route gave me plenty of time to think about my wording. Few neighbors were astir, except for a handful of children playing Keep Away with a red ball on my street. They too wanted to take advantage of the cool morning air. How I ached to be a child again and avoid the grim reality of earning money.

Giles had arrived before me. He seemed happy, quite a change from his tearful demeanor the day before. "Delhomme," he said, rushing up, smiling, "I have devised the perfect plan." He held my forearms tight. "How would you like to buy my business?"

I thought he was kidding. "Then we both shall starve!" I said lightheartedly. But the more I thought about it, the more it seemed to work. He said the sale would include his extensive client list and his much sought-after endorsement.

"How much?"

A thousand francs.

I drew in my breath. "I have no such money, Giles! And I have a sick mother to care for."

He sweetened the offer: all his tools and supplies, as well as the two uprights and one grand in the shop now. "Once you repair them, they will bring a handsome price," he said.

True, pianos were selling quickly. But I would have to figure in monthly rent, transportation costs to clients' homes, lodging, food, *and* payment for tuning lessons. Given that a tuning costs four francs, it would take years to pay him back.

He used the edge of the work bench to steady himself as he felt around for a chair. "What about a bank loan?" he said, taking a seat.

I stepped back. "*C'est fou!*" I said at his absurd suggestion.

"Think about it. Please." Giles sniffed and looked at the ground. "I have been a tuner for forty-two years. I am sixty now. If you cannot raise the funds, I will have to sell my business to someone else."

It would take some time to arrange financing. That was certain.

I shuffled home that evening, hands in pockets, head down as I pondered my situation. Any Parisian banker would scoff at my request. What would I use for collateral—my mother's house? That hardly seemed prudent, even *if* she agreed to that. What if I defaulted on the loan? Then where would she live? With me in Paris? A thousand times *non*.

My next idea was to draw upon my father's good name. I would go to the Marainville branch of the Bank of France. Surely the bankers there would remember him and accede to my loan request based solely on that. He had been a loyal customer and probably had had some bank employees as patients. Besides, loans were commonly granted to farmers since the region depended on its agriculture for food and income.

Off I went to Marainville the next day. The weather during my trip was stuffy and hot. The coach, bound for Lorraine's capital, Nancy, was crowded. We stopped several times to let off and take on new passengers. I arrived in Marainville rather late. Even so, Maman was delighted to see me and kissed both cheeks several times. The house was in order, and she had a better appetite than before. A good omen.

By the next afternoon, rain clouds had collected. Gusts kicked up. I smelled rain. I dressed in my best suit and set out for the bank armed with a sturdy umbrella and my family's good name.

The bank felt like a place that welcomed only rich people. Brass fixtures shone in the daylight. Stout bankers in stuffy silk cravats and pinstriped suits sat behind carved wooden desks.

A Monsieur Couteau greeted me politely and invited me into his office. Did he remember my father, I asked. He had just started at the bank, so, no. There went my good will. I explained in a most convincing way that I sought a loan for a thousand francs. There were more pianos in Paris than anywhere else in the world, I said, and the wealthy often bought several, each requiring tuning at least four times a year. My voice became louder with each proffered argument, ending with the fact that many wealthy piano owners had weekly soirées to burnish their status in French society. Only *la crème* was invited to attend and perform. Those pianos had to be in the most sonorant and concert-worthy condition. By now I was leaning over the desk and waving my arms for emphasis. He sat steely eyed with his hand folded on his desk.

"How much do you earn for each tuning? he asked.

"I often put them under contract for four tunings a year."

"Then, how much is each contract?"

I delayed answering. "About 16 francs." I knew he was going to ask how many clients had signed these contracts. I exaggerated: "Twenty."

He tallied the sum in his head. "That means you have assurance of 320 francs per year."

"But there are other clients who need . . . "

He frowned and shook his head.

I protested. "Surely you give loans of this size to local farmers and vintners. What assurance do you have that their crops will not be ruined by hail or heat? My earnings are practically guaranteed," I said.

No response.

I stood and counted on my fingers: "Franz Liszt, Frédéric Chopin, Friedrich Kalkbrenner . . . shall I go on? They are all my clients, and they play almost nightly at their patrons' châteaux. I will never run out of work!"

He blinked slowly and looked as if he wanted to get this over with. "Sir," he said condescendingly, "without proper collateral, this bank cannot risk the loan. Farmers have land to repossess. Your father probably had equipment and supplies as security. But, you, you have nothing but the hope of becoming a tuner one day. Future earnings are not the same. What would you forfeit if you defaulted on the loan?" He paused, then summarized his point: "Tradesmen make bad risks." (He said 'tradesmen' with a sneer). Oooh, what a supercilious . . . I had to hold my tongue while I walked away in high dudgeon. Inside I felt defeated and scared.

Despairing, I returned to my mother's house. Lili was standing on the counter swishing a rag inside the kitchen cabinets. She smiled warmly as she removed a green-checked kerchief that set off her eyes. She asked for help down. I put my arms around her slim waist and lifted her to the ground. I could have done so a thousand times and never tired.

She had made salade Niçoise with green beans and tomatoes from her parents' garden for lunch. With a friendly face and a delicious meal waiting, my anger eased.

She set two places. "I will come back tomorrow to finish cleaning the cabinets, Madame." She put her apron on the counter and turned to leave.

"*Attends*, Lili," I said, surprising even myself by using her Christian name and daring to put my hand on her shoulder. "Please join us. You brought more than enough for three." She looked pleased to be treated like one of the family and set another place.

The meal tasted like sunshine itself. The tomatoes were at summer's peak and the beans were tender and sweet. After a few bites, I was able to recount my failed trip to the bank. Maman was sympathetic but had no suggestions. As I suspected, she never offered her house or land as collateral. I certainly was not going to bring it up; it would have frightened her to suggest it.

We finished our meal; Maman retired for her afternoon nap. Lili and I drank to the dregs the Cabernet. She said Maman had perked up with more help. I again delicately asked after her fiancé. It seemed a valid question since I needed to find her replacement if she left.

He had not written her in months.

Could I do anything to help?

No, but thank you for your concern.

Of course, I was inquiring out of self-interest: How much longer could

I maintain this antiseptic distance? My competition was an invisible man who promised her security and love but provided neither. I could offer love. Lots of love.

"Let me walk you to the door," I said, hoping to spend a few more minutes in her company.

"But Monsieur, the dishes . . ."

Leave them," I said, "and please call me Beaulieu." This was an audacious request since I was really her employer. But I thought it would nurture intimacy.

We stood on the porch chatting about the storm that had passed by now. I caught a twinkle in her eye that told me more than she was able to say.

"Au revoir . . . Beaulieu." She smiled coyly.

# CHAPTER 7

# George Sand's Diary – Switching Lovers

Dear Diary,

Anyone who underestimates me does so at his peril. I *will* have Chopin. It is only a question of when and how. Only one matter threatens to bollix my plans—Félicien Mallefille. How stupid can a man be to try to control me?

Mallefille and I have been lovers for only a year. But he has become so tiresome and boring. It worked out nicely that he could work with Solange and Maurice during the day, then tend to me in the evenings. This winter he irritated me so much that I invited others to the house to avoid being with him. Balzac and Hugo came for short visits. I lost myself in those warm relationships. Delacroix also came to discuss art, and he even painted a while. He loves the ambiance at Nohant. I am considering giving him a permanent room so he can stay for long periods here, and perhaps give Maurice some lessons.

When I returned to Paris last spring, I had every intention of beginning my campaign for Chopin's heart. But I was uncertain of his feelings for me. He is so enigmatic. We exchanged kisses. It appeared we might plunge into a mad love affair, but Chopin abruptly halted its progression. Up until now, it was fine that he refrained out of respect for me, perhaps out of timidity, or even out of faithfulness to another. It was as if he were afraid of soiling our love by being carried away any further. But now I am unsure about his feelings. The only thing he does consistently is cough, although he does so quite delicately.

With our relationship still unclear, I did not want to sever ties with Mallefille, but I had to get an answer from Chopin. So, I sent Mallefille to Le Havre with Maurice to throw him off the scent of my new affair. But it was clear he was not going to be discarded so easily. The only question was how many welts would be left on his ego. I underestimated his feelings for me. His reaction was so brazen, so crass. Unacceptable!

When Mallefille returned to Paris, I saw him stationed across the street from Chopin's apartment expressly to spy on me! When he met me coming out of Frédéric's apartment, he ran at me, brandishing a pistol. He wanted to kill me! Divine intervention put a wagon between us. It gave me just enough time to run to the corner and fling myself into another coach and escape certain death by mere seconds. My heart has not stopped beating out of my chest.

Ever the gentleman, Chopin said he was frightened that Mallefille would make yet another attempt on my life and said he would accompany me and my children to Majorca. We leave tomorrow.

Of course, he has many obligations, not to mention his health, that make travel difficult. I knew he did not have much money to be gallivanting off to a foreign country without an advance for future work. So, he convinced Camille Pleyel to pay him two thousand francs for twenty-four preludes in each of the major and minor keys, which would finance the trip. Very ambitious! Pleyel promised he would ship an upright piano to our apartment when we settle. What must have seemed like a gift to Chopin was really Pleyel's insurance that he would get his preludes.

Maurice has been quite ill with rheumatism. My friend promised wintering in Majorca will do both him and Fryk-Fryk good. I should not want to hear either of them cough and wheeze through another Parisian winter.

## CHAPTER 8

# Recruitment

## Recruitment

*I* received a sad letter from Lili that I knew was inevitable.

*Cher Beaulieu,*

*I am so very sorry to tell you that your mother passed away last night. Yesterday when I arrived in the late morning, she was too weak to get out of bed or eat. I gave her some weak tea, but she refused that too. When I tried to fetch a doctor or write you about her condition, she forbade me, saying she just wanted me to hold her hand.*

*I will miss her terribly. I hope to see you soon.*

*Avec tristesse,*
*Lili*

I wrote saying I would be home the next day to arrange for her burial. The doctor said it was acute anemia. She had complained of feeling tired and faint with frequent palpitations. Her pallor should have alerted me. But, my reaction to those complaints was that of a son, thinking her gripes were due to old age, perhaps loneliness, but nothing serious. Besides, it was too odious to think I would become an orphan at twenty-four.

In her will, she left me the house, apple orchard, strawberry fields, and an acre of unplowed farmland. Papa had thought about selling it but never did. "Who knows what might happen to France?" he said. "Having workable acreage will be good insurance against hunger in dire times."

During Maman's long illness, I called on Lili every possible chance while in Marainville. She seemed to be reciprocating my attention, almost coquettish at times. I did not want to push myself on her. She was still engaged after all. Or was she? From time to time, she confided in me about her fiancé, who had all but disappeared from her life. She never mentioned a date certain for their wedding. How I longed to touch her hair, lie next to her, and savor the perfume of her milky skin but did not dare reveal my feelings. I had to resort to furtive looks.

Now, with Maman gone, I would have little reason to go to Marainville except to court her and lay bare my feelings. Her soldier's absence provided ample opportunities to woo this precious damsel. I needed to act.

Meanwhile, in Paris I was never satisfied with my tunings. Giles comforted me with his wisdom: "Perfection is a chimera when it comes to pianos. Compromise is our only recourse." He was referring to the physics that militated against the ideal tuning. "Just do your best," he said, and left it at that.

Then one day, Giles surprised me by pronouncing me proficient enough to take on some of his far-off clients.

So began my tuning career.

I traveled throughout Paris and environs building a reputation as a reliable tuner. I made some money, but I still had little predictable income. I may have five or six tunings one week, then none the next. In any event, I could ill afford to buy his business now.

To my delight, word about my tuning acumen had spread throughout the city and beyond. One day in early September, I traveled to tune a client's new grand. She lived past the Bois de Vincennes southeast of Paris. It took almost an hour to reach her home. I had not expected the work to last longer than an hour, but before starting on the new one, the woman showed me another dilapidated and woefully out of tune instrument. She asked me to fix it for her children's music lessons.

The tuning was quite flat and took two hours to correct. Then, many hammers wobbled back and forth, which required putting a larger pin into each flange—sixty-six times! And on and on throughout the afternoon. I returned home around seven to an almost empty larder. I saw some root vegetables and stale bread in the cupboard. To make soup, I first started a fire in my small stove, then went out to collect water at the nearby fountain. While the water heated, I cut the rutabagas, turnips, potatoes, and carrots very thin to hasten their cooking time. I repeatedly stirred, salted, and sipped until I could wait no longer. My hunger was so fierce that I hurriedly spooned some into my bowl, splattering hot broth on my hand. I dunked the bread to make it edible, a practice my mother frowned on but I indulged in out of exigency.

Midway through a second helping, someone rapped. "Drat," I said out loud. I expected Giles or perhaps Berlioz at this hour. Instead, there stood a stranger about my height with pudgy hands. Not a pianist, I surmised.

"*Oui, monsieur*?" I said chewing a piece of the moistened bread.

"Monsieur Delhomme, I am sorry to disturb you," he said, winded from the climb up.

He knew my name. Would he please tell me his?

"François Vidocq," he said, "humble servant to King Louis Philippe."

My eyes widened. "The *king* sent you?"

"May I come in?"

Curiosity quieted my rumbling stomach for the time being. "Please," I said, showing him in and offering my only chair while I sat on my bed of layered rags and the wool blanket my mother had given me.

A stale scent of alcohol and sweat followed him. "What could King Louis Philippe possibly want with *me*?" I said. I lit a small candle stub and placed it on the three-legged table between us hoping to burn off the stench.

"Your name was given to me by Hector Berlioz," he said. "He told me you two knew one another from the Conservatoire. I also attended the Conservatoire."

That surprised me. Hector had never mentioned this man's name, but there was probably no reason to. "Do you play the piano?" I asked innocently.

He laughed. "With these sausages?" He held up his fat hands. "I played French horn."

I laughed politely but was unconvinced. He seemed too unrefined to have had any musical training. I glanced at my steaming soup in hopes of expediting the visit. "You have no piano, then?"

"No piano, only an offer."

"It must be some offer for you to bother me at such a late hour."

"The king needs you."

"The king!" I said saucily. "Does the king need his royal piano tuned?"

He became testy at my dismissal of his mission. He spoke of unrest in the rural areas around Paris, and the threat of those agitating for better wages and working conditions, voting rights, jobs, and so forth.

I knew all of this. I did not need a civics lesson while my soup grew cold.

"We want you to help protect His Majesty," he said.

"Protect the king? He has a whole army to do that."

"Stop being flip!" An angry expression came over his face. "This is serious business. The king depends on the wealthy to keep uprisings at bay."

"And . . .?"

"We need to find out who is pro-monarch and make a list of allies."

"And . . .?"

"You have many rich clients."

I could have quarreled with the word 'many' but ignored it. "How, pray tell, does that work? Do I go into their homes and ask if they support the king?" I was not serious, but he caught none of my humor.

"Hardly, Monsieur," said Vidocq. "Just listen to their conversations. And *only* listen."

I thought this a preposterous request. Me, a piano tuner, eavesdropping on people's conversations about their political views. Such topics were not usually the subject of one's intercourse. Squeaky pedals, sour notes, missing keytops, yes. Politics? Never.

"No one will ever suspect you. So, they will speak freely."

Now I became suspicious. The king wanted to use me to curry favor with the rich—to *spy* on them. I liked it less the more I heard.

Vidocq was so large that his bulk spilled onto the wooden arms of the chair. Just last year, I had re-glued the joints, repaired the springs and cushion, and reupholstered it using some green chintz from the flea market. It was hardly meant for men of his girth. I held my breath as he wriggled to become more comfortable.

He continued: "But you can also listen to workers. That is the beauty of this plan. You easily blend in, what with your working-class togs."

"Working class!" I looked down at my tunic and (somewhat worn) corduroy trousers. "How dare you rank me with the . . ."

He put up his hand to stop me. "How would you describe yourself then?"

"Why, I am an artisan, sir!"

He waved his hand at me as if shooing away a fly.

"What matters is that you help your ruler."

Clarity finally came to my tongue. "You want me to be a spy, a *royal* spy, so I can betray my friends and acquaintances in my tatty clothing. And what danger does this present to me?" I asked.

"Absolutely none," Vidocq said with certainty.

That did not seem plausible. Spying often ended badly—death perhaps. Kill or be killed, was a spy's motto, and sacrifice all to accomplish the mission. Everyone knew that. I arose to signal the end of the meeting.

He motioned for me to sit on the bed again. "No need to get excited, Monsieur. You tune, you observe. Is that so hard?"

"You want me to 'observe' people when they have no idea that is what I am doing? That, sir, is called spying."

He squirmed again. "Spy sounds so wicked. Just assess the people you meet."

Assess. He meant spy.

"No one will get hurt. No one will find out anything. You are merely doing a favor for your emperor. Your father would have called you a hero."

He looked for my reaction at this mention of Papa. But he had gotten his information wrong. My father would never have stood for royal policies that hurt the working poor. His patients often gave him a chicken or vegetables to pay their bill. His real payment, he said often, really came in the form of pink-cheeked babies he delivered.

He railed against government policies to tax land. Such tactics would destroy farmers' livelihoods, people would buy less produce and fewer goods, schools would have more sick children; and the downward spiral would continue. Papa thought that a community was no richer than its poorest resident. Perhaps I, on the other hand, saw value in supporting all levels of society, including artisans. My family did not often speak of such things, but certainly my father's path was not mine.

That said, my face must have told Vidocq that his mission was too much to countenance. I stood again to show him the door.

He got up with a grunt. I thought he was going to leave, but instead he came close to my face and glared. "Your king has made a request," he said sharply. "There is *no* room for refusal."

Now he had my attention. This "request" had teeth behind it. And what of Berlioz? Had he been tricked into this too?

"We have not spoken about money," he said, pulling out a handful of bills.

The indignity notwithstanding, my gaze was perforce on his lips to hear of the arrangement.

For my trouble, he said, the king would pay me four hundred francs now, then another four hundred for each assignment I completed. It would not be stable income but would certainly help me buy Giles Truel's piano tuning business—the answer to my troubles. I could feel my resistance softening.

He walked toward the door. "Your first assignment after this is to become Frédéric Chopin's tuner."

A smile crept across my lips. Ah, now I understood. Berlioz was playing a trick on me! A strange man comes into my house late at night, tells me to monitor my clients' conversations and, by the way, ingratiate myself to one of the greatest musicians in Paris. How absurd! I decided to play along with this scheme. To be sure, I would pay Berlioz back with a practical joke of my own.

Red spread across his face when he saw my smirk. "You *will* serve your king!"

I could barely withstand his rancid breath and turned my head to avoid it, which only enraged him further. He drew back his arm to slap me.

I cowered. "Why me?"

He put down his hand and explained that Chopin had access to some of the richest students in Paris and played at the homes of benefactors almost nightly.

"What could I possibly say that would entice him to choose me as his tuner?"

"Your fathers knew one another," said the spymaster. "Start with that."

My memory went back to the story that Dr. Dittmar had told me about my father helping Chopin's father in Poland. I wanted details.

"Most important, he has taken up with George Sand."

"Taken up with a man?" I said.

"George Sand—a woman with a man's name. Imagine that! Her given name is Aurore Dupin. Quite love-struck, from what I hear. A real troublemaker, that one, with all that fanatical drivel she writes. It whips up workers, eggs them on to commit violence. Get what information you can about her. First step is to become Chopin's tuner. That gives you access to her. Simple as that."

I was dubious of the plan's effortlessness. The whole thing smacked of deception, which did not suit my personality.

It would, however, put me into the limelight of Paris' upper class. No matter how great the château or wealthy the owners, pianos still needed tuning. Of course, the tradeoff meant dishonesty. Then again, would withholding information about my assignment be the same as lying? I did not think so. But spying in the service of the king, why, that seemed too much to ask. Thoughts scurried in my head like squirrels at play on a tree. "I will have to think about this."

"The king is an impatient man!" he shouted and threw the fistful of money at me. The bills fluttered down. He opened the door and stepped over the threshold. "The next installment will come after you become Chopin's tuner. See that you succeed."

"Wait," I said into the hallway. "When can I meet Monsieur Chopin?"

"You figure that out. No Chopin, no money."

"But how will you know when I have succeeded?"

"Monsieur Delhomme," he glared at me through his bushy eyebrows, "that should be the least of your worries."

By now, soup cold, nerves frayed, I sat down to absorb the import of the situation. My financial troubles were easing, but France's political problems were escalating. And I had just chosen sides.

# Meeting Chopin

## Meeting Chopin

*M*y new spy mantle, courtesy of Vidocq, felt like a hair shirt as punishment for defying my father. Had it not been for my employment situation, I would have resisted. But here I sat. The very fault my father accused me of—weakness in the face of challenge—was now in full bloom. But I had made my bed. Now I had to lie in it, hair shirt and all. I was officially a royal spy.

I had built a solid reputation as a tuner by now. But still, work was slow in coming, especially in winter, when many wealthy patrons left for warmer climes. Weeks would pass before another client needed my services. But business always improved when spring rains swelled the grain causing it to go sharp. Such is the response of all wood instruments to humidity.

As directed by Vidocq, the king's envoy, I prepared to visit Chopin to offer my services. I came armed with several names of clients who would recommend me. Unfortunately, our mutual friend Berlioz was not able to accompany me, so he did me the courtesy of sending a letter of introduction. I wanted to meet the pianist for personal reasons. But I did not dare confuse that desire with my "royal" obligations. Chopin would see no guile, only sincerity, in wanting to become his tuner. Without accomplishing that goal, I would fail to do Vidocq's bidding and delay the necessary funding to buy Giles' business. But I had to gain his trust first.

Today was that day. I set my jaw, closed the door to my apartment, and headed for rue de la Chausée d'Antin.

A late March snowstorm conspired against me: Wind pushed against my chest, drifts hid the sidewalk, and ice sent me sprawling. Blowing snowflakes stung my eyes and speckled my green wool overcoat until the wind whisked them away.

I arrived at Chopin's apartment building and made my way to the second floor. Thoughts stirred in me like boys fighting under a blanket. While my intention was not to lie *per se*, I was intending to misrepresent my purpose somewhat. I paused outside his door, trying to quell the roiling anxiety over my duplicity. I heard a nocturne. *He must be composing,* I thought. *I should come back another time* and turned to leave. But my other self was stubborn. *Do it now!*

I brushed the snow from my pants and wiped my feet. My benumbed hand managed only a faint knock. The music continued. I tapped with my key ring for volume. Before long, the storied Chopin opened the door. He had a pleasant face framed by light brown wavy hair that fell below his ears. He wore a dark-colored velvet jacket and waistcoat.

"Yes," he said, "what is it, Monsieur?"

I stood in awe for a moment but regained my speech. "Good day, Monsieur Chopin." I bowed crisply as I held out my calling card.

"Good day," he replied. He took the card and examined it. "Beaulieu Delhomme, piano tuning and repair," he read out loud. "Yes, Hector said you were coming. So sorry, Monsieur, but you made the trip for nothing. I have no need of a tuner," he said, handing back my card. "Thank you for coming by." He started to close the door.

"Excuse me, Monsieur," I said, holding it open. "I am not seeking work. The friendship between our fathers has brought me here."

I held out the card again for him to recall my father's name. He studied it, then searched my face. "Yes ... my father knew a Delhomme—his first name was ... Gérard—in the small village where he grew up. Do you know this family?"

Pride swept over me. I clicked my heels and bowed again. "Monsieur, Gérard Delhomme is my father."

Curiosity must have replaced his resistance. He motioned me inside. He took my coat and hat and pointed his chin toward the drawing room as a way of inviting me in, and in a not altogether polite way either.

"Would you like some cocoa, Monsieur Delhomme? I have just made myself a cup."

I gladly accepted and warmed my hands by the fire as I awaited his return. It was a small apartment, with wine-colored velvet curtains and several rugs to dampen the sound and discourage eavesdroppers, I surmised. To the right of the fireplace stood his Pleyel grand. The music desk held an unfinished score with several staffs scribbled out and another with a nocturne, the one I had heard through the door. Normally I would have scolded a client for keeping such a fine instrument just a few feet away from a working fireplace, but this was neither the time nor place, and certainly not the person, to admonish. That would have been presumptuous.

I was eager to get details of both our fathers' bravery in Poland. Dr. Dittmar had painted a heroic picture of Papa's efforts there. I wanted to hear more about his father's experiences.

The composer glided swanlike across the room. He offered me a seat in a comfortable, dark-blue wingback chair. Thin, painfully thin, his body reminded me of a goblet with a too-fragile stem. He was taller than I by about three or four inches. He placed the cups on the small, round table between our chairs. His delicately formed hands seemed to have an intelligence of their own. We sat for a minute, he, fussing with his napkin and I, stirring my cocoa. He started to cough and sipped his drink to quell it. He appeared agitated, and I soon found out why.

I began. "How did your father fare after being wounded in the Kościuszko uprising? Papa said he was brilliantly brave to have fought in it. Of course, it ended badly for the insurgents. But Papa was only too glad to help your father get better."

Chopin's jaw dropped. "Help, you say?" He got up. "Help? He left my father all alone. He could have died."

Now it was my turn to be baffled. "But I was told he took care of him. He traveled all the way from Paris. He risked his life!"

"Is that what he told you? Then you were lied to."

I tried to remain calm. "My father never mentioned any of this. I learned about it from . . . from . . . the director of my medical school." I did not want to bring that up, but it slipped out.

"Medical school? I thought you were a piano tuner."

"Yes, well, I am now."

"Let me tell you what happened," said Chopin. He weighted his words and spoke slowly with a thick Polish accent. "My father was a twenty-one-year-old Frenchman. The Kościuszko rebellion broke out in Warsaw. The Poles thought their country was disappearing. Austria, Prussia, and Russia—they wanted to carve up our land! So, my father joined the municipal militia. He wanted to show solidarity." He paused to quell another coughing spell.

"Are you ill?" I asked, interrupting.

He signaled the unimportance of his cough. But it did not sound unimportant.

He continued: "My father was wounded." The composer got up and paced the floor as he talked. He moved as if everything hurt. "Your father cared for him for a few days, then disappeared!" His eyes were afire. Did I understand the import of what had happened? his look implied. "Your father never came back! He left him there. No way to get help. No way to get food."

This was not the story I had been told. I doubted my father would have lied to Dr. Dittmar. I dared not say anything against Chopin's father, especially when my own livelihood depended on luring him into my web. But anger overcame me at this unfounded accusation. I had to leave before saying anything untoward. So, I put down my cup, stood, and grabbed my coat off the hook. "I apologize, Monsieur Chopin, but I must be intruding on your work," I said, offering a slim excuse.

But he blocked the door. "What explanation does your father have?" he asked sternly. "Why did he leave? My father almost died!"

I turned to face him but could not meet his eyes. "My Papa did not abandon yours," I said in a controlled voice. "The tsar's men captured him. They said he was violating curfew and tortured him to get information." I looked at him without reproach. "They sent him home, ailing though he was from his own wounds. He did *not* abandon your father!" I turned and opened the door a second time. "My father knew how dangerous Warsaw was. But he risked his life to aid his friend. He was dedicated to his profession and to his friend."

Stunned silence filled the room. Neither of us was ready to apologize for the actions of our fathers, nor was an apology called for. Understanding was.

"Monsieur Delhomme, please, come sit down," he said in a mollifying voice.

I wiped my eyes and returned to the chair. We sat wordlessly. The political had become personal for both of us.

"How long have you been in Paris?" he asked after a time.

And with that simple question, we started our conversation anew, treading lightly on that brume of sorrow. We talked about performances and pianos.

"How do you find playing on the instruments of the Parisian elite?" I asked.

Happy to change the subject, he uncrossed his legs, leaned forward, and spoke with new-found energy about performing at sundry venues, which meant playing on pianos in equally sundry states of repair. Nothing galled him more, he said, than having to make do with an inferior instrument that fought him as he played. "Some have missing strings; some have noisy pedals. One time, I played in a different key to match the squeak!"

Time passed as silently as a cat crosses a room.

As he escorted me out, he sheepishly admitted that his own piano was ill-situated by the fireplace. "My tuner tells me to move it. But where?" he said, looking around the small apartment. "I want to rent a bigger place. When I have the money," he said. "My Pleyel deserves a better home."

How relieved I was that I had not uttered a word of rebuke.

We shook hands. His thin fingers did not return my grip, probably more out of protection than poor manners. How else would he speak through his instrument if they were damaged?

"If you would like, I could inspect your instrument . . ."

"Nice meeting you," he said, interrupting. "But, as I mentioned, my needs are met by my current tuner. *Au revoir*, Monsieur Delhomme." With that, he closed the door.

I trudged home in the same storm that accompanied my arrival, happy to have met a musical idol but frustrated he needed no tuner. I could almost feel Vidocq's eyes on my neck and my pockets clamoring for more money.

## CHAPTER 10

# Sand's Diary – Rating Men

Dear Diary:

Chopin's touch is so gentle, as if he thinks I might break by pressing too hard. Of course, that is preposterous that *I* would break. No one would ever call me fragile. But it thrills me to be treated that way. His kisses are so sweet and equally delicate, like being caressed by the wind.

He and I have a different relationship than I am used to. Good God, that brute Mallefille treated me like a prostitute. He had his way with me so often that the only thing missing was the payment for services. That can be thrilling, but other times, it feels as if I am on a construction crew: "George, do this. George, do that. Slower . . . slower now fasterfaster.

Chopin is like a dance partner who senses my moods and needs. I hope all my past lovers read this. Do you hear me? *My* moods and needs. Not just yours. Lovers should receive *and* give. I can tell so much about a man when we are in bed. Does he treat me like a farm animal? Or does he look at me, talk to me, tell me he loves me, and *mean* it? Behavior in love-making reveals a man's true personality and deep-seated view of women: Are they chattel or your equal? Which is it? It should be the first step in any relationship.

Sometimes, I do not even need to go through the tedious process of sleeping with them. For example, I instinctively knew that Liszt would be an aggressive and bossy beast, throwing his lover around and pouncing on her like a lion capturing a zebra, not caring a jot about her. And . . . I was right.

Chip-Chip would never demand I do anything. He cherishes me, and I adore that. I adore him.

I do not care for men who are on the other side either—too wishy-washy, waiting for me to orchestrate things. "Tell me what you want, darling." I want to be made love to! I want someone to take my soul to the moon and back, not make me feel as if I am the conductor of a train. I run the other way from those sorts.

But the worst are those men who treat the whole event like a job. In and out, in and out. No passion, no inkling there may even be a second person in the room, let alone the bed. I find it an ideal time to develop characters and plots while undergoing such quotidian maneuvers. And I may even blend the experience into a story. I call it 'secret sex' because only one of us is having it. And it is not I.

Such are the pitfalls of an untethered life. But I can be either master or mother, not both; being somebody's mistress takes too much time.

One thing I cannot abide, no matter how suave and tender, is a malodorous man. That oaf who almost raped me in the convent when I was sixteen stank to high heaven—a putrid, bitter, unforgettable smell too. It signals helplessness to my brain. Perhaps workmen like that man cannot escape such a fate because they labor in the hot sun, and perspiration dries on their bodies and clothes. But, to bring that reek into bed and then expect me to muster romantic feelings is unforgivable and certainly antithetical to their aim. What does one say to such an inconsiderate muttonhead to encourage better hygiene? For once, I am at a loss for words. I have no recourse but to expel him post haste. Smell may be one thing, but given the panic that that smell triggers, I would advise any suitor eying my bed to check his underarms first.

## CHAPTER 11

# Tailor – First Hurdle

## Tailor

That evening, spent as I was from my emotional visit with Chopin, I decided to retire early. I was too exhausted to restart the fire in the stove even to make any dinner. No heat, combined with a cold spell, meant adding an extra blanket. I lay there looking up at the beams in the ceiling. What a curious story about leaving Chopin's father in a lurch. Neither Papa nor Dr. Dittmar mentioned it. My pondering ceased with a sharp rap.

"Monsieur Delhomme!" the man roared through the door. "May we talk, please?"

I put on my robe and slippers and opened the door.

"Did I disturb you?" It was Vidocq, the rude, royal spy recruiter. It had been only a few hours since my meeting with Chopin.

"Yes?" I asked somewhat irritated.

"What came of your meeting today?" he said in the doorway.

"Come in," I said, yawning. "Neighbors have a way of eavesdropping." I offered no refreshments, a gaffe no ruder than his unbidden arrival.

The man sat down. "Well?"

I was no longer surprised he knew of my comings and goings, but I was irritated by his intrusiveness. "We became acquainted," I said, vaguely.

"Are you his tuner now?"

"Was I to do this instantaneously?"

"Yes, if you want money. The workers are restless. What should I tell the king?"

"But Chopin has no need of a tuner now," I said.

"We have a plan," he said.

Who was this 'we' he kept referring to?

"Set up a concert for Monsieur Chopin."

Set up a concert? He was daft. Such an undertaking required contacts with other performers, money, time, not to mention the consent of Chopin himself. I had to convince him I was a worthy tuner first. "Whatever for?"

"Our people will eavesdrop on audience members."

"Let me do it my way," I said, trying to delay his outrageous demand.

Vidocq remained cautious. "Get going, Delhomme! There is no time to waste when it comes to war." The chair squeaked its displeasure as he struggled out of it.

What was this war he kept talking about? I had heard nothing. But then, I was not the one worried about losing the crown.

Some weeks later, I received a letter from Lili. We had begun corresponding in the last few months and I asked her for updates on efforts to maintain the house. I was pleased at her warmth.

*Cher Beaulieu,*

*There has been less rain than usual this spring. The farmers are worried. But I see gray clouds collecting in the sky now. Their moods may improve after their crops have had a good soaking.*

*As you requested, I have been cleaning and sweeping your mother's house to make sure no rodents or spiders make a home there.*

*The next time you come to Marainville, I will give you some of my strawberry jam I put up last summer and a loaf of bread I made with the delicious hard red wheat from the nearby farm. The two go well together.*

*Please tell me how lovely Paris is now with its leafy boulevards and smart ladies in their Easter hats.*

*Affectueusement,*
*Lili*

I was happy to receive these occasional updates, hinting at her fondness for me. What would her fiancé think if he read her warm missives? After some time, the letters became more personal. She seemed increasingly interested in my life in the city. Spurred by her genial tone, I intended to return to Marainville soon to continue my courtship, but first things first. Vidocq's ultimatum rang in my ears: *"Pas de Chopin, pas d'argent."*

*Chère Lili,*

*Thank you for apprising me of the condition of my mother's house. I so appreciate your taking the time to do that and look forward to seeing you in Marainville again soon.*

*Tendrement,*
*Beaulieu*

The next day brought April weather that would tease Parisians about spring's impending arrival. The birds were returning from southern climes and set about making nests while they sang their sweet songs. The trees began greening. Invisible at dawn, buds and leaves darkened hourly as they matured. Purple and white crocuses and audacious primrose on riverbanks broke the flatness of winter. Overnight rain had rinsed away winter's fusty air. Paris was now covered by a cloudless, blue sky. Even hardened pessimists could not maintain their bleak scowls as warm zephyrs tousled their hair.

By now, after more than a year apprenticing Giles, he said I had surpassed expectations and was ready to take over all his customers.

Vidocq's suggestion to set up a concert was too ambitious, albeit potentially lucrative. But it had to wait. First, I had to convince Chopin he could not do without my services and had a plan to do just that. I walked in the fresh morning air to his apartment. I knocked. No answer. Thinking he might be in his bedroom, I knocked with more force. A disgruntled neighbor peered through her door crack.

"*Qu'est-ce que vous voulez, Monsieur*? The man is not home. Is it not obvious?"

Parisians are not known for their civility, especially when disturbed in the early morning. I told her I needed to deliver a message to the pianist. Did she know where he was, perchance?

"I saw him with a coat over his arm while wearing another one." She pointed to the window in the hallway with sunshine pouring through. "Who needs two coats on a day like this? Check with Monsieur Dautremont on rue Boulevards." She shut the door with an exclamation point.

M. Dautremont's tailor shop was a few blocks south of his apartment. I had been there last year to have a shirt mended. I hurried, fearing the musician had already left. Silver bells hanging from the door tinkled as I entered. The walls were lined top to bottom with bolts of dark Italian wools, brilliant Chinese silks, and Nepalese cashmeres. The gayer fabrics, I assumed, were for women, but I had seen some adventuresome men sporting patterned trousers. A flat iron sat face up on a trivet. The other warmed by the open fire.

"*Bonjour, Monsieur Dautremont. Il fait très beau aujourd'hui, n'est-ce pas?*" I hoped he would remember me. He only squinted in acknowledgement because his lips gripped several straight pins. He was a short, rotund, serious man, always pressed for time. He was but one of two hundred and fifty tailors serving over a million Parisians but one of the most sought after. He charged dearly for his services. For that price, he delivered skillfully constructed finery for his affluent clientele on time, no matter the deadline or occasion. The pianist was standing on a raised platform in front of a full-length mirror. The tailor was adjusting the sleeves on his double-breasted frock coat.

"*Monsieur Chopin, bonjour!*" I said, delighted to see him for the first time since our meeting on Chausée D'Antin.

He reached over to shake my hand.

"Monsieur Cho*pin*," the tailor said spitting out the pins. "No movement! I do not want to poke you. *C'est dangereux, eh?*"

"*Je m'excuse. Je m'excuse,*" said Chopin straightening and catching my eye in the mirror.

I watched as the deft, bespectacled sartor gathered the material puckering around his narrow shoulders.

"How did you know I would be here?" asked the composer, looking at himself in the mirror.

I mentioned the woman across the hall.

"People always know more about me than I think."

I said I had heard about his soirée that evening. He looked surprised. "Yes. *Chez Fourchettes*," he said. "I see Madame Busybody is not alone in knowing about my comings and goings." There was an edge to this last comment that I did not understand.

I continued: "Of course, you have not asked for my opinion, but tonight's gathering would not be a propitious venue for you, sir." I thought he might be curious enough to ask more. I was wrong. Instead, he looked irritated.

"Did you come here just to tell me that?"

I smiled feebly. Did he see me as meddlesome?

"Why, of course not. I also wanted Monsieur Dautremont to make me a new . . . a new velvet gilet," I said, fibbing. "In black. I am to attend a friend's wedding in a few weeks." I was shocked at how easily these lies flew out of my mouth.

"I appreciate your concern about tonight, but Franz Liszt will play most of the evening. There might be a duet or two." I had heard that he and Liszt often appeared together at salons to dazzle listeners.

"Oh, yes. Monsieur Liszt. How magnificent that will be, two grand masters, sitting side by side . . . "

He interrupted me. "Madame has *two* pianos. I would never play a duet with Franz on the same instrument. That would be like Mozart playing alongside Salieri." He chuckled. "There are not enough sharps for the both of us."

"Of course," I said, hurriedly agreeing. Now I felt even more ridiculous suggesting such a thing. I should have known better.

"Besides," he added, coughing hard into his handkerchief, "I am a bit under the weather today and may leave early."

"*Tournez, s'il vous plaît*," said the tailor, wishing to survey his work from the front. He buttoned the coat and smoothed down the collar and lapels, frowning. Chopin and the tailor both demanded perfection.

"Sir, my concern has nothing to do with your health." I quickly realized how insulting *that* must have sounded. "I mean, of course I am concerned about your well-being," I spluttered. But I felt I needed to explain. "My warning involves the grand piano, sir."

The tailor was finished. He gingerly removed the coat and headed to the ironing board.

Chopin put up his hand. "I have already asked Antoine to work on it, actually both pianos, yesterday. He assured me that they will meet my standards. Do you know Antoine Massot? Very fine tuner. No need to worry."

I did not like being dismissed as if I were an errant child. I wanted to seem as if I were looking out for his welfare. Perhaps he was irritated at the tailor, it was not clear, but I felt it my professional duty to continue and, more importantly, to show my concern.

"I am sure Antoine did a fine job," I said, hoping to change his mind. "But a tuner can do only so much, Monsieur. I have worked on the Fourchettes' grand. It is a Pape, an altogether average mark for an instrument, not at all like your Pleyel. I fear it will not obey your touch."

I knew a sluggish keyboard would be the enemy of his silky arpeggios and spirited scherzi. Liszt, on the other hand, manhandled every instrument he met. He would not care a whit about a slow keyboard and perhaps not even notice. Only with Chopin's music could one appreciate the quality and color of sound a piano could make. His decrescendo was as enchantingly beautiful as it was difficult to emulate. I knew because I had tried.

This Pape's unresponsiveness was a sign of cheap construction. Such pianos seemed stupid to me. They did not hold a tune very long. And worse, the Fourchettes had neglected it over the years. I knew it had had only a handful of proper tunings. What was worse, it had sat near an open window overlooking the Seine throughout its life. So, its tone had been deadened owing to rusty strings. I could give no guarantees that one of them would not break during his performance. It was better suited to living out its life as a piece of furniture. I pointed all this out, then added,

"A piano should allow you to carry a tune like the wind carries dandelion puffs silently along, Monsieur, not like a cart full of rocks that you pull uphill." I hoped he would cancel the appearance. "I want you to shine this evening, not get into a brawl with that monstrosity."

"Antoine said both pianos are in fine condition," he repeated, "and I trust him."

The tailor promised the goods by that afternoon. Chopin thanked him, put on his overcoat, and fitted his lavender kid gloves into the crotch of his fingers like a metronome counting out a 4/4 beat. "I thank you for your concern, Delhomme, but a pianist does not earn money and fame by quarreling with his instruments. Besides, it would insult my hosts."

I offered again to accompany him that evening to field any emergencies, but he declined. With that, the composer donned his top hat and slipped out the door with nary a tinkle of a bell.

## First Hurdle

The morning following the Fourchettes' salon, I had a tuning appointment with a customer who had attended the event. I could not contain my curiosity. "How did you find the performance?" I asked her.

"Chopin! Chopin!" she said, clutching her hands to her chest and looking skyward. "His fingers float over the keys. He makes the piano *breathe!*"

I probed deeper. "And did Monsieur Liszt play on the upright?"

"*Oui,*" she said, as if he were a footnote to the occasion, then continued eulogizing Chopin's performance. All the guests reveled in his stunning musicianship and incomparable melodies, it seemed.

"And the pianos?"

"Monsieur?"

"I mean, did you like their tone? Did they strike your ears as harmonious?"

She looked at me, one eyebrow raised. I surmised that she, indeed any audience member, had no inkling about the sonority or responsiveness of an instrument. While both tuner and pianist aimed for a faultless performance, the usual concert goer had no such expectation or even understanding of the mechanics involved. We technicians worked within infinitesimal tolerances; audience members would register alarm only if we had missed the mark by a mile. I feared I had made a fool of myself to Chopin, looking too eager for personal gain. Sooner than expected, however, my warnings about the lethargic piano were validated.

When I returned home at noon that day, a note from Chopin, in flawless penmanship, requested that I visit his apartment that afternoon. I replied by courier I would arrive around four o'clock.

Upon opening the door, he uttered my name in a sharp tone. I straightened. "*Bonjour,* Monsieur Chopin," I said cheerfully but cautiously.

The composer's hair was disheveled, his white tunic rumpled, and trousers still unbuttoned at the top. His eyes were swollen with sleep. I was sure his fatigue had everything to do with chasing away the exhaustion from his harrowing performance on the Pape. He headed back to his Pleyel and pounded his fist on the lid.

"That awful instrument, Delhomme. Why, I had to practically stand up to get a peep out of it. I wondered if someone had doused it with honey. Start to finish, a catastrophe."

I followed him into the salon. I tried to suppress a smile, but it was impossible. Despite my admiration, or perhaps because of it, I gave over to his mood and let him rant. It was his way of letting me know I had been right.

He went to the kitchen to make coffee and returned carrying two demitasses. "Delhomme," he said in a softer tone after he had swallowed the hot liquid. "I have let Antoine go. I cannot risk having another night like that."

I moved to the edge of the seat. "Sir, I am certain Antoine did his best." I felt I had to protest somewhat.

He did not let me finish. "*Non, non, non!*" he said, shaking his finger. "He should have warned me." He sat on the piano bench. "I should have listened to you."

"Was the hostess satisfied with your performance?" I asked.

"I do not mean this to sound rude," he took another sip, "but it does not matter what she thinks. It never matters what anybody else thinks. *I* could not play the way *I* wanted. Antoine said it was a fine instrument. He is unsuitable to remain in my employ."

I sat mum.

"My schedule is very busy, Delhomme. I give lessons, play at soirées, and compose when I can. Would you consider working for me?"

So, so sweet were those words. Vidocq's stipulation aside, I had longed to tune for this man whose music I admired more than that of any other composer. His irritation at my offer in the tailor shop had disappeared, and now it was possible to meet each other on professional ground.

He put his cup on the piano. I reached over and gently removed it lest it spill onto the strings.

"Oh, yes, I was not thinking." He sat down. "Now, about payment."

He told me in confidence that, despite wealthy students, publishing contracts, and performances, none of his money came at reliable intervals. How could it be otherwise for any artist? Even though he had been in Paris for four years now and his calendar bursting with invitations and lucrative lessons, he had gaps in income, which meant I would have gaps in mine. I was not wanting for money, thanks to Vidocq—at least for now. And once I had amassed enough tuning clients, irregular payments would not be an issue.

"I am afraid I cannot pay your regular fee either." He cited the life of an artist as the reason.

It did not feel right to skew to pettiness by haggling. After all, my goal was to sneak into his inner circle, with George Sand at its center. Until that opportunity presented itself, I could at least help him make more money. One step at a time.

# Publishing

## Publishing

Not long after being hired by Chopin as his tuner, I thought of a superb way to accomplish two goals with one idea, to wit, help him earn some money and help me buttress his trust in me. For Chopin, teaching and performing provided the bulk of his income. But composing was his first love that he could indulge only in the interstices of other lucrative activities. Publishers were hungry, hungry, hungry for his work and often expressed irritation that he would not produce more. Their sales ensured a rich return for them but less so for Chopin.

They often called at his apartment to enquire about new manuscripts. Unfortunately, their visits were for naught since he was painfully slow in penning his music. He would entice them with promises, but in the end, promises were only that. He worried so about each measure, each note, the rests, the fingering, the pedal markings. He fussed over a passage again and again as if to taste it and correct the seasoning. I admit of a highly trained ear for music, but often I heard the new version played immediately after the old one and could detect only a negligible variation. A slight pause, perhaps, or inverted notes, but my sensibilities were not of his caliber. He heard chasms of difference that spoke to his aesthetic only.

One publisher, desperate to secure first publishing rights, came un-announced to my shop one afternoon. He asked about Chopin's progress on some mazurkas he had commissioned. He was infuriated that Chopin had not delivered his work as promised. Did I know about his situation or plans to make good on his promise, he asked with pressured speech, and then quipped, "Is he still *alive*?"

"Monsieur, I see Chopin almost weekly. I can assure you he is very much alive."

"Do you see him composing? What does he *do* all day?"

At these questions, I fell silent. I did not think it my place to inform this man about any of my clients' doings, let alone about those of a man who prized his privacy.

He pulled out thirty francs, as much as Chopin charged for a private lesson, and waved the bills in my face. A doctor charged ten francs for a house call and a factory worker was lucky to earn fifteen francs a week. This emolument exposed his desperation. "Would this convince you to get some information?" he said.

I smiled, even though I was shocked at his effrontery, and disavowed any knowledge of Chopin's progress or process. I was not feigning igno-rance either. Chopin had his own timetable. This composer was not likely to increase production to suit the demands of the market. The muses sim-ply would not stand for it. Such prodding only choked them off. Euterpe, the muse of music, was jealous of her part in the process and paid no heed to the urgings from anyone, and especially not greedy publishers.

Euterpe aside, the composer on occasion did try to circumvent the muse's control. One day, I arrived earlier than usual to fix a sticking key on his Pleyel and waited in the drawing room for him to finish a waltz he had been composing for months. It was not unlike him to put away a piece to let it rest, sometimes for years. However, needing the money, he had promised this composition to a publisher by week's end, a tidy sum await-ing its delivery. Normally, during his composing, I heard nothing except the piano. But this day, I heard grunts and coughs and throat-clearing. He detested composing under pressure. He said it lent an artificial air to the piece and colored his judgment.

"Delhomme," he would lament, "why do I need to prostitute myself to the publishing world? I just want to create to feed my own soul."

No matter how much he bemoaned the realities of life, I wanted to help him increase his prospects of getting published and offered to introduce him to Maurice Schlesinger, whom I knew from my days at the Conservatoire. He would visit the school now and again to discover any gems composed by novices there. Of course, Chopin had dealt with publishers before, but never Schlesinger. This gesture of introducing him would tell him he could depend on me to help with his financial interests. I had even enlisted Berlioz to help. Given Chopin's diffidence, I imagined that he would easily be beaten down in price. I was sorely mistaken and about to see a completely different side of this man.

Upon entering, we saw M. Schlesinger sitting behind a large dark-brown walnut desk with his feet up, smoking a cigarette, and reading *Le Figaro*. He was flanked by pillars of music sheets and books. The man, probably the most well-known of all the publishers in Europe, jumped to his feet when he saw us, offering an eager hand to welcome us.

I knew Chopin was anxious about the encounter. Oh, the battles he waged for fair compensation! Both publisher and composer knew how valuable his pieces were. I thought Chopin would have the upper hand in the negotiations and could demand whatever he wanted. I was wrong. Schlesinger had, after all, published works by Mozart, Beethoven, Haydn, Weber, and so on. His reputation preceded his arrival from Berlin. He promised affordable music to the public, which meant he needed to buy it at the lowest price possible. It behooved Chopin to sell his creations to a publishing house that would dependably reproduce his works and distribute them far and wide: England, Germany, even America. He had published some works through Pleyel's company and others through Heinrich Probst, whom he called a scapegrace because he had paid a pitiful three hundred francs for his mazurkas. A pittance. But now he considered consolidating his work under one publishing house. "Better to work with one Jew than with three," was his remark.

"So nice to meet you, Monsieur Chopin," Schlesinger began, welcoming the composer. "I have heard wonderful gossip about your performances around town. It is not easy to impress Parisians."

As a rule, it never hurt to compliment someone, especially if the flattery was sincere, as I believed Schlesinger's was. But Chopin was not susceptible to sycophancy when money was on his mind.

"You are very kind to say so, Monsieur," said Chopin. His voice purred with contentment. His body, however, belied his demeanor. He stood legs astride, jaw muscles working, ready for battle. He handed Schlesinger an envelope with his latest work.

The publisher took out the composition and read the title, "Trois Valses brillantes." He looked over each one, his head moving to the beat as he read. "Very nice. *Very* nice," he said, getting up. "I can sell these easily here in Paris, and I believe Germany would also be very interested. I can offer you two hundred and fifty francs."

"You mean for each one, correct?" Chopin said.

"I mean for the set," Schlesinger said, surprised the offer was not immediately accepted.

At this low bid, Chopin flew into a rage. "Such an offer is an insult, you Jew dog! It took me months to prepare these. Months, I tell you. Months of biting my pen in half, struggling against time and illness to complete them." The composer went behind the desk and grabbed the manuscript out of his hands. "Look at this first one in A flat major," he said, pointing to the top piece. "Look at the brisk introductory bars. And look here in bar seventeen. You can feel the wheeling motion in this part. Just imagine the flowing dresses that sweep around the floor! There is vigor in the third part and tenderness in the fourth."

Schlesinger was taken aback by Chopin's agitation. "I can go as high as three hundred and fifty francs. I will grant you that these pieces are full of vitality that is unique."

Chopin shuffled the papers. "And . . . and the third one in F major— *Vivace*—see how different it is from my first? The second is *Lento.*"

I decided a word from me might convince Schlesinger. I began, "If I may say so, Monsieur Schlesinger . . ." Chopin put up his hand to block me. By now, he was so angry that I feared getting clobbered myself if I entered the fray. The only positive result of such a contretemps was the color now flushing his cheeks, something I had never seen.

"Tell me you have published anything to match these," he said, tapping the pages with the back of his hand. He put his compositions back in the envelope and leveled his demand. "I insist you pay me five hundred francs," he said, glowering at the poor man, now set back on his heels from the onslaught, "or I shall leave to find another more charitable, more sensible publisher?" He paused, waiting for Schlesinger to relent. Then he turned to me, saying, "*Eh bien, Delhomme. Allons-y,*" and started toward the door.

But before he could reach for the handle, in stepped Berlioz right on cue. He was one of Schlesinger's most frequent clients. Chopin was surprised to see him, but I had secretly arranged this with Berlioz earlier that day to add some ammunition on the pianist's side.

"Monsieur Schlesinger," Berlioz said, walking over to the desk to shake his hand. He turned to Chopin. "*Ça va?*" he said, shaking his hand and mine. "What a coincidence to see you here."

"What can I help you with, Monsieur Berlioz?" he said leaning back in his chair and steepling his fingertips.

"I came to ask, Monsieur, if you have published the waltzes Monsieur Chopin played at the Cuilllières' home last month."

Schlesinger had not attained his success by giving in to composers' demands so easily, no matter how hard they pressed. We three stood looking down at him. He met each of our eyes, slowly realizing the compromising position he was now in.

Chopin broke the silence. "I am soliciting a bid from Monsieur Schlesinger for those very waltzes."

Schlesinger picked up the score. "It will be a while before they are published, of course."

He hesitated again. "Well, Monsieur, would you please let me know when they are prepared?" said Berlioz. "The Conservatoire wants to buy multiple copies for its students." With Berlioz's endorsement and promise of future sales, the publisher gave over. He stood, stuck out his hand, and said, "*Eh bien, Monsieur Chopin,* I will meet your price."

Chopin's fury chilled. He pocketed the five hundred francs. He lifted his chin and held Schlesinger's eye, as victorious as a prize fighter. He turned to lead the way out the door.

We celebrated the triumph of art over business with caviar and champagne. Chopin had proved to be a worthy bargainer, with just a little help from his friends.

# CHAPTER 13

# George Sand's Diary – Majorca

Dear Diary,

I am exhausted! And beside myself with anger and fear. Majorca will for-ever be a synonym for disaster, illness, nosy strangers, poor planning. I am partially at fault. But I can control only so much.

It was the trial of Job to get Chopin even to commit to the trip. He is always slow to make decisions. But this time, I won out.

I wanted my dear Chip-Chip to bask and heal in sunshine. Majorca promised to deliver such a request. But I planned the trip poorly. Upon arrival, I anticipated staying in Palma, but there was not a room to be had. Where *do* visitors stay when they come here?

We finally found a villa called The House of the Wind. I could not have been more enchanted at the flora surrounding us: cacti, cedars, palm trees, olives, oranges, lemons, figs, pomegranates. The sky looked as if it had been painted by Giotto, the water shone turquoise, the mountains glowed with green. And the air! Washed by the ocean breezes. It was noth-ing like the cesspool we breathe in Paris. At night, I drank in the silence, except for the faint sound of the ocean, and took in the scent of lemon blossoms as I wrote. It was so deliciously warm that once I sat on the terrace writing until dawn.

That was until the rainy season came three weeks into our stay. Downpours, winds, dampness. No fireplace. No window glass! We resorted to using a charcoal brazier for heat. But it billowed forth noxious smoke and fumes, leaving us gasping for air. That was hardly the environment either of us needed to complete work or maintain our health. I struggled with the final part of my novel. Chopin's condition worsened. How could he compose with that incessant cough and now fever? I took him to see a doctor—three of them. No one really helped and the medicines here are only the most rudimentary.

One day, without warning, I got a letter from that cretinous landlord at the moldy villa we were staying in. He evicted us, without warning, because we were harboring a person with an infectious disease. He was certain that illness would be visited upon him and his family if we stayed. I found out that by law, doctors are ordered to report any cases of consumption or face stiff fines and licensure suspension. The owner ordered all of Chopin's belongings to be burned. As if that were not enough, he made us pay for whitewashing and redecorating the entire house to disinfect it. May God find a special place in Hell for this moron!

Moving was fine with us because we could not abide the sooty, mildewed cottage a minute more. I soon found an abandoned cloister built in 1399 at Valldemosa. I rented the cells from a Spanish refugee, who had recently vacated the premises. He was asking a thousand francs for his furniture, which was nothing less than extortion, mitigated only a little by the trouble it would have taken to find new items.

We hired two carts to move to the monastery on the hill. The three-hour journey took us through a wide range of scenery. But the most delightful of all was the architecture of the buildings in the courtyards, corridors, and chapels. Each cell—we had three adjoining rooms—was vaulted and ventilated by a small grate that cut through the very thick walls to the outside. The clay floors were covered with rush matting and white sheepskin rugs. We slept on nothing more than camp beds with straps. Each cell had a hopelessly rickety table with a lead candlestick holder, rush chairs, and a white-wood settee. Without a fireplace, we had no recourse but to use the brazier if we wanted heat. We had to cook outdoors, which was not a terrible hardship. My maid helped a great deal with this chore each day.

But, oh, what a perch to survey the ocean, fruit trees, and village below. I hoped it would provide succor to Chopin too. He continued to compose, despite immense suffering. But he had to make do, as we all had to. However, the smallest of irritants made him unpredictable and irrational. He did complete his preludes. Masterpieces, every one of them. But I must say that many sounded very mournful and reflected his sadness while there, especially the one in A minor. It seemed to crystallize and suspend in time a piece of his despair. I do not know if that was intentional.

At long last, the piano promised by M. Pleyel arrived at the port in Palma. Chip-Chip was too ill to go, so I went alone to retrieve it. Unfortunately, I had a long, unpleasant battle with the customs officials, whose avarice was unmatched in my experience. A few days after receiving the instrument, Chopin mailed off his preludes.

Some days, I felt sorry for him, and some days, I saw him as a detestable invalid. His lifeless demeanor worried me. After a few months in that climate and smoke, Chopin became markedly worse and began to hemorrhage from his lungs. He rasped and choked when he sat up and almost collapsed. I thought he might die. I fretted he would not even survive the trip home. Deeming his health had become too fragile to remain—he became too ill even to sleep—I booked tickets to sail to the mainland. I was through with the isolation and weariness of my responsibilities, anyway. Everything had fallen to me: nursing him, schooling my children, doing my own writing. I had to sell his piano, which turned into a major ordeal, since the Majorcans thought it, too, was contaminated.

By the time we arrived in Barcelona, he was coughing up bowlfuls of blood. I persevered and found a brilliant doctor, Étienne Lagerberg, who stopped his hemorrhaging. I will be forever grateful to him. We moved into a hotel to rest until he could travel the last leg to Paris.

Sadly, Majorca was not the romantic adventure it was meant to be. He has transformed into an invalid, a child of sorts. But his helplessness has made me realize how much he needs my devotion and care. This is adequate compensation for losing a sexual partner, at least for now.

The real miracle is that he composed music imbued with the very fragrance of Paradise. Life or death means nothing to him. I doubt he knows what planet he is living on. He does not seem to be aware of life as we conceive and experience it.

Oh, how I hate Spain. I have placed a hex on all Majorcans: May you all contract cholera and have to burn down the entire island.

CHAPTER 14

# The Ring – Silence

## The Ring

O ver time, Chopin's health worsened, improved, then deteriorated again, in random cycles. It was troublesome, more so for him than I realized at the time. I felt protective of his health, but soon his emotions also became my concern.

I could say Chopin and I were close, not as lovers were intimate. We connected where the emotions of music live. I instinctively knew how he wanted a piano to be tuned, regulated, and voiced. The hammers, especially in the treble, needed to sound like bright chimes. I even washed the ivories, so no dirt or oil would compromise his touch. His instrument was our garden, where he grew rare and special flowers. I tended it by weeding and emending the soil. Our goals matched: to help Chopin create beautiful music.

Often, he would say he could not bear life without my services, that I had contributed to his success. Flattered though I was, he would travel, sometimes for months, leaving me with a hole in my calendar and my heart. I felt as I did as a child when my best friend left on summer holiday. How would I cope?

One such time came when he traveled to Majorca with George Sand, a most unusual woman hailed throughout France for her literary achievements. I knew of her reputation well in advance of Chopin's meeting her. Indeed, I had many clients who attended her literary parties.

I had learned that their first meeting happened about a year before they went to Majorca, thanks to Sand's guile. Sand wanted to arrange a meeting. Apparently, she tried several avenues, even leaning on her friendship with Franz Liszt and his mistress, the Countess Marie D'Agoult, a Parisian salon hostess, to introduce her. If Madame Sand wanted to meet with him, she had the wherewithal to ask him herself with all her connections and certainly with her gumption. She had no need of using backstairs influence to achieve her goal.

Their introduction came a full five years after he arrived in Paris. At first, he showed no desire to meet Sand, aware though he was of her interest in him well before that evening's festivities. He had heard she was deeply involved with a man. He also knew of her masculine proclivities, not to mention her base and tasteless obsession with sex in her novels. He said his impressions of her were confirmed when he saw her for the first time at l'Hôtel de France. He was repulsed by her mannish mien, replete with voluminous pants and malodorous cigar. Still, suitors flocked to her like pigeons to breadcrumbs.

Sand persisted. Not long after they met at l'Hôtel, he invited her to his apartment for a musicale. Several other literary and musical luminaries would also attend, so he could easily appear nonchalant about her presence.

One afternoon, Chopin animatedly reminisced about the evening he and Sand met. Obviously, his opinion of her had changed, signaling that he too had been ensnared by her charms. As one observer said, they made a perfect, if unconventional, couple: He was very ladylike, and she was the perfect gentleman.

"She wore the most alluring outfit," Chopin told me, sprightlier than I had seen him in months. "I expected to see a woman clad in those uncomely breeches with a manly jacket and top hat. But she wore this simply ravishing Turkish outfit in red and white!" He stood with his hand on the piano wearing a rare and lovely smile. "Did you know, Delhomme, that red and white are the colors of the Polish flag?" He shook his head and sat down on the bench as if he were trying to comprehend what he had seen.

Where Chopin saw beauty, I saw artifice. I knew other women like Sand. They were calculating, controlling, and had no one's interest at heart but their own. They trampled on everything to satisfy their lust. Everyone knew about her casual morals. She had a long history of capturing men who suited her fancy, only to splay them like insects pinned in a shadow-box when she tired of their company.

Chopin may have been a brilliant composer and pianist, but he was no match for a woman five years his elder who had devices as subtle and sophisticated as Delilah's. How else could one account for the fact he showed even a scintilla of favor toward a woman in trousers? And after he had courted some of the most beautiful women in Paris. He had flitted about from flower to flower and landed on a weed. To be sure, the observations I made were away from emotion. But that cool eye could be a boon to a friend. The trick was getting that person to listen. *Tread lightly,* I reminded myself. *Ça serait dangereux.*

They started seeing one another regularly. I heard she had become alarmed at his ill health and considered spending the winter in warmer weather, the very elixir he needed to heal. Chopin and Sand finally left for Majorca, her two children and nanny in tow. They returned to Paris after spending almost a year abroad. Chopin wrote infrequently. The last letter, mailed from Paris, asked me to please tune his Pleyel before students appeared on his schedule. The return address told me he had moved to a new apartment on rue Tronchet.

When I arrived, I found a note on his unlocked door. "Please awaken me if I am not already astir," it said. I entered and found his bed chamber door ajar. I tapped lightly. No answer. "Monsieur Chopin?" I said softly through a tiny crack so as not to startle him. "I am here to work on your piano now."

"Hello, Delhomme," he said groggily. He asked me to draw back the curtains in his bedroom. He shrank from the light. He was pallid against the white linens and almost childlike with the blanket drawn up under his chin. Beholding him in such a fragile state set me to worrying about his future. I never entertained such maudlin thoughts when he was at the piano, scribbling down chords and wrestling with passages for hours on end. But today, I worried.

My medical training pointed me toward tuberculosis. Up until then, I had ignored such a dire diagnosis. The youngest of his three sisters had died of the disease when she was just fifteen and his father also succumbed to it. But it fit the pattern: a persistent cough, shallow appetite, gradual decline. Granted, he had stamina enough to teach and perform. But consumption was a progressive illness with no cure. Some patients talked about homeopathic remedies or even using a tincture of cocaine for headaches. I never asked about such personal things.

The disease profoundly affected people and could change their nature over time. It could make them care only about themselves and lead to violent mood swings. Sufferers often seemed irritable and anxious, and flew into fits of rage. Such behavior was on display when one of Chopin's students, a meek and dedicated young woman, had come at the wrong time for the lesson, due to a misunderstanding. He became infuriated. After venting his wrath, the lesson commenced, but he again became angry after finding out she had not brought the Nocturne, saying she intended to play it from memory. At this, he shouted and stomped his feet, upbraiding her because she did not know how to take private lessons. After calming again, there was a third eruption in which he found that her playing was unacceptable. She could no longer hold back tears. There was a sympathetic resolution to the episode, but this was not a singular event.

I heard others complain about see-sawing humors. Yet, all remained faithful patrons, so deep was his knowledge of music.

If he took care to properly eat and rest, he might live a long time. But his schedule was demanding. How would he, *could* he, sustain such a punishing schedule? He was in his early thirties, productive, mentally quick, and, I was told through certain channels, a satisfying lover. All these signs would call for an excellent prognosis, except for his worsening wheezing and hacking.

This day, however, he lay for all the world an invalid. I was not heartened. "May I fetch some chamomile tea, sir? It will chase the chill from your room."

He nodded.

I went to the kitchen to start the fire, then repaired to the salon to commence my work. I rolled out a cloth on which to place my tools. He had said in his letter that the A below Middle C and especially the F and G sharp above were problematic, but when I tested others, I found many wobbly unisons and the treble octaves a half-tone flat. I had predicted as much since a year of seasons had come and gone. Moreover, it had not been played during that time. Had he not noticed this overall problem?

"Delhomme," Chopin said weakly, leaning against the door jamb of his bedroom. He was bent like a half-opened pocketknife, arms wrapped around his waist to hold in the warmth. "Is my tea ready?"

I returned to the kitchen. The water had just come to a boil. I warmed the pot before dropping in several pinches of chamomile leaves and flowers, then poured in the rest of the boiling water. I placed a bone china teacup, hand painted by his mother, alongside the teapot, saucer, spoon, and honey on a tray, and took it to a small table by the fire. I foreshortened the steeping time when he began coughing and poured his cup along with a teaspoon of honey to fortify his constitution. He took his tea and sat by the window.

"*Merci beaucoup,*" he said quietly, cradling the cup in his hands. He watched the steam rise, seemingly hypnotized by its movement.

I set about testing notes in the bass to see how those strings fared. Not well, was the unsurprising answer, albeit better than those in the treble as they were under less tension.

After several minutes, he said, "Delhomme, I have been thinking . . ." he took a sip ". . . about giving you a ring I have since I have been delinquent in paying you."

"A ring, sir?" I laid down my tuning hammer to listen.

"No one knows about this here in Paris. When I was fifteen, I gave a command performance for one of the tsars in Warsaw. He gave me a diamond ring." He walked to the piano bench and sat. "A local jeweler said it is quite valuable, especially considering its provenance. Would you like to see it?"

"I should say so, sir!" I said.

Before getting up, Chopin took another sip, sighing with appreciation at the soothing liquid. He arose gingerly and made his way to the bedroom. After a time, he emerged with the gold and diamond ring on his middle finger.

I was expecting a ring with a modest diamond chip. But I drew in my breath at the brilliant two-carat diamond set in an artfully crafted gold bezel. The ring was free of other decoration, except for the fine etching of the Romanov coat of arms on the band. He removed the ring, which was quite loose on his slim fingers, and gave it to me. "Read the inscription inside," he said.

I squinted: "From Tsar Alexander."

To the Russian emperor, this may have been but a bauble, but to this tuner, it was a year's wages, perhaps more! Chopin said one time he had asked his father to sell it and send him the proceeds. "But he thought it was worth a lot more than its face value and never carried out my request," he said. "Ludwika brought it when she came last." Chopin rarely spoke of his past in Poland, although I knew he longed to return to his family, who loved him dearly. Ludwika, his elder sister, adored him and had been his first piano teacher. They occasionally played duets, until it became clear he was a prodigy needing more expert instruction.

I carefully returned the ring. "Splendid!"

"For your fiancée, perhaps?" he said.

"I have no fiancée, Monsieur."

"What about Lili? Are you not betrothed?"

I shook my head. "Soon, perhaps." I may have misrepresented my prospects with Lili to Chopin. After all, she was still engaged to that legionnaire. Stating I wanted to marry her was only a fantasy.

"How old are you?" he asked.

"Twenty-five."

"You will need to give her a ring someday," he said. I was flattered by his interest.

Was he offering me the jewelry?

He recounted more of the story of the night he received it. "I had performed and improvised on one of Ignaz Moscheles' compositions," he began. "The performance was a success. Emperor Alexander asked for a private concert in the Warsaw Conservatory." He delicately dabbed a napkin at the sides of his mouth and sat back. "The great hall had a high ceiling, with many windows and marble floors. Sound bounced off every surface and stabbed at the ear."

I knew exactly what he meant. Bad acoustics could ruin even the most brilliant performance and made tuning especially taxing.

"Thank goodness the tsar sat in the front row. He would have heard a jumble of sounds in the last row. I played a rondo, but he would have loved to hear me play scales too."

I was perplexed. Chopin knew that his music had been feted in Warsaw and now Paris. He knew everyone considered him the next Mozart. Yet, he insisted on being self-effacing about his reputation to the point of exasperation. Admittedly, that was part of his charm.

"Afterwards, I bowed to the tsar," he continued. "He then bade me come to the center of the floor, where dukes and ladies surrounded me. He then motioned to a man in uniform to come forward carrying a pillow with this ring. 'Please accept this gift,'" Chopin said imitating the tsar, "'in recognition of your outstanding performance today. I hope to hear many more.'"

He huffed some moist breath onto the stone and shined it on his sleeve. He put it back on his finger and let the sun catch its many facets. "His gift was for my art. But Poland and Russia hate each other." Poland had been brutally suppressed by Russia many times. His mazurkas and polonaises were built around melodies of his beloved homeland and served as a way of protesting and keeping his heritage alive without hazarding retribution from authorities. He had a complicated relationship with this ring. I understood his ambivalence.

He placed it on the music rack. "A ring would only click on the keys." He paused. "So, if you have no need of it, then I will give it to Aurore."

"Oh." I stiffened at the outrageous idea.

The pianist shifted from foot to foot. "I proposed marriage once to a woman from Warsaw, Maria Wodziński, before I left for Paris. She was so beautiful. But she declined." His head drooped. "Her family—that is who refused me." He took the ring to the window to inspect it, but his gaze looked faraway.

"Do you want to marry Madame Sand?" I asked, still having to modulate my reaction.

"Of course, I am proud of it," he went on about the ring, "but Tsar Alexander was evil, and Russia is still terrorizing my people. I want someone who sees its beauty, not its history." He stood silent.

I hazarded an observation to steer him away from the notion of giving his treasure to George. "It is beautiful. But do you think it would serve as a lady's ring? The band is wide and might not sit delicately upon a woman's hand." I picked up the teapot. "More, Monsieur?"

I replenished his cup; he resumed sipping. He appeared more animated, more talkative. The tea had done him good.

We fell to discussing his upcoming performance that evening at Mme Assiette's manor. She was a well-to-do Parisian socialite married to a Pole and had begged Chopin for years to play for her guests. In advance of the performance, I had worked on her Viennese-made Bösendorfer the week before. It was a stunning mahogany grand piano, well maintained throughout its eleven years. It was a suitable enough instrument to display his gifts, despite the brand's somewhat unresponsive action. The tone was brilliant, though, and I could lighten the touch. With expensive instruments, one could make a range of adjustments.

He took his teacup and went to the kitchen. The question of the ring was left hanging. When I turned my attention back to his piano, I found leaky dampers, and, to my dismay, the tuning had slipped almost a whole note. I silently cursed the fireplace at his old apartment. The wood in the pin block was probably drying out, making it impossible for the tuning pins to hold the tension on the strings. It was only a matter of time before the soundboard would crack. This caused a piano to lose its volume and possibly begin buzzing. Repairable, yes, but expensive.

I went about my work. After a time, I went to the kitchen for a drink of water and found Chopin sitting, staring at the ring. I was flattered he had confided in me about his plans with Mme Sand. I decided to appeal to his vanity, knowing that he was nothing if not a fop when making his toilet. Moreover, he liked to appear wealthier than he was by maintaining his own coach and horse instead of hiring just anyone to take him to social events.

I picked up the jewelry again and examined it. "A ring of such beauty and size would bespeak elegance, Monsieur, and would surely convey wealth and success." I hefted it. "Why not wear it over your gloved hand? Your hosts will surely notice it when you arrive and leave."

He did seem intrigued by my idea but said nothing more on the topic. "I am expecting a student in an hour," he said. "She has a full purse but no talent. Her style is so bombastic that I fear she might bloody my nocturne." He was eager for good students but tolerated many with minimal musical gifts only because they paid handsomely. He said he felt drained after they left.

My eyes fell on the brie and a baguette I had brought. "May I offer you some nourishment to withstand your afternoon labors?" I did not know if Chopin even stocked his larder. In fact, I never saw him eat. Food seemed irrelevant. I cut a piece of bread and placed it along with the cheese on the table. "Monsieur?" He paid it no mind. Instead, he ran his fingers through his hair as if to arrange his thoughts, arose, and left the room. I decided against mentioning the precarious condition of his piano until he was less distracted.

I did my best to put the piano into workable order, then packed up my tools and opened the door. Standing ready to knock was his student, a petite woman in a royal blue coat with a silver fox collar and engaging smile. Chopin greeted her warmly as I closed the door. Wealthy, beautiful, but talentless. Most men would never notice the last.

Lili grew more important to me as the days wore on. I had been to see her on a short visit home last weekend to check on the house and other matters concerning my mother's estate. She and her mother lived in a small cottage on the north side of town. Mme Millefeuille had been widowed in 1832 when her husband died during the horrific cholera outbreak that claimed nineteen thousand lives in its six-month siege. Lili was so beloved by him that he would sing songs to her, even up to the day he died. She was only eleven, but she remembered him well.

Soon after his death, both her mother and she began cleaning houses and taking care of the ill and infirm, as Lili did for my mother during her final year. After Maman died, Lili worked in a flower shop on the town square. It brought in a little more money than cleaning houses, and she enjoyed it so very much. With the help of Mme Millefeuille, she also concocted herbal remedies when customers requested a special infusion or tincture to address their illness. Despite my doubts about the efficacy of herbal medicines, I asked her what remedy she recommended for tuberculosis.

The answer arrived in her letter just before I left for Marainville.

*Cher Beaulieu,*

*Since I have not heard from you in some time, I thought to write about my day. Work has captivated my spirit lately. I see the flowers as sentient beings that speak to me each day. The daffodils say, "Good morning!" with their cheery yellow trumpets. Freesia speak softly and wish me well as I close the door to go home. But the roses—especially the red ones—chatter all day long: How is Beaulieu doing? Does he think of you when he is in Paris? You must let him know we said hello. Tell him to please write Lili!*

*Since you asked about remedies for tuberculosis, my mother recommends nasturtiums and garlic. M. Chopin can also try nettle tea made by boiling the leaves.*

*Those are the floral missives from Marainville.*

*Je t'attends,*
*Lili*

She was so lovely, so gentle and soft. I, of course, did not dare talk about marriage or my desire for a family. But if she was still betrothed, why was she writing to me?

I had long sought prospects for a wife. By now, accepted though I was throughout the music community, wealthy piano owners did not see me as an appropriate mate for their daughters. So be it. I had no idea how I could afford to support any of them in the manner they knew: fine furniture, gold jewelry, silk ball gowns, fancy bone china. Now I could indulge but one of those tastes. Instead, I sought the company of merchants' daughters and others of my social class who appreciated someone reliable, responsible, self-employed—and, if I may—not wholly unattractive. I had a full head of hair, blue eyes, broad shoulders, energetic spirit. My short stature limited my prospects. (I would feel silly courting someone taller than I.) Dainty, pretty, petite Lili was the ideal mate. We could have a passel of children and love one another forever. She could tend to our babies and forget about selling flowers.

Thanks to Vidocq and my growing business, I was more financially secure. My goal of securing a satisfactory position in society through my status as a tuner meant I could now consider proposing marriage. Would she accept?

I was contemplating my situation as I traveled to a client's house to the north of the city. The home was nestled in a wooded area with a brook running by it. I was about to knock when Vidocq jumped out of the bushes.

"Dear God!" I was so unnerved by his popping out of the shrubbery like a jack-in-the-box that I set my tuning case down to calm my heart.

The element of surprise, he would say, was half the battle to getting one's way. He wore no disguise. Perhaps, if my tuning customer saw him dressed up as a pirate or a clown, he would have some explaining to do. This way, he could pass for my assistant.

"I came to check on your progress."

"Progress with what? I have not even looked at this customer's piano yet."

He pulled a face. "With your assignment!"

"I *have* Chopin as a client," I said with finality.

"Yes, I know that. But you are only half done," he said with that menacing tone he always used. "Now on to Madame Sand and her secrets."

"Secrets about what?"

"Another uprising."

"Madame Sand lives at Nohant most of the time, almost 200 miles from Paris," I explained. "What could she possibly have to do with any political rebellion at that distance?"

He looked astounded at my ignorance of the situation. "She may not be wielding a sword," said the detective, shaking his head, "but her words are just as sharp. Now get on with it!"

## Silence

The following Sunday, I decided to take a break from work and clear my head about Vidocq and Lili and marriage and, the most challenging of all, a way to inveigle an invitation to Sand's home. I donned my box coat and felt high-crown hat for a walk in the Jardins des Tuileries, where men were squiring women in their Sunday finery.

It was an especially fine spring day. We Parisians cherished such weather because it signaled the end of snow and ice. I stepped lively down the path lined with chestnut trees and boxwood hedges. It felt freeing to stretch my legs and breathe deeply to exchange the shop dust with the aroma of redolent cherry trees. I reveled in the whoops of the children and whoosh of the water of the fountains. The park had been quiet too long.

I had been walking and daydreaming for a time when I heard my name. I turned toward the voice. M. Chopin and Mme Sand sat together on a green wooden bench. She wore an attractive cream-colored dress and a blue bonnet tied under her chin. I could not help wondering if manly pantaloons lurked beneath those fluffy crinolines. He, as always, was immaculately dressed in grey slacks, black morning coat, cravat, and silk top hat. His butter-yellow gloves were only a shade off Mme Sand's dress. A handsome couple, I had to admit.

He introduced me, although that was hardly necessary. "*Bonjour*, Madame," I said brightly. "I am honored to make your acquaintance."

I reached out to kiss her hand. But she offered none. She kept them crossed on her lap in a lady-like manner. I saw no ring.

"Please," said the pianist, moving over and motioning. "Come sit a while." We chatted superficially about the delightful weather and happy sunshine. Chopin pulled the conversation to pianos. "I hope you don't mind, Aurore, but I know Delhomme would want to hear the story about the Bösendorfer." She smiled weakly.

Chopin became lively as he recounted the tale of the famous, expensive, rare, Viennese-made piano he had been eager to play. M. Kieliszek had bought it from a dealer, who said it was one of the first manufactured. Into its tonal maturity, I expected to hear a report about its majestic sound and unique Austrian touch.

He prefaced his story with a description of the audience members who, before the concert, had been treated to meats and fruits and cheeses from all over France, along with an ocean of alcohol. "I was not terribly hungry due to my nerves," he said, "so I went to the hall and began playing Bach, as I usually do. No sooner had I sat down than the drunkest man I have ever met came teetering over to the piano. He reached over my shoulder to play something but slipped on the rug underneath the bench. And there went his Beaujolais all over the keyboard!"

I gulped. Alcohol—any liquid—in a piano action was its death knell.

"Of course, I reported it to the hostess," he continued. "She said she had another instrument that the children practiced on."

"Oh, yes, I know that one—in the sunroom," I said. "An upright. But I did not tune . . ."

"*Mon Dieu,*" he interrupted, putting his hand to his forehead. "*Quelle catastrophe.*" He chuckled at the absurdity of this whole affair, but the exertion triggered his cough. Once it was under control, he continued, "*Totalement terrible!*" Again, Chopin laughed, coughed, laughed, coughed. "Delhomme, I could not even recognize what I was playing!"

"I am so sorry," I said, touching his arm. George's eyes locked onto my hand, which I withdrew forthwith.

"Now, Liszt," he said of his composer friend, "Liszt would have just gotten up and walked away, snob that he is." I knew Liszt did not have any problem taking care of himself if things did not please him. Frankly, I found the Hungarian a bit boorish in that regard. Chopin was too well bred for such churlishness.

"I could never treat a loyal patron so shabbily. Besides," he continued, "Monsieur Kieliszek is from Warsaw. What a pleasure to speak my native language again. It made it all worthwhile."

I laughed along with him, but his bonhomie seemed forced, as if to say, "Look how happy this woman makes me!" I remained unconvinced, and Mme Sand sustained her icy façade.

A short silence left an opening to leave. I arose and said, "It will be evening soon. I will be on my way then." I turned to George. "Delighted to have met you, Madame." She had not spoken the entire time. This encounter reminded me that hostility need not arrive only on the backs of words.

Couples and families clustered to gaze at the bloody sunset through an opening in the trees. I headed east into the darkening sky. The idea of Chopin giving his diamond ring to that britches-wearing, ill-mannered slut turned my stomach, and the prospect of his marrying her, why, I gagged at the thought.

## CHAPTER 15

# George Sand's Diary – Attempted Rape

Dear Diary:

Ah, silence. What a wonderful weapon. With it, we humans can broadcast dissatisfaction against petty, obnoxious pests who somehow think I should be courteous because they know my lover. My silence in the park yesterday told Delhomme he was unworthy of my time. He pretends to be so gracious and mannerly. But I can tell by his clothes and overeager demeanor he is nothing but a flatterer who uses the Chopin's coattails to aggrandize himself. Such a small person.

By now, Chopin has become a very different person to me. Majorca uncovered a need even I cannot meet. I helped him as best I could. He has developed a sickly mental attitude that prompts fits of temper and mood swings. I cannot abide them. We share no bed anymore. How could we with that maddening cough? I tend to him during the day and find homeopathic remedies to help him sleep at night. He anticipates his burial at every opportunity, with certain pleasure. Dr. Papet thinks he is prone to hypochondria and that he will always be prone to alarm until he has passed his fortieth birthday.

Were it not for the comfort we both find in our artistic sensibilities, I surely would have abandoned him months ago for a more vigorous man to satisfy me. Regrettably, no others can satiate my lust for art as he does.

I was touched that he offered me his ring from a tsar. He said he wanted to show me how much he loved me. How touched I was. It was like a small boy giving his mommy a souvenir of himself. I will not marry him even if he wants me to. I need to love and write and enjoy the fruits of my freedom. No one will put a leash around my neck. No one.

I am not sure where my attitude came from. I keep wondering if it had to do with men, all of whom believe in the inferiority of women. One writer I sought to be my mentor told me not to even try to write. "Do not make books, make babies," he said. And he was serious!

In the convent, women were responsible for everything. If it worked, it was because of women. How safe I felt there and free from prying male eyes. We had such fun pulling pranks on others. They may not have been the most intelligent things we did, but the nuns never knew, so it was fun. We never did find where all those underground tunnels led. We searched and searched and came late to class one day. But for some reason, the nun never noticed. Such freedom.

I was fooled only one time. I never told anyone—not the nuns, not my best friend, and it goes without saying, not my mother or grandmother. I am unsure anyone would have believed me. But the shame lingers to this day.

The convent was unassailable, or so I thought. The courtyard door was armed with a grating and opened onto the echoing cloister, which was a quadrangular gallery, paved with sepulchral stones. The cloisters were vaulted, lighted by wide, arched windows that opened on the inner court-yard with a well and flower bed. On all corners, grapevines and jasmine hid the decay of the walls. The heavy doors to the cloister were closed each night with a solemn noise and a gloomy grinding of bolts.

This sad state of disrepair led the sisters to commission a stonemason to fix an exterior wall that had fallen during a heavy storm. I knew the wall had been compromised but no one had told me of the mason's arrival. And why would they? They knew our whereabouts twenty-four hours a day, or so they thought. I was supposed to be practicing piano, but instead I went to the garden to read Aristotle's *Apology of Socrates to the Jury*. I was sixteen at the time, but I still adore Socrates' resolve and dignity in the face of nincompoopery. My father quoted the famous philosopher in a letter once. Socrates' friends grieved over seeing him die an innocent man, to which he replied, "Would you have preferred that I die guilty?"

On that day, he appeared in the garden to fix the wall. The stones had fallen, but the convent was dilapidated throughout the compound. Because we girls had searched high and low for the rumored "ghosts" of the convent, we had seen more of the compound than perhaps even the oldest nun there. Which also meant we saw that the masonry and walls had not seen new mortar or repair since it had opened almost two hundred years ago.

The porter—everyone called him du Bois because he minded the entrance like a wooden soldier—must have let him in the main door, as that was the only way into the garden besides scaling the damaged wall. I was engrossed in my reading when I heard a noise. I looked over to see what made the sound. Before I knew it, a huge, smelly man grabbed me and pushed me against the wall. He started to pull down my bloomers while making this grunting noise. He then fumbled with his own pants. I screamed. He told me to shut up or he would . . .

He never finished that threat or the rape because the tocsin rang. And rang. And rang. Someone had seen him. Maybe du Bois? Sister Linnette? He pulled up his pants. I ran for the door to the main hall and never saw him again. He must have climbed over the damaged wall. He left his toolbox behind. The next day, I found it lying by the bench I had been sitting on. It was made of pine with a gray metal handle. He never returned for it. I did not dare tell anyone about the incident and avoided du Bois.

It was only the first of many lessons I learned about men: They take what they can, when they can, and as much as they can. I vowed never to be at their mercy again.

# Performing

## Performing

*M*onsieur Chopin artfully hid his difficulties with money. But as much as he sought after it, he thought performing for filthy lucre debased him. Even handling money was especially distasteful. So, he asked students to place their imbursement on the mantelpiece as he looked away. Disgusted though he was by the touch of it, he needed to teach to remain solvent.

Even though Chopin's income derived largely from composing and teaching, large recitals proved far more lucrative. Now that Chopin trusted me to have his money interests at heart, it seemed the perfect opportunity to fulfill my duty to Vidocq and set up a concert.

"We," Vidocq said, referring to his anonymous team, "will gather important industrialists and bankers in one room," especially those who had factories with many workers to ask what their plans were for beating back the fight for higher wages. How would they maintain calm in the face of deteriorating living conditions and longer working hours? Resistance among them in Paris had intensified. The king needed information.

But when I suggested this plan to arrange a concert to Chopin, he was uncharacteristically curt. "Delhomme, please, no," he said.

The memory of his last concert, six years prior, was still fresh. Merely finding a venue was time consuming: First, one had to bargain on the price to rent the hall, then publicize the concert, and finally secure outlets for ticket sales. Often, attendees expected to hear many different acts, perhaps some singing or even a duet with another pianist. Finding other musicians with whom he would not be embarrassed to perform meant cajoling a select few to appear on a given night and sharing the proceeds. Depending on the act, he may have even had to recruit and rehearse with an orchestra. He dreaded that because his delicate style was often overshadowed by their sheer numbers and volume. In anticipation of giving such a performance, he lay abed for days trying to summon the energy to attack such a task.

No wonder he preferred giving small, impromptu musicales night after night in the fashionable salons of the rich and titled. That atmosphere lent itself to his style of playing: soft, nuanced, often improvisatory. Such expressiveness was lost in a cavernous hall. Worse yet, his performances were often panned because no one could hear. Thrilled by the bombast and glitz of Liszt, audience members often complained that Chopin's playing seemed too meek. "We did not get our money's worth!" they groused. If he played a duet with Liszt, Chopin worried his music would be eclipsed by the Hungarian's boisterous playing. It was all too harrowing to repeat.

To add to his reluctance, he found performing for the masses distasteful. "I feel suffocated by the panting breath of the audience members," he said, becoming exercised by the memory. "I am paralyzed by their curious glances, mute before those unknown faces. Half the people mill around with their mouths brimming with food. Worse yet, they talk while we play! Why should I bother?"

"Because," I delicately pointed out, "you make ten times as much money by performing one evening than by taking twenty private students."

"I would sooner sell my ring." He sighed and slowly lowered himself onto the settee. "A concert is just too much trouble."

I dropped the discussion. If he did sell the ring, that would mean Mme Sand would not get it, but neither could I offer it to Lili to entice her engagement. If she refused, I could easily sell it. But then I would lose a precious memento of my dear friend. Now I understood why my mother wanted to keep my father's medical bag.

Despite Chopin's protestations, I furtively approached M. Pleyel. If the composer felt daunted by any obligation toward me, he would not be so reluctant to accept help from his friend and benefactor. Pleyel had already sponsored a young Chopin to play after having been in Paris a mere six months. He cannily saw that his own publishing company would derive much exposure by promoting this plan. I could be the unseen catalyst. Besides, I looked forward to working on any Pleyel instrument. They had been intelligently designed and the workmanship was superb. It would be like teaching a gifted student: Minor efforts purchase major results.

Some weeks later, Camille Pleyel presented the idea to Chopin, who knew nothing of my involvement. The piano maker said he would rent his hall for free in exchange for giving his pianos high visibility. He also promised to arrange for other acts to perform, hang posters, and sell three hundred tickets—all of which I would quietly lead. Chopin's only responsibility would be to captivate the audience.

"And," Pleyel assured him, taking away all of his objections, "we will not allow any eating in the auditorium!"

The piano maker and I met the next day about presenting his plan to Chopin. "There was some resistance," Pleyel reported to me in his office. "But after I offered to manage all the details, he was speechless."

"Did he suspect my hand in it?" I asked.

"I cannot say. But he did seem surprised."

None of these obstacles to setting up a recital ranked as important as a reprise of the cholera epidemic pounding on the gates of Paris. Citizens were wary of big crowds. Those who ventured out wore a cholera belt. Doctors said it warmed the kidneys and vulnerable abdominal organs. Other buildings, such as the Opéra, had taken to lining the foyer and corridors with massive vases of chlorinated water, which caused pungent, nauseating fumes to waft through the hall during the concert. Chopin begged Pleyel not to use such measures.

The public's fears were hardly unfounded. Parisians shuddered at the mention of the epidemic in 1832. They remembered the stink of putrefaction as carts piled high with bodies stuffed into white cotton sacks made their way to communal burial pits or to the morgue on the Île de la Cité. Cholera was a water-borne disease. Heavy rains resulted in deadly, fermented pools of excreta, especially in the poorer areas with their narrow, crowded back streets and labyrinth of alleyways. These cesspools were so deep that pedestrians often fell into them, almost ensuring infection.

As the concert date neared, I took great pains to prepare everything properly, including six pianos that would figure prominently in the show. Six! Tuning each one to match its neighbor was no small feat. The goal was to make them sound like one instrument. I had to fuss for days before I was satisfied. Fortunately, we had secured instruments in good enough mechanical condition so that I did not need to adjust the touch or replace any parts. Attending to the tunings was worrisome enough. To be certain they matched in pitch, I first tuned the best of the lot, then made a semicircle of the remaining five around it. I turned the master keyboard to face each one to play matching notes and correct any disparity in beats. Then on to the next, and the next. It took several days, with touchups necessary the day of the concert.

Along with all the other details, I made certain to place one of his spies next to ten guests suspected of antimonarchy sentiments. This all seemed excessive and haphazard, but Vidocq had not earned his reputation by being unimaginative.

The lights went down to great anticipation among the hundred or so people who had braved the odds to see this reclusive artist and other great masters. Even Felix Mendelssohn came to hear what would prove to be one of the most historically significant concerts ever given in Paris. Chopin played his Concerto for Piano in F minor and Grandes Variations brillantes on a theme by Mozart. But the biggest applause came after the Grande Polonaise that was preceded by an introduction and a march composed for those six pianos. What a spectacle!

I did worry about the one instrument to be used by Friedrich Kalkbrenner, whose playing could bruise even the hardiest of instruments. But Chopin insisted he be included on the playbill. Kalkbrenner also worked at the Pleyel firm, so the invitation was expected. Chopin was delighted at his acceptance to perform. In the rarest event that Chopin complimented anyone's playing, he praised Kalkbrenner, who was by most people's standards a superb pianist, despite criticism for offering accuracy over emotion. Such a failing did not seem to bother Chopin. He admitted to me one day that Kalkbrenner "is the only person whose shoelaces I am not worthy to untie."

In the next day's paper, one famous violinist said of the concert, "Simply stupefying!" Even Liszt, who was ordinarily lukewarm about Chopin's playing—due to jealousy, I thought—said the night was unforgettable. Only one disgruntled patron, probably hard of hearing, grumbled that Chopin had played too softly. This man was not the first and certainly would not be the last to cast such slights. Grumping aside, the night was a success. Chopin's coffers were filled anew.

The following day, in late afternoon because I knew he would need to rest after his concert, I brought a bouquet of daffodils with their "cheery yellow trumpets," as Lili had said, to congratulate him.

"Did you hear, Monsieur? Everyone in the market is talking about your concert, even those who did not attend."

He lowered his head and smiled. *He* was pleased with his performance. No more needed to be said.

"Your name will live forever in French history. Concertgoers can boast to their grandchildren that they heard the most brilliant pianist alive!"

"What about Polish history?" he said wryly.

"*Mais oui!*"

He accepted the bouquet with humility. He placed the flowers in a vase and started to put them on the piano, then smiled knowingly at me and placed them next to his divan.

"Thank you, Delhomme. The pianos were the highlight of the concert, and all tuned to perfection."

It was my turn to blush. I never knew if he discovered my maneuverings to set up the concert. In the end, did it matter? He earned money, Pleyel advertised his pianos, the attendees were regaled by the brilliance from Chopin and other stars, and best of all, I met yet another of my obligations to the king. Only one remained: obtaining information about George Sand.

# Arrival

## Arrival

*V*idocq was certain I could gather much valuable information about Sand's intentions if I could just get to her manor house. He wrote telling me to meet him in the Jardin du Luxembourg by the pond late that afternoon. But when I arrived, he was nowhere to be found. I looked behind hedges and down the path toward the gardens. No one. Out of character for such a punctual man. Meanwhile, I settled on a bench near the pond to watch the children use long sticks to push miniature sailboats on the water while the ducks paddled furiously to avoid collision.

Shortly, a woman who was no oil painting sat next to me wearing a long coat and large hat. "Hello, Delhomme," she said in a low voice. Startled she addressed me so familiarly, I looked closer and saw it was Vidocq! He wore a blond wig partially hidden by his pink bonnet, overly generous rouge on his cheeks and tinted lips that accentuated his yellowed teeth. I knew he was afraid of being recognized, but this seemed silly. On the other hand, I myself did not recognize him, so the disguise was indeed effective. I mused how he and *le garçon manqué* George Sand would get along in their gender-switching apparel. Although it strained credulity to consider which one would appear more convincing as the opposite gender, I had to award Sand that prize, given Vidocq's stubble.

Since Sand spent her days at Nohant writing and hobnobbing with artists, all of whom benefited from wealthy patrons, Vidocq wanted to know what they were doing to maintain their connections to their funding sources. He wanted to know what Sand was writing, to whom, and for what purpose.

"The last time I saw Mme Sand, she spoke not a word to me," I said in protest of his orders. "Do you think she will invite me to her manor home?"

The children gleefully raced around the pond to see who could push their boat to the other side with the fewest prods. Some of their screeches landed hard on my overly sensitive ears. But it was no worse than some of the cheap pianos I had worked on.

"Who tunes Chopin's piano when he is there?" he asked.

It was a good question. The composer had complained about his instrument, an upright donated by M. Pleyel, who furnished a piano each summer when he visited her residence. Even the finest instrument requires attention after shipment. He never asked me, and I never offered, to tune it, as I did not care to enter the house of that strumpet Sand.

"Tell him you will tune it for free. Say you will be in the area—I have no idea—to visit some relatives, see a piano dealer, hear a concert. Anything, Delhomme, *anything* to get into that house. Sneak in a back window if you must."

It was laughable to think Sand would let me past the front door. I would need to persuade Chopin that he could have his own guest, especially one who would better his life, which would in turn better hers.

My attention was diverted when I heard a splash and a hail of quacking. A child had fallen into the water. I rushed over, stepped into the knee-deep pond, and rescued the frightened toddler. The ducks scrabbled out of the water and waddled noisily into the bushes. The child's mother was ceaseless in her gratitude. Pleased with myself, I looked back to share my soggy victory with Vidocq. He had vanished.

The next day, I wrote to Chopin to offer my services, making up some tale about an old, ailing aunt I needed to visit in Châtre, a town neighboring

Nohant-Vic. "She suffers from gout and is not doing well," I said. Another lie to pile on the teetering stack.

"How lovely that would be!" he wrote back. "I compose with only one ear because it sounds so dreadful. But I cannot possibly ask you to spend your time here just to tune one piano."

"I would be honored." At least that was the truth.

And so, under the guise of ministering to his upright, I gathered my supplies, boarded the train, and girded my loins for an inevitable contre-temps with Sand. As difficult as it was to meet my obligations to Vidocq, maintaining civility toward Mme Sand menaced my thoughts far more.

I traveled south to Châteauroux on the newly built railway line. From there, I hired a carriage to take me the remaining twenty miles. A light May drizzle did not slow our pace.

As we passed through one idyllic scene after another, I had better in-sight into what inspired Chopin to come to the Loire valley: butterflies and bees danced on the summer orchids and daisies, and the quiet of the dense forests. It teemed with wolves, beavers, deer, and occasional hedge-hogs. The nearby river hosted dragonflies, green frogs, and newts, along with less welcome venomous vipers that hid among the ferns and grasses. He said he composed some of his best works in this peaceful setting.

I was certain that Sand had protested my coming. I made every attempt to avoid her in Paris. But given their love affair and my responsibilities as Chopin's tuner, it was a challenging goal. She preferred to be known by her pen name rather than her given name of Aurore (which I vengefully pro-nounced "Horreur"). It must have been quite a row between them about inviting me.

In his return letter, Chopin added another enticement: to meet some of their friends at a dinner party the day after my arrival. I was thrilled to be included in this circle. Artists and tradesmen rarely mixed socially. But even more so, I must admit, I welcomed the opportunity to reestablish our friendship after his many lengthy absences. Much more than just tuner and pianist, our connection was one of mutual respect and admiration, not to mention our connection through our families. He and Sand may have been lovers, but no one could understand his musical sensibilities better than I. Few relationships were as spiritually linked as ours. I remained steadfastly loyal.

Tall, slender poplars swayed languidly in the late afternoon breeze on the verdant lane to her home. The coachman drove past a few small cottages and enormous trees that embowered a tiny church. We passed through a wrought-iron gate onto the circular drive. The handsome two-story house was shaded by tall chestnuts and evergreens. The coach stopped before the arched entryway. As I alighted, a murder of crows in the catalpa tree took off as one, sounding like the day's wash flapping in the breeze. My driver kindly placed my bags next to me at the chalky-blue door. I had packed a suit for dinner, work clothes, and a gift for Mme Sand, a hand mirror with a bluebird singing among pink cherry blossoms painted on the back. Now she could admire herself *ad nauseum*. The other bag contained tools for regulating the action, as well as replacement ivories, hammers, dampers, and strings—supplies for any eventuality. On top of the tools lay my tuning hammer, packed with special care in red velvet. A tuning lever was to a tuner what a scalpel was to a surgeon, an integral extension of a skillful hand.

I knocked loudly. A man in a dirty, paint-smeared smock and unkempt hair and moustache answered. *What servant would greet a guest in such soiled garb?* I thought. He looked at me, one eyebrow raised.

I bade him good afternoon. "I am Beaulieu Delhomme, the piano tuner."

"Oh, yes, yes," the man said crankily. "I am afraid workmen must go to the service entrance around back. Meanwhile, you can leave your belongings over there." He pointed to the free-standing, two-story house to the right. He started to close the door.

"Excuse me," I said, stepping onto the threshold. "I know Monsieur Chopin..."

He smiled condescendingly. "Of course you do. He is a famous musician." He waved me off as if shooing away a hobo seeking alms and quickly shut the door.

I carried my luggage across the drive past the formal gardens and apple trees to an unmarked door. A servant answered. I explained again I had been invited by M. Chopin.

"*Oui, oui*," he said, "Madame Sand told us to expect you" and would I please follow him to my quarters. The servant opened the door to a room in the basement. It had a window near the low ceiling. The room was so small that I could barely walk past the washstand and spindly cherry table and chair to reach the narrow bed. The pillow was cased in rough hopsacking and filled with horsehair, lending an equine odor to the space. A gray wool blanket was folded and draped at the foot. I moved the kerosene lamp off the table and placed it carefully on the floor to make room for my bag. The tool case went on the chair and barely fit beneath the table. I asked the servant politely where I might find M. Chopin.

"*Oh, non, non, non, non, non, non.* Monsieur must not be bothered," he said, shaking his head. "He is composing and must be left alone, we have all been told."

I explained—insisted—I had been invited *by Monsieur Chopin* to come *from Paris* to work on his piano and would he be so kind as to show me to his studio.

He looked at me, brow knitted, then led me back to the main house and up the winding stone stairway to the musician's studio. Even through the padded door, I could hear Chopin playing on a badly out-of-tune instrument. The fourths and fifths were so tortured and octaves so strident that I wondered how he could even recognize his own compositions. Given how finicky he was about his pianos in Paris, I was mystified how he tolerated such cacophony. He would not have heard me knock, so I opened the door cautiously. The music stopped.

"Who is it?" I heard him say testily.

I peered slowly around the door. "Ah, Delhomme! Delhomme!" He stood up to greet me. "What a wonderful sight you are. Please come in."

The studio was twice the size of my attic room with a southern-facing window overlooking a wooded area with a bench and small pond to collect rainwater.

We commiserated about the arduous trip from Paris. He motioned to a seat by the piano and checked the clock. "It's half past five," he said. "What good Frenchman would pass up a glass of wine to celebrate the end of a long journey?" He went to the hallway and looked both ways for a servant. Just then a man passed by.

"Oh, Eugène," Chopin said to him. "How may I get my friend a glass of wine? I see no servants on the floor now."

The man in the paint-smeared smock spied me through the crack in the door. His eyes narrowed. "*C'est ton ami?* He told me he was the piano tuner."

Chopin looked at me, then at the man, and opened the door wider to properly introduce us. "Eugène Delacroix, I would like you to meet my piano tuner and, yes, my good friend, Beaulieu Delhomme."

I rose to greet him. "Oh, Monsieur Delacroix. I am red-faced that I did not recognize you. I have seen your work in the Louvre."

Delacroix shook my hand limply, as if I had some dread disease. "Very nice to meet you," he said, wearing an insincere smile. He turned to Chopin, "I will be happy to fetch some wine for you—and your 'friend,'" and left.

"Did Aurore greet you when you arrived?" he asked.

"Why, no. Delacroix did."

"What do you mean?" he said, surprised. "She always meets her guests." He turned away and rubbed his forehead as if that would help explain her breach of etiquette. I, too, was surprised she had not come to the door, or at least a servant with clean clothes. Even strained relations did not supersede courtesy in French society.

"And your room? I asked that you be put up next to me."

I cleared my throat. "I am already comfortably installed in the servants' quarters."

Chopin stiffened upon hearing this news. "Why, you're being treated like a stable groomer with manure on his shoes. I am so terribly, terribly embarrassed, Delhomme. I will go right now and demand you be moved to my adjoining room." He headed for the door.

I put up my hand. "I am perfectly comfortable where I am." I did not want him to squabble with Mme Sand on my account. Current gossip had it that he and Sand were quarrelling more than usual lately, and I did not want to widen the rift by complaining about my lodging. I was not certain Chopin noticed or even cared about my distaste for her, but it was not my place to voice my opinion about her now, or ever. Knowing he honored our friendship enough to risk a quarrel over such a small thing soothed my indignation.

A servant entered, poured a Sauvignon blanc, and put a plate of grapes, apple slices, and figs alongside some runny brie on a small table. He handed me my glass.

"I believe this . . ." Chopin checked the label on the bottle ". . . yes, this one is local, not far from here. Aurore told me the Benedictines developed this vineyard at their monastery in the thirteenth century. Now the peasants own it. The nobility and clergy lost control after the revolution in 1799, like everything else." He raised his glass. "Here's to a turbulent past and a peaceful future . . . And to friends who know how to tune!"

His tribute and the snack were heartily welcome. Stopping for a meal would have meant a late arrival at Nohant, so I had nibbled only on crackers and walnuts. Chopin said we would be dining alone that night. Tomorrow would be *le grand dîner*. "Did you bring proper attire?" he asked.

After a short minute in silence, he assured me I would thoroughly enjoy my stay here and became animated about its charms. "The brook is so clear. You can see small fish bunched up looking for food. Sometimes I feed them bread. You really must stroll around the grounds. Delacroix raves about the morning light," he said, "and I often wander along the paths just to hear the songbirds. They often spark ideas." He stopped suddenly and cocked his head toward the window. "Can you hear that woodpecker?" he said. "My metronome!" I did not know how true that all was, but it was a romantic notion that birds informed his scores.

We continued sipping and sampling as I caught him up on politics. Paris was restless, as was all of Europe, and revolution was on the lips of those in barber chairs and outdoor markets. He said he was glad to be away from such quidnuncs, so he could concentrate on his work. He seemed healthier. His cheeks had pinkened, the dark circles under his eyes had disappeared, and he smiled more readily.

Acknowledging that George Sand had contributed to his convalescence was difficult for me. She may have cooled his fevered brow, fed him well, and provided opportunities to create, but in my estimation, she was only too glad to use him as bait to lure other notable artists to her enclave, so she could bask in their reflected renown. Authors seek to cast whatever positive light they can on their reputations. She was no exception. Now I realized she was also borrowing on the celebrity of Delacroix, who was tutoring her twenty-two-year-old son, Maurice.

The dinner guests would include Delacroix, of course, and Franz Liszt. The Russian writer Ivan Turgenev was also invited. Chopin described him as a tall and broad-shouldered chap but restrained and soft-spoken, although "his novels were anything but timorous," he said, smiling. "I asked Aurore to invite Hector too," he said, "but he was unsure when he would arrive."

That cheered me. Berlioz would be an ally against the other haughty artists. I felt intimidated and expected to remain a cheerful but silent dinner guest. It was a promise I would not keep.

For all her writings about the common man, Sand certainly surrounded herself with very uncommon people: Gustav Flaubert, Victor Hugo, Honoré de Balzac had all frequented her home. The stream of talented men—and they were all men—who came to Nohant seemed endless. Of course, it was her right to invite anyone she chose to her table. I had no quarrel with that. I also understood that artists had a unique calling to make something out of nothing and enjoyed being among like-minded people who confronted a similar ordeal: blank pages and canvases. Are these gifts sent from on high or born of a mental illness where voices speak to them? Who can be certain? Even they cannot explain their source of inspiration. To be sure, Chopin suffered because of his gift. He closed himself up for days in his apartment, crying out in frustration, breaking quills, writing, scratching out, and rewriting. He once told me, "The pen burns my fingers."

Why would they struggle so? What forced artists to torture themselves into meeting expectations only they have created? Just as Ulysses was lashed to his mast to resist the Sirens' song, so too was Chopin ensnared by the Sirens of his imagination. Who or what decided when a work was done? As a tuner, I had the laws of physics—a string's length, tension, and diameter—to guide me. But, for artists, there were no such rules, save for the limitations imposed by language, sound, or color. One would have been excused for thinking they enjoyed their suffering.

Chopin played his latest ballade. He seemed happy with it. Perhaps after hearing the new composition on a well-tuned instrument, he would change his mind. In fact, I was certain he would.

"What do you think?" he asked excitedly.

"I . . . think you need a tuning."

"But the ballade. Do you think it is acceptable for the publisher yet? I want to dedicate it to Aurore."

"Why not dedicate it to Louis Philippe?" I said quickly.

He looked quizzically at me. "Why would I do that?"

"One can never go wrong flattering the monarch," I said, trying to stop him from aggrandizing Sand. "Besides, the aristocracy supports the king, and you want to court their favor, correct?" I needed to make sure he was squarely in the loyalist camp. But truth to tell, I was just as happy to deny her any of his accolades or admiration.

He looked undecided about the dedication. Even better, I had confirmed his loyalty to the king. But it was not his devotion I was focused on. Tomorrow's dinner party would help me gather that information.

Chopin must have seen my fatigue and urged me to rest before our light meal that evening. At precisely seven-thirty, refusing to debase myself by using the service entrance, I knocked on the door to the main house. A servant let me in. I climbed to the top of the winding staircase and rapped lightly. "*Entrez,*" he said through the door. The fallboard to his piano was closed, a sure sign he was finished composing for the day. Our food was set out on a small table by the window: cold veal, roasted vegetables, and just-picked berries with crème fraîche. If this was a light meal, what would tomorrow night's fare be? No wonder he ate so well here.

The next day, I set about my work. Thank God I had slept soundly despite the odiferous pillow and scratchy blanket, because tending to his instrument required all my attention. The pedals squeaked, which I repaired with some rendered mutton tallow to lubricate the contact points. Several dampers leaked sound, requiring delicate adjustments of the wires so they would fit snuggly against the strings. I also fixed some sluggish keys. The moisture from the spring rain and forest had swollen the wood around the balance rail pins, hampering the keys' free movement during play. This was not a complicated process, only tedious and time consuming.

Last, I set A at 435 cycles per second with my tuning fork. It was a new pitch standard recently established by the London Philharmonic, so the piano would match the reed instruments. Mozart's A had been set at 421 cycles. But raising the standard had forced piano manufacturers to replace the wooden frame with a metal one because the extra tension made the wood collapse. That change increased the weight of the instrument by many pounds but did wonders for stabilizing the tuning. Chopin preferred the higher pitch anyway because it made his pieces sound brighter and improved the harmonics. After many hours, I had restored the Pleyel to its original condition and was eager to see his reaction.

I returned to my room, tired and hungry. I opened the window and smelled the cool woodland air. I lay still. Tuning could strain one's tolerance for sounds, but the chirping crickets and hooting owls reinvigorated my weary ears. The setting sun glinted through the leaves and pine needles. My pocket watch told me it was almost eight. I dressed in my dark-brown morning coat, gilet, and cravat and crossed the driveway to the main house to join the festivities—through the front door!

A kitchen maid showed me to the dining room. The table, directly under an elegant blue and pink crystal chandelier, was covered with a white damask cloth. Seven chairs upholstered in red silk were placed around the table that had been expanded to accommodate us.

I nodded to Delacroix and Liszt, and thanked Madame Sand for inviting me.

"*De rien,*" was her perfunctory reply, the stock answer to any expression of gratitude. At least she had spoken to me.

Chopin introduced me to Monsieur Turgenev. Not unexpectedly, Mme Sand seated me at the far end as if to accentuate my pariah status. Meanwhile, Chopin was placed, possessively, at her right elbow. Berlioz had not yet arrived.

I felt uneasy about how the evening would unfurl. Flattered to have been invited, I still felt uncomfortable, like a child dining with adults. In these situations, my mother had taught me to follow the lead of the other guests. That way, nothing could go wrong. Maman was naïve on that score.

# CHAPTER 18

# First Day in Jail

## First Night

Daily life in the Conciergerie challenges all prisoners to remain calm since the exact day and time of our execution is unknowable. Yet we are all certain it is imminent.

Trials are farces. Judges and attorneys, brimming with self-importance, strut about in their robes and powdered periwigs, confident in their omniscience. Expecting fairness is folly.

At dawn, the jailers open the doors and lead us men to the open-air courtyard. Women have their own area with a fountain to wash linen. I dare not speak to anyone at this time for fear he will inform on me at trial. Vidocq certainly has enough ammunition against me already.

When darkness fell that first night, I piled some straw into a corner against the hard, earthen floor. Dread prowled in my head: What will happen to Lili, how long will my trial be, how will it feel to have a guillotine slice off my head? Will I be buried in a mass grave, as so many during the Revolution had been?

The sun came up this morning casting a few rays onto the wall. I stepped over there to let the light play on my skin but it lacked all warmth. All too soon, it moved on, and the gray cold returned. Forlorn, I sat in the corner again, arms wrapped around my knees to conserve warmth as I pitied and castigated my wretched self. I heard my father's scolds as clearly as if he were talking into my ear as he did after the medical school fiasco.

The turnkey clinked his keys in the lock. He beckoned me to follow and told me to bring my blanket. He led me down the hall to a cell with prisoners shouting and fighting. He opened the door. "Quiet down, you animals!" he said as he pushed me in and slammed the door. I looked away, not even wanting to acknowledge their presence. I felt unwelcome, but who would feel otherwise with space at a premium? Where would we all sleep?

We are now seven men with hollow expressions, stinking of fear. A worker comes once a day to pick up the bucket and replace it with a new one half-filled with lime. Prisoners of means can buy more comfortable lodging with a small bed and desk. Easily identified by their stylish clothes, which they pay to keep in lieu of the striped garb we others wore, they emerge in the exercise yard rumpled from their incommodious night. Many of their ilk arrive one day and disappear the next, perhaps having bought their freedom. All others march to the gallows with bad haircuts, including Marie Antoinette, who proudly wore a humble bonnet and prisoner's garb to the scaffold.

I slumped down against the wall in the only space available next to the lime bucket. Oh, my God, I could hardly breathe. After some time, perhaps hours—I had long since given up my ability to tell time—the heavy, black door creaked open. There stood Lili clutching a loaf of bread, a sack of hardboiled eggs, and slab of my favorite chèvre. I ran over to her.

"Darling, how did you know I was here?" I was breathless with joy.

Her expression registered her horror at the sight and smell of these unsavory ruffians, including me.

"These are for you," she said, holding out the goods as if avoiding a leper. I put the packages down. Her eyes were puffy and dull. Tears welled up. I wanted so much to kiss her. I reached out to take her in my arms, but she recoiled.

"What will happen to you?" she said.

I chose not to answer.

Meanwhile, several men made lewd remarks, and another snatched the bread and tore some off with his teeth.

"I have something to tell you," she began, but the jailer took her arm.

"Time to go, Missy," he said rudely and led her away while another locked the door.

The previous evening, the gendarmes fetched all the prisoners and led us down a long promenade to gather in a spacious courtyard at the foot of the Bonbec Tower, which housed the chamber where detainees were tortured into confessing to crimes they may not have committed.

We gathered there to hear the "evening newspaper," as it was known, read by the gendarmes who laid out the acts of accusation to the ill-fated. This reading also served as the only notice that their trial would begin the next day. Following a short, bogus proceeding and sentencing, their punishment would be swiftly carried out.

There are many fetid boils on my soul from greed. I tried to lance them by turning on that cruel spymaster and supporting workers fighting for their lives. But it was too little, and too late. Now that soul is condemned.

# Dinner

## Dinner

S and was rightfully proud of Nohant's history. It had been built in 1228 as a fortified manor. The house we dined in had been added in the mid-fifteenth century. Her grandmother bought the building in 1793, she said, during the French Revolution and then willed it to George in 1821. She had raised her two children there. She herself had spent most of her youth in this majestic home, except for the two and a half years she spent at the English Convent of Augustinian sisters in Paris to escape the conflict she had with both her grandmother and mother. (How ironic that she had been schooled by nuns.) Handsome wallpaper covered the walls. Paintings of her family hung in gold frames. She had recently installed a heating system, but no hallways were heated, and certainly not my lodging. I worried that the one blanket might not suffice on that cool May night.

The party began with laughter and stories. Sand was an incomparable hostess when it came to setting a fine table. The centerpiece had been fashioned from lilacs, hyacinths, tulips and primrose and emitted a heady scent. The goblets were cut crystal, and the dishes hand painted. It all looked so sumptuous and effortless. An empty chair was reserved for Berlioz, who, true to form, was late.

Her servants—*What? Servants in the home of a socialist?*—delivered the first course of a delicious clear broth with croutons speckled with fresh rosemary. The diners wasted no time in turning to politics. Three were immigrants: Chopin from Poland, Liszt from Germany (although born to Hungarian parents), and Turgenev from Russia, so the discussion traveled beyond France's borders.

All our homelands were in an uproar over aristocratic rule by tsars, emperors, and grand dukes. Industrialists were also under fire, due to the poor wages that forced workers to live in slums. Their cheap goods had undercut artisans' income. The potato blight had spread across Europe, turning the tuber to mush. France was less dependent on the potato than other countries, but even so, with an estimated twenty percent reduction of the crop, prices were too dear for ordinary citizens. Many lived on bread and a paltry supply of other vegetables. Any affordable meat was spoiled, causing disease and even death. They blamed the nobility who owned the farms and created unbearable conditions for the peasants. People were clamoring for the right to vote and have a say in the government. They wanted democracy.

In 1830, there had already been a rash of uprisings across Europe, including one in France, known as the July Revolution. Each revolt, in turn, had been quashed by tyrannical leaders with brutal, gory retribution. Now, as Vidocq had repeatedly warned, there were fresh stirrings among the people for equality, higher wages, and better working conditions. This unrest would mean renewed chaos and uncertainty for those at the table that night. It would have been hard to create anything when people were amassing in the streets with a *cri de coeur* for justice. Nonetheless, citizens openly discussed an incipient revolt in France. My job was to find out who would lead it and when.

"The thought of another uprising unsettles my stomach," Delacroix said, touching his belly. "The violence I saw in 1830 was quite enough."

"This time it will be different," said Sand, whose writings had been fomenting such ideas.

I perked up, listening for specifics.

"How can you say that?" said Delacroix, waving his hands as if to say, Enough! "The people have already paid dearly to express their opinion.

They were murdered in the streets, for pity's sake, and tortured to death if they were found out. And now you want *more*?"

Sand put down her soup spoon and turned to address him. "Eugène," she said drolly. "I should think you would be at the forefront of the rebellion, like the bare-breasted Lady Liberty in your painting." Here, she became more serious. "But why, pray tell, did she have to take off her clothes to lead the troops?"

"George," he countered. "I hate to be so blunt, but what else but a well-endowed, half-naked mistress would induce men to take up swords and bayonets and follow a woman into battle?"

Laughter came from everyone but Mme Sand, whose expression broadcast her chagrin at our poor understanding of women's exploitation.

Delcroix explained that since painting "Liberty Leading the People," he had turned away from political subjects. "To be honest," he said, "I hate crowds, and I am afraid of this revolutionary turmoil and hysteria." I took that to mean he would not participate in any uprising. Duly noted.

"What a pessimist you are," said Sand, touching his sleeve. She turned to look at all of us earnestly: "This time will be different. Our will is strong. We have more weapons and more organization."

"It sounds as if the revolution could happen in the next few months, the way you speak," I said, prodding her for details and breaking my vow of silence. She ignored my prompt for information. Either she did not know the timeline or did not want to divulge it. I filed it in the back of my mind.

The servants removed the soup bowls and brushed breadcrumbs from the tablecloth into a silver dustpan.

Sand continued: "How can we not fight the monarchy that has given us nothing but mealy-mouthed promises about change? We have been hearing that for fifty years. And they call him the Citizen King!" She was referring to my "boss," Louis Philippe. She motioned impatiently to another servant to replenish our wine glasses. "This government has given us only repression and usury and flagrant disregard for the common people." Her comments quickly darkened the mood. "The same goes double for women," she said. "How many times do I have to advocate for women to become equals in society?"

It was Liszt who ventured a tongue-in-cheek retort. "What more equality do you want, George? You already wear men's clothing." He looked at each of us. "Cigar, anyone?" We howled at the jibe. I must confess, I laughed every bit as hard. He poked again: "Are you not free of the restrictions of girdles and bone stays in your corsets already?"

Sand handed all that and more back to Liszt: "You had better be happy that I am comfortable in my clothes. I would be doubly enraged if I wore an undergarment that trussed my innards just so I could wear a dress that makes me look like a tea cozy."

"Touché!" said Delacroix, clapping.

A string of servants brought in lamb stew, jasmine rice, asparagus, bread, and more bottles of wine. The only thing missing was a Mozartian processional. The sourdough bread, whose aroma had wafted up to the second floor while I worked on Chopin's piano, was served warm. A green salad with bacon vinaigrette went perfectly with the stew. It could not have been a more delicious meal.

Sand tasted the lamb, then sat back in her chair, as if to take the necessary time to sharpen the barb of her remarks: "I shall work night and day until every woman is freed from those strangling undergarments."

"Do let me help!" said the ever-randy Liszt.

Sand's imperious manner grated on me now more than ever. I also found it galling to have a woman challenge men's authority. I could not resist poking a stick at her ideas about the sexes. "If I may speak for the other half, Madame Sand," I said, moderating my tone, "many men would not want to marry a woman who is out protesting in the streets for equal rights. I myself want peace in my home and a hearty meal after working all day." All eyes were on me as I continued: "Are you not forgetting what is *our* right as men? And what about the children? They would surely not be properly cared for if their mother was off colluding with like-minded women about their freedoms. I promise that we will take your opinions into consideration when we finally get the chance to vote." I saw the men shift in their seats, as if bracing for Sand's counterpunch.

"Monsieur Delhomme, you are a troglodyte of the first order!" Sand shouted so forcefully that I feared she might fling her stew at me.

"Then, what recourse do women have, Madame?" I really did ask this out of curiosity. "Will they fight in the streets? Will they threaten the king?" In case these questions could be construed otherwise, I added some humor to hide the subterfuge. "Louis Philippe wants to know ahead of time!" I laughed; she did not.

"The revolution cannot come soon enough for my taste," she said, pounding her fist on the table, rattling the china. "And where the hell is Berlioz?"

Franz intervened in the awkward silence. "Frédéric, you have been quiet this evening," he said. "What do you think of Monsieur Delhomme's ideas?" All heads turned to the pianist, who seemed pale and fragile sitting next to robust and ruddy Liszt.

Unfortunately, Liszt's question, meant to cool down the situation, only inflamed it. The political differences between Aristocrat Chopin and Everyman Sand served to further strain their relationship. He needed to tread lightly here to avoid a death blow to it.

"I . . . I agree with Aurore . . . somewhat." I could see his distress over any confrontation, especially when it came to politics at the dinner table. He said it caused indigestion. "She knows my views." But he could not leave it at that, and added, "France has had peace for some time now, even though its people have forgone some rights."

Mme Sand glowered. "Forgone *some* rights? Why is this a discussion about peaceful government *or* women's suffrage? Why can we not have both?" For a moment, I thought she might throttle him for his conservative views.

"Oh, let us not rehash all these tired arguments," said Liszt. "No one is going to change anyone's mind, so why are we debating the issue?"

"For my money—and I do mean money," said Delacroix, "I am leery about skewering the upper class. Chopin?" he said, "do you agree?"

Feeling protective of him, or perhaps just wanting to stir things up, I jumped in, unbidden, to represent his views, which we had spoken of often. "He sides with the elites." Chopin was perpetually in arrears. How could he possibly live without their largesse?

"It's not just economics," said Sand. "Of course, we want to keep our benefactors, but I am loath to preserve inequality just so I can write my next novel." She paused, then started in again. "Besides, do you really think that if we changed our government to a parliamentary one the riches of the upper class would suddenly evaporate? I will write and protest until these measures are passed."

"And what will you write about?" I asked, again without guile.

"Why do you ask these questions, Monsieur Delhomme?" she said.

"Forgive me if you think me rude, Madame, but you talk a lot about revolution. What does a person have to do to be considered revolutionary? What will *you* do? What do your servants and gardeners and workmen think?"

Chopin looked at me, his eyes pleading for me to stop riling an already enraged animal.

"Well, forgive *me*, Monsieur, but are you a royal spy? I have already told you: We are preparing the funeral pyre for the monarchy, and my writings will light the fire. That is all you need to know."

Her comment about being a spy shook me. Was I being too obvious? Certainly, I did not want to provoke any more tension between her and Chopin—well, perhaps a little—but I needed to know: Was there a date certain for this supposed funeral pyre? I may have needed to bring back the information to Vidocq, but if a bomb was going to explode, I myself wanted to know where and when. After all, I depended largely on industrialists to manufacture pianos and on wealthy customers to buy and maintain them. Chopin was sustained largely because of his well-to-do students, and who did Delacroix think was going to buy his paintings? The flea-bitten wretches living in squalor on the streets?

"Maybe George has a point," said Liszt, taking the floor again. He leaned back in his chair and sipped his Beaujolais. "Look at America. Wealthy people are flourishing in that democratic society, so why not ours?"

The mention of America brought peals of derisive laughter. That country's government had barely hit the half-century mark and was regarded by most Frenchmen as a crude attempt at social equality. "Americans are so crass and uneducated," said Delacroix, "that they have no artists to support! What difference does it make *what* kind of government they have?"

More nodding and snickering.

Quiet until now, Ivan Turgenev, who had emigrated to France precisely because he had seen brutal crackdowns in his native Russia, said that Tsar Nicholas had opened fire on the rebels in their Decembrist revolution in 1825. Those who were not killed in battle were either hanged or sent to Siberia.

He continued: "Nicholas imposed very strict censorship on the people and set up a network of spies and informants to force people's loyalty. It was sickening."

... 'forced' people's loyalty . . ., I thought, *Is that what Louis Philippe is doing? Forcing my loyalty by paying me to spy?* Vidocq had not stated clearly that my assignment to observe others was compulsory. I considered it temporary, merely an expedient to making money in the short term. I thought I could back out any time. Was I mistaken?

"Equality in America is a joke," said Turgenev. "They have *slavery*, for goodness' sake. Their so-called democracy is pathetic!"

This comment was disingenuous to say the least since his mother had well over five hundred serfs on her estate in Russia, Chopin told me later.

Where the hell *was* Berlioz?

Truth to tell, I had heard about some piano manufacturers in America that were flourishing under such a system. Chickering & Sons out of Boston and William Knabe & Co. in Baltimore were manufacturing and selling pianos to those on the east coast and in southern states. But Turgenev was right. Democracy in that new country was in jeopardy. I had heard some states were threatening to secede over slavery. President Polk, a slaveholder himself, handily won election in 1844. So, it was hard to see how the status quo would change over that issue.

In contrast to a roiling Europe, England was peaceful and thriving. That country had ended two costly and bloody battles with America in 1783 and 1812. Memories of war do not fade quickly, and England was more interested in keeping its citizens safe now.

"As for America being a place for uncultured buffoons," Chopin added, trying to inject some humor, "I was thinking of going there myself. So, there would be at least one artist in residence." He elbowed Liszt with a twinkle in his eye. "Franz, I have a wonderful idea. Come with me, and we'll double the census."

Flustered by the lack of support for her revolutionary spirit, Sand sighed and theatrically threw down her serviette, muttering something about checking on dessert. As she arose, a sparkle from her necklace caught my eye. She was wearing Chopin's diamond ring on a gold chain! I was aghast, and admittedly, covetous. He had offered that ring to *me*, for *my* fiancée when the time came. Now she had it. I picked at the asparagus to squelch my choler.

"We can laugh," said Franz about the gloomy prediction, "but Alexis de Tocqueville says that the United States will be one of two main global powers, with or without artists."

"And the other one?" asked Chopin.

"Russia."

At the mention of his country, a pie-eyed Turgenev waved his glass and exclaimed, "*Na zdorovye!*" as he toasted Tocqueville's forecast. Perhaps he had forgotten his reason for emigrating to France in the first place. So much for the horrors of slavery.

"Democratic ignoramuses versus oppressive tsars," said Delacroix. "God help us all."

Just then, a breathless Berlioz stumbled into the dining room with disheveled hair and torn clothes. He almost bumped into a servant pouring coffee.

"Hector!" said Sand. "Where have you . . ." she started to ask, then signaled one of her servants to bring him a plate of food.

"I was being chased by someone!" He said he was not sure what they wanted. This was indeed unusual behavior from a man who was not exactly stable and measured but never given to illusions.

I saw Chopin and Liszt exchange knowing looks. Chopin had told me that one time Berlioz had become insanely enamored of some woman who had no idea who he was. He had driven himself so crazy with desire that he set off into the forest. Chopin and Liszt, along with Felix Mendelssohn, found him before he had a chance to do himself in.

He finally married that woman, an actress and a drunken one at that. Oh, such troubles they had. The more he composed, the more she drank. There was no peace in that house. People knew of his volatile home life but looked past the gossip to savor his musical gifts. Such individuals were not judged by the same standards as ordinary folk.

George, in her motherly way, calmed him down. Tending to a needy soul placated her as well. Still huffy, though, she rejoined the table. "Monsieur Delhomme," she said, placing her napkin in her lap again. "You are in the working class. Do you not see your people as unfairly treated and the industrialists taking advantages of their workers?"

Now it was my turn to chafe. How did she reckon they were *my* people?

"*Excusez-moi*, Madame," I said, "I make my living with my hands and proud to do so, but there is a difference between a worker and an artisan. I am the latter," I said, perhaps a bit too defiantly.

"George!" shouted Berlioz, as bits of food shot out of his mouth. "Delhomme went to medical school with me—and the Conservatoire. Stop calling him a worker."

I hardly saw myself on the same level as a peasant or factory worker. It had taken me years to perfect my trade. I dealt with wealthy landowners, bankers, even royalty. Apparently, some others at this table did not see me as one of their own. Certainly not Sand, who had repeatedly reminded me of my station at every turn on this visit. I wanted to take this opportunity to embarrass her. Badly I wanted that. But my upbringing would not allow me to behave in kind, at least not in public. Besides, it would have embarrassed her in front of her guests and, worse, would make me look petty and coarse, just what they would have expected from a loutish bumpkin. No, I chose honey, not vinegar. Above all, I wanted to mollify the woman. But I planned to serve my own hearty meal of revenge later, when it would hurt her the most.

Berlioz spoke, now a bit more stable from nourishment. "This talk about politics and class is so boring. Let me recite some *Hamlet* for you." He wiped his mouth with a napkin, stood, cleared his throat, and began with an outstretched arm:

"To be or not to be . . ."

Sand interrupted. "Hector, Hector. We all love Shakespeare, but could it wait?" she said. He could hold forth for hours, putting everyone to sleep.

I returned to her question about my place in society. "Of course, I want everyone to earn a fair wage as befits their skills." I looked at Chopin. His worried glance warned me against setting off an explosion by contradicting Sand. I softened my tone. "But artists must stay above the fray. They must remain unrestricted. Art means exploring the fringes of thought. The muse of creativity is a jealous mistress. Just ask Chopin. One can never trap, summon, or brow-beat her. Lord knows, he has tried. The aristocracy understands that and supports your efforts. Certainly, I want equality for workers, but I also want you artists to feel free to create."

Chopin sent me a look of gratitude for not goading her into upending the table.

"Well spoken, Monsieur Delhomme," said Liszt, raising his glass. "Let's drink to . . . to . . . *liberté, égalité, fraternité!*"

We stood, clinked glasses and roared our approval. Berlioz raised his glass too, although I was sure he had no idea why.

The guests retired one by one. It was almost midnight and the excesses of alcohol had brought Morpheus to all of us, except Sand, who, as was her practice, went to her room to write until dawn.

# Snooping – Reporting Out

## Snooping

*I* could not leave Nohant without gathering the juicy morsels of information Vidocq sought. Delivering them would surely release me from his clutches. With Sand's full-throated pronouncement that an uprising could not come soon enough, Vidocq would certainly be drooling for proof: dates, names, addresses, and reports of her writings.

The next morning, I decided to investigate while she slept. Chopin was happily composing on his freshly tuned instrument, and Delacroix was painting in the garden's mellow morning light. I had heard Liszt and Turgenev drinking shots of vodka late into the night and singing their national anthems. They would surely not arise before midday.

I first went to the kitchen and chatted with the cook. She told me to help myself to tea from the pot. I took my orange pekoe and tiptoed upstairs to Sand's office next to Chopin's studio. I placed the saucer on a table by her desk and made haste, all the while being mindful of the inkpot off to the side of her writing space. Three shelves on the desk held stacks of paper. I began there.

A thick sheaf on top was a manuscript for *The Country Waif*. (Not an autobiography, I presumed.) Bills occupied the next shelf down. Tucked on the bottom shelf were letters. The one on top was addressed to

Alphonse de Lamartine, yet unfinished. I had read his poetry, but now he was a prominent politician with moderate views.

She wrote: "My heart is bursting, and my head is aflame. All my physical ailments and personal sorrows are forgotten. I am alive, strong and active, and do not feel a single day over twenty." The letter mentioned "the event" planned for late February but without gloss. It had a tone of urgency and the last part swore her to secrecy. Under that letter was a several-page tract listing demands like those she had mentioned at dinner: universal suffrage, a ten-hour day for Parisians, the abolition of slavery in the colonies, something about establishing a government-run program for the unemployed. Surely that much was meaty enough for Vidocq.

Chopin opened the door. "Here you are!" he said, startling me. "I have searched high and low for you."

"Oh, Chopin. Good morning." I fumbled with the papers as I returned them to the shelf. He had caught me *in flagrante*.

"What . . . That is Aurore's desk. What are you doing?" he asked. It was a rhetorical question. I had no excuse. "Boredom led me to have a peek at the next great book she is writing." I was not a good liar, and this weak excuse proved it. I tried to appear collected, as if one rifled through one's hostess's papers all the time.

He looked dubious and bade me follow as he left the room. No rebuke. It was his gentle way of telling me I had overstepped the bounds of decency. My queries of what she was writing about coupled with my challenges to her revolutionary words and actions made me worry that he would awaken to the fact I had misrepresented my offer to tune his piano.

Out of earshot of any servants, he told me to leave immediately. I was not certain if he would report me to Sand. But in the coach back to Paris, I remembered the teacup I had left by her desk. Those tattletale cooks would surely reveal its owner. There would be hell to pay. Of that I was certain. But even if I was revealed to be a spy, I would have completed my assignment and would no longer be associated with that role.

## Reporting Out

Once back in Paris and eager to tell Vidocq of my findings, we met near the newly built Gare d'Austerliz in southeast Paris in a library. The place smelled of dusty books and was morgue-quiet. He was in the corner, his head down reading.

"Bonjour, Delhomme," he said without looking up.

"How did you know it was me?" I asked.

"I heard your cheap shoes scuffing on the carpet," he said, turning a page.

Was there anything this man did not know?

As if he heard my thoughts, he looked up. Today's disguise included a black patch over his left eye. "What have you got?" he said.

We sat in a secluded corner, but I paused to look around for eaves-droppers.

"Well?" he said, raising the brow over the patch.

I recounted *sotto voce* that Sand had written a tract for some newspaper and a short note to Alphonse de Lamartine. I paused to see if he knew the name. He gave an exasperated sigh, as if to indicate he already knew that.

"And on a third piece of paper," I continued, "she wrote a list of de-mands the rebels wanted addressed. And something about an event in late February."

This piqued his interest. "Event? What event?"

"*Je ne sais pas*," I said.

Vidocq showed no emotion upon hearing any of this, although I thought the information was extraordinarily interesting and useful.

"What else happened?" he asked.

I told him about the dinner, the various attendees, and their views. This information did not seem quite as revelatory as Sand's writings.

He rubbed his hands together. "Excellent work, Delhomme."

His pleasure at my findings emboldened me to apply pressure.

"Now that I have given you the goods on Sand, I will be leaving your service," I said, flatly. I knew that was not an option, but it set the boundary for negotiation. I held out my hand to thank him.

But this man, with his pitted skin, greasy hair, and rumpled shirt, stood and leaned over the table. His face reddened. "Death," he said, wag-ging his finger. "That is your way out! We are hardly done with you. Now go find out when the plan will be executed, who will lead it, what they plan to do, and how."

If Vidocq wanted to intimidate me, he was succeeding. Having the weight of the monarchy behind him, along with his own heft, was plenty of incentive to comply.

But this spymaster had taught me another thing: Manipulate your opponent into a corner, then set your demands. I pressed on. "Then I want more money—a thousand francs before beginning the next stage and another thousand after I deliver the information." I hid my trembling hands under the table.

"*C'est impossible!*" he said, his one eyelid twitching with anger.

"Sir, you never told me this assignment would last forever."

He softened after realizing his goal—Mme Sand's seditious plan—was nearly at hand. Killing me, as he said he would, would be self-defeating. Certainly, the king would not be pleased. He could ill-afford to have such a stain on his precious reputation and to be beaten at his own game at that! It was the peppercorn that broke the camel's back. My ruse had worked.

He held my gaze with his one eye. "Meet me at your apartment tomorrow night at eight. I will bring the money." He left forthwith. I stayed seated until my heartbeat subsided.

# Confrontation

*M*y mood was buoyed by the news that my wealth would increase by two thousand francs. I would still have to deliver the goods, of course, but now I could propose to Lili. After all this time, her so-called fiancé had not married her. She never spoke of him and had been writing me more warm, affectionate letters. I considered her engagement defunct. It was high time I asked for her hand.

The next morning—it was too late to send her a note—I took a coach to Marainville. It was heaven to let my mind wander, to recite my proposal. *I must be bold!* My head swam with thoughts of sweeping her into my arms and kissing her until—I could not see beyond such ecstasy.

The coach rumbled on. I arrived in Marainville before the sun set. I directed the coachman past my mother's house, her neighbor's stone wall delineating his fields now brimming with yellow wheat, and his barnyard donkeys ever-braying loudly.

As the coach neared Lili's house, I saw a couple on the porch. They were sitting much too close for an unmarried couple. I squinted to identify the man. Hirsute, barrel-chested, uniformed. Was that her soldier beau?! I had no time to array my thoughts. I jumped out of the still-moving coach to confront him and stumbled, breathless, up to the porch.

I stammered like the town imbecile as words jammed in my throat. "G-g-get away from my Lili!" I shouted. My warning carried more spittle than threat.

I went over to him and grabbed his thick forearm to pull him off the chair, but he just grinned and wrenched it away. "Who are you, anyway?" he said.

Lili sat horrified at the unfolding scene.

"I am Lili's betrothed," I said, pointing to my chest for emphasis. Those words shot out of my mouth without counsel. What a clumsy way of proposing!

"I see no ring to signify that," said the burly churl. "Besides, I have known Lili much longer than you." He stood slowly, all six feet of his muscular frame. "Now step back." He pushed against my chest. "She is *my* betrothed."

My anger tumbled out. "How dare you!" I said. "You disappeared for months on end. Never a word about your return!" I was done defending myself to this insensate beast. "Come, Lili." I motioned for her to go inside with me. But the legionnaire blocked her.

He said, "I have been off fighting in Africa."

Lili had mentioned he was in Algeria. I despised the admiration I saw in her eyes when she talked about him. I wanted her to look at me that way.

He crossed his arms. "What have *you* been doing to defend your mother country?" he said.

I had no reply. It hardly seemed a strong argument to say I was a piano tuner, fighting battles with Vidocq and Sand. None of it had to do with colonizing a foreign country.

This man had lied to Lili ever since I had known her. He was drinking and whoring around the world in the name of his homeland. I just *knew* it.

I said, mustering courage, "You shelve her until it is convenient for you to claim your pretty prize."

Lili pushed us apart and stomped her foot. "Stop it! Just stop it! I am not a fatted calf for either of you to cart off to your celebration."

I was relieved she intervened. This Goliath was seconds away from pummeling me into the dirt.

Mme Millefeuille heard the commotion and stepped onto the porch. The situation was manifest: We stood with hands clenched, teeth gritted, each of us marking our marital territory.

Meanwhile, her daughter stood with arms crossed and back turned.

Madame's fury was palpable from her low, measured speech. She spoke, first to him:

"You, Alexandre, have caused my daughter great suffering while you traipse around parts unknown being a soldier. She heard nothing from you—*nothing*—for months on end. You promised her a life together. Yet your long absences have left her sitting alone month after month. You keep delaying the marriage, saying you have to fight the enemy. 'Next year, next year,' you kept saying. She has no desire to be engaged to a vague promise."

Then to me: "Beaulieu, you have not offered Lili a future either. Yes, perhaps some love letters and occasional visits." (The soldier glared at me.) "She needs you to hold her hand and take romantic walks in the park. Promise her children and a happy life together. Where is your offer to provide these things?"

I looked at the ground. I should have proposed sooner and not just blurted it out during a set-to between two suitors on her porch. She deserved better.

Lili's mother went on: "Neither of you has shown how you would take care of her."

I made my bid. "Madame, my financial situation has brightened. I have a profession and will make a wonderful home for your daughter."

She turned to Alexandre for his response.

"Madame Millefeuille," he began, thrusting out his chest, "I have the respect of the French Army and the skills of a warrior."

"But what will you do after you leave the army?" she asked.

He had no good response. He was trained to kill, a talent that did not translate into much else. A farmer, perhaps, where he could slay rodents munching on his lettuce. Or a blacksmith, where he could hammer on hot metal all day with his muscle-bound arms. And if he stayed in the army, that would mean more long absences. She would wilt of loneliness.

Mme Millefeuille landed the defining blow to the discussion. "Lili wants a family. That does not happen when you are off expanding the French empire, now does it, Alexandre?"

This time, brawn lost. Mme Millefeuille saw to that.

I started to take Lili inside, but her mother stopped me, shaking her head. "Return when you have a plan, Beaulieu."

She took Lili inside.

I had assumed Lili was mine for the asking. Now, who was the arrogant one?

I walked slowly back to my mother's house to check on her vacant home and fallow fields. Hard work lay ahead to capture Lili's heart and devise a plan to convince Mme Millefeuille I was good enough for her daughter, a plan that would begin with getting Chopin's ring.

## CHAPTER 22

# George Sand's Diary – Regrets

Dear Diary,

I am still seething at Chopin for his trickery at dinner last night. I let him invite that silly piano tuner, that contemptible red-haired ninny with dirty fingernails and condescending manner that Chopin reveres so much, only because he needed work done on his precious piano. Certainly, he can find a tuner here in the Loire suitable for his summer tunings. Is not one tuner just as good as another? It is a piano, for God's sake, not a human body that requires a trained surgeon. I scream at his solipsism.

I allowed Chopin to invite Delhomme, but I forbade him to join our party. I planned this special gathering weeks ago and did not want some-one with no interest in the arts to spoil our conversation. What would he possibly have to say? Yet there he was holding forth about women's rights and how men would vote our interests. *Merde!* It became such a row be-tween us that I finally gave in so people could properly digest.

What complete madness the night was, as I predicted. Someone asked him what he thought about the political situation, and he had the temerity to defend Chopin's laissez-faire attitude toward the king's autocratic rule. "All artists need to eat," or some such animal dung that he spouted about keeping the status quo to keep money flowing to us artists. Where is your spine, sir? He is just like Chopin—weak and unconcerned about people who are suffering. How ironic that the name Delhomme means 'of the man' but whose meaning has totally escaped him. Perhaps he is taking his name literally since he belittles women's role in society. I hereby change his name to *De-la-femme*!

I can only hope he never returns to spout such trumpery again. I would surely lose control.

C. continues to enervate me with his persistent cough and relentless need for care. It is as if I have a third child in its infancy.

Two days ago, he ignored me, said nothing the entire day, as if that would improve things between us. Our relationship has been seriously damaged by his immature behavior.

And his politics! I abhor C.'s passive acceptance of the status quo. He is no groundbreaker, that one. He talks quite patriotically about Poland and the struggles of his people, and I thought, judging by his extremist friends, that he would have similar inclinations. But France does not engender the same feeling in him. In fact, he fits all too comfortably in the cradle of luxury of the aristocracy. I do sympathize that he would be biting the hand that feeds him if he did advocate for change. Who else has the means to support artists but the well-to-do? But it is a growing rift between us. I, who feel equality in my bones, must work hard to overlook his meek, uncritical acceptance of the state of affairs. It pushes me toward yet more radical views when I hear his shallow and reactionary opinions. His positions seem a bit odd to me since his own father fought in the 1830 Warsaw uprising *and* the one in 1794. At every turn, he becomes stranger and stranger to me. It is as if I am reaching into the mist to find who he really is. There is nothing of permanence to grasp about him except his cough.

I do not understand how he could have such heartache for the people of Poland and yet be so blasé about those of us in France who yearn for the very same freedom. Is he not sentient? How could he not be enraged by a government that kills people who merely want to eat and live without disease and vermin in their apartment? Who want more than just bread and potatoes? This is not a humane reaction to such suffering.

I am nigh on to shoving him out of my bed for harboring such royalist sympathies. It assuages nothing in me that he has given me a ring. I admit my attraction to a man with such an aristocratic bearing, but his backward-looking attitudes to these many social and political ills show he is unsympathetic to my ideas.

Work goes apace to collect my coterie of people interested in protesting against the current government. I do not know where we will go with our anger, but I can at least write about the inequities against the working class and the outrageous liberties that the bourgeoisie take with their money and power. Lamartine is the engine behind all this. I so admire him. We must amass so we can become a large enough political force. But we must do it quietly. The monarchy has big ears.

Soon, though, we will need to bring in people beyond our circle if this is going to work. We must have a blueprint. It does not make any sense simply to revolt.

I dare not have a meeting at Nohant since that would draw attention to all the parties involved. Not even Solange and Maurice know of my activities. It would endanger them to know too much. C. would not approve, so of course he is shut out from my thoughts and plans. It is not as if he notices anyway.

I listened last night with great interest about the troubles of surrounding countries: Poland, of course, Germany, Spain, Italy, even Russia. How fascinating that we feel similarly about being oppressed regardless of country and government. Once again, it proves that those in power will do what they can to subjugate others, regardless of geography. Power corrupts, but I am hardly the first person to make that observation.

My plan is to write even more tracts outlining the complaints we have against the king for ordinary citizens. They will see how their feelings and suffering are being recognized and put into words. Nothing is more stirring than to see someone care about their plight. People are dying in the streets! People have nothing to eat, and their children are covered with scabs and lice. They pay taxes, yet no one cares about them. Could there be any more basic frustration with life in France today?

Women's right to vote will be a centerpiece of my work, too. As I tried to get through the dense skulls of those morons last night, letting women vote will help everyone in society. I had to restrain myself when that dunderhead tuner uttered the view that a woman's job was to cook and have children, so men could do what they want. And Chopin agreed! So, there you are. I am a servant to take care of his needs. My patience is waning. I am not his domestic, nor his mother, nor his do-good slave. The only reason we have lasted this long has to do with his demands on how *I* should behave. If his needs are answered, he does not care what I do. So much the better! I will continue to plot my exit from this relationship and my plans to engineer the next revolution. Life is intolerable under this regime and Chopin's endless list of needs.

Exhausted. Simply spent. Chopin has wrung me dry of sympathy. He is behaving like a squalling infant. I have two children already and no want of a third.

CHAPTER 23

# Concert – Uprising

## Concert

Tonight would be Chopin's last performance in Paris. And what a *tour de force* it promised to be. Where did he find the strength to prepare for such a demanding program? I also wondered how we—Pleyel and I—could have been so ignorant of his situation and weakness. It never occurred to me that Chopin would not regain his health, even though he had been ill the entire time I had known him. It could not be that he would ever die. Some days his coughing almost strangled him. Other days it was the grippe or rheumatism, making it impossible to move his fingers. He smelled homeopathic flasks from time to time. And took opium drops on sugar and gum-water to deaden the pain during lessons and rubbed his forehead with eau de Cologne.

Alas, his adoring public wanted to hear more of this genius, no matter how he felt. So, we two greedy fanatics suggested setting up another concert for him at Salle Pleyel. He raised every conceivable objection. So, we wheedled and pleaded: Yes, we will invite other performers to accompany and spell him; of course, we will sell the tickets; no worries about the pianos, and so forth. "You just need to come to the concert hall and play," said Pleyel, "and I will even send a concert piano to your apartment so you can practice in comfort."

He finally relented. After a brief announcement in the press setting the date on February 16, just two weeks hence, three hundred tickets sold out within two days. Thirty alone had been purchased by the royal family. Six hundred people were willing to pay in advance for a possible second appearance. In retrospect, we were selfish, really, to drag him off his sick bed so we could feast our ears on his music one more time.

Even unburdened by details, he indulged in plenty of *Sturm und Drang* when deciding on attire: which tail coat to don out of the dozen or so he owned, the finely pleated evening shirt or a ruffled one, a white bow-tied neck cloth or cravat, and finally, the more proper white kid gloves or his beloved pink ones?

At precisely eight o'clock on that cold February night, his driver pulled up to the Salle Pleyel, 20, rue Rochechuart. I helped him out of the coach. He said nothing. I knew he was focused on his performance. Once inside the building, I watched as he strode down the flower-bestrewn aisle, carrying himself like the noble prince he was. Aside from his ashen color, no one had an inkling he was ailing. Applause continued for several minutes. He bowed to accept their appreciation. The other performers joined him among the baskets of fresh flowers that M. Pleyel had placed there.

The house grew quiet. He threw his coattails behind him and sat on the bench that I had adjusted to his preferred height. He put his hands on the keyboard and paused. Three hundred pairs of ears were turned toward the master. No one dared breathe.

The first piece was a trio by Mozart for piano, violin and violoncello, and the last three movements of his Sonata for Piano and Cello. He had also chosen the Berceuse, Barcarolle, and the D flat Major Waltz. He played as only he could and as he always had, with restrained emotion. That same idea could be expressed with the paintbrush: One notices primary colors right away, but it was the ethereal tints of the pastels that added depth and luster to the painting. He never dominated the piano but partnered with it, caressing the keys and coaxing out their secrets. He had learned to substitute technique for power, executing crescendos without the muscle.

Nonetheless, he had chosen demanding works: mazurkas, preludes, and other gems he had composed. He listened attentively to the passionate singers who punctuated the program.

He played brilliantly through the first half, but I could see the strain it was taking on him. During intermission backstage, he was close to prostration. After resting, he continued. But our thirst for his virtuosity could not be slaked; the thundering applause beckoned him back to play three encores. The audience roared each time he reappeared. When he did not return for a fourth, I went to the green room to congratulate him. I knocked, then opened the door to find his collapsed body next to the divan.

"Monsieur!" I said. "What happened?" I knelt to assess his condition. His brow was damp, his hands icy cold. He had a weak heartbeat and was barely breathing. My medical training had taught me how to do mouth-to-mouth resuscitation, so I began rhythmically pushing breaths into him. After a few minutes, his eyes opened.

"Where am I?" he asked.

I thought it best he not talk. I covered him with my coat to conserve his energy.

By now, several admirers had collected outside. "Please let us in," someone shouted. "We want to congratulate Monsieur Chopin!"

"He is resting," I answered through the door. After an hour, he was still too weak to walk on his own. I put his arm around my shoulder and helped him to the coach, making certain no spectators saw him in this debilitated state. I had sent a message for his doctor to meet us at his apartment. His head lay in my lap on the way home. He shivered as I carried him up the stairs. The doctor's prescription was the same as always: rest and good food. I helped him into bed and said I would make some tea then return the next day with provisions per doctor's orders.

His condition improved slowly, but he had little stamina. I prepared several meals for him over that next week. He was partial to soups and custard flan. The local baker gave me some baguettes, and even some madeleines for his famous neighbor. Soon he began sitting at his piano scribbling down ideas he had developed as he convalesced. Irrepressible, this man. But he was far from his old self and spent most of the day in bed.

As usual, the reviews were glowing. *Le Ménestrel* called him "the sylph of the piano, the ineffable artist, attached to this mortal world by the merest touch of a finger and nourished by dreams from on high." His playing was compared to the "sighing of a flower, the whisper of clouds, or the murmur of the stars." But no one would ever know what that performance had exacted, nor could they know that he would never grace a Paris stage again.

## February Uprising [1848]

As he was convalescing, I went to his apartment several times, saying I had to work on his piano, but it was really to check on him. He needed food, something he was capable of neither buying nor preparing. For him, just eating it was a feat. Caring for him kept my hands busy while I mulled over what to say to Vidocq about quitting. Would I honor my parents' teachings to be true to myself and honest in all dealings or become mesmerized by the allure of money?

Counting on Chopin's recovery, Camille Pleyel arranged a second concert for March 10. Political fate intervened, however, and quashed those plans. Paris had become a whirlpool of chaos. The unruly rabble forced the government to outlaw the gathering of people in public places. But, Parisians, not being ones to blindly obey anything, skirted those dictates by organizing a campaign of so-called fund-raising banquets. They were lively affairs: Prominent politicians spoke, people exchanged ideas, neighbors visited with one another.

Threatened by the power that could be wielded at these banquets, Louis Philippe banned them, too. At this denial of their rights, agitators spilled onto the rainy streets. One soldier accidentally fired his rifle, igniting the crowd's tinderbox of anger. Pockets of violence erupted. Over fifteen hundred barricades were built from overturned carriages, ironwork, furniture, and trees cut down along streets and parks. They then set them on fire to melt lead for bullets. Lanterns were demolished, streets torn up, stores looted. It was shocking to see such damage to our fair city.

Before long, crowds gathered in front of the Foreign Ministry, heckling the soldiers. Newspapers reported that one young armed guard, apparently shaken by the tumult, accidentally shot his musket into the angry mob. Then the rest of the soldiers joined in. Fifty-two people were killed in just that one incident.

It became known as the February uprising. But poor Chopin, abed with a headache and neuralgia, could do nothing but listen to the fighting and gunplay. He said all he could do was tremble. I watched from my apartment. I did not dare go outside. It seemed the world was ending.

The uprising lasted three gory days. The final day, Louis Philippe, unprepared for such a violent reaction and lingering animus toward him, went to review his troops in the Tuileries but was met with belligerent mobs. He quickly abdicated and fled with his queen through a secret passageway leading out to the Place de La Concorde and absconded, leaving behind a city in turmoil. In short order, the demonstrators invaded the palace in the Tuileries, tore down mirrors, broke statues, fouled his bed, and stole clothes and jewelry. A small contingent went to the wine cellar. After puncturing the casks, they became so drunk they drowned in the several feet of wine that flooded the chamber.

Only a few days after the uprising, Vidocq commanded my presence on the outskirts of Paris. It was impossible to move within the city limits. Streets were torn up. Donkeys trudged through the streets pulling wagonloads of dead bodies plucked from barricades and gutters. So very grim.

He came into the café wearing a beret and a huge gray knitted scarf wrapped around his nose and mouth. I sat on the edge of the chair.

"Coffee?" he asked. "Excellent coffee here."

"Vidocq . . .," I started.

"Shhh." He put his finger up. "No names in such a crowded place. Call me Raoul."

"Let me be direct . . . Raoul," I said. "I want out."

"I told you. There is no out."

"What do you mean?" I said. "The workers have just fought a battle to overcome the monarchy and chased Louis Philippe out of town. The new republic will not need spies. So, I have no intention of doing any more royal prowling." I stood to leave.

"One moment," he said, holding up an index finger. "Louis Philippe may be gone but now we have a provisional government."

"Yes, and soon we will have the Second Republic. You hear that? A *republic!* There is no more reason to spy!"

"You really are a dunce, Delhomme," he said calmly as he pulled the scarf down to take a sip. "The new government will *also* want you to spy on likely enemies. Heads of governments may change, but threats to their power never do."

The truth gripped me hard. "So, you are working for Lamartine now?"

Yes, he replied. Lamartine, the poet-turned-politician, the very name I had seen written in Sand's handwriting! He had been appointed head of the provisional government until a constitution could be finalized. My mind spun: Vidocq himself had used the information I gleaned from Sand's desk for his own purposes, anticipating the ouster of Louis Philippe and wanting to know the next leader so he could ingratiate himself. "Your allegiances are slippery," I said, "to say the least."

"Never you mind about my loyalties. Now, on to your next assignment." He laid a piece of paper and sheaf of francs beside it.

I looked hungrily at the money and had to stop myself from grabbing it. I felt so uncomfortable doing his loathsome bidding. "And if I refuse?"

He peered at me over his scarf, narrowing his beady eyes. "Then we will get your attention."

"Meaning?"

"Want to find out? Because we can make it quite difficult."

"And I am asking you *how* difficult." I wanted to see the trade-off.

He took the saltshaker, sprinkled some salt onto his palm, and licked it off. "We know about Lili, your delicious *amie blonde* in Marainville. We know her address. We know where she works. We know what she means to you."

I shook my finger at him. "She has nothing to do with any of this!"

"If you value her nice round little arse, then you had better take this assignment." He turned the paper toward me and pointed to some dates and times. I heard the words 'club' and 'Auguste Blanqui' but nothing else. My ears were paralyzed. My dear, sweet Lili was caught in this web of intrigue of my own doing. He was asking me to choose between her love and, well, I was not sure what else. I comforted myself by saying that Lili lived too far away. He would never travel to Marainville to bother her.

"You can have your snooping and your disguises. I quit!" I threw the bills at him, grabbed my coat, and slammed the door behind me.

Not twenty-four hours later, I received an urgent message from Lili's mother, saying her daughter was in the hospital and might not survive such a savage attack. "She is asking for you, Beaulieu. Please come."

Damn you, Vidocq! God damn you!

I took the next coach to Marainville and went directly to her house. Her mother answered, sobbing. Her grief made me wonder if Lili had died. She took me by the hand upstairs to her room.

One did not need medical training to see that Lili had been seriously hurt. Her eyes were black and swollen from the beating and her right knee had been mangled with an iron rod. The doctor said she was having trouble breathing, probably from a broken rib. I was sickened by my own part in this.

Hanging between life and death, she barely recognized me.

"Who beat you, my darling?"

She tried to talk but nothing came out. Her mother drew me away, afraid I would only upset her more. We went downstairs to the kitchen. She went through her well-worn habit of making tea, something that could occupy her hands in a sea of helplessness. "Thanks be to God she is still alive," said Mme Millefeuille through hot tears.

She said that a shopkeeper had heard a scream. She said, "He ran to the window. He saw a man push Lili down. Then he whipped her face and legs with a cane." I put my arm around her shoulder. The merchant ran out to stop him, she said, but the man had left. He helped Lili inside and sent for Mme Millefeuille and a doctor.

I asked if the police knew who had done this (as if I had no idea). She said it was a random attack on a pretty girl going home after work. "Probably some angry unemployed factory worker," she surmised.

What about the assailant, I asked. Was he old, young, tall, short?

The witness said he wore a stocking cap over his ears and baggy coat. The attacker had to be a hooligan in Vidocq's employ.

My forehead perspired, stomach churned, legs quaked. I excused myself and went outside to manage my reaction by leaning on a tree to steady myself. How could I right this? *If* Lili survived, she would live a hellish life, crippled and scarred. But if I did not comply with Vidocq's orders, I feared he come after her again. For him, maiming Lili was just his first salvo. This man, devoid of conscience, was as dangerous as an unlit bomb.

## CHAPTER 24

# George Sand's Diary – Shaken

Dear Diary,

I am shaken to the core by the latest event. Paris is enraged over the government's unfair practices towards workers. People are starving, for Heaven's sake. Many live in the streets, begging for food. More than half the residents are out of work. It is time to act. Of course, this has been brewing for many years, but punishing policies brought on these hostilities. I have no sympathy for Louis Phillipe. Even though his father was killed in the Reign of Terror, that gives him no right to treat citizens so viciously.

I heard the unrest quickly became a horrible scene. Mobs crossed the bridge to the Place de la Concorde. They were beaten back, but when they retaliated the next day, barricades were put up all over the city. Hordes stormed the Ministry of Affairs. Imagine! People being shot in the streets of my own beloved Paris! The people threw Louis Philippe's carriage into the Seine. And who would blame those who invaded the palace and carried off his throne to the Place de la Bastille to burn it?

I left Nohant as soon as possible, just a few days after the uprising.

I knew very few details but was devastated when I arrived in Paris. The destruction and anger were still rife among the citizens. Was it safe here? The people are drunk with happiness to have fallen asleep in the mud and awoken in heaven. I have been agitating for this exact thing for years, but I am repulsed by the government's cruelty. I must support my people and usher in a government that addresses inequality. Lamartine will be a good leader.

This is not the end of the unrest; of that, I am certain. I cannot fight with weapons, nor would I, but my pen can be just as deadly. I will write a series of documents that explain to my compatriots what is at stake and how we should fight. The government has become too powerful, too heavy with rulers insensitive to workers' needs. We want to rule ourselves, not have people who wear lavish fur coats and live in gold and marble palaces make decisions about our lives.

Things moved quickly after I arrived from Nohant. A mass funeral was held for those poor souls who had died on the barricades. It was fine, simple, and touching. Four thousand people pressed together from la Madeleine all the way to the Place de la Bastille. I hope the government noticed that there was not a constable to be seen, and yet not a foot was trampled on, nor a top hat dented. It was admirable. I was profoundly moved by the events. I turn to writing in such times. Politics is a man's power game in which we women dare not participate lest we be considered promiscuous. Better to work on our liberation in the home sphere. I will fight to have laws of the household changed so we can more easily attain power over that realm.

Recently I met Alexis de Tocqueville. For such a famous intellect, his eyes were also blinkered to the suffering of the poor. I spelled out the difficulties they were experiencing. He said he understood, but I know that look, when people want you to think they agree when they are only being polite. People of his class are inured to the suffering of the lower classes. I doubt he spoke to even one worker to get a first-hand account. That shows how restricted and protected he is by his social class. He will learn. He will learn. He did correctly assess the situation when he said that the French were sleeping in a volcano and that a storm was on the horizon.

No sooner had I returned from the funeral when I had another upsetting event of a completely different nature. I unexpectedly met Chopin. It had been almost a year since we had seen one another. But the only letter I received during that time chided me for how I had raised my children. How dare he criticize my mothering!

He told me Solange had given birth to my first grandchild, Jeanne-Gabriel. To have him deliver such wonderful news to me, the mother and grandmother of these two people, was embarrassing, humiliating. Of course, I had not seen Solange and Clésinger, that monstrous, avaricious husband of hers, since that horrible row at Nohant last July. He said he expected me to mortgage Nohant to pay for his debts after they married! They also demanded an allowance to cover their lavish lifestyle in Paris with servants, parties, a carriage, and hothouse flowers delivered daily! I suggested they might economize, but he became furious. He had revealed nothing about such debt beforehand. Another albatross.

To make things worse, Clésinger has no work. He had mentioned before the marriage that he had just completed a commissioned work titled *Woman Bitten by a Snake* sculpted out of marble. I saw it just before he delivered it to the patron. Dear God, I had all I could do not to shout my disgust over its licentious theme. The figure is lying on her back with her breasts and pudenda on clear display and a snake whose head directs the viewer's attention to her private parts! One might think she is writhing out of agony, but knowing his lascivious mind, it was more likely to represent an orgasmic pose. I do not shock easily, but this sculpture had gone too far. My eyelids fluttered as if trying to edit out the content of his sculptural pornography.

Obviously, Chopin and Solange have chosen sides against me. Why else would she tell him about this momentous event in her life before me, her own mother? I told him he could return to Nohant but only if he agreed never to see Solange and Clésinger again. Chopin refused, calling me hard-hearted and accusing me of abandoning her on the eve of her womanhood. I am wounded to the quick. I doubt I shall ever recover from this betrayal by both.

When we met that night by his apartment, Chopin seemed in a rush and left rather abruptly. I wanted to ask after his health, so I followed him down the stairs. He said he was well, but after pressing his trembling, cold hand, I knew otherwise.

Chopin is a stupid man. He always shied away from any talk about the revolution and feared violence of any sort, while his own Polish compatriots were struggling to free their people and yet crumbling from the same entrapment. Frankly, I found his views quite backward-looking. I believe he liked the hierarchy in his homeland.

I may be shy to appear in public with my views, but I will shout them at the top of my lungs in print. Chopin never shared my passion for these matters. Indeed, that is, in part, why we separated. Besides, I found him childish and petulant.

In the end, even with C.'s abrupt departure that day by his apartment, I must admit that I have regained my freedom from a man whose narrow and domineering ideas I constantly fought against. I remained chained to him out of pity and fear that he would die of grief. For nine years, while full of life, I tied myself to a cadaver. I admit I have been unfaithful to him. I accept responsibility for those moral failings. But how could anyone deny me my pleasures?

We may have shared an artistic soul at one time and a love for our work. But he never deigned to reach down to the common man to see his struggles. If people criticize my resistance to joining public life in lieu of putting my power behind my writing, then Chopin must also be criticized for remaining behind his keyboard. He composed mazurkas and polonaises as his sole effort to show solidarity toward his people. But at least mine were aimed at improving the lives of people in a very tangible way.

Perhaps his constant battle with his health prevented him from turning outward to see others' problems. However, that does not excuse his behavior toward me. After all I had done for him—taking care of him day and night, answering his every whim and need—he still insisted on communicating with Solange after I expressly forbade it. I never caught them together, but I suspected they were in love. How dare he. This behavior was untenable. She is *my* daughter and responsibility, not his. I reared her and gave her succor and motherly guidance. Her allegiance belongs solely to me.

I cannot abide these critics. Let me alone. Please, just let me be.

## CHAPTER 25

# Entanglement – Club – Galvanized

### Entanglement

The streets were filled with carnival gaiety after the insurgents' victory in the February uprising. So hard-won was the new re-public that people could not believe they were still standing. The king had fled to England along with his high-handed notions of how French workers should be treated. Now, men had the right to vote. Bread would soon appear on every table—or so they thought. Before long, though, the jollity dissolved into uncertainty when they faced the hard part: choosing leaders. What new policies would emerge in the aftermath of the chaos a month ago? What should the new government do or say? What taxes would they implement?

My task was to continue gathering intelligence for Vidocq if I was to keep Lili safe. He had made that clear. His next summons came several weeks after her attack. I was ordered to go to an abandoned sawmill on the outskirts of town.

I pulled up to the dilapidated brick building with missing roof tiles and peeling paint. The main door was open. I stepped carefully around the rodent feces speckling the floor. Little sun shone in through the dust-caked windows.

"Vidocq," I called out several times. Nothing. Then, a tap on my shoulder made me gasp. I quickly turned. As my eyes adjusted to the light, I made out Vidocq, dressed as himself, whatever that meant.

He offered me a seat on a dirty crate, but I declined. He sat and asked me how I had been and what I thought of the uprising, and so forth. He acted as if nothing had happened!

I could not contain my anger. "You went to Marainville and assaulted my sweetheart!" I stood over him, but he sat, unperturbed, cleaning his fingernails with a sharpened stick. He never apologized. Thugs never did.

He looked at me with those beady eyes. "Monsieur Delhomme, you have no idea who I am, do you?" He pointed to the crate with his stick. "Sit."

He recounted tales of when he had been a ruffian and was locked up with criminals. He said he escaped after many attempts and hid out in a small French village where a band of thieves threatened to blackmail him. He escaped their grasp and managed to stay hidden in another town for many years until he presented a clever plan to the police there to become the head of detectives. If they agreed, he said he would hire those same blackmailing crooks as snitches to ferret out yet more crooks, but only if they did not punish him for escaping jail. Thus was born the world's first detective agency. He bragged he had rid Paris and other cities of swindlers, murderers, and robbers.

"I am rich, I am fearless, and I am loyal to no one except the man who pays me," he said. "And now that we have ousted Louis Philippe, that person is Alphonse de Lamartine. You deny his wishes, you suffer at my hand."

Vidocq followed the scent of power as eagerly as a dog tracks the spoor of a chicken. His allegiances were malleable, his morals for sale. "I see you have deftly ridden the political winds. Quite an opportunist, you are."

He smiled at that the perceived compliment. "You have gotten your money, he said, darkly, "now you *will* do as I say."

I bristled at his haughty tone. I could see that threats to quit were futile. I put my mind to finding another way out of this quagmire. As long as Lili was safe and the money still flowing, I had time. Bucking Vidocq would, no doubt, carry grave risk for Lili and who knows who else, but it was a risk I needed to consider.

The assignment was to visit a club meeting. Clubs let people hear speakers and voice their own opinions on political events. They had mushroomed just since the uprising. After only three weeks, almost sixty clubs had sprung up. That number tripled by mid-April. A mass movement had taken root. I had heard that there were almost one hundred thousand members spread amid the eighteen most popular clubs. Many met three times a week or more. I heard that George Sand had come back to her Paris apartment and found herself locked out. Not one of the three locksmiths she tried to summon could be reached because all were attending a club!

All this flurry of excitement was to elect the provisional government, which would write the new constitution. Lamartine led the way, but he was turning into a tyrant. Sand was highly sought after for a position in that government, but she refused. Strange woman: She was so active in inciting discontent around the city, then demurred when asked to follow up with governing in its aftermath.

"I know of many clubs. Which one should I attend?" I asked Vidocq.

"Auguste Blanqui," he said. "Sources say he is preparing a strike force. Very dangerous man, this Blanqui. He thinks change in government can never be done peacefully. We want to infiltrate this club. And that means you, my friend." He poked me in the chest with his stick. "Visit his club. Listen to his talk. We want to know what people think. And for God's sake, find out what is he planning. You know, detective work."

No stranger to a jail cell, Blanqui had repeatedly been locked up by Louis Philippe for espousing the dangerous, anti-monarchical idea that the people should rule. A strident, left-wing socialist, he had been released after the February uprising, then promptly founded the Central Republican Society, one of the first and most radical clubs to assemble after the February uprising.

"Will I be the only spy there?"

"Spy . . . stop using such a pejorative term, Delhomme. The answer is no. But, just between us, he is unreliable and morally suspect. You . . . *you* are reliable. Because I know of your love for Lili." He smirked at his clever plan to ensnare me further into his plot. "You would not dare mislead me."

The intimation was clear: Comply or regret the consequences. I already knew what he was capable of. What a disgusting, vile man.

My job—my *life*—would be imperiled if any attendee, especially at that club, found out I was a spy, so rabidly anti-monarch were they.

## Club

The following evening, I disguised myself à la Vidocq in a large-brimmed hat, ill-fitting wool coat, and knit scarf to cover my mouth but skipped the wig and makeup, as I feared it would draw attention to my injudicious use of either. It was early April, so this kind of roomy garment would go unnoticed in the cold and rain. I had to assume there were others spying on me. That was the Vidocq way. When one became a spy, *no one* could ever be trusted. I, like Vidocq, needed to protect my identity because I did not want anyone to associate me with this radical group headed by Auguste Blanqui. I could not be too careful.

The legacy of the February riots left Paris half denuded of her lush, tree-lined streets in the service of the barriers, many of which had still not been dismantled. Where were the work crews to tear them down? Who would plant more trees to restore the cool shade and sumptuous silhouettes of our boulevards and byways?

Women begged with children hiding behind their skirts. Men sat idly on park benches. Others were rushing to club meetings to pass the time. They were free, after all, and who knows what ideas for finding work they would glean there?

I arrived at the large auditorium early to secure a seat in the top row to increase the chance of my anonymity. Candles lit the stage, but the steps to the upper rows were barely visible. A crowd of four thousand or more buzzed. People milled and greeted friends while others carried on fiery arguments even before the speeches began. The hard-of-hearing jockeyed for seats near the front.

I had not been there long when none other than Chopin's protégé and favorite student, Adolf Gutmann, sat beside me. He recognized me even with my disguise.

"Delhomme! I have not seen you in ages," the young German said.

We had met from time to time in Chopin's apartment. He reached out to shake my hand. "A Blanquist, eh? So very radical of you!"

This was not a good situation. I had now been loudly identified, in front of many attendees and branded as a Blanquist. Even though Blanqui's ardent followers were fine amid like-minded clubbists, they were often subject to ridicule when surrounded by those from more moderate groups. I decided to act normal, even though my stomach turned.

"I had heard so much about these clubs, I thought I would attend one," I said striking a light tone with Gutmann. "He is the leader of the opposition to the government, right?"

I knew about Blanqui from the newspapers. He had indeed opposed the monarchy and was captured and imprisoned for leading five hundred armed revolutionaries in a surprise attack on the l'Hôtel de Ville in 1839. He had been condemned to death, but the sentence was commuted to life imprisonment. He had only recently been released from prison—four years of which were served in solitary confinement. Prison conditions had been harsh, with no possibility to find a comfortable sitting or standing position. He left jail only two months ago, gaunt but unrepentant.

"Yes. Yes. He is very dynamic. Very compelling," said Gutmann.

"I warn you, I resist indoctrination of any kind," I said, laughing, but I added that I would leave if the people started shouting and orating.

"There is the occasional fight, I will give you that," said Gutmann. "But nobody cares if you leave."

"What do they fight about?"

"Everything!" he said.

"How do I know that spies will not take my name and note my face to report my being here?" I asked. I had no idea whether Vidocq would back me up as one of his "employees" or just let me twist in the wind with the authorities thinking I was a Blanquist.

"There are no spies!" Gutmann said, smiling. "So what if there are? Do you think you will be arrested?"

The large auditorium warmed quickly with the throngs of men young and old, some foreign born but mostly French.

"Blanqui will be very inspiring, I assure you," said Adolf. But by eight o'clock, with Blanqui nowhere to be seen, the crowd began shouting, whistling, and stomping. "*Où est Blanqui?! Où est Blanqui?!*"

I feared his ill health would prevent an appearance. But when the bearded revolutionary, shirtless under a filthy black topcoat, finally emerged, people applauded and roared encouraging words about their fight against the government. The crowd hushed as he rose to speak.

He leaned into the podium and silently scanned the audience before beginning.

"The Republic means the emancipation of workers; it's the end of the reign of exploitation," he said, raising his arms, "it's the coming of a new order that will free labor from the tyranny of capital." Some began clapping, but others stilled them for fear of missing his words.

Powerful leaders were always charismatic, and Blanqui was no exception. His dark eyes commanded everyone's attention, even the ones seated far from the podium. His passion for equality and worker's rights matched that of George Sand.

His views were quite radical, almost frightening in their demands. He repeated the statistic that over seven hundred thousand people had lost their jobs in 1847, thanks to some bad economic policies. There was a clear division among the attendees: The radicals shouted and whistled and clapped. The quieter conservatives just wanted work.

Blanqui was interrupted several times by moderates and revolutionaries, bourgeois and proletariat sparring with each other over his ideas, even coming to fisticuffs at times. I soon saw that these clubs, or this one anyway, were not a place for reaching consensus but to air grievances and frustrations.

The speaker came from behind the podium to the edge of the stage. "It is the end of the reign of exploitation, the coming of a new order that will free labor," he said with the passion of a preacher. "We are France's workers, and we are united!"

The room thundered with applause and chants of "Work and bread! Work and bread!"

The pain in the clubbists' voices rang through my head. After all, almost fifty percent of Parisian workers were jobless. I comforted myself with the thought that none of those worries touched my life. I had a job, and my client list was growing. But their suffering was on clear display tonight.

The meeting continued for two hours. When the clock struck ten, I asked Gutmann, "How long do these meetings last?"

"Maybe 'til midnight," he said.

Just then, I saw a company of the Mobile Guard enter through the side door. That was the newly created professionalized militia of men under thirty years old established to maintain order. They visited the clubs known for excessive rowdiness and extreme views of its speakers. Vidocq had put me in an untenable situation: If a clubbist found out I was a spy, I would surely get socked in the mouth; but if I was identified as one of the attendees, I could face trouble of another sort. One guardsman began climbing the steps to our row carrying a musket and wearing a cartridge-belt wrapped around his red tunic and a kerchief around his forehead. I pulled my scarf up to my eyes and looked straight ahead. This cadre had surely been sent by the government. Whose side did they think I was on? Even more important, whose side *was* I on? I had professed a liking for the status quo—for the government to maintain a safety net for the rich, but Blanqui's ideas were making a lot of sense. Was Sand right after all?

"Stay calm, Delhomme," said Adolf, seeing my reaction. "*There are no spies!*" he reassured me, laughing at my absurd fears. "The club movement has been sanctioned by the government. They even set up places for meetings, including this one. Why would they do that if they felt threatened by them?" He spoke with such certainty. But I knew otherwise.

The wiry Blanqui paused before ending his talk. Not one sound was heard in the auditorium. He spoke slowly but powerfully:

"There is no brotherhood when the worker drags himself to the door of palaces with his starving children. It is not enough to change words: Things must be changed!" he said, "Or else! There is no freedom where there is no bread. Work and bread! Work and bread!"

The room erupted in chants as I got up to leave.

I worked my way along with the thick crowd to the exit. Guardsmen were stationed by the door looking at people. One young man studied me intently, as if to memorize my face. I pulled up my scarf as my pulse and pace quickened. Others hunched into their ragged coats against the night chill and tucked gloveless hands under their armpits.

Gutmann caught up to me. "Delhomme, what did you think of Blanqui?"

"I was surprised by so many angry men," I said.

"Why surprised?" he said.

"I used to be a monarchist," I admitted, now out of earshot of any guards or clubbists. My thoughts cast back to Nohant when I had spouted pro-royalist beliefs to Sand's dismay. But at the club tonight, I saw the results of those policies furrowed into countless weathered faces. "These men are suffering under the boot of royal policies. I saw Blanqui's words give them hope they can recover."

Gutmann clapped me on the shoulder. "Welcome to our side!"

There. I had said out loud what I had been thinking all during the meeting: The bargain I had made to exchange money for espionage was intolerable now. My conscience burned. No more lying, no more spying. I would find a way out. But first, I had to make things right with a very special person.

## Galvanized

Before dawn the next day, I gathered my suit, packed a lunch, and put something very special in my pocket. The coach to Marainville reached Lili's house by dinnertime. "*Bon soir*, Madame Millefeuille," I said. Surprised, she held the door open as I stepped in. "May I see Lili?"

It had been two weeks since her attack. From her letter (her mother had taken dictation), she tried to sound positive, but I knew she was suffering.

Madame shook her head when I asked to see her. "She is asleep, Beaulieu." Besides, an unmarried woman did not entertain men in her bedroom.

I stood awkwardly holding my hat and looking deeply into her eyes. "Just this once," I said. "I think you know what I want to ask her. I will tell you about my plan later."

She must have felt my urgency and moved aside. "The last door on the right. Only a few minutes, Beaulieu. You can stay tonight in the room across the hall," she said.

I climbed the narrow, creaky staircase and tapped on her door. "Lili," I said softly as I cracked it open. She lay in bed covered with a red and blue quilt her mother had made. She opened her eyes and smiled. I fixed a pillow under her shoulders so she could sit up. She held the blanket modestly under her chin. I brushed back some strands of hair off her face. The swelling had gone down, and her smile was almost the same. She was still unable to speak clearly.

My heart seemed untethered. I knelt by her bed, took her small hand in mine, and asked her to marry me. "Tomorrow," I said. "Tomorrow I want you to become my wife." I touched her belly. "I want lots of babies, too—sons, daughters, I have no preference." I saw only beauty through her scarred face. "Do you also want that? Will you have me?"

She nodded and whispered something I could not make out. I leaned closer. "What is your plan?" she said, smiling with her crooked lips. If she felt good enough to poke fun at her mother's comment on the porch that day, then I knew things would work out. "I love you, Beaulieu."

Tears welled in both of us. "Then tomorrow we will start our new life together." I lay next to her and stroked her hair until she fell asleep.

I lay awake all night to savor my new resolve to live an impeccable life, although that goal would take some time and finesse in dealing with Vidocq.

When morning dawned, I sent a message to fetch the priest while her mother helped Lili into her church-best pink cotton dress with a white lace collar. Meanwhile, I went to the woods to gather blue forget-me-nots, a red wild rose, and her namesake flower, lily of the valley—colors of the French flag. I knew she would like that.

Our pastor was more than happy to marry his parishioners on short notice. He stood by the old chestnut tree holding a Bible open to I Corinthians. Lili's mother supported her as she hobbled toward us, clasping her bouquet. I held her fast as we two faced the priest, just as we would face life's trials.

The priest read:

*"Love is patient; love is kind.*
*Love is not envious or boastful or arrogant or rude.*

*It does not insist on its own way: it is not irritable or resentful;*
*It does not rejoice in wrong doing, but rejoices in truth.*
*Love bears all things, believes all things, hopes all things, endures all things.*
*And now faith, hope, and love abide,*
*and the greatest of these is love."*

At his prompting, I took her hand and slipped my mother's silver wedding ring onto her finger. I kissed my beautiful wife. I swept her up and carried her slowly back to the house. A skylark sang. The sun peeped over the trees. The grass twinkled with dew.

A small but persistent voice kept asking if I had felt obliged to marry her. After all, Lili would never have been hurt had it not been for me. I did love her and had thought about marrying for many months. But now that she was scarred and lame, who else would take her? Certainly not that haughty legionnaire. But her pure heart had not been defiled. I will cling to her goodness to counteract the baleful influences of Vidocq.

## CHAPTER 26

# Resistance – Tea – Regaled

## Resistance

*I* had to return to Paris without Lili, difficult though that was. Her mother could care for her until she had become stronger, which the doctor assured me she would. Otherwise, I never would have left her side. I wrote her faithfully; she replied in her cheery way.

> *Mon Cher Beaulieu,*
>
> *We have such beautiful weather in Marainville. It makes me think of our wedding day just two weeks ago. I am so eager to move to Paris, to start our life together. Do you know how much longer it will be? I dream of walking my babies in the Tuileries. I long to cook your favorite meals.*
>
> *Please let us set a date. Please, my darling.*
>
> *Beaucoup de baisers,*
> *Lili*

Giles Truel had long since retired after receiving the balance of the money I owed for his tuning business. I had repaired and returned all the pianos in his shop to their owners, hoping to move nothing but tools and supplies to my new place.

I wrote that I had found a new apartment with an attached shop in the fourteenth arrondissement, south of the city. Modest but practical, the apartment had a narrow kitchen on the first floor with a nook for a small table for meals, a small bedroom upstairs, and an adjacent shop that could accommodate two grands or three uprights. I was not certain how easily Lili would climb the stairs, but I could not afford anything else that was this convenient.

One evening after I had moved in, someone came to the door. I peered out through my kitchen window and saw Vidocq on my doorstep yet again. *Go away!*

I blew out my two candles and crept up the stairs. He knocked again. "Delhomme, I know you are in there!" he shouted. A consummate thief, he picked the lock and let himself in. He correctly surmised I was hiding upstairs. He tromped up the narrow steps. I cowered in the corner of my bedroom.

"England," he said, after he hauled me downstairs by my collar and threw me into a chair in the kitchen. "Pack your bags. You leave next week."

"My English is very bad, Monsieur Vidocq. What could I possibly accomplish there?"

He explained that Napoléon Bonaparte's nephew, Louis Napoléon, was a rising power. "This is urgent. No shilly-shallying! Lamartine wants to know what his plans are."

"Plans for what? Dinner?" I asked, trying to rile him. It worked.

Vidocq pressed his lips together and frowned. "Plans to wage a civil war, you lunkhead, to assert his right to the throne."

I squirmed. "How do I do that?" I asked. "Should I burst into his office and ask if he has any plans to overthrow the French government?"

If Vidocq heard my derisive tone, he ignored it. "Praise him. Tell him France needs him to carry on the Bonaparte dynasty. Incidentally, he has a German accent because he lived in Switzerland. But make no mistake: He is French down to his little toe."

I started to get up, but he had more instructions.

"Tell him his compatriots long for the return of the imperial age." He impersonated a king, waving a handkerchief and twirling around on his toes greeting his minions. "Flattery," he said after his theatrical display, "works on everyone."

He picked up his hat. "You will need an excuse to tell your clients. That is why you need to convince Chopin to go with you."

As usual, Vidocq stressed the non-negotiability of these requests. "You *will* do this, Delhomme! We are counting on you."

"But Monsieur Vidocq . . .," I said in protest. "How can I convince Chopin to return to England? His sickly lungs will be marinating in coal dust." It made no sense to propose an idea that would injure the very man who could link me to Sand.

"Quit manufacturing excuses and get on with it."

I prepared a three-pronged argument to present to Chopin. First, the trip would help him re-enter bachelorhood since he was no longer with Mme Sand. He had seemed quite sad: His playing lacked the usual brio, and he only tinkered with his manuscripts. Nine years was a long-time to have the attention of a woman who had unceremoniously cast him out like a rotten banana peel. Distraction always worked well in these circumstances.

Second, I would suggest that the British piano factory owner set up some concerts. Londoners adored his music, and his appearance would surely fetch a tidy sum. Frankly, I had no idea why concerts in London would be any less arduous than Paris, but I would suggest it anyway.

I would save the strongest reason for last: escape an uneasy Paris, with its constant churn of political events and unrest. Leaders were tense about the upcoming election of the Constituent Assembly. Club meetings were rallying more and more workers. Blanqui, especially, kept attacking institutions and whipping up sentiments about equality and suffrage. Citizens were growing impatient at the discord.

I mentioned each reason when we met. After presenting the final one, I added, "Your affluent students are fleeing the turbulence, and my customers are doing the same. It all smells of war, Monsieur."

He coughed a few times, then nodded his assent.

I had no intention of visiting Louis Napoléon. I had promised myself to lead a life free from lying and spying for the king from now on. Vidocq's arms may have been long, but they could not reach across the English Channel. I could just say the prince was not in town and be on my merry way. He would never know the difference. I was so stirred by Blanqui's speech that I wanted to put up resistance to Vidocq and his merry band of snoops. Count me out!

I intended instead to visit my nephew, Marc. He had been living in the Gentle Lamb orphanage for three years. Giles knew M. Broadwood through his work.

"Would you please ask Monsieur Broadwood to take on Marc as an apprentice?" I said. "That way he can learn a trade and have ready employment when he leaves the orphanage."

Marc had written only one letter since moving to the Gentle Lamb. It was filled with forced cheer about his warm surroundings.

"I have a wonderful time playing with all the other children," he wrote. His mother had taught him to be hopeful and positive. But no one ever equated orphanages with sunny days and nourishing food. When I told Marc about my upcoming visit in April, his quick reply expressed great anticipation. "I can take you on a tour of the factory, Uncle!"

Although Chopin never spoke of intimate things, sources told me that his breakup with Sand after their almost decadelong affair had devastated him. The effect on his health, even after a few months, was manifest. He neglected his diet and renewed a heavy schedule of evening soirées. His cheeks were sunken and sallow. The chills and cough continued. He looked thinner, haunted. I hoped this trip would cauterize his emotional wounds and set him on a path to better health.

We could have made the trip to London in one day, but I doubted Chopin had the stamina. First, we took the new train to Boulogne, then another hour or so by carriage to Calais. We then boarded a vessel that set sail across the channel. Gales and swells buffeted our ship the entire trip to Folkstone, giving Chopin a touch of seasickness.

After the crossing, he wanted to rest in Folkstone and continue to London by train the next day. I was happy to oblige. The next morning, we ordered an "English breakfast" not knowing that it comprised enough food for four Frenchman: eggs, beans, toast, sausage, some tomatoes and mushrooms. Chopin turned green at the sight of such rustic fare on his queasy stomach. He left to wait at the train station behind the hotel. I finished but a quarter of my meal, paid, and joined him there. The train to London pulled in at precisely ten a.m. The engine belched steam as riders poured onto the platform, juggling baggage and babies.

Once in London, Mlle Jane Stirling met us on the platform. She looked elegant in her light-blue wool coat with an ermine muff, a boon in London's chilly weather. "Monsieur Chopin, how wonderful to see you," she said, with a look in her eye that said more than just hello. Chopin kissed her gloved hand and introduced me.

"How have we missed meeting in Paris, Monsieur Delhomme?" she said. "And here I have been a student of this brilliant musician for so many years."

"I am the poorer for it, Mademoiselle," I said, bowing.

Chopin told me that he had begun tutoring Mlle Stirling shortly after he arrived in Paris, adding that she was "charming but talentless." I am not certain how much romance played a role in their relationship, but it was not for lack of trying on her part to kindle any. He dedicated his Nocturne No. 9 to her three years ago. But I also knew that dedications were a common way to repay generous benefactors. So, one should not conclude much beyond that. When rumors spread about their imminent wedding, he told me, "I am nearer a coffin than a nuptial bed." An unsettling comment, to be sure.

Truth to tell, many women had swooned over Monsieur and fancied more from him than was possible—possible in the sense that he lacked time and endurance to spark another relationship.

Mlle Stirling led us out of the station to her coach. Lining the path were vendors hawking wares, such as warm chestnuts, mince pies, boiled eel. I watched as customers hurried to eat the fish so the merchant could rinse out the cup for the next hungry patron. That water looked none too clean, and I certainly had no penchant for eel, boiled or otherwise. At the end of the path, I spied a cart with a delicious-looking drink.

"Is that tea?"

"It's called saloop," said Mlle Stirling. "Would you like to try it?"

Thirst and curiosity made me say yes. She paid the man and handed me the cup. I swirled it. It looked thicker than tea. "Odd consistency," I said. I took a sip and spat it out in a most indecorous fashion. "What is it made of?"

Mlle Sterling laughed. "Ground orchid root."

I put down the remainder of the sludgy drink. We French did not drink beverages made from orchid root.

Her carriage driver pulled up. I picked up my bag to place it inside when the driver wrested it from me. "Oh, pay him no mind, Monsieur Delhomme," Mlle Stirling said. "I told him to make you feel at home." My notion of making someone feel welcome did not include prying a suitcase from one's hands. But I gave over. Imagine my delight when he grunted as he lifted my hefty tool satchel.

Within only days, Mlle Stirling had settled Monsieur into a lavishly furnished suite of rooms at 48 Dover Street, near Piccadilly. His drawing room was large enough for the three grand pianos provided by Pleyel, Broadwood, and Érard, manufacturers vying for his imprimatur.

"How do you choose which one to play?" I asked, after we had been there a while.

"When I am indisposed, I play on one of Érard's pianos and there I easily find a ready-made tone. But when I feel in the right mood and strong enough to find my own tone for myself, I must have one of Pleyel's pianos. I love its silvery tone and slightly veiled sonority." As for the Broadwood, he seemed unsure, or perhaps diplomatic. "I need more time to become acquainted."

Chopin had not yet set his schedule, so I had a free morning to tour the city. So, the next morning, I planned to visit the British Museum. I ordered tea in a friendly café and a lardy cake, which turned out to be a small, hard, tasteless piece of bread. I dunked it in my oolong to avoid cracking a tooth. My mother would have been appalled. I left the café and set out on my route. I rounded a corner when someone snatched me by my collar and dragged me into a doorway.

"On your way to visit Louis Napoléon this morning?" It was Vidocq, sans disguise. (No one knew him in England.)

"I . . . I planned to call on the prince, er, tomorrow."

"Please, Monsieur Delhomme, your lie is too brazen. I made an appointment for us. Today. Right now."

"Why not go yourself?" I said, pulling my arm from his grip. "You can get the information directly from him. Am I not superfluous?"

"Part of this assignment was to see if you *would* do what I asked. A spymaster cannot always count on his men to do their duty. Now are you coming with me, or must I visit your nephew at the orphanage?"

His threats tormented me. He had already mangled Lili, and now he had Marc in his thuggish sights. Why did I keep underestimating this man who had a violent history and the full power of the government behind him?

"Come," he said. "We will meet the prince together." He explained that Lamartine had told Louis Napoléon politely but firmly to stay in London until Paris calmed down. He did not want him to return before the elections for the National Assembly. His bloodline accorded him great popularity and power, even without holding an office. "We need to know his intentions. You conduct the meeting. He knows me, and that would color his answers," he said.

He hired a hackney to take us to the modest accommodations that Louis Napoléon shared with his mistress. Tea was served. He was a man of regal bearing, medium build, about forty, with brown hair and beard, and blond moustache. His head seemed sunken into his large shoulders. Over the decades, King Louis Philippe, afraid of this man's power and notoriety, had kept him at bay in prison in the north of France. One day, he disguised himself as a laborer carrying a load of lumber and walked out of jail to freedom. A carriage took him to a boat and off he fled to England. No wonder Lamartine wanted to monitor his activities.

His office was rather small but elegantly furnished with leather captain's chairs, linen wallpaper, and glass bookcases. A small fireplace was to his right. His black-lacquered desk sat directly across from the door so he could see who came in, I assumed. One window to the left of the desk looked out onto a park with well-manicured shrubs and trees.

I had hoped Vidocq would start the discussion. But he elbowed me to begin. "Sir," I began, "thank you for seeing us today. We have come on behalf of Alphonse de Lamartine."

He laughed. "Let me guess. Lamartine wants to know if I will try to usurp the throne if I return to France."

"Why, yes, Monsieur." I was talking about things I knew little about. But with Vidocq sitting next to me, I had no choice but to ask verbatim what he said. "He also wants to know if you will start a civil war."

At this, the prince laughed so hard he cried. "A civil war? Why would I do that? Louis Philippe has been sent packing, and the people want a republic so they can speak for themselves." He stood and leaned his arm on the fireplace mantel. "I find it ridiculous that Lamartine sent both of you across the English Channel to ask me these questions that are not even relevant. No, I will not try to usurp the throne, and no, I will not cause a civil war." He seemed perturbed.

These were not frivolous questions. He had planned a coup against Louis Philippe eight years before but failed. Current leaders were justified in their wariness.

"What are your intentions, then? Do you plan to return to France and participate in the new government?" I asked. By now I was curious how a man of Bonaparte lineage would see his role in his native country.

"That I might do. But I can swear to you I have no plans for a military coup." He seemed genuine in his words.

Later, after we had walked several blocks out of earshot, Vidocq said he thought otherwise. "I can only report to Lamartine what I heard," he said. "But the Bonapartes are crafty rulers. It is hard to believe they would sink back into history and let others reign."

We rounded a corner to an empty street. Vidocq pulled me up sharply and dug his fingernails into my hand. "Are you defecting from my service? Tell me the truth!"

I pulled away from his grip, but he had drawn blood. "No, I am *not* defecting." That, of course, was a lie. Tracking me down in England—and all the other times he knew of my whereabouts—was to assure me he was watching. Very, very closely.

"When I tell you to carry out an assignment, you *do* that assignment right away. You will not shirk your responsibility again or you will be sorry. Do you hear me?"

"What could be worse than battering Lili?" I shouted. "I am not afraid of you, Vidocq!" Not true. I was very afraid. Vidocq sneered and walked off.

It was too late to visit the museum since I had an appointment with

Chopin at the Violet Tea Room in midafternoon. Already three, I checked a map and hurried off in that direction.

## Tea

I walked quickly to the tearoom. Chopin and I were to plan the weeks ahead. The owner directed me outside to an area surrounded by a well-tended garden. A handful of small tables was placed on the gravelly ground. I was surprised to see Berlioz sitting across from Chopin, who had told me about their falling out some years ago. I approached them, but they were so deep in discussion that I stood for a minute before either acknowledged my presence.

"Delhomme," Hector said. He got up and put his hand on my shoulder. "*Mon ami*, it has been too long."

We bathed in the London sun, which had broken through a blanket of clouds to pay a rare late-April visit. On the table was an eye-catching bouquet of lavender and baby's breath set off by a white linen tablecloth and napkins. The owner graciously brought us a plate of small sandwiches, chocolate eclairs, scones, and, thank heavens! no lardy cakes. "On the house for you fine gentlemen."

His vanity never on holiday, Chopin was dressed in a starched white shirt, dark blue cutaway, and boots. His hair had been curled, probably by his servant. Berlioz, whom I remembered as an upbeat, energetic fellow, seemed panicked and sad at the same time. I had noticed over the years that he often swung from frightening intensity to a state of joylessness. I had come in the middle of his explanation of his current plight:

"Only the choristers, the orchestra, and the workmen are paid on a weekly basis," Berlioz explained, "so that the theatre can continue to function. Yet Jullien sold his music shop in Regent's Street only two weeks ago for nearly two hundred thousand francs, and I have yet to be paid! Everybody—principal actors, the set designer, the coaches of the singers and the dancers, the stage manager. A fine kettle of fish. Can you imagine?"

His position as the opera conductor at the Drury Lane Theatre had been terminated, all due to this Jullien person's mismanagement. But, with no job in London and his French sinecure funding evaporating due to the unrest there—the very outcome that Chopin and I had warned about at

Nohant—Berlioz was nigh on to destitution. His sadness was underscored by sunken lips due to many missing teeth and a chesty voice from persistent bronchial ailments. His hair had turned dark russet with age. Here I sat with these two great composers, ailing and scrabbling for money.

They soon got on to the subject of critics, which always raised hackles. Chopin had been savaged by one, who had called him "a morbidly sensitive flea." He rolled his eyes. "Another said my playing had 'too much refinement, which sometimes made his playing a little mannered.'" He drew his finger across his throat to signal that critics should all be done in.

Berlioz, known as an innovator among French composers, had caught the wrath of others who mercilessly and caustically attacked him. "One time," he began, "I fooled them all by publishing something under a pseudonym, and they loved it!" He laughed and wiped his hands together as if rubbing off dirt to signal his triumph.

Chopin poured us tea and spooned some sugar into his own. As he stirred, he casually announced that he had been asked to play with the London Philharmonic Society. "One of my concertos," he said. He sat, legs crossed, staring into the swirling beverage, looking disengaged from the world.

Berlioz, who had not been extended a similar invitation, looked envious at this news and offered his own explanation for that. "I think the principal conductor of the Philharmonic saw me as competition," said Hector. "But, you, Chopin, are a pianist. So much the better."

Chopin's fame in Paris and throughout continental Europe was indubitable, but to hear of this great honor bestowed on him in England was wonderful news. "Now you are the toast of London too!" I raised my cup of Earl Gray.

"Thank you, Delhomme, but I have declined."

I put down my tea. "But, Monsieur," I protested, "the Society has denied such an honor to no less than Kalkbrenner and Hallé."

"I understand that, but their orchestra is like their roast beef or their turtle soup—strong, pungent and nothing more," he said.

Chopin's arrogance irritated me at times. How could anyone be so off handed about performing with London's premier orchestra? Was he too jaded after playing for Tsar Alexander and Louis Philippe? And to do so in front of the now-unemployed Berlioz, who probably hungered for such an opportunity. Sometimes, I could not fathom this man. But I reminded myself yet again: I was no Chopin.

"I will have no chance to rehearse with the group before the performance," he added.

Ah, *now* I understood why he declined the invitation. I noticed his increasing need, of late, to control things. His comment about the overpowering orchestra may have spoken more to the energy needed to avoid being drowned out. It was too daunting. The last time I heard him play one of his concertos with an orchestra was just after we had met. Now, he could not even manage a flight of stairs on his own.

In the end, I decided it was his fatigue speaking. He did perk up after some refreshments. "I tell you, Delhomme, my days flash past like lightning. I have so little time to play that I worry I will lose my edge."

No sooner had he complained about all this when, in the same breath, he reported he had been invited to play for Queen Victoria. So dispassionate was he about the news that it might as well have been an invitation for tea and crumpets with his landlady. This news set me wondering about preparations. "When will you perform? How many people will be there? What piano will you play?"

"Not to worry, Delhomme. All is in order. It will be a matinée in a private home in front of a much smaller audience. Maybe eighty people."

Berlioz perked up. "May I come?"

Chopin had no love for Berlioz's music. One time he took his pen, bent back the point, and then let it rebound. He said, "This is the way Berlioz composes—he sputters the ink over the pages of ruled paper, and the result is as chance wills it." He often leveled criticism at other contemporaries. For instance, he scorned Wojciech Sowinski once as "the height of artistic chicanery and stupidity and short of brains." He described him as someone who "bangs the piano, leaps all over the place, crosses his hands, and hammers away at the same note for five whole minutes with a clumsy finger that looks like it should be wielding the whip and reins for some farmer out of the Ukraine." Such was the rivalry among composers.

I pressed the matter of his choice of piano: "Of course, it would be an insult to play on anything but a Broadwood before Her Majesty."

"But the Broadwood . . .," he started to say, but I interrupted.

"I know, I know—you will have to turn into a banger like Liszt," I said. Berlioz laughed at that characterization of his Hungarian friend. Chopin abhorred such crude tactics. His exquisite *pianos* and *pianissimos* were relative to his *forte*, which was not loud to begin with.

"To play with great strength is German," he told a Parisian woman who sent her eight-year-old to him for lessons once. "Never let the child play loud," was his advice.

Chopin chimed in. "One critic said Liszt leaves a slaughtered piano behind at every concert," he said, smiling.

"But," I said, returning to the matter at hand, "you *do* want to please the queen. So, the Broadwood it is. I will make the necessary adjustments." He looked delighted that I could read his thoughts. It was one of the great joys of our relationship, of my life, really. With both men feeling better and the sun once again taking refuge behind the clouds, we left the tea garden and went on to our evening's activities.

I settled into my workspace that M. Pleyel had arranged for me and commenced conditioning the Broadwood to Chopin's taste. I put the action on the workbench and began quickening the touch by tightening the springs in the repetition levers. Older pianos did not have this feature, and its invention in 1821 by Sébastien Érard changed piano playing forever because it allowed a pianist to perform rapid trills, as Chopin's music required.

Regulating dampers also affected the touch. If a damper lifted too early in the keystroke off the string, it would add weight to the touch. That was easy enough to fix. I softened hammers, so the sound would not stab the eardrums, especially in the treble section. Such a boisterous sound would have suited Beethoven with his Germanic sensibilities. But he was going deaf, so the barky tone suited him.

## Regaled

James Broadwood, the largest piano manufacturer in Britain, invited us to dine at his handsome town house in Bryanston Square, an area also known as Millionaires' Row. As expected from the name, his home was lushly furnished: oriental carpets in every room, chairs and sofas upholstered with the finest linens, silk curtains drawn back at the floor-to-ceiling windows. White-gloved servants stood erect as they offered aperitifs and hors d'oeuvres on silver platters. We were treated to a scrumptious meal of roast beef and vegetables. Dessert was a splendid pudding called spotted dick with treacle sauce. I had the temerity to ask for seconds and ate more than I should have in polite company. Broadwood knew some French, and we, little English. Occasionally, Pleyel would translate, but the night belonged to the two men, giants in the field of piano manufacturing, who wanted to catch up. I would have loved to eavesdrop on their shop talk.

Few companies had benefited more from industrialization and England's burgeoning railway system than John Broadwood & Sons. The firm had gained worldwide notoriety and admiration because of its superior production methods. His company averaged over two thousand pianos a year while manufacturers in Marseille produced only four hundred and exported one hundred fifty of those. Alas, success at production does not always assure a superior tone. Even the best pianist could extract only what had been built into the instrument and nothing more. They were musicians, not magicians.

Broadwood was handsome for a man in his seventies. He had wavy gray hair and distinguished lines around his eyes. He was no stranger to manual labor. As a young man, he had worked in his father's factory, which his brother and he inherited. Perhaps because of that background, he retained a common touch and welcomed me as a tradesman at his table. What a contrast between him and my hoity-toity compatriot George Sand, who had made me feel like a flea-bitten cur begging for scraps.

After dinner, Mr. Broadwood offered us brandy and "a special treat." Chopin looked exhausted and feigned enthusiasm. Nonetheless, we dutifully took our snifters and followed the Englishman. The rooms were lined with tapestries and oil paintings of his ancestors, I supposed. With a flourish, he opened double oaken doors. There stood a large hall filled with thirteen pianos lined up like soldiers on parade.

"I keep my most expensive instruments here for artists to play," he said.

My eyes grew large. Concert grands made of Indian rosewood, baby grands of Indonesian mahogany, uprights with carved music desks and brass candlestick holders were just waiting for the perfect pair of hands. One piano looked out of place.

"You are right, Monsieur Delhomme. That piano is about forty years old, made before the repetition levers were invented."

"And before pedals too," I added.

He nodded. Chopin's music gained much of its nuance because of the sustaining pedal, which lifted all the dampers letting the notes ring and resonate with overtones that would be unimaginable without it. It made possible subtle washes of color and heroic storms. Even the low bass notes sounded light and pillowy, the essence of Chopin's style. One reviewer quite smitten with Chopin's work said he had made the pedal into a third hand, creating intrigue and subtle shadings and refinement of tone. His students were exhorted to follow his pedal markings to produce these same results. Nothing was superfluous on his scores.

"*Mon dieu!*" said Chopin. His face cheered at seeing such an impressive collection of keyboards just waiting for his expert touch. Without asking, he slipped onto the bench to play a few notes on the odd-man-out piano. Since the repetition lever and sustaining pedal had been invented only twenty-five years ago, he had practiced on such a piano in his youth.

After a few bars of a scherzo, he smiled at the unhurried return of the keys, slowing his tempo from allegro to andante. "It feels like a harpsichord!" Maybe Bach and Mozart could express themselves without the faster keyboard or pedal, but not this pianist. It was the first time I had ever seen Chopin display such delight over an instrument.

As we stood in the front door about to leave, I asked Mr. Broadwood if I might tour his factory while here. "Of course," he said. "Will Monsieur Pleyel accompany you?" he said. I detected some nervousness at the prospect of another manufacturer stealing his production methods. I assured him I would be alone, adding, "I only repair pianos, not make them, so your secrets are safe." Convinced of my discretion, he offered his cabriolet and driver to fetch me in the morning. "You will also need a guide to show you around. I will have my master tuner . . ."

I interrupted. "Oh, no need, Monsieur. I already have a guide."

"Is that so?"

"Yes, my nephew."

"Which department is he in? I do not recall a Delhomme working for me."

"He is my sister's child. His last name is Montgolfier."

"Of the Montgolfier brothers?" he said excitedly, referring to the inventors of the hot-air balloon.

"Unfortunately, no," I said, but I enjoyed his child-like enthusiasm over such a possibility. "Marc was orphaned and was assigned to your factory."

He sniffed, an Englishman's lash of disdain. An orphan was a scapegoat in this society, generally regarded as someone with no past, connections, or status, and prone to criminal activities.

"Splendid," he said coldly, and closed the door leaving us on the other side.

He had not slammed the door, but it felt as if he had. What a strange reaction from a man profiting from my nephew's labor. I intended to get the full story from Marc tomorrow. After three years, I very much looked forward to seeing him.

## CHAPTER 27

# George Sand's Diary – The Snub

Dear Diary,

Visited a Club of Women meeting today where a man—a *man*!—spoke about women's suffrage and divorce. And I was elated to hear someone address the problem of prostitution. I think men believe prostitutes want to be prostitutes and cannot imagine any of them having another motivation to carry on such a dreadful life. Of course, women want to have sex with sweaty, fat, snorting pigs who believe the woman really *wanted* to lie with them for the few minutes it takes to relieve themselves. How self-serving an explanation.

This is how I see the situation: We deprive her of an education, give her no civil rights, and then excoriate her for turning to the only form of labor that she can do. The hypocrisy is rampant. To make matters worse, a faction of men stampeded the door of this club meeting and shouted vulgar unpleasantries. They heckled the speaker and burst into laughter meant to ridicule the proceedings and us women. How can one argue against someone who is braying like a donkey to proclaim his male dominance?

Sympathetic though I am to women and their issues, I need to draw the line somewhere. A newspaper edited by ladies has nominated me as a candidate for the National Assembly, without my knowledge or consent. I refused and asked that no one vote for me and told them I do not have the honor of knowing a single one of those ladies who form clubs or write papers. Without my own acknowledgement, I cannot allow myself to be taken for the standard-bearer of a coterie of women with whom I have never had the slightest association, pleasant or otherwise. As I have told everyone, I do not seek any office.

If this little joke were hurtful only to my self-esteem, by attributing to me a ridiculous pretentiousness, I would let it pass, as with all such jokes, of which any one of us in this world may be the object. But my silence might lead people to believe that I adhere to these principles of which this paper seeks to become the instrument.

My strength is in my writing, not governing. I know they feel slighted. But I must do my duty where I can shine and make the most difference. Almost forty percent of the manufacturing workforce is women, yet they receive half what men do. They have suffered along with men in these uprisings, and many died. My work toward those goals was to write about all these issues, not to be political. Now it is time for someone new to take the reins of the Assembly. How ironic I could be asked to run for a position and be elected by men—the only ones who have the right to vote—so I can speak on women's issues. I doubt they would listen. Such is the state of affairs in France now.

# Factory – Je Suis Français

## Factory

*T*he day after our splendid dinner chez Broadwood, I was taken to the factory on Horseferry Road in Westminster, a less afflu-ent area than Millionaires' Row, to understate the contrast. The coach bumped along the poorly maintained streets as it passed row after row of ramshackle apartment buildings with laundry hanging from win-dows. After a time, the factory hove into view. The redbrick, four-story complex of buildings spanned several blocks. Train tracks ran behind the main building for easy shipping of finished instruments to eager pianists and dealers. Huge stacks of wood were piled outside for seasoning.

My nephew was sixteen now. The last time I saw him was in France, when he was a friendly, rambunctious twelve-year-old. When his parents died a year later, the state placed him in an orphanage where education consisted of learning skills for manual labor like blacksmithing or working as a footman. Learning my trade would better his earning prospects. I was happy to have given him a boost in that direction and hoped that in three years, he would have made great strides toward that goal. Today, I would check on his progress.

The entrance to the factory looked anything but exceptional. Plain, white double doors opened into a large foyer leading to the factory's finishing area, where pianos were fine-tuned, polished, and inspected before shipping.

"Uncle Beaulieu!" Marc shouted as I entered. I would not have recognized him with his poor haircut and ragged clothes. We hugged. His back felt bony. I told him how much he looked like his mother. He managed a faint, sad smile.

"How have you been?" I asked, but his appearance told the story: gaunt and short for his age, with blemished skin, lifeless eyes, and dull, dirty hair.

Eager to show me around, he steered me toward a wide staircase leading to the second floor.

"Does your supervisor know you are doing this? I fear you will get in trouble."

Yes, he had gotten permission. He took me first to the room where workers made wooden cases for grand pianos. Several strapping men, with forearms shiny with perspiration, worked like a well-oiled machine to coordinate their movements. I had never witnessed such an ambitious undertaking.

"It takes six men to bend the long piece of wood," he said, shouting over the pounding and grinding. "They put it around an iron pattern, then place metal blocks against it to keep its shape while it dries."

"What happens to the case after that?" I asked.

"They install a soundboard inside the rim." He pointed to a room. "Over there." The wood in a soundboard was as crucial to a piano's quality as to a violin's. Seasoned spruce was glued together in strips. It was imperative that the direction of the grains match so the sound could easily travel. Then it was planed to measure three-eighths of an inch. This was the surest way for it to be flexible and maintain a crown that would resist flattening when strings were tightened. "The metal plate rests on top of that."

"Where are those made?" I asked.

"At another factory with a special furnace to melt and shape the iron." It made sense that many of the thousands of parts making up a piano were shipped to the factory for assembly. No manufacturer was big enough to make everything.

We were just leaving the case-making room when a man with a bulbous nose and short forehead hastened over to us. His breath and demeanor told me he was a mean alcoholic. His harsh words to my nephew confirmed my assessment. He was an overseer patrolling that area. He caught Marc by the arm and yanked him into the corner. The boy was in trouble, that much was clear. The man shouted and slapped him several times. Marc turned away. But the man pulled out a stick and beat his back and shoulders. I rushed over. By now, Marc was curled up on the floor, covering his head to protect it. *"Arrêtez! Arrêtez!"* I said to the brute.

"Shut up!" he said, shoving me away. He raised his arm to deliver another blow on the poor child. This time, I blocked him. I shouted to Marc, *Couris!* Run!"

The paunchy, double-chinned swine was easily overcome. I was younger, stronger, and more agile. We struggled to the floor. Then I kicked him in the stomach.

"Oof!" He writhed in pain.

"Some of your own medicine!" I said.

A crowd had gathered. Someone helped the bully up. The monstrous ogre turned and spat at me. "Bloody frogs," he said, as he limped away.

I spat back. Decorum did not seem to rule these people; I was only behaving in a way they understood.

Marc's right cheek was red from the smacking, but blood from a bigger cut on his nose flowed into his eye. I ripped off a corner of my shirttail to dab around the wound. I may have helped with the physical effects of the beating; I could do nothing about his battered soul.

"We had better find Mr. Broadwood," I said. I wanted to find out why he had been beaten. We carefully descended the stairs, Marc pressing on his wound all the while. His face and eye were puffy. Mr. Broadwood would be met with quite a sight.

We returned to the reception area. "Mr. Broadwood, please," I said to the secretary. She answered me in English. I looked at Marc for the translation. "He will be back shortly. We need to sit over there."

"Is it still bleeding?" he asked.

I peeked under the cloth in a caring way, as I believed he needed pampering more than a medical opinion. I said it looked very good. I smiled and mussed his hair. By now, his one eye was swollen shut. "Keep pressing on it," I said. Wanting to distract him, I asked, "You never told me what you do here."

"I make sure the stringers and bass-string makers have enough wire," he said, proud of his responsibility. "I go to the supply building with a horse and wagon, load it up, and then take it back. If they run out, I get punished.

"How so?"

"The foreman beats me. If they run short, it halts production. It is an important job."

"How often are you beaten?" I asked, but I could see he did not want to answer. I took that to mean often and without much provocation.

"Are you the only orphan who works here?" He shook his head and pointed to several children sweeping floors and running errands for other workers. Some were barely seven years old.

"They—*those kids*—work here?" I said.

He nodded. "The older ones work as many hours as the adults, but none of us are paid. They also beat us if they find us sleeping."

"Is that even legal?"

Mr. Broadwood came in. We stood. He shook my hand but never acknowledged Marc. "How was your tour, Mr. Delhomme?" Marc stood by my side but looked down.

"Very impressive," I said. "This is my nephew, Marc. He restocks the strings for your workers."

"Looks like you had a bad fall, son," he said, looking at his blackening eye.

"Yes, that is precisely why I want to talk with you," I said. "May we speak in private?"

He led us to his warm, roomy office, removed from the hubbub of the factory. A large writing desk with a gilded chair sat just below the bay window. I stood in the doorway waiting for an invitation to step onto the plush maroon and navy Oriental carpet spanning the width of the wooden floor. In stark contrast to the workers' tunic and baggy pants, our host wore a dark blue jacket with brass buttons, beige knee breeches, and polished black leather boots. The trappings of his office and dress demarcated the bright line between the powerful and powerless, the tutored and unlettered.

"Mr. Broadwood, my nephew did not fall. His foreman beat him."

He looked unconcerned and defended the foreman. "He must have seen some irregular behavior."

I continued probing with what I hoped was a neutral tone: "Marc said he had permission to give me the tour. Is that correct?"

Mr. Broadwood nodded, saying he himself had alerted the head foreman.

"But was the supervisor on the second floor told as well?"

The owner looked dismayed. "The communication may have been faulty," he said. No apology though.

I asked him about the children. "Oh, we have had orphans working here for years," he said breezily. "The government limits children your nephew's age to twelve hours a day. The younger ones work only eight. But they can stay as long as they want. It is warm, and they feel needed. A damn sight better than that hellhole they call an orphanage."

This was state-sponsored slavery!

Accentuating his greed, he boasted about his improvements. "I had gas lighting installed about a year ago." His pride was obvious. "It allows employees to work fourteen, fifteen-hour days instead of stopping at sunset. That way they can earn more money."

This detail about the lives of working men and women—and children!—reminded me of Blanqui's words in the club that night.

"What did you think of our tuning and regulation department, Monsieur Delhomme?"

"We never went there," I said, pointing to Marc's swollen face.

"Well, then, follow me. I will show you myself."

Again, no apology. My bad impressions of the British were mounting.

The regulation room was filled with activity but no noise. Several technicians were hunched over their workbench, preparing actions by turning screws, bending wires, and leveling keys. Some were installing hammers and dampers. It was exacting, painstaking work. Each key required several adjustments within miniscule tolerances so each would feel exactly like its neighbor. There was no such thing as adjusting an action quickly, especially a new one. I watched Marc's eyes track the movements of the various workmen.

"Have they taught you how to regulate an action yet?" I asked him.

"Oh, no," Mr. Broadwood interrupted. "He is much too busy for that," he said.

"Would you like to learn?" I asked him.

Mr. Broadwood intruded again. "Let us move on to the tuning department. Right through this door." He pointed to double doors that would accommodate a grand piano at its widest part.

As we walked through, Marc said close to my ear, "I want to learn, but Mr. Broadwood says I am not old enough."

This was the exact time to learn these skills when the mind and hands were supple. "Let me talk to Mr. Broadwood about that." I patted his hand.

In this big room, several pianos were receiving their first of six tunings so new strings would stretch enough to hold the tension. I had to cover my ears for the din. I required complete silence when I tuned. This work would have given me a headache.

We continued across the floor to a separate room where several men were making copper-wound bass strings. The machines were steam driven. Steam was an efficient method of providing power, but it was ungodly noisy. I watched one man clamp a steel wire at both ends of a machine. Then, he attached copper wire at one end and set the string spinning at high speed. He held the copper wire taut as it coiled tightly and evenly around the rotating steel core from one end to the other.

"Would you like to do this?" I shouted to Marc over the noise. He shook his head. I could understand why. The monotony of making bass strings hour after hour, day after day—my God, could there have been anything more alienating, enervating, and mind-numbing than that? Paid by the piece, Marc said workers seldom took lunch. The shop foremen patrolled the work area to ensure quotas were met.

"*Magnifique*, Mr. Broadwood," I said as we returned to his office. And it was magnificent, just not for the people working there. I told him I admired the efficiency of the production and marveled at their skill under pressure.

"How would you like a job here, Mr. Delhomme?" Broadwood asked in French. "We could use your expertise. Nice, steady work, and I would pay you handsomely. Marry yourself a pretty English girl who can have your babies and cook good English food." He raised his eyebrows as if to say, "How about it?"

After he told me how much I would earn, I pretended the offer was generous and never mentioned I already had a perfectly good French wife. The salary was more than I made in Paris, but to trade in my independence and peace of mind for spiritually deadening, deafening, hot factory work where one's aesthetics were continually compromised was far too expensive for my soul. And for what? So he could profit from my misery to pay for a fancy house on Millionaires' Row, gorge on tin after tin of caviar, and swill champagne every night? I put up my hands in surrender. "No speak English. No English," I kept saying, as if my poor language skills were the sole reason.

After that day, I reconsidered the views I had espoused that unfortunate evening at Nohant. Where Broadwood saw nothing but fair skies ahead as the boom in piano production continued, I saw workers who had been turned into empty shells with lifeless eyes and shambling gaits. People needed fulfillment, a purpose, a ray of hope. It was a major shift to admit I had been wrong, but after seeing these workers suffer, I felt protective of them—and certainly of the children—against this barbaric treatment.

## Je Suis Français!

Marc walked me to the waiting carriage outside the factory doors. I climbed in and was about to wave goodbye when he held on to my arm.

"Uncle," he said, "would you like to come to Sunday dinner?" His look was so pleading that I could not refuse.

"*Bien sûr*," I said without hesitation. I wanted to show him every kindness.

The orphanage encouraged visitors because everyone was a potential adoptive parent. But come October, Marc would be seventeen and need to fend for himself. Where would he go? What would he do? I could see the panic in his eyes.

That Sunday, the coachman pulled up in front of Gentle Lamb orphanage, a commanding building made of sooty brick. The foreboding façade did not spark optimism. As I entered, the stench was unbearable: urine, sour milk, unwashed bodies. I saw shoeless children with dirty faces wearing ill-fitting, ripped, soiled clothing running pell-mell, screaming, and hitting one another. Dinner was served at four. That gave us an hour to make plans for his release in October.

The visitors' room by the main office had three chairs and a couch whose working springs were only a memory. Marc came to greet me. We talked until the dinner bell rang. He got up to leave, but I stopped him. "I almost forgot," I said. "This is for you. I held out a small sack of cheese, a bottle of milk, some bread, and two bars of chocolate. He peered into the bag and then shoved it inside my coat.

"Uncle," he whispered, "the head matron does not allow us to accept food. She will surely seize it."

We wended our way through the narrow halls, past closed doors leading to dormitories—girls slept on one level, boys the other—and downstairs to the mess hall in the basement. Three rows of tables ran the length of the room. The residents vied to be first, and not politely. Once in line, each child eagerly held out a bowl as several pinch-faced women doled out the fare: porridge, milk, and a hunk of bread. Sunday dessert was the usual rice pudding, his favorite. The noise level decreased sharply as the orphans slurped their gruel and swabbed leftover bits with bread. I ate to be polite, but it was disgusting food. Greasy, thin, and tasteless. No second helpings, either. Marc did not say much, only that he missed his parents; he missed France.

After dinner, I asked to see the sleeping quarters. Visitors were not allowed, he said. They were probably as ghastly as the meal. Instead, we walked around the grounds and found a bench perched on the top of a small hill leading to the woods. The sun dodged behind the fast-moving clouds then peeked out again once they passed.

"Have you ever thought about running away?"

"They lock us in our rooms at night. I got out through a window once."

"Where did you go?"

"It was night. I stepped on something sharp and cut my foot. So, I waited till morning to go on. I slept with the horses in the barn. But the matron found me and put me in the punishment room straightaway."

"Where is that?"

He turned and pointed to the attic with blackened windows. "I slept on the floorboards with only a blanket for a week. Two meals a day and no one spoke to me."

I was quite disturbed to hear about this cruelty. I had no hope of bettering his life at the orphanage, but I did plan to talk to Mr. Broadwood about teaching Marc to regulate actions, so he could become a salaried employee when he turned seventeen. I started to get up from the bench, but Marc pulled me back down.

"Uncle, do you think I could come live with you in Paris?"

"Marc, Lili will be coming soon to live with me. Until then, there would be no one to prepare meals or wash your clothes."

"But I can cook! Maman taught me how to make boeuf bourguignon, and stewed chicken and . . ."

"Marc," I interrupted, "what will you do? You have no skills except hauling wire around." I regretted sounding so patronizing.

He thought, then responded, excitedly. "I could be your apprentice! I could clean your shop, organize your supplies, and do whatever you want."

Excellent point. By now, I had enough business to keep us busy and could easily train him to tune and repair instruments. He seemed bright and eager. It would be better instruction than he was receiving at the orphanage. Giles took me in as an apprentice when I had nothing. Now was my opportunity to send my gratitude forward.

Moreover, taking him back to Paris was the one way I could help just one poor, suffering, emaciated individual, orphaned through no fault of his own. I could share my knowledge and wealth with this fine young man. He was blood, after all. I felt a swelling desire to protect him from the abuse of people like Broadwood. Only, where would he sleep when Lili came?

Then I remembered why I had wanted to come to London in the first place. "There is unrest in Paris," I told him. "How can I, in good conscience, bring you home to such a dangerous city?"

"I will stay inside. No one can hurt me."

I explained how rebels roamed the streets and threw rocks just to be disruptive. I recounted how his own grandfather had been abducted by militia in Warsaw during an uprising there many years ago. "War is dangerous and unpredictable. Many people have died, and most have nothing to eat. Everyone is angry."

His eyes filled with tears.

I tried to discourage him. "Why would you want to leave peaceful London and endanger yourself?"

He stood up and pointed to his chest, *"Parce que je suis français!"*

That reason was good enough for me. I slapped my thighs and got up. "Well, then, let's go back to Paris where you can be as French as you want."

In my haste to rescue Marc from this misery, I put aside the worry about sleeping arrangements.

A week later, my coach arrived at the orphanage on a cool morning. As soon as Marc saw me, he burst through the glass doors and bounded down the steps as if fleeing a monster.

"Where is your suitcase?" I asked, opening the carriage door.

He shrugged. With only a look of great expectation, he scampered aboard, and we set out for Folkstone. It took several hours to cross the channel due to fierce winds. The boat docked in Calais by late afternoon. As I stood on Gallic soil again, pride surged within me that I was returning this boy to his homeland. But without warning, that emotion melted into a frisson of dread: The smell of war filled my nostrils anew.

## CHAPTER 29

# George Sand's Diary – Memories

Dear Diary,

I dined with Alphonse de Lamartine this evening. He has risen handily to power in the Constituent Assembly installed after the February uprising. It looks likely he will take charge of the Provisional Government in a few days. Although a bit too moderate for my tastes, he has a steady hand; things could be much worse. Now we can steer our country in the right direction. But our work is not done yet. I have been busy behind the scenes to do that, but I am lending my voice to two Government circulars, one of which is the *Bulletin de la République*. It is anonymous, but surely clever readers will figure out who wrote it.

   My thoughts are addressed to people in the rural districts. The *Bulletin* comes out every other day, and mayors in each district can post or distribute them. In the latest one, I praise our citizens for their bravery in erecting the barricades in the February uprising and urge them to manifest their will. *Aux armes, citoyens! Formez vos bataillons!* I hope to arouse their nationalistic spirit, so they will rise again. We have no time to waste. The election for our next government will be in a few weeks.

No sooner had I felt myself regaining my strength from the turmoil here than I was weakened anew by the odor of that dastardly would-be rapist. Today, as I left my apartment, a poor man with ragged clothes cowered in the alcove of the doorway. I smelled that horrid odor of sweat and days-old filth. My head throbbed with anger and helplessness. I almost swooned. Nothing frightens me more than losing control. It has been almost thirty years since that incident; yet it remains as fresh in my memory as what I ate for breakfast. I have spent my life trying to be self-sufficient and vying for respect from men on their terms—by dressing and acting like them. And I have succeeded. How can one whiff of that odor be my undoing?

# CHAPTER 30

# Homecoming – Turned – Church Work

## Homecoming

"*L*isez la Presse! Lisez la Presse,*" the newsboy shouted waving a newspaper on the quay as we made our way to the train to Paris. I was eager to learn about the political situation in France, having left six weeks ago. I put six centimes in the boy's hand. The news was jarring:

### POTATO BLIGHT CONTINUES

WORKERS demanding bread, voting rights, no taxation
Workers being phased out

That last item was worrisome. Exasperation must have marked my face.

*Qu'est-ce qu'il y a, Oncle?*" said Marc.

"We have trouble—*again*."

"Does it affect you?" he asked.

I had no desire to alarm him but thought he should know the situation. "After the February uprising," I explained, "the government wanted to create jobs for unemployed people. So, the government started a system of workshops to build railways and repair roads. The swamps needed draining. And in the last uprising, people cut down trees to use in the barricades, so they learned how to plant new ones."

Marc said, "Did they do that for free?"

"Twenty-three francs a day. That much buys some bread and vegetables." The problem, I said, reading from the article, was that the idea was "too successful."

He looked perplexed. "How can something be too successful?"

"It says here that 'Over one hundred thousand unemployed laborers from all over France poured into Paris demanding work. Paying for the project meant imposing taxes on farmers and peasants.'" I turned to Marc to explain their resistance. "They wanted no part of supporting the urban poor."

I continued, "But no new taxes meant they had to end the program after only a few months. Now people are" . . . I looked at the article for the exact word . . . "discontented."

That seemed an understatement since it said large crowds were threatening another uprising like the one in February. To parry that menace, the government passed a harsh new law stating that unarmed crowds would be "forcibly dispersed" after three warnings, meaning they would be shot dead.

I saw another article under that news report by none other than George Sand. She wrote: "I cannot believe in any republic that starts a revolution by killing its own proletariat."

For once I agreed with her. Governments had a responsibility to take care of their citizenry, not kill them because officials had made bad economic decisions.

Marc looked worried. "Now what will happen?"

I had no idea. Several pro-worker leaders had been jailed while we were in England, dimming hopes for a larger voice in the government and presaging trouble.

Now, even though the situation was a *fait accompli*, I questioned the wisdom of my decision to bring him home.

Our train passed fallow fields usually planted with corn and wheat by now. What was the use of planting anything when farmers could not earn enough money for their produce or had to watch it rot from disease? As we approached the outskirts of the city, we saw beggars pleading for a sou. At the station, I dropped some change into the open hand of a woman with a crying baby.

I retained a carriage and transferred my bags. It was late evening when we arrived at my apartment at 15 rue Daguerre with my piano shop next door. Marc looked as if he were beholding the Château de Chenonceau, which it most certainly was not. A tear on his cheek shone in the moonlight.

We settled into a comfortable routine. Meals were quiet events. Marc spoke only if asked a question and sometimes not even then. He would nod and resume eating, crooking his left arm around his plate and wolfing his food.

"Marc," I said one morning, "you need not guard your food from marauding hordes anymore. Please, eat as much as you like."

And eat he did. He consumed twice my portions: four sausages at breakfast, over half of a baguette with two bowls of mushroom soup for lunch, and a half chicken for dinner. His help as my apprentice relieved me of some tedious tasks and increased output in the shop. He swept up sawdust and put away tools. I taught him how to level piano keys. That involved feeling minuscule differences in key height between its neighbors and adding paper punchings to achieve a smooth surface. What is not noticeable to the eye feels like mountains to the pianist. He did that well, and I praised him for it.

His assistance helped pay for the larger grocery bill. But his protective, oversensitive behavior extended far beyond our meals: He startled at loud noises and tiptoed around, apologizing if so much as a floorboard squeaked. He would flinch, as if anticipating a thrashing for his infraction.

But on other kinds of tasks, I noticed he had difficulty following directions. When asked to do something, he would nod as if he understood. But later it became clear he did not. His one chore was to keep the fire lit in the kitchen stove. He was shown how to fetch kindling from leftover millwork in the shop. But he often forgot. It meant breakfast was delayed. His inability to follow instructions rankled me most during tuning lessons. I explained what to do, then showed him several times, but after two weeks, he had absorbed nothing. Whether his disregard for my directions was due to willfulness, a hearing disorder, or brain damage from multiple beatings, I could not tell. Suspicion mounted whether he was even teachable. But I also had to remind myself he was like an abused animal that cowers even at a raised hand.

I loved his smile when he heard about the tricks his mother, Marie, and I had played on one another. Once he even laughed out loud when I recounted how I had taken her doll from her bedroom. Marie cried and cried because she had to go to bed without her precious Mimi.

Earlier that day, I had hidden the doll in my mother's sewing room and fashioned a black sack for the doll out of some leftover cloth. Then, as Marie slept, I crept up to her bed and waved the shrouded figure in her face shouting, "I found your doll! I found your doll!" She screamed so loudly that it woke our parents. My father whipped me for my prank as she looked on, smug and triumphant.

The day after our arrival, Marc and I set about organizing the shop. The space was three times as large as my living quarters but even more crowded with pianos especially when I took them apart to make repairs. A ladder led to a small storage area for supplies. He took special pride in organizing the wire. Resuming my routine calmed my anxiety about the waxing menace in Parisian streets.

I hoped reorganizing would create a living space for Marc in the shop so Lili and I would have privacy. The only space left was under a grand piano. He probably would have consented if I had asked. But it seemed too punitive. The poor boy had endured enough. I hoped Lili would see it that way too. I wrote her the next day.

*Dearest,*

*I have returned from England, where the weather was as bad as the air. Chopin suffered so very much. Many people there care deeply about him and fussed over him. As always, he worked too hard. I fear he will suffer a relapse.*

*I have some news about Marc. My visit to the orphanage was dispiriting. Dreary rooms, unpalatable food, and unruly children made his life miserable. What is more, his status as an orphan at the* piano factory meant ineligibility for any professional training. All he did was fetch wire from the supply depot.

He begged me to return him to France as my apprentice. He would have had to leave the orphanage in only a few months anyway.

I know I promised to move you to Paris soon, but as you know, my space is quite limited. Marc and I sleep in the same room, so it would not do to have you stay with me in our conjugal bed, as much as I would like that.

I was torn by this decision, but it was thrust upon me because of his imminent release. What would he do? Where would he go? Life was so very grim for him at the factory and the orphanage.

Please try to understand. I will write soon about an alternative date for your arrival.

Je pense à toi, toujours, mon amour.
Beaulieu

Lili's curt reply came soon thereafter.

Beaulieu,

I sympathize about Marc's situation. It must have been horrible to have to endure such cruelty after having lost both parents. But I would be remiss if I did not express my disappointment at how you have put your nephew's needs ahead of mine. I will try to understand.

Please do not make me wait much longer. Pretty women are everywhere in Paris, and I cannot compete with them from afar.

Ta femme,
Lili

She signed "your wife." Was I a bad person for choosing to save a lost soul? I resolved to ask Chopin for the ring since he and Sand were no longer together. I would send it to Lili. Then she would see how much I love her.

# Turned

Even though the Provisional Government had resulted from the February uprising, it lasted a scant three months. Worry gnawed as I tried to reconcile my role in supporting the government that legalized such ruthless policies against workers. At least we were done with "Citizen King" Louis Philippe, that pompous buffoon with gold-braid epaulets and military medals festooning half his chest.

People began whispering in salons and saloons about yet another uprising. Vidocq had heard about it, too, and sent a message to meet him at the Gare du Nord train station in the tenth arrondissement. The large crowds and noisy engines would muffle our conversation. Once again, my inner voices warred. My father demanded we children be honest. But, whom should I be honest to now—myself or Vidocq?

The spymaster and I sat on a bench inside the entrance. He had chosen our meeting place well: Crying children, travelers bent under huge bundles as they rushed to their train, and conductors shouting out destinations and announcements to board easily masked our conversation. "The rebels are planning to assassinate Carvaignac," he said over the pshoo of the trains releasing steam, "but I have no information."

It made sense why insurgents would target this man. Carvaignac was the ruthless general just appointed Minister of War in the provisional government. This tyrant clamped down on rioters without compunction.

"Tomorrow morning, go to that market." He pointed to crowded marketplace across the street. Give this envelope to the fat woman in the southwest corner. She sells peonies. She will be expecting the note and will give you one in return that will say when, where, and who will lead the attack. I will come by tomorrow to fetch it."

"Does she work for you?" I asked.

"She is just a go-between. We have discovered that her corner of the market is the favorite meeting place for the resistance. Use those highly trained tuner's ears to gather any other information. Try to be a real spy for once. And report back, *toute de suite!*"

He looked sternly at me. "If ever there was an important errand, this is it, Delhomme." He shook his finger to punctuate each word: "Do—Not—Botch—This."

I was heartened to hear that workers were planning to fight the government's harsh policies. But I knew I had to play along yet again.

The next morning, I walked to the southwest corner of the market. Merchants sold everything from spring greens to sponges to silk scarves. It bustled with mothers buying provisions for dinner and children playing tag among the mounds of fruits and vegetables.

I combed the area but found no peonies sold by anyone, fat or thin. I panicked. Vidocq would surely want that envelope.

Defeated, I turned to leave when I saw three men huddled in the southwest corner engaging in what looked like a conspiratorial discussion. They were not merchants but men with scraggly beards and soiled clothes. Their voices were low; they leaned in, sometimes covering their mouths when they spoke. I edged closer. I overheard the words 'bomb,' not the usual vocabulary in a Saturday morning marketplace.

I inched closer while pretending to inspect some leeks and artichokes. The man with the bald head looked at his watch, then pointed to a piece of paper as he said, "*Carvaignac. Dimanche. Le train d'Orléans à six heures.*"

If I understood correctly, these men aimed to kill him as he alighted from the train from Orléans at six o'clock Sunday evening—*tomorrow!* The plan was to rush onto the train and plant a bomb in his boxcar. One of them quietly made the sound of a big explosion. They laughed.

I left immediately to alert Vidocq. That way, he would see I was cooperating, even though I had not retrieved any envelope.

But on the way home, I reconsidered my quandary with Vidocq. I had said I would quit several times and tried to dodge the meeting with Louis Napoléon. Those things only enraged him. But this time, *I* had the upper hand in this situation. Vidocq's directive was to feed him information. That did not mean I had to tell him the *correct* information: I would tell him the bombing was set for *Monday*, not Sunday, so Vidocq's henchmen would miss the train by a whole day. That would allow the resistance to kill him on Sunday. I could just say I had misheard the conspirators. Two could play at this game of spying. How would he know I had lied?

When we met again to debrief about the market, Vidocq was very interested in my information and wrote down every detail. He seemed uncharacteristically thankful. Saving Carvaignac would make him look indispensable to Lamartine and win his respect. I knew that was important to him. It all seemed so easy.

Sunday, I wanted to witness the bombing. Gare d'Austerlitz, the southern-most station in Paris was dedicated to trains to and from Orléans. The late-afternoon air felt heavy and still under low-hanging clouds. I did not dare enter the station but secreted myself in a grove of trees within sight and earshot of the station. I thought it imprudent to show my face (disguised or otherwise) as it would have raised questions about why I was there on Sunday when I had reported the event would occur on Monday. Vidocq's motto: All warfare is based on deception.

The train chugged into the station right at six. There was a screech of the brakes and the hiss of steam. I waited and waited.

Boom!

Train parts shattered the station's roof. Shards of glass blew to the sky. Big hunks of metal rained down, landing with a thunk. People screamed and ran out of the station covering their heads. Sirens sounded. Policemen appeared on the scene quickly, perhaps too quickly. Were they already at hand, perhaps *expecting* a bombing? And if so, why did they let it go forward? They should have—*could* have—stopped the insurgents if they knew about it. A few minutes later, a pair of men led someone (Carvaignac?) with a blanket over his head to a police wagon. The man did not look injured. So, how did *they* know that Sunday was the day he would come? I had explicitly said Monday. Surely, the conspirators in the market were disappointed that this madman Cavaignac was safe.

Vidocq could never say I had not told him about the plot. I just lied about one fact. He would not dare blame me for that infraction, would he?

## Church Work

On a mild Tuesday morning in June, Marc and I had just finished breakfast and set about our work restringing a customer's piano. In the three weeks he had been here, I went from alarm about his inability to learn to blaming myself for expecting him to know everything upon arrival. That morning, we were working as a team: I removed the strings and measures the width of each one with the micrometer screw gauge and recorded its size.

We were well into the process when a messenger delivered a note from Father Bernard, the head priest at my church: Would I please come this Friday to work on the newly acquired upright for the young parishioners' summer solstice celebration? It had recently been donated, which always meant it had been neglected. No one gave away good pianos. He wrote that it "did not respond to my touch" and "some keys were missing." I hoped he meant keytops and not the key itself. Making an entire key would require tools I did not have. His late notice would upset my schedule, but I decided that denying a request from a priest would not turn out well, either in this life or the next.

The night before we were due at the church, I readied supplies and provisions for the long day ahead and stoked the fire to be certain we could carry on with breakfast without waiting to start a new one. We turned in about nine o'clock.

Around midnight, I was awakened by scuffles and shouts outside my window. I smelled gunpowder, too. Although these sounds and scents concerned me, I could do nothing about them and returned to bed.

I arose at dawn. Raindrops quickened down the windowpanes. I planned to leave for the church before traffic grew heavy. The streets were certain to be slippery and passage difficult, especially in the poor arrondissement where the church was located. As I descended the stairs to the kitchen, I remembered the midnight disturbances, believing they had most probably been alcohol-induced skirmishes. That was my first mistake that day.

We ate breakfast, hitched the horse to the wagon, and arrived at the church by eight o'clock, enough time to complete our work by dinnertime. I brought a bucket of oats and another of water for the horse. Fr Bernard greeted us and led us to the basement.

"*Voilà,*" said the priest, proudly pointing to a beaten-up instrument. One side had been marred by careless movers. The other had faded from repeated exposure to direct sunlight. God only knew what torment its innards had endured.

"I kept meaning to notify you, but time slipped away," said the priest. I smiled and said it was nothing. "I will fix it to help your children sing like the angels they are." A bold promise, that, since it needed two tunings before it would hold the pitch, some ivories were missing, and several keys were sluggish due to spilled liquids and years of accumulated dust, not to mention broken parts from exuberant pounding.

We worked all day without stopping, except for lunch. Three tins of sardines (one for me), crackers, and fresh berries. He remained his laconic self, but his company was agreeable. After testing my tuning and repairs by playing some Chopin that would show up some irregularities, especially in the fifths and octaves, we gathered our tools and supplies and left the rectory just a hair before five p.m. with dinner on our minds.

The sun had dried up many of the puddles by that time.

Our carriage stood by the rectory door. I turned to load the toolboxes when Marc said, "I can drive the wagon, Uncle."

I looked at him.

"Remember?" he said, "I used to transport piano wire at the Broadwood factory," he said. He did not wait for a reply and climbed up to the driver's seat and grabbed the reins. I thanked my great good fortune at having brought him that day, but I would soon rue that decision too.

Since we had been working in a soundproof basement, neither of us had heard the commotion swelling in the area. We set off for the main street. As we neared, I heard raised voices and horses clippity-clopping as their riders shouted for people to put their weapons down. I did not care to join in the fray. "Turn around," I said. "We'll go another way."

We doubled back, passed the church, and rounded a bend in the street.

He drew up the reins. "Uncle," he said, "the street is barricaded!" I got out to inspect the pile of paving stones, glass, and junk collected from the streets.

"Can you go over it?" I asked.

"The wheels will break."

I told him to go over by the side where there was less debris. I held on to the horse's bridle and tried to coax her over the rubble, but she refused. I gave up. "Better return to the church."

Fr Bernard was only too happy to see us again. He had just learned that the government had announced the official dissolution of the workshops that day, depriving all those workers of any means of support. The news had radiated throughout Paris. He said the government anticipated chaos and sent out guardsmen to disperse the one hundred thousand workers gathering across the town. "I fear not even God can keep you safe today," he said.

Back on church grounds, Marc curried, fed, and watered the horse while I arranged sleeping quarters for the night. Surely, the route would be safe if we left before dawn.

The next morning, Marc readied the horse. I climbed into the back of the wagon, expecting to be home within the hour. We approached the main street. Marc pulled up sharply. I stood up to see what he saw. In the blue dawn, a much larger swirling mob carried banners. A rhythmic chant became louder. They poked the air with metal poles, knives, and pistols.

Suddenly, sparks and reports came from guardsmen's guns. One insurgent fell into the crowd. Women screamed. Another was carried away on a bloody stretcher. This time the crowd seemed much larger and more agitated. I had to keep Marc safe. I caught his eye and pointed toward the church. He jumped off the wagon. I put my arm out to slow his pace to a walk. "We dare not attract attention."

We had gotten about halfway when I heard hooves. I glanced back and saw a soldier galloping toward us. He took us for rioters and was coming after us. "Run!" I shouted to Marc. "Run to the church!"

I ran fast. Quick breaths stung my chest. I looked back. The rider drew near. Gunshot. My calf burned. I screamed and fell. My head hit the ground. I looked up and saw Marc reach for the church door. One more shot. He yelped and dropped. The guard dashed off.

I put my hand on my wound to stanch the blood. Marc lay still.

The priest ran onto the street. "I heard gunfire," he said. "What has happened? Are you all right?"

"Please, Father," I cried, "Marc . . . Look after Marc. He was shot, too!" Fr Bernard rushed over to him and knelt. His robe dragged in the pooled blood. He picked up Marc's arm to check for a pulse. He put it down, crossed himself, and said a short prayer.

"No! No!" I shouted as I dragged myself to Marc's side. This most precious boy lay crumpled, his head twisted back with an expressionless face. "Father, stop. He is not dead! Please. No last rites!" But my shouts could not drive off the truth.

The priest came to my side. He moved my hand off the wound. He ripped a strip of cloth from his frock and tied it tight above the torn flesh.

"Can you stand?" he asked. He put my arm round his neck and helped me to the church. I paused in the doorway and looked back at Marc's body on the cold stones.

"Let me stay with him. He should not be left alone. Not again." *I* was to blame. *I* had not protected him.

Fr Bernard guided my shoulders. "We will pray for Marc soon. We must take care of you now."

The priest took me to the kitchen and helped me down onto a wooden bench. He opened a cabinet and pulled out a roll of dressings and a small bottle. With deft hands, he cleaned and dressed my wound.

I admired his medical skill. He said he often helped doctors treat wounded patients in local hospitals. "The bullet only grazed your calf," he said. "Tore the flesh, but you still need to see a doctor," he said. "You dare not take chances with an open wound."

I shivered from shock. He went to get a blanket and placed it around my shoulders. Then he pointed to the blue bottle on the table. "A teaspoon of this will ease the pain."

"What is it?"

"Laudanum, a tincture of opium." He poured a teaspoonful and said, "You might find it a somewhat bitter." He was right about it being bitter. I had all I could do to swallow it. He smiled knowingly and turned to tend to Marc.

"Let me help you, Father," I said, trying to stand but fell back down.

"Give it time. It will heal."

The wound would but not my heart.

Marc's death was but one of four thousand killed in the three-day uprising. Six thousand were wounded, maybe more. Brave insurgents held their own against four times as many soldiers and National Guard troops lobbing grapeshot, shells, and incendiary rockets. The government's henchmen took those who had surrendered or been imprisoned. They massacred them, some as they were being taken to jail, some in public gardens. Others were thrown into the Seine and killed. Those who made it to prison were shot through the bars if they dared make a peep. Officials estimated that twenty-five thousand people were detained, eleven thousand in long-term custody, some deported to Algeria.

What had the workers won in exchange for their spilled blood? It was too soon to know.

*Paris, 22 June 1848*

*My Dearest Lili,*

*Marc was killed in the latest uprising this morning. My emotions are jumbled: guilt, grief, anguish, rage all flood my head. Crying is pointless.*

*Our beloved France is in tatters. Many loyal citizens died seeking bread. Sand was right: "No one could believe in any republic that killed its own workers."*

*I will come to Marainville soonest to be with you. We can return to Paris together.*

*With all my heart,*
*Delhomme*

## CHAPTER 31

# George Sand's Diary – Lament

Dear Diary,

The fight for our rights has been defanged. Since the June Days uprising six months ago, a faction of murderous bourgeoisie has been elected to run our "Republic," along with Prince Président Louis Napoléon, who was swept in on his uncle's coattails. He has shown his stripes, and we do not like them. We want a real Republic! They have imprisoned more than two hundred women who fought nobly on the barricades, bringing ammunition to the insurgents and designing ruses to sneak food to them as they fought. They devised ingenious ways to spy on the enemy. The government said that out of forty to fifty thousand combatants, "no more than" fourteen hundred were killed or mortally wounded. Everyone knows bureaucrats lie when reporting numbers. Surely there were more than that. *Affreux*!

Allowing Louis Napoléon to come back from exile in England and electing him to the Constituent Assembly means we are headed for a semi-monarchical restoration, at the very least. It all smacks of a yearning for the Empire. For some reason, the people equate *me* with bedlam and mob rule. I detest politics. It is a stupid and insincere business. I am done. I need rest. I only want to write.

I heard Delhomme's nephew died in the melee. What a waste.

CHAPTER 32

# Theft – Death – Rest

## Theft

*I*t was September, more than a year since Marc's death and the June uprising. Lili helped arrange his funeral and shove aside my regrets to focus on our new life together. She was now happily ensconced in our new home and had already imposed order on both our apartment and the shop. How did I get so lucky?

Now, however, Chopin lay dying. There was no hope of recovery from consumption, although no one would acknowledge that reality. The pianist's generous friends had paid the staggering sum of four hundred francs a month for a luxurious, sunny apartment on Place Vendôme.

His window looked out on the expansive courtyard, built by Napoléon I. In its center stood a column with bas-relief bronze plates fashioned out of European wartime cannons. A statue of the emperor wearing a laurel wreath topped the column. He clutched a sword in one hand and globe in the other, upon which stood Winged Victory. A noble, if self-serving, piece of art but true to his character. The apartment was much closer to medical care than his previous one, his doctor only minutes away. The poor soul had become very weak in his last year. He was a proud man. Being carried upstairs was the height of ignominy.

On a balmy early fall morning, a month before his death, I paid him a visit. By now, he was confined to bed. He could no longer compose or play in those aristocratic circles where he basked in the congenial atmosphere of the attendees. Even as early as January of that year, he said he had to lie down ten times a day. He could still sit up and eat, but the latter required coaxing. His eyes looked dull; his skin, loose and flaky, and he was, oh, so pale. His relentless cough sounded soupy, as if he were drowning. But his mind was sharp. He asked about the latest piano I had worked on. Was I still practicing accented scales and learning new music? Which of his preludes did I find the most difficult to play?

That last question I answered quickly: "Your last Polonaise in A-flat major, without question," I said. "Those powerful left-hand staccato octaves are . . . well, did you know Liszt said playing it was 'a danger to health'?" He loved being told his works were wickedly hard. He smiled, because we both knew Liszt was no stranger to exacting pain with his own compositions.

Then, without warning, his expression turned somber. He handed me a note. I opened it and read: "As this earth will suffocate me, I implore you to have my body opened, so that I may not be buried alive."

Impending death brings the realization that time can no longer be squandered. But for me, such a request showed he had accepted his fate much more readily than I.

He must have seen my shock. "Please, Delhomme. Promise me."

This note and his deteriorating health were difficult to abide. I excused myself, explaining I had an appointment. I needed fresh air to absorb the shock. I opened the door to leave. Standing there, ready to knock, was Mme Charlotte Marliani. We had met when Chopin and Sand lived next to her in the Square Orléans.

"*Bonjour*, Monsieur Delhomme. How is he today?" Her arms were overflowing with packages and a small basket of food.

We traded places in the doorway. "No improvement." I tried not to sound ominous, but such news could not be construed otherwise.

I offered to help with her bundles. "You are such a gentleman, but I can manage," she said. "Though, would you help me with one thing? I received a letter from George last week asking about him." She nodded toward an envelope sticking out of her coat pocket. "I think she should know. Would you mind posting my reply?"

I hesitated, not wanting to help George communicate with anyone, but then agreed. "Of course," I told her, "with pleasure." I put the letter in my breast pocket and offered again to unburden her.

"Thank you, no, but I will ask you to close the door behind me."

I did so, then rushed down the steps and onto the sidewalk. Gusts of cold air made me button my coat. I leaned against the building to catch my breath and watched tourists crane their necks to look up at Napoléon's statue. I took Mme Marliani's letter out of my pocket. It was addressed to George at her Paris address. How could she possibly not know Chopin was sick? Thousands of Parisians, even people the composer had never met, were whispering about it. How could a woman who had spent a decade of her life with him not have heard?

I stood frozen by a divided mind. On the one hand, Chopin's friend had entrusted the letter to me. I was therefore honor bound. On the other hand, Mme Sand's reprehensible behavior toward Chopin in the final months of their relationship two years ago sickened me: cheating on him, lying about her feelings, taking his ring under false pretenses. She even had the temerity to write a roman à clef, *Lucrezia Floriani*, modeling the buffoonish, parasitic invalid after him, without much attempt to hide the resemblance. Meanwhile, her heroine, a free-wheeling libertine, had four children by three lovers, all of whom she was dating *at the same time!* This lack of taste, ladled liberally throughout the book, was no surprise, but its sweeping disregard for my dear, defenseless friend was vulgar. It reeked of petulance for having to care for an invalid for so long while her needs had gone unmet. She even had the nerve to read the book aloud to Chopin and Delacroix, as if to rub his face in the excrement of her prose. Delacroix said he cringed as she read but added that Chopin showed no emotion.

I vowed to inflict revenge. No punishment would be too harsh for someone who derided her lover to his face and in a book to be read by thousands—perhaps millions—of her devotees. The only question was whether withholding this letter would be enough reprisal for her depravity.

But grace and compassion were not expected. *What would it accomplish for Sand to know that Chopin was dying?* I asked myself. He was almost senseless now. Would he even know who she was? Besides, I thought it might upset him to see her after their turbulent breakup. His name was not even to be uttered at Nohant! More to the point, I blamed her for his decline and death—casting him out like rubbish and all because of some silly row with her daughter. This sole act dwarfed all her other transgressions against Chopin. She seemed to know enough to write those incendiary rallying cries to foment an uprising. And still she declared she "knew nothing" of his illness. In the end, George always got what George wanted. Her solipsism had devastated so many. She had harrowed her daughter's life and most certainly that of her son. Yet she refused to acknowledge any of it.

I cast the envelope into the wind. It twirled away over the expansive plaza. *Let someone else mail it,* for I could not.

I had my own transgressions against Chopin to answer for. I deeply regretted using him to reach Mme Sand for to satisfy the monarchy's thirst for knowledge. How could I have abused my friendship like that? Was it my own voracity for attention to compensate for my father's contempt and disappointment? Was it a desperate need to feel important while standing in the shadow of someone so beloved and admired? How pitiful that decision was. How out of proportion to the gold of Chopin's friendship. Now, with his demise imminent, I felt a clamp around my chest. Perspiration collected on my forehead. I needed to make right what had been spoiled by my own deceitful actions.

## Death

I visited the musician almost daily after that. He never lacked for friends, who by now had to wait their turn to visit with him. I went to his apartment late one evening. Mid-October asters, dahlias, camellias, even some sunflowers rescued from marauding crows, filled every corner and surface, including the piano. I thought to remove them lest water spill but decided to let the bouquets stay. It seemed a fitting honor to this and all pianos. For they had been his voice for most of his thirty-nine years. His world would soon go dark and his hands would never again grace another instrument.

The mourners moved slowly. The shades were drawn. The clock struck midnight. Candles were clustered around his bed. He had worsened considerably. Blood trickled out of his mouth with every wrenching cough, followed by a gurgling, crackling sound as he struggled to return air to his lungs. His arms were slowly turning purple from being deprived of oxygen for so long.

Hardly bigger than a twig, he had been too weak to work much since our debilitating trip to England last year. In the months that followed, students told me he would lie on the couch while they played. One said he remained like that the entire lesson unless he became irritated, especially if the pupil took rhythmic liberties, such as using rubato on more than one measure. He demanded purity from his pupils. No adding what he called *smalec,* which I took to mean excessive sentimentality. He never wanted his music to sound mawkish.

Every note of his compositions had a point. There was no padding. "Keep elbows close to the sides," he would say, "and use only finger touch, no weight from the arm." If a student violated these rules, he would jump up and push the person off the stool to demonstrate *"la méthode Chopin."* Then he would return to the divan, pale, perspiring, gasping for air, and ask, "Who taught you to play like that?"

To worsen his situation that year, his servant, Daniel, a dim and unpleasant man from Italy, had been too profligate with Chopin's money, had stolen it, really. He had spent it with abandon and whittled down Chopin's savings. Now the composer was indigent, sick, and dependent on his friends to support him. Fortunately, they did this gladly.

His remaining hours turned into minutes. Mourners huddled beside him. Each person wanted to be the last to touch him.

It was well past midnight. He lay still as each person said parting words. His clouded eyes slowly opened and closed, each breath a victory. It was my turn. I sat by his side and whispered his name. As if some spirit suddenly overtook him, he looked at me: "Delhomme!" he said in a raspy voice.

I begged him not to speak. I feared he had only a few breaths left.

Then he said, "Aurore?" as if expecting to conjure her up with his words. I was not sure how to respond. Was he delirious? He repeated her name. Perhaps, I had misunderstood their relationship. Though Chopin often spoke bitterly about her, it seemed they had a bond that transcended malice. I now saw I had erred in confiscating Mme Marliani's letter. Sand had every right to know he was ailing.

"Madame Sand will not be coming, Monsieur," I said, delaying the inevitable confession of my theft of the letter. Not mailing it seemed a good decision at the time, but now I had to answer for it.

"*C'est toi, Aurore?*" he said, feverishly tossing his head back and forth. "Do you still love me?"

"She has no idea you are sick," I said. Chopin held my gaze for a long time, trying to absorb what I had said. "I never told her."

There. I said it.

But he did not seem to understand. "Where is Aurore?"

"She never heard about your illness," I repeated.

He searched my face, as if fighting to see through a veil, trying to assess the import of such an admission.

"I want her," he repeated. Then, he slipped into a daze again, his empty eyes turned upward. He would not last much longer. It was possible he was not even aware I was there.

By throwing away Mme Marliani's letter, I had ensured that George Sand would not learn that Chopin was *in extremis*. Was I right to deny her the opportunity to say goodbye? If I agreed with that, then I should have also admitted to turning into the very person that the diners at Nohant thought I was: an ignorant intruder. I was mortified at my own conduct.

"Delhomme," he whispered, rousing his head, then lowering it slowly. I stroked his hair ever so gently. He opened his mouth as if to speak but no sound came out.

"Please, please forgive . . . ," but my words caught in my throat. I could not continue. I took his hand as lightly as possible. He winced but did not pull away. "Let us not part as enemies." My tears fell on his wrist. A salty absolution.

He paused, inhaled to speak: "*Pierścień, pierścień.*" His voice drifted off and exhaled for the last time.

"Monsieur!" I said loudly, as if that would call him back. I held his hand a few more seconds, too stunned to accept that he had slipped away.

I was jolted out of my thoughts when Father Jełowicki, Chopin's childhood friend, asked for my seat to begin his ritual. I put my hand on his shoulder. "Father, what does . . . ," I began, but he shook it off. He crossed himself and tended to his duties. I would get a translation later. *Pierre's chin, Pierre's chin*, it sounded like. I repeated it a thousand times.

For three or four hours after his death, mourners wept and prayed. Our numbness was pierced when two photographers barged into the apartment. I did not recognize the trespassers.

"Excuse me, gentlemen," I said. "No uninvited guests."

The larger of the two men put down his camera equipment and looked at me. "We are here to take photos of the deceased."

The "deceased." Had he referred to Chopin by name, I might have relented. "And on whose directive have you come?"

They looked at one another. The shorter man said they had heard a famous man had died and wanted to record his passing for "posterity." Before I could respond, they pushed me out of the way, grabbed the four posts, and began shoving the bed toward the window—with Chopin still in it!

"Whatever are you doing?" I said.

"We need to catch the first light," the one said.

Repositioning the death bed to take photographs of someone they did not know while he was still warm was too macabre to countenance.

"No, no, no! You will not catch any light! And you may *not* move his bed!" I said in raised voice. I pushed the vultures toward the door and hurried them out. The audacity!

## Sunrise

Morning sun leaked around the edges of the drawn blinds, lightening the room. The mood changed from sorrow to practicality. Solange arrived with Auguste Clésinger, her sculptor husband, to make a cast of his face and hands. This act we found more appropriate. At least he knew Chopin. When I saw the finished death mask, I was pleased it captured a face free of pain. Surely Clésinger had doctored it, and with good reason: No one wanted to remember his agony, only his elegance and style.

The cast revealed a surprisingly small hand. His piano students told me they, too, were astounded how he could play the wide intervals that he himself had penned.

"Fingering," his answer. "Raise the fingers high, then the thumb will pass by the action of the muscles alone," I heard him instruct one young pupil. "Watch," he would say as he demonstrated. "Pass the third or fourth finger over the fifth. You can then be prepared for the most difficult scales and arpeggio passages without effort."

With such attention to detail in his instructions, I was dumbstruck when a few weeks ago, Adolf Gutmann, his favorite student whom I had seen at the Blanqui meeting, stated his intention to destroy Chopin's unfinished manuscript about his piano teaching theories and methods.

"How can you do such a thing, Adolf?" I said. "What purpose will it serve?"

"It was his wish, Delhomme," he said.

I asked if he could at least take some notes or summarize the content. I was frantic about such a trove disappearing forever. After all, Chopin's music came to life through his own techniques. "I have learned his technique," he said. "Perhaps someday I can write it all down."

I turned away to hide my shock. Gutmann was indulging in fantasy to think he even came close to imitating Chopin's style, what with his prize-fighter's fists and sensibilities of a bricklayer. And he even had this manuscript! Emulating Chopin meant a keen knowledge of harmonic change, modulation, rhythmic transformation, and especially ornamentation, not just getting the notes and fingering right.

Gutmann had a bad reputation within the Parisian music world. We knew he ranked as Chopin's pet student, but no one fathomed why. He thumped the piano with no regard for his teacher's tastes. Other students were roundly chastised if they played that way. Accordingly, he felt he alone could wear the mantle of Chopin's legacy. Nonetheless, I was heartsick at the prospect of burying these gems along with their creator.

"Where is the manuscript now?" I asked.

"Chopin said it was among his things," he said.

*What things?* I wondered. He had brought so few items to this apartment, I wondered if it had inadvertently been left behind or stored in a special place?

Dr. Jean Cruveilhier, Chopin's trusted physician, came to oversee the transport of the body to the medical college where he taught.

"May I accompany him?" I said.

"Let him make this last journey alone," he said. "Besides, we do not allow observers during the autopsy."

In that, I had no interest! The doctor assured me he would give his heart to Ludwika, as Chopin had requested.

Now, with the sun well into the sky and Chopin and his mourners gone, I perused the apartment for any valuables left behind, just as I had when my own father died. I found his pink kid gloves, along with a memorandum-book for the last year on a shelf in a small closet. I opened it and out fell a blue silk envelope embroidered with the initials GF, George and Frédéric, I presumed. Inside was a folded piece of cream-colored paper with the inscription "Hair of George Sand." I was tucking it into my breast pocket when the door opened.

*Not more photographers,* I thought.

No, it was a team of people to remove the bedding and clean the apartment. As the two men dragged the mattress off the frame, a sheaf of papers bound with a ribbon fell on the ground. The manuscript! He must have worked on it in his waning days.

I leafed through the pages. He suggested playing Bach's Fugues, Hummel's compositions, and Clementi's *Gradus ad Parnassum*. "Training in these composers will befit training for my own works as well," he said.

I read further: "The thumb has to be accommodated for every piece. If one plays a scale, it must reach under the other finger easily. If it cannot, then the passage will be uneven. That is unacceptable. Maintaining the tranquility of the hand is imperative. No tension! . . . Trills are to be done with three fingers, four if practicing."

One student told me that Chopin made him play scales with a lot of sharps before he even tried C major with none because that scale gave the hand no way to pivot onto the next white key. And that also explained why he composed pieces with so many flats and sharps to help him negotiate the keyboard and compose what he wanted.

These pages were spun gold, in my opinion, his gift to the world that should never be destroyed. I tucked the papers under my arm. The envelope I would return to Sand, the manuscript to Adolf, never!

After the autopsy, the body was taken to a funeral home and embalmed.

On the third day after his death he was laid out amid tiers of flowers, so a few of his closest friends and relatives could say goodbye in private. I looked for the last time at his curled hair around a pale, expressionless face. I tucked his pink kid gloves beside his body. It would not do for the great Chopin to arrive in heaven without them.

## Rest

Late October weather usually brought snow flurries or worse. But today, on this sad day of Chopin's funeral, the sun sparkled, belying our grief. The façade and doors of the stately Church of the Madeleine were draped in black velvet adorned with the composer's initials in silver embroidery. Close friends and family made the arrangements and issued black-bordered cards to limit attendees. In addition to the nearly four thousand seated in the pews, thousands more uninvited mourners stood outside. Coachmen in their smart liveries jammed the streets from the church all the way to Place de la Concord. Sand was invited but did not come.

Solange was inconsolable. My handkerchief was soaked before the funeral began. "He was my salvation," she told me once. Chopin had accepted her as she was, unlike her mother, who called her "queen of sloths."

That was just one of many insults Sand leveled at her. Chopin's admiration was returned in full measure. He reveled in her attention. She would come to his room to read or eat candy and listen while he composed. Solange was special. Maurice, on the other hand, was Sand's favorite. Chopin found him flat and boring, creating yet another rift between the two lovers.

Mourners listened to Chopin's Sonata in B-flat Minor from his own funeral march as they found their places. As the casket was placed in the mausoleum, Mozart's *Requiem* began. He had requested it, unaware it would delay the service almost two weeks. Women were not allowed to sing in parish churches. After much pleading and negotiating by powerful friends, female singers, most notably mezzo-soprano soloist Pauline Viardot, sang behind a black velvet curtain. Chopin loved singing. He thought the human voice was the most beautiful of all instruments. Pallbearers included two Polish princes, two musicians, Eugène Delacroix, and Camille Pleyel. The six men carried the coffin up the aisle to the strains of Chopin's preludes in E Minor and B Minor. Many attendees had heard Chopin play those very pieces in their own homes. After the service, the organist played a voluntary of themes from his works, while the subdued crowd left the church.

The cortège wended its way toward Père Lachaise cemetery, some three miles from the church. His English friend, Jane, and Ludwika sent their carriages on ahead and walked. Hundreds joined them in silence. Chopin asked to be buried in between the great Italian musicians Vincenzo Bellini and Luigi Cherubini. His sister sprinkled a cup of Polish dirt over his casket as it was lowered. Mourners threw in garlands and flowers as the gravedigger went about his work. As requested, there were no pronouncements over his body. He was buried under a fine marble marker with weeping Euterpe sitting atop. Clésinger had chiseled a handsome profile of the composer into the side. A grand tribute, indeed.

His heart, preserved in cognac, was smuggled under Ludwika's cloak to avoid questions at the border and delivered it to Warsaw's Church of the Holy Cross. How telling that he left his body in France but sent his heart to Poland.

Our souls had been stitched together, Chopin's and mine. Now, death had rent that bond. In the following weeks, I met my work obligations only out of habit. Food was tasteless, sleep was broken. For months afterwards, I visited his grave and laid flowers atop the growing mound. At times, I would stand across from his apartment on Place Orléans expecting a mazurka or nocturne to float out.

In the aftermath of that emotional day, one mystery remained: Chopin's final words, "Pierre's chin." After church on the Sunday following the funeral, I found Abbé Aleksander Jełowicki, who had given Chopin last rites.

"Oh, yes, it means 'ring,'" he said. "Why do you ask?"

I explained that those were his last words to me. "Do you know the ring he was referring to?"

"Chopin told me he received a diamond ring from a tsar a long time ago. I know of no other," said the priest. "He never wore jewelry."

What a strange thing to mention as one is dying. But I was certain it had everything to do with Chopin wanting me to have it. Why else would he have said that on his death bed? My next step was to explain to Sand why the ring meant so much to me. I had dim hopes that she would accept such an explanation. Then I remembered the envelope with her lock of hair. This seemed a plausible trade-off for the ring. I planned to set up a meeting with her soon.

# CHAPTER 33

# George Sand's Diary – Sorrow

Dear Diary,

Dear Chopin has died. I do not recognize these emotions. They are pitching back and forth in my chest. They leave me spent. I can identify sadness and loss. But the other feelings are knotted together. Anger. Frustration. Relief. How can these live side by side with my love, even though that love has long since been extinguished?

I was ambivalent when we lived together. We had a rare, rare understanding of one another at a fundamental level. No language required. Once my heart was captured, reason was shown the door, deliberately and with a sort of frantic joy. I accepted everything. I believed everything. No struggle, no suffering, no regret or false shame.

We were artists, he an extreme type. He made a single instrument speak the language of infinity. His music was full of nuance and the unforeseen. Sometimes, it was mysterious, even tortured. Although he had a horror of what could not be understood, his excessive emotion carried him away, without his being aware of it, to regions known to him alone.

Perhaps I was a bad guide for him (he would consult me the way Molière consulted his housekeeper). I identified with every fiber of my being.

He was devoured by the dream of an ideal. He accepted nothing of reality, both his vice and virtue, his grandeur and his misery. He was the same in friendship, enthusiastic at first sight, then becoming disgusted and correcting himself. He lived on infatuations for those who were the object of them, and on secret discontents which was an exception in his life. We respected each other's creativity and need for solitude. But his illness often overtook him and caused him to be irritable and unpleasant company. That was why he was never a refuge for me in my own sadness.

When he was angry, it was alarming. We had cross words with one another only once, but he always restrained himself around me, treating me with devotion, kind attention, grace, obligingness, and deference.

As time went on, though, I began doubting he really knew me. He just wanted to be around someone—*anyone*—so as not to be alone. My friends who collected at Nohant and at my apartment in Paris came there to be with other like-minded people—people who peeled back the mundanity of life and the callous disregard most have for its rich fabric. Many complain about work. But work is not man's punishment. It is his reward and his strength and his pleasure.

My children and my country must come first. Chopin never understood that. I must fight for their rights or die trying. My pen is my voice. I know people blame me for fomenting revolution in the same way Chopin's piano was his power, urging fellow Poles to revolt against repressive tsars and demand civil liberties. We shared those passions so there was never anything that needed to be said when thinking about our countries.

But Chopin never knew the bliss of having children, nor the selflessness it engenders in parents. That is why I became so angry when he split Solange off from me and sided with her. How dare he, after what I did for him! I shared his bed before he became a consumptive wraith. Even then I nursed and coddled him as if he were my child. I owed him that.

I am angry that he died. I miss him dearly.

# Quarrel

## Quarrel

*I*t had been some years since that stormy dinner at Nohant, but I still rankled at Sand's treatment of me and, more importantly, for her part in Chopin's death. She had tossed him aside like wilted lettuce when she decided he was no longer useful.

To be fair, Mme Sand could not be blamed entirely for his decline. He neglected his diet and stayed out late after teaching seven, sometimes eight, students each day. England's foul air worsened the deterioration, although Paris' skies were equally foul. That did not excuse the humiliation he endured from her indiscretions with other men, the loss of the emotional mooring, and the abandonment in his fragile state. He never returned to Nohant after that summer. Their breakup was official the following year. He ate poorly after that and slept little. In two short years, he would be dead.

Despite my antipathy for Sand and her bluestocking temperament, I finally saw her wisdom in supporting workers. Witnessing the way M. Broadwood exploited his employees was a triumph of greed bested only by the indentured slavery of the orphans. How could I, in good conscience, not protest these injustices? After all, anyone who bought, played, or tuned pianos made at his factory had profited from the misery of the underpaid workmen and abused children, not the least of whom was my nephew. I could no longer look away. That visit had shaken me out of my self-serving cocoon of ignorance when witnessing their suffering.

I decided to ask Sand's advice about how I could help the cause. Only mutual animus stood in the way. She had fought for workers' rights, then turned around and contemned me. Her behavior mirrored the same dichotomy in my father: He cherished his fellow man yet chided me for being weak and stupid.

But how to lure her out of her lair? Since Chopin's death a month ago, she had retreated to the shadow of her quill. No longer involved in politics—she even turned down a nomination to the National Assembly—it was hard to believe she had abandoned her cause entirely, since much needed doing.

With trepidation, I wrote asking to meet the next afternoon at l'Égyptien café near her home in the ninth arrondissement, about a twenty-minute walk from mine. I said I had something that belonged to her but did not mention the embroidered envelope. To my surprise, she replied with a curt acceptance.

L'Égyptien had only ten tables. Its windows had frosted over, but inside was warm and fragrant with tempting delicacies like *petites brioches* and *pains au chocolat*. Each table was covered with a blue and white checkered cloth. I hung up my overcoat and summoned the waiter to bring a pot of chamomile tea with honey and almond madeleines. It comforted me to eat food that put me in mind of my cherished friend.

I fidgeted with my serviette and smoothed the cloth under the vinegar and oil carafes several times. A young couple gazed intently at each other in the corner. The walls were painted with murals of Egypt—the sphinx, the pyramids, a caravan of camels. On such a cold day, these desert scenes should have warmed me, but today, my flushed face came from the rage I felt when Sand demeaned me in front of Chopin and her friends.

Today, I hoped both of us could put away that rancor for now. I was no Blanquist, but my experiences at the piano factory and orphanage had opened my eyes to the oppression of the voiceless. I wanted to ask her how to resist the new government. I feared she would see my change of heart on politics as a ploy. But about that, I was sincere. The initialed blue envelope could act both as a gesture of good will and, I hoped, an inducement to give me the ring in exchange.

After twenty minutes, just before I gave up hope, the door opened and in came a young man. I erroneously assumed he wanted to purchase baked goods. But rather than approaching the pastry counter, he walked directly to my table, took off his hat, and told me that a woman was waiting for me outside and would I please meet her there.

I did not take my coat, hoping my shivering would persuade her to come inside. Sand sat in a coach across the street. She gave an anemic wave with a gloved hand to beckon me. As I neared, she, without any greeting, put the door ajar, stuck out her hand, and asked for the object I had promised her.

I told her I wanted to discuss other things. "Please come in. It's frightfully cold out here."

She seemed irritated. "No, you get inside the coach." It was clear she wanted to do this on her terms.

Bundled in a black wool cape and matching felt hat, she looked less like a famous author and more like a charwoman who emptied ashes for a living. She appeared tired and unkempt. Perhaps she did not find it necessary to dress in special attire just to meet me.

She said impatiently. "So, Monsieur, what is it that you want to return?"

"Madame Sand," I said, shaking from the November cold, "could we please go inside? I have ordered tea. This conversation would be so much more pleasant in the warmth. Besides, I left the item in the café."

Begrudgingly, she told the driver to wait for a few minutes.

I held the café door open. She entered in her queenly way.

"*Garçon*," I said, "*encore une tasse pour la madame.*"

She held up her hand, "*Merci*, I will not be staying long." She stood by the table, expectantly.

"Please, Madame. Have a seat."

She hesitated.

"*Asseyez-vous, s'il vous plait*," I repeated with emphasis and motioned to the white metal chair.

She removed her hat and coat. As she sat, Chopin's ring swung from a chain around her neck. Spleen cascaded through my body. I was unprepared for that reaction. Why would she wear a souvenir from a past lover? Then, I remembered I too had taken my father's watch and Saint Raphael medal as keepsakes. Perhaps we both wanted to honor something we admired in their owners, even though the relationship was fraught with anger and shame. I stayed focused on my task.

The waiter brought the cakes and teapot. I poured a cup and handed it to her. She accepted it. Turning down hospitality was rude, although that had never stood in her way before.

We sat in silence for a minute, sipping and eating. "I believe we have much in common now," I said.

"Oh?" she said, challenging my opinion.

I recounted the atrocities I had seen at the piano factory, the children working there, the brutal fifteen-hour workdays while the owner lived in a mansion and rode in luxurious cabriolets pulled by matching horses. Meanwhile, workers walked home, fell asleep, then returned the next day to repeat the relentless grind.

"Seen the light, have you?" she said, with an edge, then sighed. "I have given up trying to influence political events. Besides, even after two of France's bloodiest fights this year, we still have a Napoléon in charge. He will end up giving sugar to the rich and a whip to the poor. Mark my words."

Louis Napoléon had gone from political exile in London, where I had met him with Vidocq, to the newly installed Prince Président of France's Second Republic. Despite lip service to bettering the plight of the destitute, he did nothing, and what's more, he restricted male voting rights and even implemented a three-year residency requirement before voting privileges were bestowed. He never uttered a word about women's suffrage.

"Some republic," she said. "Twenty thousand people killed in protest of the government," she said, drumming her fingers, "and this is our lot now."

I nodded and sipped, trying not to stare at the ring. "You sound defeated," I said.

She folded her arms as if closing herself off.

"Did you know I brought my orphaned nephew back from England?"

Yes, she knew. Chopin must have told her.

"Did you know he was killed by a National Guardsman? Dead at sixteen."

She knew that, too. "My sympathies to your family."

I looked for a sign that she saw a connection between the violence and her inciting words. *She* had fomented the rage that led to the chaos but uttered not a word of sympathy. Again, I had to quash my vitriol if I was going to gain her cooperation.

"Are you still writing about politics?" I asked.

"I write what I want," was her clipped response. She said the secret police were flushing out and punishing provocateurs. She had little incentive to put herself in jeopardy by writing any more instigative tracts.

*My nephew died because of her actions*, I thought, further incensed. I sipped my tea to wash down the bile at her abdication of responsibility. "Tell me, Madame," I began in what I hoped was a civil tone, "what else did you do to further the workers' cause?"

I must not have succeeded. She looked at me, "Are you implying, Monsieur Delhomme, that I did not contribute enough?" Her dark eyes flashed.

I had to dam my ire, so I began anew to broach the subject of politics. I wanted to learn from her, see what her thinking was. "You wanted equality for all people, correct?" I wanted so badly to launch off into a diatribe about her self-righteousness, what with her own servants and fancy lifestyle. I thought it a fair question. After all, *I* had gone to England and witnessed the workers' dreadful conditions. *I* had brought home an orphan to give him a better life. What exactly was her contribution other than whipping people into a mutinous frenzy? But I stayed mum. Impertinence would not serve my purpose. "What have you done besides write about inequality, Madame Sand?" I said without rancor. I must have missed the mark again.

She blinked back disbelief at my comment. *She* was the great George Sand, respected author known throughout France and beyond. "How dare you question the sincerity of my intent," she said. "Now please give me what you promised to return, and I shall take my leave."

"*Je m'excuse,* Madame." I used my most conciliatory tone to win her onto my side. "I merely wanted to find out how I can help fight the resistance."

"Oh, come now, Monsieur Delhomme," she said. "Do you really think I am so easily manipulated by your tawdry sweet talk? You had nothing but contempt for my position at Nohant."

She had called my bluff

I *wanted* to accuse her of doing nothing, of retreating into her writing. Nothing about those uprisings had touched her. She had remained an un-apologetic patrician, who felt entitled to treat others beneath her social status as hoi polloi. So haughty, so self-righteous. I had no recourse but to confess my real aim.

I said in a tone much milder than my thoughts, "I want justice for my nephew."

"Then you have come to the wrong person." She slouched back into her chair and sighed. "I quit."

"What do you mean, you 'quit'?"

"I have no more fight in me," she said. "You will have to find your own way to avenge him."

"Why did you refuse to run for election to the Assembly? You could have helped change laws to protect the working class and help women."

"Have you taken note, Monsieur, that the legislators are *all men*?" she said through tight lips. "I would be nothing but a curiosity to amuse them, even if I wore a dress. They would have as much regard for women's issues as a pack of wolves arguing about the rights of the poor little lamb," she waved me off. "What else but futility would await me?"

*Futility, yes, but also a fresh stable of lovers, perhaps?* I thought but did not say.

Aware she would not budge, I changed the subject. "What did you think of Chopin's funeral?" I asked.

She turned her head aside as if to deflect the question. "I had no idea he was sick."

*Absurd!* I thought. She had kicked him out of her bed *because* he had been a millstone cramping her debauched lifestyle. Even as she housed and fed him, she went swanning about looking for other men to bed. And bed them she did. Right under his nose! No loyalty. No conscience. And all the while keeping his ring.

"What is it that you really want from me, Monsieur Delhomme? Respect? Admiration?" She held my eye as she stroked the ring like a talisman. "I loved Chopin. Yes, he was ill, and I cared for him, but he left me. I thought of nothing else but his welfare day and night," she said, her face reddening. "His care became too much for me. I am not a nurse!" She started to get up.

I knew one reason they had parted. Chopin had taken Solange's side in a terrible row between Sand and her daughter over excesses in spending. Yet other gossipry said that she saw Solange as a seductress angling for Chopin's affections. Ultimately, Sand accused Chopin of having an affair with Solange. Whatever the reason, she then terminated relations with her daughter and never forgave Chopin.

I pushed aside my tea and cleared my throat. Just as I opened my mouth to deliver my unvarnished opinion of her actions, she stood and began gathering her belongings. The owner rushed out of the kitchen wiping his hands on an apron tied around his waist.

"Madame Sand," he said with strained smile, "would you care for anything more?"

"*Non, merci!*" Sand said sharply. "My coach is waiting."

"One more thing, Madame. Why did you keep the ring if you fell out of love?" I said, agitated.

"I have no need to explain anything to you, Monsieur Delhomme." She put on her coat. "What went on between Chopin and me is private." She squinted her eyes and asked, "Why are you so interested in that ring? Were you his lover too?"

That was it. I jumped up. My chair fell back. I laid the embroidered envelope with the strands of her hair on the table and pushed it toward her. "Here," I said. "This belongs to you." My fingers remained on the envelope a few moments. *Should I? Should I take what is rightfully mine? I had remained loyal, she had not. Besides, he had offered it to me first. What right did she have to this jewel when she treated him like an annoyance?*

She leaned over to take the envelope. I yanked the ring from her neck.

Her mouth flew open in surprise.

I had finally gotten the ring—and her power of speech.

I snatched my coat and left the café clutching the diamond ring as blowing snow stabbed my cheeks. Whether it was a fair trade was of no interest to me. Chopin meant for me to have it. *Pierścień*, he had said on his deathbed. *Pierścień*.

## CHAPTER 35

# Arrest

## Arrest

*T*he death of both Chopin and Marc pulled me into a crushing despond. My marriage to Lili did lighten some of those pockets of gloom. She had made steady progress since our wedding and now walked without aid but slowly. We wanted children, lots of them, and now, finally, at thirty-four, in demand for my skills across the city, I could support them. I wanted to settle into my home life, attend concerts, and look at my precious Lili by firelight. We had tried, so far unsuccessfully, to conceive. That too darkened my hopes for the future.

Hope for a democracy had also dimmed to nothing by now. The so-called Second Republic had restricted male suffrage yet more, and working conditions remained as punishing as ever. So, we had returned to the same sad situation before the bloodshed. All those deaths for naught. Like Sand, I too had abandoned the idea of fighting the government. What was the use? Its power was too great. And to think that I had betrayed my beliefs all for the love of money. I had not heard from Vidocq since I was ordered to visit the fat woman in the market. I hoped he had seen that my interest and need for his money was waning. Let him find another gullible mark.

In the music world, people hungered more than ever to hear Chopin's works. Many pianists attempted to emulate him, but for those who had heard him play, these imitations fell short. Adolf Gutmann played all his music, perhaps not brilliantly but serviceably. How could anyone else succeed when even Chopin was often unsatisfied with his own performances? Perfection was an elusive goal for him, especially when its definition kept changing. What was acceptable one day was dross the next.

Of course, Gutmann never knew I had Chopin's manuscript about theory and technique. So, I assiduously studied the instructions in his manual:

> "Fingering is everything. It is difficult to describe here, but he must practice all patterns so there is no inequality of sound, especially in a very fast scale. So, if the beginner is being taught that fingering is not important, he needs to remedy that attitude, especially if he intends to play my compositions. Fingering is calculated to attain results. Often my students tell of teachers encouraging them to treat their fingers as if they were little hammers. Fingers are not hammers! They are individual digits of varying length and strength. But they must not be considered a percussive instrument. Other basics, such as use of the pedal and arm positioning, must be explained. Everything starts with technique."

Evenings before retiring, I redoubled efforts to improve my technique, but my fingers did not often seem acquainted with my mind. I wonder what he would have said if I had been his student.

My daily routine resumed: shop work in the morning, home visits in the afternoons. My chore for the day was to restring a harpsichord. I wanted to begin first thing. The morning started slowly. Lili was off visiting her ailing mother in Marainville. Already seven o'clock, I descended the stairs, yawning and stretching to ready my body of the labor ahead. I went to the kitchen to light the fire. I stacked some kindling and was just about to light it when someone pounded on the door. I expected to see Vidocq on the other side with another assignment. This time I would stand firm and tell him no—no more supporting this punitive government!

I opened the door, but instead of Vidocq, two men stood solemnly in the dark-blue uniforms of the royal constabulary.

"Good day, gentlemen."

"Are you Beaulieu Delhomme?" one said.

"I am."

"You are under arrest." One lunged toward me and grabbed my shoulders while the other pinned my wrists behind my back and trussed them with rope.

"What are you doing?" I struggled against their grasp, but it was futile. "What have I done wrong?"

"No idea," said the other.

I defended myself. "What about Monsieur Vidocq? He will vouch for me!" I said struggling against the restraints.

"He is the one bringing charges," said the first.

So Vidocq was exacting his pound of flesh. "Stop!" I commanded. "I have things that need doing. You have no right . . ."

"We have every right," the more rotund officer said as the pair pushed me outside and shoved me onto the bed of an empty, windowless police wagon. I tried to sit, but the coach lurched over the bumpy streets. I kicked the sides of the carriage and shouted, "Let me talk to Vidocq!" I shouted. "I must tell my wife where I am!" They ignored me because their job was not to reason with prisoners, only to deliver them to the jail. Hot tears burned my eyes when I realized there was no recourse now.

Soon came sounds of the wheels crossing the bridge to the Île de la Cité. Most certainly it was bound for the Conciergerie, the most brutal of all prisons in the city. Candidates for the guillotine had been sent there since the revolution. I was not sanguine about my prospects.

The wagon stopped. The door opened. I struggled as they pulled me feet first to the edge. With my arms still bound, they stood me on the ground. I kicked one in the shins.

In response, the man swore then trussed my ankles and dragged me, like a rolled-up carpet, down some steps, and across the stone floor through the vaulted-ceiling passageway to the booking room. One of them shoved me inside with his boot. "You can have him!" he said to the official, snarling.

A noisy, smelly place that area was, too. Prisoners shouting, officers manhandling suspects wearing bloody clothes and horrified looks. An officer removed my restraints and motioned to the seat. A grumpy man with several chins recorded my name, address, and occupation in a book, never glancing up once. How many thousands had sat in that chair, yearning to be seen as human?

The next room held gray and white striped garments made of nubby cotton.

"Strip," the man said, handing me my set. They were none too clean. Why bother? The next poor wretch would have to sit in a filthy cell anyway. My only concern was whether they had been worn by men at their execution. I unbuttoned my pants. They fell to the ground. I saw the Saint Raphael medal I always kept with me fall out of the pocket. I picked it up. "May I keep this?" I asked. I laid it on my palm to show him.

"No!" said the officer with finality. "No personal effects." He reached out to grab it. But I turned away and quickly swallowed it. He hurried from behind the table, pried my mouth open, and moved my tongue from side to side looking for it. He soon realized it had been sent southward. He grunted.

Now, name recorded and clothes changed, I was ushered down a long hall with cells on either side. The small, bent man took out a large key, opened the door, and gestured for me to enter.

"You're a lucky one, you are, to have your own room, at least for now. We need to move you as soon as they get rid of a few next door."

In other words, as soon as they carted them off to the scaffolds.

"Where is my bed?" I asked, naïvely.

"Bed is extra," he said.

"Extra what?"

"Money, of course. Eighteen francs a month. Pay in advance."

From what I had heard, no one stayed longer than a week before he was . . .

I could not even finish the statement in my own mind. He started to close the door, then added, "See that window?" He pointed to a small rectangular opening. "Beg for food through that. Unless someone can bring some." He threw a horsehair blanket at me. "Here." It smelled just like the pillow at Nohant and felt just as scratchy. It seemed insufficient for January's freezing temperatures.

The dirt floor was covered in fresh straw, my new "free" bed. The small window threw a patch of light on to the opposite wall for the nonce. But no amount of breeze coming off the Seine could rinse away the stench of dung.

I took shallow breaths as I paced. How could I get word to my beloved Lili? She would have no idea where I was.

What had I done wrong? I would soon be amid thieves, murderers, and rapists. No one could accuse me of any those crimes. My sins were but venial: unquenchable greed for Chopin's admiration, abusing his trust, spying on George Sand, stealing the ring from her (which really belonged to me), disappointing my father, not sending Mme Charlotte Marliani's letter to Sand alerting her of his dire state. But my loudest sobs were reserved for Lili. I had failed her. Indeed, even her injury was due to my relentless pursuit of Vidocq's money to achieve a better station in life. These transgressions rang in my ears, but none warranted imprisonment. Still, shame wrapped tightly around my soul.

Most merciful God, relieve me of this torment! Had I not saved Lili from that unreliable soldier and taken good care of her until now? Had I not cared for my mother and saved Marc from that abominable orphanage? I had applied myself to become a respected tuner and tried my best to help workers to regain respect and improve their lot. Yes, I disobeyed Vidocq's orders, but it was in the service of the workers. How could he know I had done that?

After some time, I lay trembling, more out of fear than cold.

The sun was high by the time an official came to read me the charges. He spoke through a hole in the wooden door. "Delhomme, Beaulieu?" Once I confirmed my name, he came in, checked my name off a list, and looked at me, "You are in serious trouble. Treason, you know, is punishable by death."

"Treason?" I said, recoiling.

He looked again at the paper. "Looks as if you will be visiting our guillotine. One-way transport only." He looked up and winked. Gallows humor. I needed none of that now. "If you want the executioner to sharpen the blade, it will cost you." He pointed to his palm and raised his eyebrows. I never could have asked Lili for such an execrable favor.

I had gone from stringing a harpsichord to facing execution, all within a half day. "When did I supposedly commit this treason? And against whom?" I asked.

He brought the paper close to his eyes. "Club meeting, it says here, with August Blanqui. Something about preparing to overthrow the government?" He seemed uncertain.

Now I was convinced there was something amiss. Only two people knew I had attended that meeting: Gutmann and Vidocq. Adolf seemed an unlikely tattler. If he had told, he would have been charged with treason himself. But I heard nothing of his imprisonment. How could I be blamed for doing something I was ordered to do? Vidocq had *paid* me to carry it out. Then it struck me: It must have been George Sand! How vindictive she was just because I had stolen that ring. I was hardly surprised, given the callous way she treated her own daughter. But then I remembered the officer had said Vidocq was the one bringing charges. Confusion reigned.

"It also says here," the man squinted, "that you took part in an insurrection in June . . ."

"That is false! I never participated in any insurrection!"

The jailer held up his hand, leaned outside the door, and motioned to someone. In stepped Vidocq, the ubiquitous spy, wearing that same self-congratulatory grin.

The man handed him the papers. Vidocq turned to me and continued reading, "Second, you refused to meet with Louis Napoléon. Third, and worst of all, you failed to *accurately* report an assassination attempt of Louis-Eugène Carvaignac. Yes, Delhomme, it was a trick. I told you to gather intelligence at the market. The men said it would happen on *Sunday*, not Monday, which is what you told me. You lied. I had suspected your disloyalty for many months. And now you will get your comeuppance." I began to protest, but he just spat on me and left.

I stood stunned. It would have been pointless to argue. I needed to convince the judge of my innocence.

I was weak from hunger. I stuck my hands out the window into the cold wind to beg for sustenance. After an hour or so, a kind passerby gave me a boiled potato and some moldy camembert. I willed myself to eat all of it. The hunger pangs subsided. Now my mind was clearer to wonder about Lili. What would she think when she came home to find me gone? There was no way she could know I was in jail. What would happen to her after I was gone? I agonized about that more than my own fate.

The endless boredom was interrupted at sunset with the arrival of five new prisoners. More came the next day, making thirteen of us. I hunkered in my corner atop the matted, damp straw, not daring to converse with anyone. What does one say to a murderer or thief or kidnapper? What should I have replied when asked about my violation? 'I was a spy against the monarchy,' I could say. Better I admitted to rape or arson, something they would understand.

After an uncertain number of days, stinking, and starving, I opened my rheumy eyes one morning to the old, stooped jailer saying through the door slot: "Beaulieu Delhomme?" I slowly raised my hand. He opened the door and waved me out. "Off with you. Trial starts today."

# Trial

## Trial

My addled brain reckoned it was mid-January by this time. I was led into the courtroom and taken to the defendant's box. Blessedly warm, well lit, and clean, this place, with its majestic marble floors and gilded doorways, made me blink back the glare. France had gotten used to such flagrant displays that defined divisions between power and poverty. Both the prosecuting and defending attorneys were dressed in black robes. The judge, with his groomed white moustache and matching powdered peruke, peered down from his large desk high above the proceedings.

I scanned the audience to find a familiar face. My eyes fell on Lili. She was sitting in the front row. "Lili!" I cried out. She held out her arms. Her face was streaked with tears.

Some charges were read aloud and my "not guilty" plea was noted. The defense attorney, whom I had never spoken to, wasted no time in calling the first and only character witness, Hector Berlioz. I was so happy to have someone speak in my defense. Dressed in a fine suit, he looked natty and serious, despite his tangle of hair.

"You will find no more loyal, genuine, earnest individual anywhere," the composer said. I winced at his hyperbole. "Monsieur Delhomme and I have been friends for many years. We went to medical school together," he said, nodding to reassure me.

But the prosecutor was not about to let that affirmation stand and sprang to his feet. "But, Monsieur Berlioz, neither of you is a doctor, am I right?" the prosecutor said.

"No, but that does not diminish him . . ."

The judge interrupted him: "Excuse me, Monsieur Berlioz. That is not for you to decide."

Then the defense attorney asked: "Do you know, Monsieur, if the defendant attended a meeting where Auguste Blanqui spoke?"

Hector said, "He never mentioned it," and looked at me apologetically because he could not do more to bolster my case.

"But just because you do not know . . ."

Hector stood up in the witness box, and said forcefully, "I am certain Monsieur Delhomme is innocent of all charges! He was the tuner for Frédéric Chopin, for God's sake. He would never betray his country!" he said, thrusting his finger into the air. This theatrically impassioned outburst was pure Berlioz.

"Would you stake your life on that?" asked the judge.

Berlioz looked down. He could not, under oath, confirm that. He was excused. He paused by me and put his hand on the rail. We exchanged knowing looks as he took his seat.

The next witness was George Sand. She was dressed in a somber, black silk dress with a bejeweled crucifix providing the only color. She appeared drawn, fatigued, much as I had seen her at l'Égyptien a few weeks ago. I assumed she was testifying for the prosecution. Although our views on government policy were now aligned, we had not left on good terms.

So far, the trial had nothing to do with theft. Sand never mentioned that I had rummaged through her papers at Nohant. Apparently, only Chopin knew, and he must have kept silent. Of course, I did leave that telltale teacup by her desk. Surely, she had asked the kitchen staff whose it was. Or perhaps Chopin removed it. Whatever the case, I hoped she saw that our political views were now aligned. I was sincere in describing my political turnabout, from the overbearing behavior of Mr. Broadwood, his treatment of his workers, and my nephew's death. Such experiences tenderize the soul. She had to grant me that much.

The shifty-looking, gangly prosecutor approached the witness. "Good afternoon, Madame Sand."

She nodded.

"If I may begin by asking how you know the defendant, Beaulieu Delhomme," he said.

"Monsieur Delhomme and I shared an acquaintance with the composer Frédéric Chopin. He served as his piano tuner for many years."

"Did you know that Monsieur Delhomme attended a meeting of the Central Republican Society led by Auguste Blanqui?"

She paused, looked at me with those inscrutable dark eyes. "Yes. I knew. It was during the provisional government after the February uprisings in 1848."

"What was the business of that club?"

"Monsieur Blanqui's mission was to overthrow the government and gain a foothold for the insurgents."

"How do you know the contents of Blanqui's speech that night?" asked the attorney.

She straightened. "I know everything that goes on in this city."

Yet she claimed ignorance of Chopin's condition! She could not have it both ways. Her indignation rang hollow.

She then added, "I have always been attuned to politics. Monsieur Blanqui was too radical for my tastes. Yes, I advocated vociferously for the rights of women and workers, but I certainly never plotted to overthrow the government." She looked at the judge. "*Never* did I do that, and I hardly believe that the defendant was the sort who would either." No one surpassed Sand in expressing outrage.

"If you thought Blanqui was very radical—too radical even for you to attend his meeting—and you knew that Monsieur Delhomme was there, can you say for certain that he was *not* plotting to overthrow the government? In other words, was he there because he supported Blanqui or because he wanted to spy on him?"

She did not answer right away. "You are asking me to speculate on his reason for going to the meeting. I can speak only to his having been Frédéric Chopin's piano tuner and to his having attended the Blanqui meeting. About the object of his spying—whether it was for or against the king—I have no idea." She paused, then added: "He told me once that he very much supported the monarchy." She let that comment hang for others to think through.

I wondered why she never mentioned our recent meeting at l'Égyptien about my full-throated capitulation due to my nephew's poor treatment and death at the hands of a soldier. Was she trying to hide my possible motive? She was a complicated woman!

The prosecutor showed her a newspaper. "I have here an article you wrote only two months after the February 1848 uprising during the time of the Constituent Assembly:

"'If the elections do not ensure the triumph of social truth, if they are only the expression of interests of a caste, torn from a trusting people, then these elections, which should be the salvation of the Republic, will undoubtedly be its end. In that event, the only road to salvation for the people who raised the barricades would lie in their expressing their will a second time and setting aside the decisions of a body unrepresentative of the nation.'"

The prosecutor turned to her: "Are these not words to incite revolution—a coup d'état—that you so coolly said was beyond the pale?"

She leaned forward and held up a finger. "*Attendez*, Monsieur. You have omitted my final line," (which she quoted from memory): "Let us save the Republic at all costs. We still have it in our power to save it without schism and upheaval." She paused and sat back, looking self-satisfied, then added, "I will thank you not to twist my words, Monsieur," she said, her chin held high.

"My question to you, Madame, is this: Since you flocked with Communist birds, are you not then also a Communist like Blanqui? After all, he is in jail now for his radical views."

"Pray tell, Monsieur." She leaned forward, then said with a calm, measured but contemptuous voice, "Am *I* the one on trial here? Should I be persecuted for thinking that people should not be treated like chattel in the workplace? That they should have civil lives, be proud citizens of

France, and enjoy her fruits as do all others? If that is your accusation, sir, then lock me up!" She held out her wrists together for handcuffing.

The courtroom erupted in applause, which the judge had to gavel into silence.

Sand had flattened his implication that poor people deserve less and are inferior. It was a pitch-perfect diatribe.

Seeing he had been outsmarted, the lawyer said, "I am done with this witness, Your Honor." The judge turned to Sand, "You are excused, Madame."

But Sand squared her shoulders and persisted with one last comment. "Monsieur Delhomme has told me he now supports the Prince Président Louis Napoléon, who has shown great wisdom with his new policies."

That, of course, was a lie. But a good one and delivered at the right time. She and I both knew that this latest Napoléon would soon reveal his intention to return France to monarchical rule.

Again, my attorney stayed mute. Was he being paid by the prosecutor to scotch my defense?

The last witness was none other than François Vidocq. He swaggered satyr-like up to the witness box, wearing a black suit, white cravat, gold earrings, watch chain, diamond studs, and white glacé gloves. If this was supposed to be a disguise, it failed to mask his aging face, jowly cheeks, and squashed nose with flared nostrils. Some women discreetly fanned their nose to ward off the smell. Surely the courtroom would require fumigation from his foul breath and body odor. His wife must have the patience of Job to put up with him. He sat down, all five feet, six inches of him, with his thinning brown hair and buttonholes of his vest straining across his paunch. He smirked as his eyes swept across the audience, meeting mine at the last. I had no chance when the king's right-hand man prepared to lambaste my character and actions. My body went limp.

It was beyond me how the court system would think that Vidocq was anything approximating a reliable witness. He had robbed—even from his own family!—and been jailed numerous times. He changed allegiances as often as women change clothes. He drifted from the employ under Charles X to Louis Philippe to Lamartine. Now he was courting the favors of Prince President Louis Napoléon to employ him.

Those loyalties crossed a range of political ideas, none of them his own, I would wager. Given his opportunistic habits, I expected him to color himself in the best possible light regarding my situation. Surely, I was expendable, a means to aggrandize him and his vaunted detective agency. He had no morals, no cause, no loyalties. Vidocq's sole interest was Vidocq. His word, however, would still hold sway over all other testimony.

The prosecuting attorney smiled as he approached his star witness. His testimony would make short work of me, and he could be home in time for a hot meal of veal and dumplings.

"Good day, Monsieur Vidocq. The court appreciates your taking the time to help us today."

Vidocq flashed that ingratiating smile that had fooled me once.

"How do you know the defendant?"

"Monsieur Delhomme was in the employ of my detective agency for several years."

"For what purpose?"

"We were monitoring the comings and goings of various people."

"And by 'we' you mean who?"

"Why the government, of course." He grinned at the gallery as if he were giving a performance.

"Why did you think Monsieur Delhomme would be of any help?"

"Because Monsieur Delhomme was very poor, so we offered him a lot of money. And he was desperate for praise and attention which we gave him in full measure."

Cutting words. But I did not dare let any of that register on my face.

The prosecutor continued: "What was his assignment, exactly?"

Vidocq crossed his chubby legs and tugged at each finger of his gloves. He pulled them off and laid them on the railing of the witness box. He explained the dangers behind the disgruntled workers who rose up and the need to monitor the views of both the wealthy and the working class.

"Did the defendant execute his responsibilities faithfully?"

"In the beginning, yes, but always under protest. He said he wanted to stop working for me several times."

"And why was that?"

"Laziness, I assume."

What control I exhibited when he said that!

"And you gave him money in exchange for this service?"

"Correct."

"What exactly is your complaint, Monsieur Vidocq?"

"Often in my business some become counterspies. That was what Monsieur Delhomme did."

"So, the defendant willingly took your money and then promptly spied for the other side?"

"Yes."

"How do you know this?"

"Our first clue was his attendance at the club of Auguste Blanqui."

I stood up and shouted, "You lie, Vidocq! You *ordered* me to visit the Blanqui club. *You* wanted me to spy on him and his supporters!" I was certain now that Vidocq wanted to preserve his reputation. He could not very well have people disparage his skill as the supreme royal detective.

The judge rapped his gavel and warned me to be quiet. Two guards pulled me back into my seat.

The prosecutor continued: "As I understand it, Auguste Blanqui is in jail at this moment for his own illegal behavior during the time of the provisional government. True?"

"Yes," said Vidocq. "Blanqui's radical ideas were too threatening to the new Assembly. So, they imprisoned him—where he belongs, I might add."

"What other evidence do you have that Monsieur Delhomme was a counterspy?"

"The second time came in London, I sent him to meet with Louis Napoléon to find out whether he was coming back to France or staying in England. Monsieur Lamartine wanted to know."

Vidocq conveniently left out his disdainful thoughts about the House of Bonaparte's lust for power, something he had witnessed when Napoléon I crowned himself emperor when Vidocq was only twenty-four, only six years younger than the emperor himself.

"I waited for Delhomme to appear, but he never came. and I had to go find him. In my agency, an assignment is an assignment." He looked right at me, glaring, "And that, my friend, is *treason!*" He pointed his finger on the railing for emphasis. "This was an extremely important duty. Monsieur

Lamartine, who headed the provisional government at the time, needed that information to make further decisions."

"I see," said the attorney. "Go on."

"The third time, he knowingly fed me false information about a planned assassination of Louis Carvaignac. In fact, we had set it up as a loyalty test to see if he *would* report the information. He did not report it, at least, not accurately." He sniggered as he looked at his fingernails.

"Was there anything else?" prompted the prosecutor.

"Oh, yes," he said, leaning forward to deliver the fatal blow, "he participated in the June uprising. Ask him to show you the scar from his bullet wound. I know about it because my soldier had to shoot him in the leg when he saw him escaping."

I gasped. It was *his* man who shot me? Then surely it was *his* man who killed Marc! I leapt out of the defendant's box and charged Vidocq. "You killed my nephew! You killed Marc, you bastard!" I shouted as I grabbed his fleshy neck. "And, you beat my wife senseless too!" I began shaking his head back and forth.

The judge rapped his gavel. Lili screamed. I continued my tirade as the guards dragged me back to my chair and tied my hands to it: "Look at my poor wife. She can barely walk. Vidocq is a horrible man, Your Honor. *He* is the one who should be on trial for war crimes, not me!"

The judge called for silence a second time. When calm finally reigned, the prosecutor continued. "Monsieur Vidocq, what possible motive would the defendant have had to defy the government and risk the difficulty he is facing now?"

Vidocq lifted his chin to straighten his tie. "Fear. Spite. Remorse. Change of heart over the mission. Those are the usual reasons to subvert a government. Ask him yourself."

After being excused, the pudgy trickster picked up his gloves, got up, and glided back to his seat in the courtroom, quite amused with himself.

Vidocq's mendacious testimony and misdirection had hurt my case. Berlioz's words were hardly an antidote to such chicanery. And Sand's valiant attempt to scuttle the prosecution's cheeky questions ended up humiliating him but did not successfully discredit the charges against me. The judge called me to the witness box.

"Monsieur Delhomme," he began. "You have been accused of the heinous crime of treason against our government. Have you any words in your defense?"

"I am innocent, Your Honor," I said in a measured voice.

The courtroom exploded in laughter at my stock answer.

"What is your relationship with Madame Sand."

I paused. What *was* my relationship? It was best to paint it as neutral.

"Madame Sand and I have met on a few occasions. I was a guest" ... I had to steady my voice at that word ... "at Nohant, her manor house, and recently, we met at a café."

The judge continued: "What did you and she talk about at Nohant?"

"Economic hardships, the workers' predicament."

"Is that all?" asked the judge.

"I said that I feared that both Monsieur Chopin—in fact all artists, including Madame Sand—would suffer if the government were to take money away from the wealthy."

"And you and she fought over such views?"

"Disagreed, your Honor. Disagreed is more accurate."

"Is it correct to assume that you gave Madame Sand a reason to accuse you of treason?" he said.

"Not at all, Your Honor!"

What was not in dispute was my attendance at the club meeting. "Yes, I was there but I had no malign intent towards the government or anyone else. I went because I had been so ordered *by Vidocq*." I looked at the judge when I said that. Treason, this was not.

"What was your opinion of the government when this happened?" asked the judge.

"I supported the monarchy."

"But you then came to disagree with the new provisional government. Is that true, Monsieur Delhomme?" He peered over his spectacles. "You were afraid that the new liberal policies would destroy your livelihood."

I was growing increasingly frustrated. "*At that time* I believed that," I told him.

The gawky prosecutor summarized. "You were happy to take Vidocq's money when you favored the government? Is this correct?"

His words became jumbled in my starved brain. My forehead and hands grew damp. I trembled, then cried out, "My nephew died." Tears welled up. "Vidocq killed my nephew!"

"And?" prompted the prosecutor. "What may we understand from that tragedy?"

I tried to calm down to explain: "I was in favor of the monarchy before I was against it." This comment made more sense before it left my lips.

The prosecutor whirled around to face the audience to register his comedic reaction to the absurdity. "So, Monsieur Delhomme, you are conveniently switching sides now that your life is imperiled."

I was tongue-tied.

Guards returned me to my cell that afternoon. I was too numb with disbelief even to feel the cold floor. I could not even muster tears of self-pity. The other prisoners looked at me. No one asked about the trial: Everyone knew the charade would be perpetrated on them as well. They merely laughed and asked if Lili would come back with more food after I had gone. "I loved that cheese!" one joked.

I could not even muster a smile.

Such was the company I would keep for the last hours of my existence. Stinking, rowdy, crude outlaws. Perhaps they considered me of the same ilk. Nothing mattered now. I lay my head on the straw for a fitful night's rest.

# Final Hours

## Final Hours

The trial had ended. My fate was certain. Now, all I did each hour, each minute, in this cell was to weather the chaos, endure the smell, ignore my hunger, and blot out the fear of dying. Trying to control one's senses and thoughts took extraordinary effort. It helped to worry my father's Saint Raphael medal for hours with my thumb. I had retrieved the medal—with some ado—after having swallowed it in front of the guard. Its worn surface comforted me. My goal was to keep to myself, concentrate on the good, and sleep when I could for a blessed reprieve from my fate.

Such an aim was made difficult with men squeezing in and out of the cell. Some went to trial, others faced torture or the dread guillotine. As many as fifteen men had been packed into a twelve-square-foot cell at one time giving us hardly any room to sit. Fear saturated the air.

At night, we lay jammed together. No one could move lest we poke a neighbor. The only benefit was shared warmth. Before dawn, the man next to me kicked off his blanket and flailed his arms. "Get away from me! Get away!" he shouted in his sleep. "Shut up!" the others shouted back. Yes, we all needed rest for our busy day ahead sitting in our cell trying to fight off reality.

This same man had arrived late yesterday evening, just as we were arranging the straw to make a "pillow." He was stooped with a white beard and a few strands of hair that played on his bald head. His hands had blue veins that ran like ropes under translucent skin. He must have been at least sixty years old. He seemed confused of his whereabouts.

This morning, the old man sat next to me. He tugged at my sleeve. "I am so afraid of dying," he said, trembling. "Please talk with me."

I turned to look at him. "What about?" I said, irritated. "There are many other men here. Why choose me?" I had my own troubles.

"Because you have the face of an honest man," he said, looking at me with bloodshot eyes.

I softened. Could I not spend some of my last moments with him—one condemned man commiserating with another?

He told me he had been captured by a guardsman for betraying his country. "But I would never, *ever* betray my beloved France!" He said this as if I could influence authorities to pardon him. I put my hand on his as much to feel the warmth of another human as to comfort him. The world was cold, indeed.

That afternoon, the man clung to me as we marched to Bonbec Tower for the reading of the newspaper. No one spoke. It felt heavy and eerie, like the sullen mourners who moved as one behind Chopin's casket. The gendarme began handing down the acts of execution: "Jean de Ville, Gérard Cross, Beaulieu Delhomme..." His voice trailed off in my head. I expected this announcement, but now it was real. I sucked in my breath and broke through the crowd to steady myself against a wall. Tomorrow.

Now I needed to seek out the old man to comfort me. Where was he?

The hours wore on. Death was nigh. I wept, then stared into nothingness. I fought to stay awake to taste the last morsels of life. But worry soon overcame me. *What will become of Lili? Who will provide for her, love her, tell her she is so pretty? Life will be impossible for a widow.* My stomach churned with worry over her plight. *Will she ever forgive me?*

Morning came too soon. A jangle startled me. *Is it the turnkey with my shackles?* He entered. I pushed through the others to go to the far corner. He was here for one reason: to haul me off to the guillotine. "Go away!" I shouted and hid my face. I frantically reached for my Saint Raphael medal by the window and gulped it down. I wanted it with me when I died.

He neared. I cowered.

He reached around and grabbed my wrists. I struggled against his grasp, but I was too weak. He trussed my hands behind me with a twine that cut my skin. He led me down a long hallway and steadied me while we descended the stone stairway for my final ignominy: a haircut.

The barber sat me in a chair and hacked at my thick curls with his dull scissors to clear the nape for a clean cut. The rusty blades pulled at my roots. *Please, God, make the guillotine sharper than these scissors.*

The wagon was waiting. Two men heaved me in headfirst. One latched the back. The blinkered ox plodded along with no thought about my fate. It had no conscience, no way to judge what it was doing. I forgave it.

The other prisoners said the guillotine was preferable to hanging. It was more humane because it was quick. No dangling at the end of a rope for minutes on end as the life drained out of the ill-fated prisoner. The guillotine was thought to signify equality among citizens—royalty could die the same way everyone else did.

The logic of using 'humane' to describe any execution method escaped me. Whether something aimed at taking a life was humane or cruel seemed but an intellectual argument. For the hapless scoundrel awaiting beheading, no method had any merit.

I worked my way to a sitting position to peer over the edge of the wagon as we approached. The crowd—perhaps fifty or more—milled about while the executioner stood chest out, arms akimbo. *The blade will be the last thing I feel on this earth.*

The sun was blocked by rain clouds. The crowd quieted as the wagon drew up to the steps. My beheading was their theater. The back of the wagon opened, and I was pulled out feet first. Standing, hands tied, head down, I was led up the stairs. I felt one, then two, then more raindrops on my face. *God's tears.*

Several men placed me face down on the bench and guided my head through the lunette that would hold my neck still.

I tried to ignore the sight of the bloody basket below with a sweet memory of a late summer Marainville day, when cooler mornings melted into balmy afternoons. Feathery swallowtails with their yellow forewings and black tiger-like stripes, zigzagged across the blooming meadows.

Lili was still engaged to her soldier. But I longed to steal her heart. I had said nothing to her about my feelings, although such scorching ardor was hard to hide. Could she not feel its heat? For the time being, it was enough to be near her.

The day before, she had asked if I would help her pick apples to make a tart for Maman's birthday. I said of course but sat down so my knees did not give way.

That morning, she wore a moss-green bodice and broad straw hat. A few purple asters were woven into her blond braids. I grabbed an empty wicker basket, and off we went to the grove.

The flagstone path was covered with papery leaves. We giggled as we kicked them out of our way like children. The sweet scent from the last of the strawberry patch hung in the air. The warming sun, still low in the horizon, shone on the bedewed spider webs stretched across the hedges. Vapor rose from the pond into the cool air. Deer, foxes, rabbits, red squirrels, and migrating storks often drank the clean, cool, rippling water fed by an underground spring. Papa said he saw a wild boar there once and warned me to mind such beasts. They can attack if surprised. But I was eager to help all our forest friends. In winter, I used to hammer out a hole in the ice so they could drink.

I asked Lili ever so gently about her fiancé as we walked, but she brushed aside the question with "I have no idea." That was a good sign.

We inspected the apple trees for the best candidates. She spied several high up and directed me to fetch them. Willing to please, I crept out onto several branches, plucked the ripest ones, and tossed them down.

"Enough, Lili?"

I made my way to the lowest branch and dropped to the ground. She applauded my derring-do.

"Anything for my fair lady," I said, bowing in playful chivalry.

Basket brimming, I started back to the path, but she gently held my wrist. She turned her face up and closed her eyes. I bent down to kiss her. Her lips felt like pillows. I drew her close. After some moments, she gently pulled away, her cheeks flushed. My breathing stopped. Hand in hand, we walked wordlessly home.

I was jolted out of this reverie by the pounding of hooves on the cobblestones.

"*Arrêtez!*" the man shouted. "*Arrêtez l'exécution!*" I heard him halt his horse and rush up the steps to the platform. I saw out of the corner of my eye a soldier waving a piece of paper high above his head.

I tried to turn my head to see. "What is happening?" I shouted. "Someone tell me what is going on!"

# Qualms

here is much to dislike about Delhomme. The few times we met, he seemed peevish and argumentative. But now is not the time to dwell on that. Perhaps aging has shown me that grudges are too burdensome. I have been battered by many disappointments and betrayals. Solange has forsaken me, Chopin left this world detesting me, and I have been politically stigmatized and am completely ignored in Paris. When I travel to Nohant, people threaten to burn down my house. They shout, "Down with the Communists!" as I pass by. I seek goodness, beauty, and truth. Is that too much to ask?

Did my writings cause others to die, as Delhomme charged? The answer is not so black and white. Life is change. I am transformed because of motherhood, the uprisings, my lovers. Maybe Delhomme has changed too. Our meeting at l'Égyptien only a few days before his arrest was rancorous. But he desperately wanted a keepsake of Chopin. Why not? He loved him, had served him well. I admit I wanted to keep the ring just to deprive Delhomme of it. But, with my attachment to Chopin having been extinguished long ago, I no longer need it.

Since meeting him at the l'Égyptien café and seeing him at trial, I now sense his sincerity about fighting the ruinous policies against the working class. Yes, yes, at Nohant, he spouted all that twaddle about not wanting to marry a woman protesting the right to vote because *he* wanted a hot meal waiting. And then he so very charitably stated that men would take women's opinions into account when casting their ballots. Is he a misogynist or just plain stupid? God forbid he be both.

But now he faces death for doing what I do—confronting the tsar's ruinous policies. I wage war with my quill; he did it by flouting Vidocq because he saw the injustice of those policies that touched the lowly orphan. Thank goodness he was able to save his nephew from certain destitution, who was then ironically killed at the hands of the tsar anyway. That alone led me to sympathize with his cause. Turning against the monarch was not treasonous. It was heroic! I applaud his valiance.

Once I witnessed such bravery, I saw that his values were *my* values. Perhaps I could save Delhomme, just as he saved his nephew. But I had to act fast.

I hatched a scheme to rescue Delhomme from the guillotine when I whiffed that sickening smell after Vidocq passed by me in the courtroom. It was the same smell as the would-be rapist at the convent who grabbed me and ground my cheek into the wall while he grunted and fumbled with my skirt. My stomach tightened at the smell; hot blood rushed to my cheeks; my heart pounded in my ears. I was powerless. Delhomme must have felt the same way when Vidocq said he had murdered his nephew. Of course, he was enraged. Everything had worked against him.

That smell awakened my primal rage and focused my plan: I would ask Prince Président Louis Napoléon to pardon Delhomme, as I have done in hundreds of other cases. I needed to get an audience with him about this urgent matter.

My first thought was to meet with Vidocq. He said he knew Napoléon. I wanted his hints about how to approach the new ruler about Delhomme's situation. However, I wanted no part of appearing in public with such a coarse man. I steeled myself.

Sentencing was held the day after Delhomme's trial. The courtroom gallery was full, and spectators leaned over the balcony, all awaiting the news. The magistrate entered, sat behind his desk, struck his gavel, and asked the defendant to rise. "On the charge of treason against France, this court sentences Beaulieu Delhomme to death by beheading two days hence."

Lili let out an animal scream. Poor thing. Onlookers gasped and whispered to neighbors. I was not surprised at the outcome due to Delhomme's lackluster defense and Vidocq's deceitful testimony. Only minutes later, I overheard Vidocq tell the prosecutor that he was to meet with Louis Napoléon at four o'clock that afternoon to tell him the results of the trial. I saw my chance.

I approached the spymaster. "Monsieur Vidocq," I said in a friendly way. "I would like to ask your opinion." His eyes twinkled at a woman needing his expertise. "But it would not be proper to ask you here. Might we have lunch?"

I led him to a restaurant down the street that served peasant fare: hearty potato soup with garlic and herbs along with some good, crusty rye bread. Just right for his rough-hewn manners and language. The ceiling was fashioned from chiseled beams, and the walls were a whitewashed plaster. Long wooden tables accommodated several diners. I chose to sit at the end of an empty one where our conversation would remain private. I ordered a bottle of Pinot Noir to complement the dish. The establishment was a local favorite, too crowded and noisy for my taste, but the chatter would cloak our conversation.

Before getting down to business, we—well, *he*—talked about his escapades as a detective. I let him go on and on and used all my charms to appear captivated, a skill I kept in reserve for just such situations with men. I mustered fortitude to take in his sickening, treacly odor. He had meat-hook hands and a nose crisscrossed with red lines from excessive drink, although that fact could be verified from his exhale alone. Nevertheless, I knew he was a powerful man who had earned the respect of many a French leader and miscreant alike. His longevity as lead detective paid testament to his ability to reinvent himself and perform brilliantly. If I played my hand well, he would be my entrée to the Président's office. We chatted amiably. It was he who dove into the matter at hand.

"So, you want my advice, do you?" he said smiling.

"You work for Louis Napoléon now."

He corrected me. "I would say I am negotiating for a permanent position." That fact did not change my plan. He downed the last of his second glass of wine. I poured another.

"You have such a fascinating job," I said with my chin in my hand looking up at him. "All those dangerous criminals wanting to kill you before you kill them. I am in awe."

His chest puffed out at the praise. It took no sixth sense about men to see that flattery was the true arrow to hit the bull's-eye of this man's vanity.

"I would like to talk to Louis Napoléon," I said.

"About what?" he asked.

Now I had to step gingerly. "I have some information about Delhomme. Surely you would like to bring him information that he needs to know. You want him to rely on you, trust you, right?"

"What information?" said Vidocq, frowning. "The trial is over. Delhomme got paid to spy, he turned his allegiance, and now he will die." He tore off a hunk of bread, then dunked it in his soup and crammed the whole piece in his mouth. I gripped the table to divert my attention from his lip-smacking and slurping. Focus was everything now.

"I was in the courtroom too and heard the same evidence you did, but . . ." I began.

"No 'but,'" he said. "No one can quit. Ever. Spying is not for milksops!" Some bread sailed from his mouth at that last word.

Yes, Vidocq. We all know how *important* your job is to spy for kings and princes, how morally bankrupt you are. Selling your soul so your boss could murder the poor to further his ends. Congratulations. What was a spy but someone sanctioned to carry out a job whether it be lawful or criminal. Now who was the sinner?

I smiled at him, praised his hard work. "Tell the truth—you asked Delhomme to perform duties, and he carried them out. True?"

"Well, yes, but he . . ."

"I just want to know if that is true. I must get my facts right, Monsieur Vidocq. I think he was wrongly accused. I want to seek a reprieve."

Oh, he did not like that idea one bit. It flew in the face of his testimony and his irrefutable position as a spymaster and confidant to France's new ruler.

I needed to regain his trust. So, I slathered on more honeyed words. "I believe we should let honorable men live. Men like you. Let us toast the Republic's honor!" He needed no encouragement to comply and drank deeply. I breathed shallowly as I leaned toward him to gain intimacy.

"Tell me more about your life," I said, returning to the gambit of letting him puff about his ruses. "Your stories are so amusing." This gave me time to gather my thoughts. There was one last idea I had to trace out in my mind.

He went on and on about his disguises, mother's milk to this Thespian detective. "I was a horse dealer, archbishop, duchess, colonel of the Hussars, and a Russian general. No one ever suspected it was me," he said, beaming at his prowess.

"One time," he continued, "I pretended I had dropsy—an old trick that inmates used—that got me into the prison hospital."

I interrupted. "You were in prison?" It was hard to fathom a criminal being so revered by the monarchy.

He batted away my query. "Long, long story," he said and continued. "Sister Françoise—she was a big, fat nun who came to the prison every day. I thought, what a brilliant costume to escape in! It was so big that I could easily wear my clothes underneath. So, here is what I did." He lowered his voice to a loud whisper. "I bribed an inmate to charm her out of her habit, who then gave it to me. That way, she would have no idea who was using it. I put it on, stuffed my hair under the headdress, and then it was up and over the wall to sweet freedom."

I could only imagine how one "charmed" a nun out of her clothes. None of the sisters at *my* convent would have ever fallen for such a prank. I opened my mouth to comment, but he had more to tell.

"No one can fool me. I can identify any man even if he is disguised as a woman!" Then he leaned over to me, looked at my chest, and said with a lascivious leer, "I can tell *you* are not a man."

Such a lewd comment was not out of character for him. I hid my indignation and threw my head back to laugh. "You are ingenious!" I motioned to the garçon. *"Encore du vin, s'il vous plaît."*

"Monsieur Vidocq," I said in my tenderest tone, "or should I call you . . . Eugène?"

He smiled at the intimacy of the question. We French do not dare advance to first names so soon, although many a quaff of spirits has sabotaged that custom.

When the waiter returned, I asked the time. "Nearing four, Madame."

Vidocq jerked to standing. His napkin fell. "I have to meet the Président," he said urgently.

"May I come with you?" I asked.

He objected. "This is a private meeting."

"I would love to hear more stories," I said without guile. "I can wait in the coach while you have your meeting. Please, Eugène."

He was too frantic to disagree. We drove across the bridge to l'Hôtel de Ville. I feigned shivering just as we arrived. "Madame Sand, waiting in the coach will be too cold. Come inside, just to warm up."

"Do you think it would be all right?" I said innocently.

"I insist," he said in a manly voice and held out his hand to help me alight.

L'Hôtel de Ville was a grand building, so impressive in its French Renaissance majesty. Parquet floors shined to a mirror-like finish, paintings of cherubs and soldiers and flowers on the ceiling and over entryways to rooms, long windows with silk curtains, crystal chandeliers, magnificent alabaster sculptures, and furniture that had belonged the Sun King himself—a miniature Versailles. It was where the mayor of Paris had his office, but all leaders have used it often for official purposes since the mid-thirteen hundreds.

A soldier approached us. Vidocq, a familiar face, received easy passage. But he motioned for me to wait on a bench. I protested: "I am George Sand, my good man. The Prince Président knows my name. He surely will be happy to see me." The soldier shook his head and pointed to the bench a second time. I sat fuming but quickly formulated my next move.

The two men turned and walked down the long hall. Then, when they both went into the Président's office, I slipped in behind them just as the soldier announced Vidocq.

The soldier turned when he saw me said sternly, "Madame, I told you to . . ."

But the Président immediately recognized me and came from behind the desk holding out his hands to greet me. "Madame Sand, what a wonderful surprise," he said warmly then kissed my hand.

Vidocq, not one to be taken advantage of, acted as if it had been his idea. "It is my honor to present Madame Sand, Monsieur Prince Président," if a little late.

I hurried to explain my presence. "Monsieur Vidocq was gracious enough to invite me. He knows how I admire your patriotic views." Flattery works on *all* men.

He stood beaming. "Please, come sit by the fire while he and I talk for a moment." He offered his forearm and led me to a gold chair upholstered in vermillion silk with legs that tapered like fluted columns. The armrests met the front of the seat in a carved scroll, a style carried over from the reign of Louis the Sixteenth.

He kissed my hand and said, "You have brought great honor to France with your books and plays." I felt special indeed. Perhaps he, too, knew the power of blandishments.

"You are too kind, Monsieur Prince Président," I said as I sat. "I know you will lead France with a benevolent hand."

He cut quite a figure with graying goatee and dramatic moustache that ended in waxed points. He stooped a bit in the shoulders but still looked dashing in a blue cutaway uniform awash with medals and set off with a red sash. We French have always loved our uniforms.

Louis Napoléon looked at Vidocq, eyes sparkling. "Vidocq, I had no idea you were interested in literature."

With obvious frustration that he had been out maneuvered (and by a woman, no less), he stepped forward. "Monsieur Président, you requested an update on the trial of Beaulieu Delhomme."

In the meantime, I sat ladylike while the two men talked, awaiting my chance to speak.

"Guilty," Vidocq said.

"When?" asked Louis Napoléon about the execution.

"Day after tomorrow."

"Remind me what his part was in the uprisings," said the Président.

"He defied my authority," Vidocq said.

"How so?" asked the Président.

"I ordered him to visit you in England. Remember? Lamartine wanted to know your intentions to the French throne."

"I remember him now," said the Président. "Short man. Red hair. He hardly seemed menacing. Again, why is that a problem?"

Vidocq explained that Delhomme had never planned to see Louis Napoléon until the spymaster caught him going in the opposite direction of his apartment in London. I could see Vidocq was irritated at having his judgment second guessed. He went on with his other complaints: "He never reported an attempted attack on Carvaignac. It was a trick I devised to entrap him, to prove that he was a traitor," the spymaster said excitedly. "But when he reported back to me about the details, he told me the wrong day! I was certain he was lying, proving he had joined the other side!"

"What other side?" he asked.

That was my opening. I leaned forward. "The side that fought *for* people's rights, Monsieur Président, against poverty. We do not have to agree with people to defend them from injustice, but, sir, you even wrote a book about that very struggle—*The Extinction of Pauperism*, not five years ago."

His eyes lit up.

"You said it was necessary to give workers ownership," I said, "since they have no other wealth than their own labor . . . that it is necessary to give them rights and a future and to raise them in their own eyes by association, education, and discipline."

The Président moved his lips along with these words and nodded, coming to realize that, by these sentiments, he was on Delhomme's side and not that of his very own employee, Vidocq. He stroked his goatee. The President was conflicted: Should he agree with me in principle or agree with Vidocq on protocol? I could tell what he was thinking: How would it look if someone—Delhomme—who had championed the poor was guillotined, when the Président himself had promised the downtrodden to be their protector?

Now the emotional part. I stayed seated. "Did you know, Monsieur, that Delhomme's nephew was killed on the directive of the previous administration?" (I intentionally left out Vidocq's name as the one who had ordered his death.) I went on, being careful to maintain equanimity: "Delhomme was wounded in that attack, and his wife was crippled by a beating earlier that year. He wanted to help get the poor out of their filthy hovels and frightful working conditions. You were also falsely imprisoned at one time, exiled at others. So, you know what it is like to suffer and fight for freedom. You want France to be great, as do we all. But, sir, I hardly think Delhomme's infractions deserve death."

Vidocq's face turned crimson at having his authority challenged.

But the leader was cautious. He walked back and forth behind his desk, hands behind his back, head down in thought. After some time, he sat and tented his fingers. "I should never go against the court's decision to execute anyone, especially someone whom Vidocq says is guilty."

That soothed the spymaster to hear.

"But Madame Sand is right. I fail to see how this warrants execution, especially since he has already suffered."

"I agree that it might be unusual to repeal the sentence," I said, maintaining a steady tone. "Of course, the judge's decision should be given serious consideration." I was loath to overplay my hand but felt it necessary. "Monsieur Delhomme has been a hard-working patriot," I said. "He was Frédéric Chopin's loyal and highly respected piano tuner. He brought his nephew back from London to save him from the squalor of the orphanage."

"And that was the boy who was killed?"

"He was killed for no reason," I said, without a hint of accusation toward Vidocq, but I knew the Président could figure that much out for himself. What is left unsaid is often the most potent argument.

The Président shifted in his high-backed chair and pinched the ends of his moustache into needlepoints as he thought. We sat silent. Then he said abruptly, "The court has spoken. If I reverse their decision, the judiciary might look expendable. I cannot sanction such a thing lightly . . ."

Vidocq wore a victorious grin.

". . . but Madame Sand has a point that Delhomme was acting out of charity, not vengeance," Louis Napoléon continued. He then stood and walked from around the desk to address us. "Advocating for the poor is an act this government should honor, strive for. Perhaps my predecessors thought otherwise." He looked at Vidocq. "Day after tomorrow you say?"

He nodded.

"I will consider your views, Madame Sand, and notify you both of my decision. Guard!" He motioned for the soldier to show us out. We thanked him for his time and followed the soldier out of the building.

On the plaza in front of l'Hôtel, clumps of downy snowflakes played in the January breeze, landing on my cheek like cold cottonwood fluff. I hailed a carriage and got in. Vidocq looked defeated. He had been humiliated, this man who ran roughshod over anyone under the guise of the government authority. He started to get in the carriage. It seemed he had intentions that did not match mine. I quickly closed the door, almost pinching his fingers.

"Good night, Monsieur Vidocq." I waved goodbye as the driver pulled away.

He stood looking confused and forlorn.

The cabriolet drove past the Conciergerie. I thought of Delhomme, fretting in his cell about how to meet death and worrying about how Lili would cope. Everything was out of my hands now. The carriage traveled across the Seine and over streets that had been consecrated by blood from the uprisings. I drew my cape snug and leaned into the corner.

# Le Petit George

## Le Petit George

oday, I lie on a sun-warmed blanket listening to the Madon babble and eddy. Many happy days were spent here as a child sifting through the sand for beautiful stones. "Papa, look!" I squealed when I found my first piece of quartz. It felt cool, so cool that I thought it was ice. Sunlight passed through it to create a rainbow on the sand. He explained that quartz is sand changed by heat and pressure to become a beautiful, clear gem. A violent transformation.

The warm blanket on the soft grass lulls me to sleep. I close my eyes. Soon I am flying over the river, where tadpoles cluster in calm havens away from the swirls, where beavers upstream pile logs, sticks, and shrubs around a water door to the river. My father lovingly washes my small hands before our picnic. He kisses my cheek and says he loves me. I feel happy. My mother has arranged a meal of ham, cornichons, salad, and grapes on a striped cloth. The food will nourish me and make me strong. It is the surest sign that my mother loves me, too.

I hover above Chopin at his grand piano scrawling musical notes for a sonata, then scratching them out and rewriting. He is happy and hale, and he welcomes me to his home and offers me coffee and chocolate. He laughs and chatters on and on about how he has just written the most dev-ilishly difficult piece of his whole life—"Not even Liszt can play this!" he says, proud that he has finally vanquished a foe. Lili looks at me as if I am the most important person alive. She does not limp, and her skin is smooth and glowing, and she rubs her distended belly, happy to bring a child into the world because she no longer fears my death. I watch myself broadcast seed on rich earth and use water from the Madon to nourish the wheat I will harvest to make flour, so Lili can bake good bread for supper. Pride surges as I scythe the grain. A cloud passes by and asks if I am tired of flying. No, I say . . .

But a small hand pushes my shoulder again and again awakening me. "Papa, Papa, *qu'est-ce que c'est,* Papa?" the boy asks in his two-year-old way. He is holding my father's Saint Raphael medal. It must have fallen out of my pocket while I slept. He is so radiant with goodness and innocence and love for me. He starts to put the medal in his mouth.

"No, George!" I say trying not to sound alarmed. "Give Papa the medal, *ChouChou.*" George runs away on his stubby, shaky legs, daring me to give chase. I pretend to dash after my quarry. He whoops at the pretend danger. After some minutes, I "catch" him, and he gives me the medal in trade for a trip on my shoulders, high above me, where he can feel supe-rior, as if sitting atop a mighty steed to rule his domain, with his father at his command.

"Beaulieu! George!" Lili says. *"Mangez!"* I reach back to hold his arms fast as we gallop back to our picnic. He thumpity-thumps at my every stride, screaming with delight. Once we arrive, still holding his arms, I bend down and flip him over my head and place him on the blanket. Lili applauds our circus antics.

She was pregnant during the trial, although I did not know it. The stress caused our son to be born early. He already speaks several words. Lili wanted to name him after her father. But I overruled her wishes, explain-ing that George Sand saved my life. If it had not been for her, he would have been born fatherless. Life would have been difficult for Lili: Her limp slows her pace; her scars have stolen her beauty. Guilt clings to me for all my sins, but worst of all for being gulled by François Vidocq into compro-mising my morals for money. I violated the lessons my parents had taught me: Be honest in all dealings. I had misrepresented myself to Chopin and Sand, and had lied to Vidocq, although it hardly seemed a transgression to lie to a liar.

As for Vidocq, I heard that he is to be tried not only for overcharging clients at his agency but also for spying on Napoléon, abducting young women on instructions from their parents and placing them in convents, and worst of all, colluding to assassinate a politician with his *machine infernale*, an invention that could fire three hundred bullets a minute.

He will wriggle out of these charges, as he has all his life, because he lies and cheats as easily as the robin sings: He stole money from his family, he lied to escape punishment by authorities, even his disguises were a kind of lie. For all I know, these accusations leveled against him now are a ruse to put him back in the Conciergerie to befool yet another unsuspecting wretch into losing his freedom with feints and fabrications. Danger lurks in this man's wake. He is the most noxious, amoral, conniving person I know. Thank God I am free of his shackles.

As for Mme Sand, she has kept her word to remove herself from politics and remains secluded at Nohant with her quill and inkwell. I wrote a letter thanking her for interceding on my behalf to Louis Napoléon; I never received a return communication, odd for a woman for whom correspondence is a staple. It must be her way of admitting she had done nothing heroic. She merely defended someone wrongly accused. I still have Chopin's ring. She has never asked for its return. Lili wears it around her neck at times. Such power that piece of jewelry had. It has since lost some luster for me, perhaps because it symbolized what I did not have—love.

Our hard-won Second Republic was dissolved in three scant years. Louis Napoléon, faced with a law stating he had to step down after his term was up, staged a coup, then promptly crowned himself Napoleon III, emperor of the France's Second Empire.

It was as Sand had predicted. Clearly, he had lied to me when we met in England at Vidocq's behest to ask if he had any plans for a military coup. "*C'est fou!*" he had said, throwing his hands in the air to emphasize how crazy the idea was. All those lives wasted fighting for freedom, only to have this wily man re-erect the House of Bonaparte.

He deserves credit, though, for solving the horrendous problem of our overcrowded, polluted streets with inadequate gutters. It took a year, but he redrew the entire map of Paris that would end the labyrinth of narrow, fetid, airless routes that could no longer support our million or so population. Instead, he proposed widening boulevards and promenades. He billed it as a beautification effort, but I knew it was really to prevent future attempts to barricade them. Even so, I hope to live long enough to witness the transformation.

Marainville suits me with its verdant pastures and the rolling foothills of the Vosges, whose snows swell our rivers in the spring leaving behind rich silt for crops when the waters recede. Swallows nest under the eaves of our barn. In the evening, tawny owls signal to their mates with a tremulous hoo-hoo-hoo-hoooo. My father was right to want to spend his life here among farmers, whose ploughs release the petrichor, earth's heady scent after a rain.

He was wrong to speak condescendingly of them: "I hope you have a good, strong spine, because you will need it to wield a scythe when the wheat crop comes in," he told me after I quit medical school, as if farming were a vocation pursued only by those who could do nothing else. Now I have chosen to work the land I inherited. For now, the bitter memories of Paris—my difficult quest to be accepted as an artisan, the deaths of Chopin and Marc, the trial I endured because I selfishly thirsted for money and recognition—that has all been wiped away now in this bucolic setting where the rustle of trees in the wind replaces the clatter of carriages on cobbles. The Madon flows majestically north to the sea, as it has for thousands of years. Paris was where I became a man, but Marainville is where I will live as one.

M. Argent recognized me right away when I returned to his store after so many years. Nothing has changed: The bags of seeds are stacked as they always were. There was even a young man sitting in my same hard, wooden chair stamping receipts and looking bored. That could have been me and *would* have been had I not learned to tune. Now, I would be the one purchasing those seeds to farm the land, work I had never considered nor honored. I told M. Argent that I hoped to gain the respect of my neighbors through hard work and sweat. He smiled knowingly.

Now I purchase these embryos of hope, to sow in the fecund soil and beseech the skies for rain to coax out their bounty to feed my family and countrymen.

Like the quartz I found by the river, I experienced my own turbulent transformation. But that education has forged my soul into a beautiful piece of quartz.

I occasionally tune a piano for a neighbor. I miss bringing out the best in instruments and pleasing their owners. But now, my greatest pleasure comes from playing Chopin's piano that he bequeathed to me. I give a "recital" each evening for my family. Sometimes, George sits next to me and puts his tiny, soft hand on top of mine as I practice scales. He especially likes the ones with a lot of black notes. He laughs then scampers onto the lap of my precious, radiant Lili and sits spellbound while I play my favorite pieces. These concerts are not followed by the thunderous applause from madding listeners I once hungered for. Now I hear two dimpled hands clapping. And when my playing lulls him to sleep, I carry him to bed, gently kiss his warm, soft cheek, and lower him into the crib, afraid he might break.

I watch him breathe and weep at this magnificent gift of life.

# FIN

# PROFILES OF
# MAJOR CHARACTERS

**Hector Berlioz** (1803-1869). French composer, critic, and conductor of the Romantic period, known largely for his *Symphonie fantastique* (1830), the choral symphony *Roméo et Juliette* (1839), and the dramatic piece *La Damnation de Faust* (1846). His last years were marked by fame abroad and hostility at home.

**Auguste Blanqui** (1805-1881). French socialist and political activist, notable for his revolutionary theory of Blanquism. He was repeatedly jailed during the 1830-1848 reign of Louis Philippe. He was condemned to death in 1840 but that sentence was commuted to life imprisonment. Eventually, he was released from jail in 1848 only to resume attacks on the government after the February uprising, but it failed. George Sand sympathized with Blanqui's ideas, but she thought his practices were too radical.

**Frédéric** (a.k.a. Fryderyk, François) **Chopin** (1810-1849). Polish-born composer and pianist who left a legacy of music that, it is said, is being played every minute somewhere in the world. He revolutionized fingering technique, style, and musical form. His major piano works include mazurkas, waltzes, nocturnes, polonaises, etudes, impromptus, scherzos, preludes, sonatas, and two piano concertos.

**Alphonse de Lamartine** (1790-1869). French writer, poet, and politician instrumental in the foundation of the Second Republic and the continuation of the Tricolore as the flag of France.

**Emperor Napoléon III** (a.k.a. Prince Président Louis Napoléon and Napoléon le Petit) (reign 1848-1852 and the last French monarch 1852-1870) (1808-1873). He accomplished many positive infrastructure projects such as widening the streets, expanding the French railway system, and establishing modern agriculture that helped eliminate famines and even allow farmers to produce enough to export. He also allowed workers the right to strike and organize, and allowed women to matriculate at the Sorbonne.

**King Louis Philippe** (1773-1850) (reign 1830-1848). Louis Philippe I was King of France from 1830 to 1848. As Duke of Chartres he distinguished himself commanding troops during the Revolutionary Wars but broke with the Republic over its decision to execute King Louis XVI. He assumed the throne after Louis XVIII. As economic conditions worsened, he fled under disguise during the 1848 February Revolution.

**George Sand** (a.k.a. Lucile Aurore Dudevant, née Dupin) (1804-1876). French author and political activist. Her political life waned as she aged, preferring instead to focus on her family. Still very popular in France and beyond, she is one of the most notable and prolific writers of the European Romantic era. She wrote 58 novels and 13 plays; a two-volume autobiography; numerous stories, essays, and articles; and twenty-five volumes of correspondence. She was also an accomplished gardener, cook, draughts woman, and painter. Some of her works are on permanent display at the Musée de la Vie Romantique in Paris.

**Eugène François Vidocq** (1775-1857). First director of France's crime-detection Sûreté nationale as well as head of the first known private detective agency. He wore many disguises and was a convict, escape artist, and fugitive. Authors Victor Hugo, Edgar Allan Poe, and Honoré de Balzac, were inspired by his colorful antics. His reputation survives to this day in the Philadelphia crime-solving club called the Vidocq Society. He died of cholera at age 82.

# Minor Characters

**James Broadwood** (1772-1851). One of three sons of Scottish joiner and cabinet maker John Broadwood, who, in 1770, founded the oldest and foremost firm of English piano makers, which eventually became John Broadwood & Sons Ltd. The firm has built pianos consistently for over 250 years. John Broadwood is credited with inventing the sustaining pedal, using wound bass strings, and extending the keyboard to six full octaves in 1794.

**Auguste Clésinger** (1814-1883). French sculptor and painter trained by his father. He first exhibited at the prestigious Paris Salon in 1843. At the 1847 Salon, he created a sensation with his erotic "Woman Bitten by a Serpent." He made Chopin's death mask and cast of his hand. He also sculpted the figure of Euterpe weeping on top of his funerary monument.

**Solange Sand Clésinger** (1828-1899). Daughter of George Sand and Casimir Baron Dudevant. Married Auguste Clésinger in 1847.

**Dr. Jean Cruveilhier** (a.k.a. Cruveillé) (1791-1874). French anatomist and pathologist. He became professor of anatomy at the University of Paris in 1825 and was the first occupant of the chair of pathology at Paris. He tended to Chopin in his final days.

**Eugène Delacroix** (1798-1863). French Romantic artist regarded from the outset of his career as the leader of the French Romantic school. He is remembered for his "Liberty Leading the People" and "The Death of Sardanapalus." He employed principles such as the division of tones and the harmony of contrasts.

**Adolph Gutmann** (1819-1882). German pianist and composer. He was a pupil and friend of Frédéric Chopin.

**Friedrich Kalkbrenner** (1785-1849). German-born pianist, composer, piano teacher, and piano manufacturer. He began studies at the Paris Conservatoire at a young age. He was once considered the foremost pianist in Europe. He died just four months before Chopin.

**Franz Liszt** (1811-1886). Hungarian composer, virtuoso pianist, conductor, music teacher, arranger, and organist of the Romantic era. He was also a writer, philanthropist, and Hungarian nationalist. A prolific composer, he wrote 12 symphonic poems, two (completed) piano concertos, a variety of solo piano pieces, and several sacred choral works that reflected his love for the Catholic church. He was deeply influenced by Chopin's poetical style of music.

**Félicien Mallefille** (1813-1868). French novelist and playwright born in Mauritius. He wrote several plays, including "Glenarvon," "Les sept enfants de Lara," "Le cœur et la dot," and "Les sceptiques," along with two comedies and two novels: *Le collier* and *La confession du Gaucho*.

**Countess Charlotte Marliani** (1790-1850). Wife of Spanish politician and author Manuel Marliani, and confidante of George Sand. She held salons for Chopin to play and helped introduce Sand and Chopin.

**Felix Mendelssohn** (1809-1847). German composer, pianist, organist, and conductor of the early Romantic period. Mendelssohn's compositions include symphonies, concertos, piano music, and chamber music.

**Camille Pleyel** (1788-1855). French virtuoso pianist, music publisher, and owner of Pleyel et Cie, a French piano manufacturing firm. He also ran a concert hall, Salle Pleyel, where Chopin played the first and last of his concerts in Paris. The youngest son of Ignace Joseph Pleyel, he studied with Czech composer and pianist Jan Dussek.

**Maurice Sand** (1823-1889). French writer, artist, and entomologist. He studied art under Eugène Delacroix and also experimented in other subjects, including geology and biology. He was the elder child and only son of George Sand. One of his passions was creating several hundred hand puppets used to entertain visitors in the Nohant theater.

**Maurice Schlesinger** (1798-1871). German Jewish music editor and publisher. In 1834 he founded a society to publish both classical and contemporary music at reasonable prices that included works by Haydn, Mozart, Beethoven, Hummel, Weber, Meyerbeer, Berlioz, and Chopin.

**Wojciech Sowinski** (1803-1880). Pianist, composer, and writer about music. He studied in Vienna under Carl Czerny (piano) and A. Jirovec and Leidesdorf (composition). He moved to Paris, where he worked as a music teacher.

**Jane Stirling** (1804-1859). Scottish amateur pianist best known as a student and friend of Chopin, who dedicated two nocturnes to her. She took him on a tour of England and Scotland in 1848 and took charge of the disposal of his effects and manuscripts after his death.

**Alexis de Tocqueville** (1805-1859). French aristocrat, diplomat, political scientist, and historian. He is best known for his works *Democracy in America* and *The Old Regime and the Revolution*.

**Ivan Turgenev** (1818-1883). Russian novelist, short story writer, poet, playwright, and translator. He wrote *A Nest of Gentry*, *On the Eve*, and *Fathers and Sons*, one of the most acclaimed Russian novels of the nineteenth century. Due to a politically stifling climate for writers under Tsar Nicholas I during the 1840s and 1850s, Turgenev left Russia for Western Europe. He also had a lifelong affair with the singer Pauline Viardot.

**Pauline Viardot** (née García) (1821-1910). Leading nineteenth-century French mezzo-soprano, pedagogue, and composer of Spanish descent. An outstanding pianist, she often played duets with her friend, Frédéric Chopin, and sang at his funeral.

**Stefan Witwicki** (1801-1847). Polish poet of the Romantic period. Chopin set ten of Witwicki's poems to music, including "The Ring," in Opus 74, *Seventeen Polish Songs*. It was published posthumously in 1855. Two other songs were added in 1910. The nine remaining poems were written by three other Polish poets.

**Maria Wodzińska** (1819-1896). Childhood friend and eventual love interest of Chopin. Her parents were skeptical of his merits as a husband for their daughter because of his whirlwind social life, frequent ill health, and status as a composer. They gave him a year to prove himself a reliable prospect, but in the end, they refused his proposal.

# RECOMMENDED RESOURCES

**Atwood, William G. (1980).** *The lioness and the little one: The liaison of George Sand and Frédéric Chopin.* **New York: Columbia University Press.**

Atwood focuses on and extensively footnotes the relationship between George Sand and Frédéric Chopin, especially their attitudes toward one another and their artistic passions. It includes excerpts from correspondence between Sand and many of important people in their lives.

**Eigeldinger, Jean-Jacques. (1986).** *Chopin: Pianist and teacher.* **Cambridge, U.K.: Cambridge University Press.**

This trove of (translated) information provides an invaluable resource for anyone wanting to read about Chopin as a teacher through the impressions of his students. It provides accounts by Chopin, as well as his students and contemporaries, about his insights into his technique, musical style, aesthetic beliefs, and interpretations of his music. Especially interesting to pianists are the fingering and annotations in the scores of pupils.

**Fenby, Jonathan. (2015).** *France: A modern history from the revolution to the war with terror.* **New York: St. Martin's.**

Fenby provides a comprehensive account of the transformation of France from the defeat of Napoléon Bonaparte at the Battle of Waterloo in June 1815 through the following two centuries. The book is richly footnoted and describes in detail the struggles of both the government and its people during France's turbulent past.

**Huneker, James. (1966).** *The man and his music.* **Dover: Mineola, NY.**

James Huneker was born only eight years after Chopin's death. He was a prolific writer and newspaper critic and put his skills to use in this book, first published in 1900. This updated volume has been footnoted by Herbert Weinstein, who corrected inaccuracies and planed down some of Huneker's passion for Chopin, the musician. The first five chapters recount his birth-to-death story. The next nine give a thorough analysis of Chopin's études, preludes, mazurkas, nocturnes, sonatas, and polonaises. Included are others' impressions of his works. The book speaks to pianists as well as music lovers and students.

**Loesser, Arthur. (1954).** *Men, women & pianos.* **Mineola, NY: Dover Publications.**

The pianoforte has played an integral part in the social history of Europe and America since its invention around 1700 by Italian Bartolomeo Cristofori. Pianos soon replaced harpsichords and clavichords and grew in popularity to become commonplace in many homes by the mid 1800s. This book is an excellent overview of how the piano affected Western culture throughout that time.

**Morton, James. (2004).** *The first detective: The life and revolutionary times of Vidocq criminal, spy, and private eye.* **New York: The Overlook Press.**

and

**Vidocq, Francois Eugene. (2003).** *Memoirs of Vidocq: Master of crime.* **Oakland, CA: AK Press.**

Eugene Vidocq is one of the most fascinating characters in French history. The novelists Balzac, Hugo and Dickens all created characters based on the quirky detective. The quintessential opportunist, he started out as a criminal then saw that his skills could be sold to the monarch to help catch criminals. He pioneered the first private detective agency that served kings and other French leaders until his death at 82. Morton touches on every part of his life—from his parents to his extraordinary life as a criminal to his death due to cholera.

Vidocq's own (translated) account of his life is engagingly written and provides many details not found in other books. He takes the reader on a tour of the circuses, pirate ships, jail cells and women's bedchambers that were all part of his life.

**Niecks, Frederick. (1973).** *Frédéric Chopin as a man and musician* **(Vols. 1 & 2). New York: Cooper Square Press.**

Niecks has written an exhaustive, two-volume set of account of Frederic Chopin as a musician that is couched in the society that revered and supported him. The book includes a helpful appendix of Chopin's published and unpublished works with opus numbers. Excerpts from letters, newspapers, scores, announcements, drawings, and other ephemera round out the reader's picture of this man.

**Opienski, Henryk (collector). (1988).** *Chopin's letters.* **New York: Dover Publications.**

This extraordinary (translated) collection of 264 letters to and from Chopin's friends and family provides insight into Chopin's thoughts and emotions starting from the first letter he wrote celebrating his father's name-day greeting in 1816 to the final undated entry he wrote in pencil imploring someone to open his body before he is buried. Although George Sand is mentioned in many letters, virtually no correspondence between the two exists today since Sand burned most them.

**Sand, George. (1991).** *Story of my life (Histoire de ma vie).* **Albany: SUNY Press.**

Much has been written about George Sand. She has her own say in her (translated) autobiography of 1117 pages covering her life from birth up to (briefly) her affair with Chopin. Readers will get a bird's-eye view of France and the country's travails throughout Sand's life.

**Szulc, Tad. (1998).** *Chopin in Paris: The life and times of the romantic composer.* **Cambridge, MA: Da Capo Press.**

Szulc's very readable account of Chopin's life winds through the important musical and personal parts of his life. He even recounts the years of his father born in Marainville, France (Lorraine), and how he found his way to Poland. From there the book concentrates mainly on the composer's 18 years in Paris until his death. Interesting are the numerous tales of the artistic luminaries that passed through both his and George Sand's life: Berlioz, Turgenev, Hugo, Balzac, Liszt, Stendhal, Delacroix, to name a few.

# ACKNOWLEDGMENTS

*I* am indebted to Don Wilson, the tuner/technician who taught me with patience and good humor; Dr. Steven Lagerberg, generous to a fault with his encyclopedic knowledge of Frédéric Chopin; Scott Driscoll, nonpareil writing teacher to whom all his students genuflect; Colin Mustful, my eagle-eyed, tireless editor; Rob Birchard and Mary Jane Ferguson for their thoughtful suggestions and insights; Susan Irving, pitch-perfect writing and character development coach; Durinda Wood, famed Hollywood costume designer for helping clothe my characters; and Austin Irving, quintessential photographer who somehow found my best angle.

# ABOUT THE AUTHOR

**Nancy Burkhalter** is an educator, writer, journalist, linguist, and piano tuner. She holds a Master's degree in journalism and English education, as well as a Doctorate in linguistics from the University of New Mexico. She has taught composition for many years in the U.S., Germany, Saudi Arabia, Kazakhstan, and Russia. Her overseas work led to an interest in comparative education, especially critical thinking. Both observa-tions and research led to her book and blog, Critical Thinking Now. In 2019, she was a recipient of *Go Back, Give Back*, a fellowship through the State Department to train teachers in St. Petersburg, Russia. A resident of Edmonds, Washington, Burkhalter loves to travel, write, and learn languages.

CPSIA information can be obtained
at www.ICGtesting.com
Printed in the USA
FSHW020102200620
71228FS